I-

TRIAGE III:

Treatment of Rampant Individualism Against Global Extinction III

What if you had a quantum computer that could access your alternate lives in parallel universes?

What if your planet was under threat from within and without?

What if you couldn't trust even your nearest and dearest? But what if only you knew the rules of the game that could save them all?

The gauntlett is down.

Will you rise to the challenge of

I-*Mage* and play?

Also by the same author

TerraRise

TriAge I:
Treatment of
Rampant
Individualism
Against
Global
Extinction
I

PsycheSomatic

TriAge II:
Treatment of
Rampant
Individualism
Against
Global
Extinction
II

I-Mage

TriAge III:
Treatment of
Rampant
Individualism
Against
Global
Extinction
III

By

Rowney Marshal

Cover Design: Rowney Marshal

Illustration 'Metron Lily': Nancy Knight

ISBN 978-0-9561190-2-5

Date of first publication 2008

This book is a work of fiction and, except in the case of historical or scientific fact, any resemblance to actual persons, living or dead, is purely coincidental.

Printed and bound by CPI Antony Rowe, Eastbourne

Fonts:
Titles-Atlantis MF-Richard William Mueller
Main body-Calisto MT-The Monotype Corporation

Publisher: Rowney Marshal Ltd
Registered Company Number: 6747111
Contact: Rowney Marshal Ltd
P.O.Box 3419
Bowthorpe
NR5 5AA, UK
e: contact@rowneymarshal.co.uk
www.rowneymarshal.co.uk

Chapters

A: Prima Materia:
Solutio and Separatio

Zelas was singing to her 'imaginary' friend. Well, that's what the grown-longs said ... *had said* ... she was. Normally, she sang silently, using the ancient heraldic forms that conceptualised her thought most coherently for her listener, but today, too upset to focus, she was babbling in Common, aloud, emitting a great fountain of bubbles.

The response-tone echoed in her mind, fibrillating her sonar-melon, elongating to a pause. 'Slow down!' was the implicit instruction, but wielded gently, a nudge not a command. Zelas obeyed nonetheless. She unfurled from the foetal position, rotating to slip out of the niche snout-first, if upside down, and struck for the surface. She had had plenty of air left, but it was bracing to erupt into the cool night and her upturned nostril quivered as the surface winds scoured the salt from her face, her pupils contracting under the glare of the full moon reflecting off the dome of the deep ocean. She hung motionless, mesmerised by the lunar eye, supported by the only mother she could now know, the buoyant sea itself. Finally, when she had regained control of her heart and its drumming was less urgent in her ears, her friend 'spoke' again. This time it was an interrogative and a puzzled behest. 'Tell me what happened! From a beginning.'

Beginnings are hard to locate from final destinations at the best of times, but when you're alone and distraught, teetering on the edge of the abyss, how you got there is usually lost within the eddying paths of your journey thence. But Zelas wasn't the Foremost Hydraen Knight for nothing. She centred her mind into the Heraldic Harmonics, rehearsing her status for stability of purpose.

'I am the Tripodial of the Hydradesic. In the Common, I am BarbShark. I am the Ray between predator and prey, the shortest classical line between 0 & 1 in a swirling, coursing, eddying, tridimensional maelstrom of environmental dynamics, the one who is trusted to cut through the contours of detour.' *Trusted! But why? Why? When the Whorlingas knew I was Fey. How often have they reproached me for my lack of concentration? Why deliver their lives unto me through blind faith?* Images of blood and spilled guts and torn flesh spooled through her, the taste of familial fluids, the scent of death lacing the salt, the maddening pulses of frantic sonar in the inky cloud of the feeding frenzy, the aching wails that reverberated to ring her bones.

Again came the *adagio* chord. She didn't slow. This time she stopped. What had happened? Really. It was difficult to translate her memories, all embedded in aromatic differentials and sonic mappings, into the colourful layers of heraldic visual-signifiers and harmonic-emoters, the antique language of the Ancient Knights, of which her order was the Aquatic one, but, although her friend shared a marine environment, her Common and her senses were so separately evolved, their joint communication had to be Heraldic. *It was how she knew without question that her friend was far from imaginary. What figment of one's own disordered mind would require linguistic recoding?* Ordering her thoughts for translative-compression was steadying though. *Alright, here goes.*

'I was questing with dogs. Well, I was supposed to be. That bit was easy. I could have scented that seamount from an ocean away the place was so heaving with sexual hormones. It was just a question of timing it right to be around when the squid come up at nightfall to mate. Then all I had to do was drop an ink sac into my wake and blast it with directional sonar down my route to the place, so the Shoal could track me, and then just stay alert to send the Call at the right time for the upstream-hunters to come and corral the prey during their dawn dive back to the depths. Two tasks and a whole night inbetween them.' *I've never been any good at waiting. But it wasn't that.* Primate curiosity. That was it. An atavism from another world. *That was why the Whorlingas called her 'fey', meaning both whimsical in the derogatory sense of unreliable and inspired in the way of the Ancestors. (But it was their own lack of curiosity that had put their lives in her span.)*

An inner bell sounded recalling her to the current. 'What did you do?'

Well, actually it wasn't entirely unfettered license. She was both following the hominin fascination with intricate colourful patternings of information, *succumbing to curiosity*, and was also back-architecturalizing conceptual-design into media-conduit, *engaging an algorithm she'd been developing to translate the cephalopod communication*, to construe the Realisation of the Common, *Meaning*. But the confession was more shame-faced. 'I was playing with the food.'

Her friend might be worlds away, but she shared the Shoal's sense of *dis*taste in this respect. The *legato* fractured, there was an instant of *mosso,* and Zelas sensed the restraint behind the *calando* that replaced it. The mores of sentient predation were offended. Having sent the full Blazon by now, it was no use trying to excuse any part of the action, but Zelas did, guiltily, try to explain.

'I know I got the dogs to separate that poor squid from the crowd, and it disrupted the flocking-to-reproduce behaviour for a little while, but there were millions of them and they barely noticed really. And we were just going to eat them anyway. I just wanted to know what level they were at. You know I think they're sentient. That the chromatophores in their mantle are flashing far-from-primitive communications. Well, I know I shouldn't, but I justified a a little experimental 'cruelty' to accelerate finding the basic *"HELP!"* ideomemes of the language. You have to start the decoding process somewhere. After all, if I can prove their sentience meets Conduit criteria and thus has Meaning in Common, they could be removed from the list of acceptable prey. And I've a hunch they're more than that. Maybe even Shell of Arms status. I definitely sense at least a basic Reef coating. It was just a starting point. I wouldn't have done it twice. I...'

Rinforzando recalled her from apologia. 'You could have done all that and more by mere observation, and you know it.'

'Yes, but my optics aren't up to their standard. I'd have had to use my Mantis Shrimp and details they see get lost in translation.'

Maybe it was the chill air evaporating off her exposed back, but the ambient mental temperature seemed colder too. *Enough excuses. I know what I did. Tell it.*

'I took my attention off the dogs.' She frequently broke protocol like this, so confident was she in her supersonar alerting her to her own and the shoal's downstream endangerment. Well, she had to, to do anything like *science*. It wasn't merely frivolous. It was research. It was also a point of principle.

Everything living possessed its own definition of Meaning, and most spoke soporifically into the background waveform, part of the Fluid ambience, but Shoaling promoted the concept of the-part-in-the-whole, which in turn mandated a protoindividuality, *the Message*. Even unintelligent swarms transmitted internal reports to act *en masse*; more complex entities evolved communicating, cultured, societal Shoals.

The content, whose smell or ink or charge or sound or light, might be indecipherable swirls in the unending babble of the ocean to all but those of the same species, was readable to a ScentScouter, at least the Gist of it was. The full Hydradesic Knight, being faster, honed, practised-unto-fractally-geloid, got First Blood and therein the Meat of the Meaning. The terms were ancient, referring to the times when all information was contoured around survival, but sentience had turned taste to metaphor and the hunt was now for knowledge.

However, Zelas knew that she was something more than the foremost Knight. That was why she was here, playing with a food in which she sensed its own complex intelligence. It was also the one aspect of her quest-successes she had been desperately trying to keep from the Whorlingas. Although she might despise the priestly collective, with its aspirations to achieve a state of Eddyless Calm, *iconographically a Solid concept, denying the reality of Flow*, she suspected they had already inhaled more than a whiff of her abilities.

The trouble was she would never know if they had. If they suspected she was the embodiment of their mythic being, they would behave with the utmost caution. In accordance with their tenets, which required them to turn their snouts away from interaction, for fear of disturbing the unfolding of the prophesy, they would allow the myth to play out, as even direct observation was forbidden. The most they could be doing was suspecting and collating open source data and analysing the statistics thereof.

Of course, if she *was* a fabled hyperD-Ray, a tuner of the liquid harmonies, with the potential to sound the depths to ring forth nautilus-chimes, the long-awaited Tachyon-Siren, then she was the kind of archetypal myth that was only safe for the shoal to expel to its boundary eddies, and then only if she was deemed to be sufficiently empathically-boid-braided not to Dance even a swirl of danger towards the Shoal. If she were not deemed enough of a team player, banishment was the historic requirement.

It was fair enough. Zelas understood her skill to be extreme sensitivity to stimuli and enhanced pattern-recognition; ordinary abilities to all, just tuned higher in some individuals to enable an almost-mystical, instinctual aptitude for the Quest. But if such an Aquamancer found too many engaging patterns out there, she could lead the group so far astray that the worldwaters she was meandering over, in between dizzying spurts of speed, could take the Shoal into extinction-threatening vastnesses of barren sands just as often as into favoured lagoons of largesse with their leisurely largo notes.

Still, someone had to lead and discover the changes inherent in the Wave, and Intelligent Predators also know they face a lot of complex moral choices, such as those surrounding prey and symbiote interactions. So Zelas was licensed to experiment and tradition kept that activity at current-width from the Shoal, her method unobservable as a prerequisite for faith in any of her results. Hers alone would be the conclusion; her translation of any communication with any other species the definitive version. From then on, judgement lay with the Whorlingas. It was their decision as to prey or not to prey. However, Zelas, being both fey and studious, had concluded from a metastudy of old data that this was an ill-advised way of developing science.

Anyone could train to be a Knight, but intuitive Aquamancers were rare in each generation. At best, waiting for them to be born and reach their potential and attain knowledge was chancy and very slow. At worst, they had chaotic overloaded minds and random results that had led to some of the worst Whorling Edicts, such as the Long Talk, when everyone tried their hardest to 'gist' polychaete worms, or the ban on eating krill for two generations, leading to famine and infertility. And sometimes the priests impeded progress through prejudice and ignored the findings of the very Aquamancer in whom they protested such faith. *This was a sore point at the moment. Zelas had uncovered the amazing visual capabilities of the Mantis Shrimp but they'd stayed on the prey-list despite all her pleas. All she could do when enshoaled was set an example.* She stroked the bonded pair that she now wore as a badge on her crown. *Between them and the dogs, her hunting success had increased fivefold.*

But Zelas was also engaged in an unprecedented solo crusade against those who had upheld Heraldic traditions for all the generations of the Order. And it was regarding this issue of being the One. She knew she was special, every fibre of her being thrilled to the touch of the world, but hypersensitivity is not knowledge, and neither does faith so easily convert to truth. Zelas felt that knowledge and its gain should be shared endeavours, so that the multiple observations of the shoal would be a heavyweight counterpoint to the flimsy singular view of the one. It had to be wiser to subject the new solutions found by mavericks such as herself to stringent tests, not least the reproducibility of the chord. The faith that the Aquamancer had honed in upon the *right* Note was dangerous and was such pressure to bear alone, out here, beyond the Song of the Shoal.

Plus Zelas was pretty certain already that it didn't work like that. The world they inhabited was fluid, and it was no use hoping to find the saltsea of perfect buoyancy, that Eddyless Calm, for that was simply reversion to the evolutionary throwback of landlolling, *gravity on solid diagonally reciprocated as the aspirational nirvana of spiritual calm*, the single note.

No, it was not that Zelas heard the timeless call of the One Note of cosmic destiny for all, but that she had to cope with the worrying responsibility of the realization that there were an infinite number of One Notes omming within every thrum of the waves in an infinity of quantum foaming seas.

Thus she felt she had No-Choice imposed through an innumerability of Perceived-Choice Horizons, and, awfully, that this Undecision was no worse for being random and wanton as a method of 'choosing', than if she had put any effort into 'plotting a course'.

If she had been completely free to explore becoming Siren without still having to lead the Shoal, perhaps she wouldn't have been feeling so confused. Being out here in isolation, she had no markers for her own stability. *Was this perception of multiplicities erroneous? Perhaps her sensed Tachyon-Siren status was hubris? Perhaps she had just gone mad beyond the orbit of her pack? How would she tell?* And the recognition of an immeasurability of Chords, that thrummed of a deeper Harmony whilst sounding in any Now like an amusical cachophony, was as paralysing to her mind as an eel sting to her body. So she compromised.

She went with the flow whenever it smelt symphonically-shapely. Not, *of course – she was not a novice,* when it yanked with the passionate forces of mucosoidal attraction, when the charge overloaded early at the brainstem, flooding the frontal cortex into submission, *at least not often, not just because some topological composition of entrancing intra-twinings beckoned her to loose herself down their intricate rides into the unretraceable unknowns.* No, she had enough sense of duty not to be self-indulgent or reckless, but she felt that both sides of she-to-shoal umbilical, the one and the many, were owed the controlled whimsy of *duplicated* experimentations. She was still feeling her way after all. She felt she still had much to learn.

Abruptly, her latest lesson had come upon her. Only this time she hadn't remembered to include the new term in the equation. Not the statistically-unexpected but predictable, great white shark - where they'd just come from that was part of the inevitable background noise which couldn't have slipped under her radar - but her own unbroken dogshark, unleashed for the first time within a surfeit of food.

It had gone into a frenzy, and, although it knew from its training that it was only meant to corral the prey, within the pack all working together under Zelas' instruction with minimal crackles of electrical discharges ringing the foodball, it was yet unable to restrain itself from breaching the sphere and snapping wildly into the cornucopia of flesh.

Inevitably there was blood. Inevitably the great white noticed, but Zelas' pridefulness had already made the Call to her Shoal and inked the map of the shortest route back along the sum of her tracks, before she had Mused for long enough to establish the amplitude and steadiness of the local note for safety. So the Shoal arrived into the open maw of a giant, grinding its way through whatever its momentum swept into its teeth.

Zelas was beyond the dark-rainbow cloud that the squid made in their frantic dissipation, trying to harness and quieten the sharkpup and round up the rest of the hounds, so it was only when she tasted familial blood, dense and thickening the indigo shadow of ink to garnet-sulphur stormbreakers, that she understood, in a gel-instant that would replay on all senses forever, just what her inattention to the Here and Now, that fabled, still location of the golden age yet to be achieved, had cost all who had believed that she could be trusted with the siting of it.

The site was not wrong, not in space nor time, only in my calculation of the speed at which that splace could pass or be passed or be past or, as in this case, be wantonly distilled into the chaos of dispersion of the previous pattern.

And it was she that had failed to cherish above all the pattern that now was so horrifically lost to her: her entire clan, mutilated, killed outright if they were lucky, spiralling up to flop their last breaths out to the sunlight, plummetting as the air absorbed their final screams of pain; a dozen pairs of huge bright eyes dimming upon her in distress and disbelief. It was worse than simply a rabid shark. Over the following few hours as she tended the lingering wounded, she thought it was their inability to compute their loss of faith in her that made them give up and die, rather than face her guilt-ridden succour betraying afresh her betrayal.

Apparently, there had been no point to the self-deceit that she was modestly confirming her status as an Aquamancer before stating herself to the Whorlingas. Apparently the whole shoal had known, before she herself had. Known erroneously! No doubt, because of hope and a long famine followed by the sardine glut which she had found serendipitously and which had saved them all so recently. And it had led to unreproducible, invalid, premature faith. Now demonstrated, in the result of their deaths, as an hypothesis too far.

And then the recriminations of their pain were gone and she was forever fixed on the boundary without a central eddy to leash her, like her dogs, into a shoal-orbit, and she was alone of her kind. There is no such thing as a sole shoal, even one with attendant hounds.

'And' she finished, twisting to and fro with the pain of it all, 'all the time I just wanted to be unleashed to explore being an Aquamancer, and now there's no one left to be one for, and I can't be one or they wouldn't be dead, and I can't put it right, and I don't know how to be alone, and I'm only young, and the years ahead are long and dark. I just wish I'd died with them. I should have died for them. Not like this, not like this. It shouldn't be like this. I shouldn't be.'

The *doloroso* sympathy that had been chiming with her mood as she had unloaded the tragedy was being overlaid by a more vibrant, strengthening melody. 'Don't give up. There is cause, then effect.

Then the effect and the prior causality are reduced to mere history. You are not dead. Life is always worth celebrating.'

Zelas rallied enough for a rebuttal. 'You say that, but it's that kind of thinking that got me here. If I hadn't put cephalopods before *Homo aquaticus*, we'd all be here to celebrate our life, munching on juicy squid oblivious to whether or not whatever thoughts they had on life died with them.'

'And in a branched-off universe, no doubt you all are. But in your Here-and-Now, you are alive, alone, and upstream are decisions that only you can make already flowing your way.'

'I don't know what to do!' It was a howl that would travel eight hundred lengths without dissipating in her ocean, would have circled her friend's world. Even mentally it was deafening.

It was met by a stern response. 'Do what you can, Survive. Be what you are, Tachyon-Siren.'

'You still believe I am?'

'These are hominin concepts I do not share. But I do know that you are extraordinary within your genus. That is why you are not truly alone, for you hear me. I do not think it is this that will save you though. I think it is your curiosity that will bring you to a new home, for you will be unable to resist seeking out others to bond with, new ideas to taste.'

'The Whorlingas say that the last sounding of any other of our kind was two centuries ago. We are all but … I mean, now we are … extinct.'

'It is a big world. It may not be so. And anyway, there are still some among the Landlubbers that would recognize and welcome a Knight of the Ground Real.'

'There are?'

'Oh, they have different names for it. Like the Water of Life and the Blood of Light and the Breath of the Vacuum. It depends which race of humanity they come from. And there are few Questers within any of the four tribes, but these days they are coming together. Perhaps to find and join them is your challenge, or perhaps the challenges on the journey are the quest.'

'I have thought I sensed Heraldic motes in the air from time to time, but so faint, so distant, so fuzzy, that I thought I imagined them. The priests said only we kept the faith, that the Landlubbers were degenerate and had turned against the true stream so much so that they could not even see they were poisoning the waters. How is it you know more than the priests? Was it in my mind?'

There was a pause, as if the friend were weighing her information before sharing it.

'Yours is not the only Terran mind to be communicated with by us.'

'Us? It's not just you then. I thought you were your world's communicator. Your world's equivalent of Tachyon-Siren.'

'There is also my brother.' Zelas sensed well enough that this revelation was even now given with reluctance. She forebore to press the matter of why, her excitement was directed elsewhere.

'Does he talk with another Aquatic?'

'No. We both commune with humans.'

'Day humans? But they don't Think!'

'There are atavisms in all species, ancestral throwbacks that enable new phenotypic pathways to develop. Some Days have a certain amount of telepathic capability, although mostly they disbelieve their own talents, more 'imaginary friend' diagnoses.'

'Don't try to insinuate I have anything in common with Days. They are the planet-killing enemy of all life, for Deepsake. These are the people you think I should Seek? The destroyers of the Ground Real? I would have nothing to say to them other than words of Mordant-Morte Harbinger. What can you have to talk about with them?'

'Much. But that Meat is for another Splime. Gist-say, I planned to introduce you and my human - my brother communes with another and words and reality do not gel within that bond, though strong it is - but you were not ready. Maybe you are not yet, but if I understand your Heraldic constructions correctly, the Conceit now behoves the Ludus Puerorum. Are you in the Game or out?'

Knowledge is mutable, as flexible as memory. But new data is as a stone thrown into a pond, ripples will fibrillate the world around it no matter who wish it not so. To call any idea a Conceit is to declare a Challenge to the possessor of knowledge. The challenge is, literally, Child's Play, the Game of Children, *ludus puerorum.*

In general life, in Common, there would be no obligation hidden in the phrase, there would be Choice. That is why it is the child's game, undertaken only as do the young, who play, or not, at will, freely, but throwing themselves into the current, without course-set, learning through doing, not plotting; the Game the thing, not the destination won. To a Knight there was an obligation to play, which meant enjoining the quest for, usually, more knowledge. To anyone purporting to think themselves worth the title of Tachyon-Siren, the challenge was more to understand why they did not already possess this knowledge, the No-Choice of Need-to-Know All-there-is-to-Know. To Zelas, this was not a challenge at all, it was an ultimatum. Either she was Tachyon-Siren, the Aquamancer who might find but will seek the Ground Real, the Source of the Waters of Life, even if in splime there is no longer anyone left to find it for, or she was ordinary.

'I Re-Solve.' She declared, in the ancient untongued. 'I will Cast.' In Common, she thought, with the familiar thrill of anticipation for the hunt upstream, *Game On!*

Jake heard the shout of 'Game on!' erupt from the room across the corridor, accompanied by the hearty burst of self-congratulatory clapping he was coming to recognize as far from indicative of true success. That, *of course*, was the *sole* reason that prevented him from rushing back into the throng of tech-heads to ingratiate himself with collegiate air-punching, and why he turned back to the coffee machine with an indulgent smile.

'It's not back to work for you now, then?' asked the latest addition to the Institute. She was petite, with the most vivid and luxurious curtain of red curls he had seen outside of forties' movies, and her face was symmetrically flawless. Pale, yes, but pretty with the transluscence of fine china, although it was the acute jade eyes you noticed. And, when she gave that slightly-uncertain, amused twist to her mouth, the curve of rosebud lips. He realised he was waxing dangerously lyrical towards his new colleague and managed a casual shrug.

'It's hard to believe, but Americans do actually live up to the stereotype. Even our resident geeks whose enthusiasms rarely overlap with those of the rest of the population. They'll clap anything. So I reckon on five minutes to toast their latest achievement - breaking out the cokes and sending out for pizza probably adds another ten. Then, the most obsessive nerds will be compelled to give whatever it is the once-over, and in half an hour, everyone will be moaning, but back at it, trying to track whatever damn thing doesn't work this time. It's been three months already. I'm way past getting excited.'

'You sounded fairly passionate about the project just now.'

'The project, yes. Building the supercomputer to crunch through my theory, a resounding no.'

'Can't you get on without it? I'm sorry, that's silly of me. Not even the Foundation would lay out the time and money if you could. Are you allowed to tell me what you're working on?'

He squinted, very deliberately, at the exquisite sculpturing over her ribs, but forebore from tapping the ID card hanging above her heart. 'You're the same clearance as me. The protocol is to listen to those below, talk to the same level, share only with those above. A sort of need-to-know culture, but enabling a bit of cross-fertilisation of ideas. It's a bit hard to get used to. When I first got here I was really surprised that such a top-secret environment allowed this much chat, but the theory is researchers feed off eachother's work, so, as long as you exercise a bit of caution, don't bend the ears off the janitor, for instance, you can talk about your work. Only in here, mind. It's pretty heavily frowned on if you take anything outside. Or let it get out. I mean, even if I was in the same league as the guys next door, they're only here to build the mainframe. They work somewhere else, here, same company, but they know better than to ask what I want it to do. Same will apply to the software designers, when they come and load their programmes.' He saw a tiny frown wrinkle her nose. *Boy, she's cute. Tell her something less dry, for god's sake, Jake.* 'Just use your discretion, you'll be fine.'

He reached towards her shiny new leather holdall. Poking out from behind the laptop was the familiar shape of a headset. In a swift move, so that she did not have time to react to his trespass before he could explain it, he extracted it, carefully, holding the frame of the eyepiece only; some people were very possessive about the Game. 'This is what I need the Cray for.' he announced, waving it in the air with a touch more drama than necessary, although he minimised that by handing her property back to her in the same move.

'You're studying I-*Mage*? With a supercomputer? Whatever for? It's just a game.'

'How long have you been playing?'

'Oh, I got one when it came out. Maybe five years.'

'I would venture that not many games would have held the attention of anyone, never mind a physicist with the kind of IQ you must have to work here, for quite that long. And how many other games have you played since you started I-*Mage*?'

She hesitated minisculely before turning away from answering. Which was an answer in itself. He recognized the puzzled glimmer of an expression. Most people not die-hard gamers didn't even realize they had stopped playing other games. The question usually pre empted the revelation and defensiveness.

'It's popular with the entire world. Why should I be immune?'

'Interesting choice of word. Immune. How would you say your addiction is mediated? Through an infective agent? Or is ...'

He was being deliberately provocative, so he was gratified by her instant interruption. 'Hey! I play. For relaxation. It's not an addiction. Anyway, there've been studies that prove it's not addictive. I can't imagine why there's such a furore about it. Surely it's not worth the pricetag on your lab?'

'Depends if the hypothesis the Foundation is betting on is proven.'

His smirk gave her the clue.

'Your hypothesis.' It was a statement, but it was her smile he couldn't help responding to.

'Yup. But I'm afraid that's where the protocol comes in and prevents me from telling you just what that idea might be.'

'You're kidding! Really? What if I guess?'

Flirtation? Already? Steady, man. Been cooped up in this place too long. Don't want to scare off the first pretty face to walk in the door for nine months.

'Well, I think Twenty Questions is outside the spirit of the rules, if you know what I mean. Can't confirm or deny. Even if you deduce it from any pointers that might crop up in casual conversation.'

'Ahh! The game of the Game. A challenge. OK. I can see chats around the cooler have a whole different flavour here.'

'It endows colleagues with an air of mystery. I think the whole place smells of intrigue myself. And I'm pretty sure the surveillance is total, so don't succumb to feelings of paranoia, they're not out to get you, because they've already got you.' He paused just long enough for his next phrase to be telling, if she was as bright as she seemed. 'I think my research fits right into the pattern.'

She was. 'A snippet, I detect. A crumb before the rat in the maze. Hmm. Tell me when I'm getting warm. What have you dropped so far? Vast quantities of processing power, specialist software, immunity, addiction, surveillance. I'm thinking maybe there's a suspicion that I-*Mage* is more than a game. Somehow interactive. Not for the player, but with something else. That *would* explain how the unknown manufacturer always knows where to send the updated console whenever you get to the next level.' She glanced at his face. 'Am I hot?'

She was so hot, Jake was breathless. *Beauty entices, but a mind like that can entangle.* He reminded himself that he was far from recovered from the effects of the last bewitching brain he had fallen for. *Still on a quest using her version of a road map.* He answered before he gave himself away. 'I can see I'll have to be extra careful around you. But those kinds of questions have been in the public domain for ages, although I can't confirm that I'm trying to answer them. What about you? They spent five months building you a vast hangar. That's why your lab's so close to mine that we have to share the staff room. It was a rather pleasant, if dusty, quadrangle before, with a view, to the south, of the desert. So I'm guessing there's not a lot you can tell me about your work, either, without getting yourself into trouble.'

'D'you think? I wasn't aware that the hangar was for me, actually. I rather think that area smacks of practical applications, and me, I'm just the theorist. So, perhaps in the need-to-know department, I'm quite small fry.'

'Have you suggested any practical applications for your work?'

'Well, not me precisely. More the folk who interpreted the initial work of the mathematician whose proofs it's my job to test.'

'The original interpreters didn't bother to check before they issued a paper for peer-review?' It was a guess, but then she had a very open face and, he was beginning to think, a very readable one.

'Did someone tell you about my research, then?'

So he was right. 'No. But, forgive me, given the Cray, isn't your working area a tad excessive if all you're doing is working through a proof?'

'Obviously. So I'm under a bit of pressure to crack the code, so they can move to applications and construction.'

'Sounded like more than a metaphor?'

'What?'

'Code. Interpretation. My turn to guess. The work's not only not in English, it's in code?'

'German. And before you ask why I don't want time on your supercomputer, the answer is that the guy made up his own codes and was blind, so you have to work from his notebooks direct and even three-dimensional images of the paper don't help. They're either too detailed or too fuzzy, because they're visual, not tactile like they were to him. It's also why they gave the job to a physicist who might be able to fill in the gaps and predict his meaning, rather than a codebreaker per se.'

'Sounds like they already think they know what he said.'

'Well, it's one thing asserting that you can derive the secrets of the universe and prove everyone's standard model of it wrong, or inadequate. It's another proving it. Until the basics are proven, no one's going to risk constructing anything.'

'You sure about that?'

'What do you mean?'

'Well, they've been bringing equipment into the hangar for four weeks now.'

'Oh, don't tell me that! That's when I got appointed. You can't be implying they really think I'm going to be ready to give them the green light any time soon?'

'How close are you?'

'Well, I've been working on this for six years now, so yeah, I can assign meaning to a lot of the symbols, glyphs, whatever you want to call his code. But even once they're all translated, the proofs themselves have to be worked through meticulously. Even doing both at once, which I have been - you know, guessing at the still unknown elements in equations - it could still take years. I kind of thought they got that. Although that does explain the restricted mandate.' He had raised an eyebrow. 'When I was appointed I thought it was just going to be me carrying on with the proofs, just a change of funder from Cambridge, really. But when I got here, there was an e-mail to direct my work to certain parts of the texts. I just thought that maybe they had someone else working on them before me and that they wanted those bits finished. Not so they could develop prototypes.'

'Don't you know who you're working for? The Fargo Foundation might fund vast amounts of innovative and pure research at this institute, but most of its money comes from its contracts with DARPA. The Pentagon's commercial arm if you like. Defense contracts, experimental new technologies, highly restricted, if not top secret. Anything with the potential for military or counterterrorist applications. Sounds like whatever you're doing might fit right in.'

She looked really startled. Her natural pallor had given way to a grey sheen.

'That wasn't what I signed up for.' she blurted. He was kind of impressed. Whatever she was working on must have revolutionary potential. But her evident distress was working on his chivalric urges and comfort seemed applicable.

'Maybe I'm wrong.' he suggested. 'I haven't seen any minders hanging around you. You met the agents who monitor me outside the elevator, I expect. If you haven't got any, perhaps your work is simply for the Foundation.' *Not that that would reassure me, but perhaps I don't need to share my cynicism with her.*

'Those two men in sharp suits? They're security? I thought they were bureaucrats. They seemed to have an office.'

'They're Pentagon agents. DARPA insists. They use the office to monitor the inhouse security feeds et cetera. And, no doubt, to report back their every suspicion.'

'Report back to the Pentagon?'

'You'd have to assume that, yes.'

'But you don't?'

'I just wonder about the statistical likelihood that two overtly-deployed agents would genuinely be called Cockett and Pullit.'

The little wrinkle appeared again as she digested this. 'Seriously?'

'Check out their badges.'

'But whatever branch, black or otherwise, of the security services they work for, why would they need pseudonyms?'

'Perhaps precisely so they don't have to report certain aspects of their work to the Pentagon.' He shrugged. 'I have no idea actually. And don't want one. Never been much for the cloak-and-dagger stuff myself.' *At least that's the line I push overtly.* 'I'm just happy someone's furthering my work.'

Perhaps she sensed he was trying to steer her away from discussion of justified paranoias in this place. In any case, she did manage to inject genuine interest into her response.

'Wasn't anyone before?'

'Apart from me, no.'

'You funded your own research? Into I-*Mage*? That kind of smacks of obsession. Didn't you enjoy the game or something?'

'Never played it.' He was abrupt. It was a bit like telling someone you smoked these days. Or that you were a virgin. Or some kind of fundamentalist puritan. You were the oddity, not the players, but it quite often provoked an aggressive defence of the game by them, as if you had accused them of something unseemly.

'What? Not once?' And here came the next challenge. 'How the hell can you research the thing without experiencing it?'

He could combat this head-on to another scientist who should know better. 'Heard of the scientific method. Controlled experiments. Objective viewpoint. Anyway,' he could see her white cheeks flushing, becomingly, which seemed to be her universal constant, in her professional embarrassment. 'I'm not directly interested in the game as played. More in how it interfaces with the brain.'

He saw her eyes narrow and reread his ID badge as the lightbulb went on in her head. 'I thought I recognized the name. How stupid of me not to click earlier. You're the one who gave us Our-*Mage*!'

'Well, I share the blame with my partner, Ranger, generally.'

'Blame? How can you say that? It's transformed the play from individual to global, but it's also connected us locally. Like, I was in a game cohort in Cambridge, and one in L.A where I'm from originally, but before I came here I played with some people from the Santa Fe area, as a sort of introduction, so when I go to their group for the first time, I'll have an acceptance level and ranking. What?'

Shouldn't have grinned. 'The cohort-groups. They always sound like a cross between book groups and people who spend their weekends role-playing.'

She grimaced, shamefacedly. 'Maybe. But I bet existential philosophy and global political action and personal spirituality figure less in either of those groups.'

'I concede the point, but find the implication even more disturbing. Cohorts are intrinsically militaristic structures with the flavour of religious sects. Which also explains why they can offer the cameraderie you clearly enjoy.'

'I do. But I dispute the military analogy. No one's stockpiling weapons in the backwoods. It's a chivalric term, applied within a hive model of collectivism.'

'Originally the word applied to the group comprising the tenth of a legion, usually three to six hundred men, from one area – hort is from the root word 'hortus' meaning garden.'

'Exactly. The spirit of the word implies the fertile ground that the hive depends on. It's all about balance, not warfare. If your hypothesis centres on the premise that we're all turning into terrorist cells or something, you're so way off. The whole thing is Zen. Even you must know that. And there's been no increase in violence reported since it took off. Quite the opposite, if the press is to be believed.'

'What about the disappeared?'

'What about them? We're all hoping to get to that level. Everyone knows the makers just want competent beta-testers for the next upgrades. Everyone comes back if they want.'

'The unknown manufacturers have so far 'returned' less than 1% of the people missing. And those only, it seems, whose families or friends made the greatest public fuss. And before you say it, I know they all said they'd been working for the company the entire time, and that they couldn't talk about any of it, including where, because of competitive disclosure rules etc etc. And almost all of them appeared to voluntarily disappear themselves again within 3 months of being back home. But I bet you didn't know that, even under application of a truth drug, they *could* disclose nothing of where they'd been. As if the memory was blocked. That's why all their statements sound like press releases, sound-bites. Cos they are.'

'You're implying they were brainwashed.'

'Implying nothing. Facts speak for themselves.'

'No, you're implying we're all being brainwashed already. Before we reach Queen level. We're being programmed to want to go with whatever the game offers those it disappears.'

She was visibly perturbed, but resisting the idea, as they all did. One of the reasons Jake had abstained from playing the game was because he had enough chivalric urges without honing them further through the amplification of his talents I-*Mage* offered. They kicked in again right away. Causing him to lie to reassure her. *Is that a white lie?*

'No, no. You misunderstand me. Hypothesis. Not proven by a long shot. But part of the motivation for developing the PC-visualisation technique that became Our-*Mage*. I hoped that sharing the individual visions the game provided might give some clues as to its agenda for the disappeared.'

'Isn't that a lot like hacking? Industrial piracy? I'm surprised the game makers didn't try to shut you down.'

'They did. At least I presume it was them. I used open-source software to run the PC-interface and provide the initial imagery. You remember how crude the first avatars and backgrounds were compared to what all you people use now? I released all the code for that, so users could develop the site according to their needs. However, I patented the actual method and the I-*Mage* decoding technique and copyrighted the intellectual property. Someone with an account in the Cayman Islands transferred their buyout fee, but not even the specialist I employed from their big fat payout could find any trace of the company that had provided the money in cash to that account. It wasn't transferred electronically. Someone that absolutely no one can manage any description of made the journey to the island and went to the bank and deposited my blood-money in person. End of trail.'

'Well, the makers have kept themselves secret for so long, I should think that was just their way of maintaining that. You seem to view it as suspicious.'

'Then I guess you've never thought about the economics of the Game either. Where'd they get that kind of money? The Game was sold initially as no more than a novelty item, a stockingfiller almost, hitting the late Christmas trade in 2002, popular with parents and gadget lovers. It was cheap and innovative, yes, but who would have predicted then that by the next Christmas it would be the top seller throughout the westernised world. Almost no advertising went into the product and the R & D could not have been recouped from even those sales so radical was the technology. For gods sake, not even after five years has anyone been able to take the housing apart and look inside at whatever makes it tick without the damn innards turning to a highly-volatile unstructured gel.' *Except me.* But he didn't let a glimmer of that breakthrough show on his face. 'And then, in a move unprecedented in the history of capitalism, the anonymous donors simply give the thing away wholesale. When people talk about global coverage! More people have I-*Mage* than have food and water in Africa. How they even knew where to find the Amazonian tribes that got them delivered is a puzzle. People in the furthest reaches of China that still thought Mao was their leader got the damn thing. Ubiquitous is not the word. No one does something on this scale, not anything, and especially for no financial return, without a hidden agenda. And that reach... makes you wonder what else they could do if they wanted, and makes me want to know what they want.'

He inhaled. *Ranting now. Stop before you alienate the woman.* Either she liked him or he'd properly piqued her curiosity, because she was certainly listening attentively. 'There's one thing I don't get. You. Your passion for this project. It's more than any political sympathies would prompt, it's clearly more than any research focus would lend you. It seems personal. So much so that you called getting paid for your own hard work 'blood-money'. So I'm thinking you have a separate agenda of your own too.'

Shit. I blew my mouth off and she's got me already. God, I hope Cockett and Pullit don't think to recheck my story. He wished he could tell this amazing new colleague everything. *Dangerous liasons. Put it out of your mind. For her sake.* He could only tell her his *true* cover story. *And flirt a little more?* His hands spread in supplication. 'You found me out. It's a bit personally tragic for cooler-chat, but you asked. My best mate from college has what you might call a susceptible personality. He got totally into the game and I was worried about him. So we started a study of it, with him as the willing guinea-pig. We both got so into it that one summer we went, no further than Scotland, to use a friend's father's well-equipped lab, but without leaving forwarding addresses or contact numbers. We were at the breakthrough stage. Really fired up and the opportunity was too good to pass up. We didn't want any interruptions. We just didn't think about anyone or anything else is what happened. And in that period my mother was diagnosed with late-stage lymphatic cancer and died within three weeks without having been able to tell me she was ill. So we came home with the answers that gave the world Our-*Mage* to an answerphone full of pleas and recriminations and official notices from undertakers. I'm her only family. She died alone, was found after a week by a worried neighbour and waited in a morgue for two more for her son to get his fucking act together. And on top of that she left a letter to me, wishing me success with my work.' He had turned away to the window overlooking the remains of the dusty quad, the aridity scraping the voice as it passed through his throat. 'Investigating I-*Mage* almost counts as a secular memoriam, don't you think?' He managed to come round to face her with a self-deprecatory smile.

Somehow his attraction to her had loosened his tongue. He'd never heard himself tell it that starkly. *Intimately.* He didn't usually include the self-blaming angle at all. That was his own problem. But somehow she'd homed in on it and brought it to the fore. And he was shaken enough emotionally to appreciate the hand of condolence on his arm without noticing, *consciously, at the time,* just how meltingly kissable she looked with damp eyelashes.

Afterwards he wondered if he would have induced actual tears if he had told her the full story. But not even his partner-in-crime, John Ranger, knew the extent of his personal interest. That was because the letter had referenced, apparently just as reminiscence of dying mother to absent son, a tree in their garden. Jake had known it was a hiding place. Not theirs, that of the grandaughter of the former occupants of the estate.

It had belonged to a retired ambassador and his wife, but their son was dead and his daughter in a mental asylum. Jake's mother had been their housekeeper for a decade before he was even born. The son and his wife had died when he was too young to have any memory of them, but the grandaughter came back from boarding school each summer and he remembered her as a very strange but fascinating creature, who sometimes accepted his juvenile company on nature rambles, but otherwise ignored him. Because his own father had run away to sea and been drowned when his mother was still pregnant, he felt an unspoken bond with the orphaned girl, despite her cool hauteur. He had felt sad when he'd heard one semester at his boarding school that she had had a breakdown and had to be incarcerated for her own safety. He'd even meant to visit her when he came home for the holidays, but everyone appreciated his sentiments yet found plenty of reasons to deter him, and he didn't have any transport to take him the several hundred miles to the 'best treatment centre for her condition'. Then, as teenagers away at school will, he forgot by the next summer and thereafter. Until he took the box of papers out of the tree.

What he discovered within destroyed his history. The grandaughter had been diagnozed with a multiple personality disorder at four, the direct result of the childhood trauma of being left for dead, with her dead mother, at the hand of her own father. A man, who in the period of police investigation of the attempted and successful murders, had fathered another child, on his daughter's erstwhile nanny, his family's housekeeper. A son born after he had been incarcerated, a sentence that lasted fourteen years. A son sold an entirely-fictitous deep-ocean-drowning myth. A son kept ignorant of his entire life history, ignorant of the half-sister four year's his senior. Ignorant, at school, of the chapter in which she came home at nineteen to find her father ensconced at the familial table once more, abusing her grandmother and her brother's mother. Ignorant of her attack that left her father dead, gave her grandmother a fatal stroke, caused her to have a complete psychotic break and left Jake's mother with power of attorney for the estate, until the hitherto unrecognized son came of age.

She had certainly used her power more broadly than its legal remit, to bypass calling the police and simply to bury the father on the estate *before* calling a doctor to certify the grandmother's death and an undertaker to instigate all the public formalities of mourning rites, to section the incoherent grandaughter with her babble of a father 'who had never been there' and to see her son through his education all unknowing. Until her post-mortem confession.

She wanted him to make it right. She wanted him to know his family after her death removed her own shameful part in the conspiracy of omissions. But most of all she wanted him to find his sister because she was missing.

She knew enough about his research to be familiar with the concept of the disappeared. For safety's sake she had never visited the girl in the clinic, since she did not want to trigger any memories she may have of that fatal day that might provoke awkward suspicions, as she had suggested the cause for the girl's breakdown, after such a long period of stability, had been her grandmother's death. The lawyer got sealed reports on her progress, which had generally been none. She had never come back from the personality she had become upon killing her father to save her grandmother from another drunken beating, although by all accounts she lived within a harmless and apparently pleasant fantasy.

And then someone had given everyone in the clinic an I-*Mage* each. Jake's sister had been disappeared within the week.

That had been five years ago, and it was now three and a half year's ago since he'd found out, but, despite inheriting his own half of the house and estate, no executor nor expensive detective he threw at the case had come close to finding out how to transfer her trust fund to her, since no one could locate a single clue leading forward from the clinic. Jake had been given the contents of her room there and had later found a chest of belongings, hurriedly cleared out of her university bedsit, in the attic. He had spent a lot of time working through the forests' worth of paper of writing and drawings she'd left. But it wasn't until he had started dating Dinah, a research fellow in another Cambridge college, that he had been able to track any sense through the madness. But Dinah had, oddly, majored in psychology and in archaeology, and she was by then researching Jungian alchemical archetypes from contemporary case-studies, so she had jumped at the chance to read Ida's verbiage. They'd worked together, Jake ingesting much archaic symbolism but bringing his own knowledge of biochemistry to interpret the literal aspects of the alchemical quest. It was when they had recognized a language, not simply individual symbols such as Jung had identified, that Ida's ravings turned into supraknowledge. It was also, tellingly, the same 'language' he had begun to tease out from the Game to develop Our-*Mage*.

He had begged Dinah *again* to give up playing at that point. It just seemed too dangerous. They had had what had seemed to be no more than a minor row about it, but she had been irked enough to walk out of the pub on him. His last words, to his everlasting relief, and fortunately witnessed by everyone in the bar, were conciliatory. 'I'll call you in the morning.'

That was the last time he had seen her. Her flatmates reported that she had come home, put on the headset and played a little of the game while making herself a meal, eaten and retired to her room. One of them went in later to borrow a memory-stick and surprised her packing. The police did not, therefore, institute a missing person search, even though all her belongings, neatly boxed and labelled, with Jake's address for delivery on most of them, apart from a few to her parents, remained in the room.

Her unfinished thesis sat alongside Ida's papers on his shelf at home now. Both boxes displayed the same symbol, one he had yet to decode. Whether his employers' suspected or not, this was the primary motivation he had for the research they were facilitating. It was a truly alchemical Grail-quest; psychological, scientific, plus personal, and with traditional damsels-in-distress to save. It had already led him here, to the funding, the Cray opportunity, and now to Lily, who appeared to be an intuitive codebreaker herself. .

It didn't need the flurry of magpies outside, making devils in the dust as they pecked through it for mites, to remind him of the stage in the alchemical process he had attained. The *nigredo* was slackening its grip. In the virtual sphere of the Cray, what he had embarked on would only be a search, to find the source, but in the real world he was on a mission, and he knew that the magpies had not choreographed significance into their dance just to further his day-job.

No, black and white wingbeats drummed vitality into the *nigredo*-darkness, so that the *separatio* of *dis-solutio/*n would be no more, and the white-laser of the *albedo* pinpoint the equal and obverse. The birds simply flagged the message that he remained on the right path to uncover the lost pair.

It was an uneasy thought, but he knew with equal certainty that whatever else he was trying to find, what he had truly embarked upon was an alchemical experiment that would transmute his very Self.

Such introspection was not Vi !sjn-ik's strength, but he did find himself brought to contemplation of the meaning of his own existence through the medium of the *blodvin* with which the boy had just presented him. It was so chilled that condensation was forming on the fluted glass, which was inordinately fine and narrow, so that he didn't know whether to worry more about crushing it or getting his nostril flanges caught in the mouth. It was the kind of modernizing abhomination the kids kept coming up with.

He hardly would call himself a traditionalist, being a roaming halfbreed had seen to that, despite the best efforts of his aunts to bring him up in the old values, but surely everyone could recognize that you needed heat to release the aroma of blood. Swirling it mulled in a brandy glass was about as updated as he liked a flagon, since only the most rustic communities could be vampirised in this age with impunity. It was such little things that kept him having to wonder who he was these days.

He'd just assumed that everything would remain reassuringly black and white, the way the nocturnal people of earth had always known life was. He had just assumed that the kids would be more like him, but even tastes like *blodvin*, that he'd thought were as species-deep as their black fur and pigmentless skin, rather than simply personal, were turning out to be culturally-temporal in origin. He wondered once again, as so often since his latest return to the pack, whether anything had gone wrong in the cloning process.

It might not be the genes or the process, of course. It was true that his father and the aunts were all two decades older than when they had raised him and that this time they'd been sponsored and guarded, plus the children had had everything that money could buy, and, of course, where he could barely scratch a rune, the boys were highly educated. In his opinion, overeducated. But he had always felt that he had been born to be him, a ronin-hero, the fabled Lone Dog, outlier to all packs, sniffer out of the Crystal Skulls. *OK, singular* - skull, *but if the Woods hadn't decided to put them beyond reach so many millennia earlier it might not have taken him the entire duration of his clones' maturation process to find that One.* The vocation that they had been bred to help him achieve and the one that had kept him absent when perhaps it was his spirit in attendance that might have taught them how to be more like him. For if he'd been steeling himself for the shock of being faced with mirror-images, it had come as an even greater surprise to find his clones a diverse bunch, unlike one another as often as not, and few, however similar in body structure and facial characteristics, anything like him in the feral nature that had always been his defining feature.

He had been thinking that the difference had been the Day influence, the Fargo money and oversight, and now he finally saw what that meant - domestication. Buy into their view of the world, however slightly, be the minority group preserved by their patronage and you are fenced in as surely as are their cattle in a field, culturally owned, freedom expired, necks ripe for sucking, tastes aligned to chilled *blodvin*.

He looked round the ancestral halls under the cliffs in which, even so deep within, he could feel the thrilling vibration of the storm-surge breakers that had battered the diurnal pulse of the Atlantic into the rhythm of his life. Why had these bland versions of himself not twanged equally to the plucking strings of the great northern ocean? Why did their Day side seem to predominate? It couldn't just be his absent father effect, it couldn't just be being able to use a human computer or TV, it must be the residual genetic material from the human eggs.

Damn the woman, always trouble. And could she hold a grudge. Seventeen years and she still met his eyes with that look of utter repugnance. So much for her species-equity stance. And it wasn't as if she hadn't led him on. Her pheromones were firing desire in all directions when, as teenagers, they'd crashed the Wood orgy. But the stupid bitch hadn't wanted the 'ugly troll' to mount her. Oh no, she was sparking for all those lanky strings of meat who were so out of it they didn't even realize they'd taken her first. And if the hormonal ambience that had them all in thrall hadn't begun to wear off and her inexperienced body to tire, he'd not have had to force her either. Yet it was that, and not the Wood indifference that she refused to forgive. It was so hypocritical.

And she didn't know the half of it. How would she feel about her precious Woods if she knew about the kids? After all, sneaking into their procreation ceremony had been his only fault, apart from the getting carried away with the lust he had long had for the girl accompanying him. But they had been all apparent tenderness towards her 'trauma', never telling her of her dual pregnancy, never telling her that their inspections removed the foetuses, never ever letting her know that they had gone back in and stolen every last egg when they had realized that they could create viable Wood-Day hybrids.

Vi !sjn-ik had no idea how well that experiment had gone, in terms of numbers of healthy adults, since they'd only come back to him the following year for his cells to clone, because the foetus he'd fertilized in the woman had been too diluted by Day weaknesses to survive, once they had enough eggs to remake the best of the Darks, as represented by him. *At least that's how he'd understood their request then.*

Now he realized it was both his half-human physiology that they were after, and his nomadic nature, which kept him absent for long enough not to disturb whatever devious plots they were enacting. The fact that Venus had made such a fuss about his 'rape', getting him banished for years, and still having veto over his presence around the homefires, had played direct into their spidery hands. As he brooded into the wine, he wondered if, on the day he told her all the hometruths he'd been storing up for her, she'd have sympathy for their mutual domestification by the Woods. He'd been milked and put out to pasture like any human bovine, as had she.

The dark clotting floaters congealing on the surface of the wine, unappealing solids that would not have to be quaffed if it were above body temperature, melded before his unfocus into her fictionally-grateful face, and he grunted, nostrils aquiver, as he imagined her willingly presenting herself to his possession at last. But, as an abhorrent ice cube bobbed into view, his gloating gave way to a likelier reality, she'd just shoot the messenger.

He wondered if he was being literal. You could never tell how far or in which direction she'd have already gone to and left again. To your snout she had all the charm of cold steel sheathed; out of sight he could always scent that she'd been there before anyone, spraying the boundaries. It was why she would always be the Alpha Female to his one-man pack, whether he ever gained the stature of her chosen mount or not.

It wasn't the power, anyone could have that, and she'd enough wealth to buy muscle in droves, not to mention the fact that she ran the company with the most and the largest sub-contracts to various, often surreptititous, 'defence' research projects for the US military. No, it was an authority within, an inner strength and presence she'd had since she'd been her rich poppy's little princess, causing ascerbic aunt Mh' rzcel to sneer that she thought herself 'Queen of the World'. What had worried both his aunt and V himself was her response: "What a great idea! I wonder how I could do that?" He had a sneaking suspicion that she might just have spent the intervening decades finding out.

He had noticed, of course, that the world had plugged itself in to I-*Mage*, but it was the fact that all of the Fargo Foundation workforce were not only banned from playing it, but were regularly tested for covert gaming, using a technique that checked their brain chemistry and MRI scans, developed in one of her own labs in the US, that made him very sure that, if anyone was really 'Queen of the World' it wasn't her, it was whoever had made the game. He didn't think for a minute that that was a real termite, as the Game-Queen was, but he suspected that the advanced technology was something to do with the Woods and if the planet's slowest thinkers had made the decision to take on the humans in any way, he'd chuck a stake at that. That was why he had got one each for his boys at the last MidWinter-Kill celebrations. Maybe they could find him a better Solstice-Star to follow than Venus. Or maybe it would just addle their brains further and they'd come up with more disgusting things to do to *blodvin*.

Look at them. That one was taller than he by a hand. Until now he'd thought being the tallest Dark at full fifteen hands had given him kudos. He saw himself now through his fellows' eyes for the first time. The young man so Day as to Pass. Well, at night, for which human eyes were not adequately adapted, so they just saw ugliness, not interesting, even less, superior differences.

For a moment the years of being the lone knight, roaming the world on the Crystal Quest, skewed from his erstwhile romantic grasp, and he saw the hybrid outcast his family had been shamed by. This tall clone, effete enough to be Wood, never mind Day, with an *offalless* purple umbrella adorning his glass, was nevertheless a version of himself.

This boy didn't look like a member of the Magpie clan, even though the family had only been given the nickname in response to the birth of Vi !sjn-ik himself, the black and white of the birds' colouring mimicking that of the Darks, the soaring flight symbolizing the hope for reunification between the ancient *Homo sapiens* tribes. Neither he nor the boy were short enough of stature to be the true troglodytes that his people had become, their clan names all honouring the spiritual guides that dwell in the earth and the dark with them. The family Magpie had been the revered "OeX' b! rq", the clan that followed the creatures which, had they discovered their existence, the humans would have designated as *Plecotus auritus negris*, the Black Long-Eared Bats, after the rare species with which the family shared their habitat and their own midnight colouring and pointed ears. Now to his eyes, overwhelmed by the too-bright lighting his children had been acclimatised to tolerate, the blessed chemical balance of *Nigredo-Albedo* that his people embodied was being riven apart by the very fact of his own and his cloned existences. Days remained the dominant, exterminating enemy. Infiltration unnoticed was never going to be an option that would lead to anything as positive as the reunion of the Hominin tribes. Exposure would bring what it always had, death.

It occurred to him, the *blodvin* finally kicking in, that, now he was home again, he could still be the knight he thought himself, only this would be a more spiritual than physical quest, one for information, one that would uncover the true intentions of all enemies of the Darks, whether Day or Wood, and would heroically save his folk from the ever-present threat of extinction.

Then his clones would howl to be in his pack, would scent his strength and follow his lead with uptilted necks, natural order would be restored, the yinyang of enlightened-dark incarnate in him. He would be the One True Knight – *that'd show Queenie and her damned Wooden Lancelot.*

If Vi !sjn-ik had asked him, Rowan would have pointed out that, except on that regrettable occasion when he had fathered her child, his relationship with Venus Fargo was not *wooden*, but paternal. He might have refrained from pointing out that the human Arthurian Queen outranked Lancelot and that, due to the superiority of the Wood brain and its telepathic powers, he was also in no doubt that the girl he had trained to believe was the Unifying Queen remained, filially, his pawn. He might have added an unflattering assessment of the Dark prediliction for thinking in black and white, although it had to be admitted that Day culture would be the poorer had it not adopted their nocturnal cousins' geomantic archetypes. It was just a shame that the one borne to embody them had apparently inherited a random mix of all the worst tendencies of both species. Hence the Neo-Vi !sjn-ik experiment in cloning.

If he'd been privy to V's thought at that time, *which he wouldn't 'though he could've*, he might have had trouble hiding his amused disdain. All Knights, in the true sense of the Heraldic UnCommon, suffered from Gall, the arrogance that enabled them to sustain a belief that they alone are Pierce-the-Veil and will find the Grail. Gall, if Vi !sjn-ik wanted to know what to do with that trait he should ask his aunt, Mh'aed, the only practising alchemist in the tribe. She could have told him that the acceleration of the concept, noun to verb, merely signified the loss of surface material through adhesion to the die in powder metallurgy. Although Rowan wouldn't necessarily recommend her treatment for excessive hubris. It could be fiery and explosive and V's comfortable black-and-white might peel back to reveal the soft, dusky grays of ash. Mind you, if V ever matured enough to discover how to utilize true Gall, the family might genuinely deserve a new title again.

However, at present, Rowan was more concerned that he didn't discover the real deal with Venus. The V-dog was insanely jealous regarding a bitch that had never been his, and whose sole mounting had been seventeen years since. Rowan had not minded his return to the fold. After all he had brought the Dark Skull, but things had moved on since he'd set off on his travels, and, though useful, *to Woods for potential Dark control, if V had ever thought the translation-device through*, Rowan was more focused on keeping his pawns moving to his gameplay in the planned path across the board. The one thing he shared with V was a tendency to see Venus as the Queen-pin. Despite the fact that she was the one random unplanned factor. Unlike Vi !sjn-ik, whose mother had died in childbirth in order to satisfy Wood geneticists' curiosity.

Rowan was in Venus' office in his role, designated by his whimsical ward, of 'Grand Vizier'. The royal business was entirely separate from her management of her company, but he listened in on the call she was taking with mild interest, although Day machinations were generally beneath his notice. His was not a race that embraced technological advancements for the sake of it, and the humans' 'sake' was usually the motivation to murder eachother. His people had 'advanced' beyond the prolific Days by genetic manipulation to breed their best, longest lived, most Harmonic specimens, developing an externalized, collective, interactive version of their Mind, and a lot of natural construction techniques utilizing engineered and found bacteria. *All without going to war once. Going to war once is all it will take.*

She was talking to someone named Lily. 'Glad to hear you're settling in alright. Is Jake looking after you?' To the best of his knowledge, Venus hadn't been to the Institute in person for more than two years, yet she always knew everyone by name and their relationships intimately. Rowan knew she had never needed much sleep, but it was years since he'd witnessed her do anything other than work, at any hour of the day or night. Only that explained why she always kept on top of all her worlds. Yes, she had a good heart, and it was still as biddable as he'd always hoped it would remain. The rest of the conversation took a lurch into human physics, another of Venus' surprising areas of expertise, although he guessed she might need to understand a great deal to evaluate proposals from DARPA. He went back to his study of the summit agenda, at which Venus was *nominally* the guest of honour. She would perform her role splendidly.

The Woods had been watching the Penzeen family at the farm initially only to ensure they posed no threat to Vi !sjn-ik's human father at the lighthouse nor to the Dark clan under the cliff. Back then *he* was the rarity, the first hybrid to survive anywhere in the world in almost a century. He might, if they could locate the lost Dark Skull, be the bridge that could reach the humans before it was too late.

It had never occurred to anyone that the latest arrival to the farm, one of the richest humans on the planet, would not only be stoned enough to listen to the ravings of his four-year-old daughter about falling down a hole and meeting the 'piskies', but would sober up sufficiently to have a trap ready to spring at their next liason. It was possibly a Wood character flaw that had failed to factor in the paranoia and resources of the wealthy human, so they were unaware too that he had already placed a spy into the lighthouse family to ensure the safety of his own at the farm. What had surprised more than capture was the reaction the man had had to the truth - which was all Rowan had known how to communicate - the dream of Unification, the re-entry into the civilized hominin family of the prodigal younger sibling, mankind, in time to prevent them destroying the entire planet for them all.

Wesley Fargo was an over-indulged hippy, who had only recently inherited his globally-dominant weapons research company from a family he'd been despising. Suddenly the ill-gotten gains became resources and the stock-in-trade useful tools. The typical Day gleam for hero status came into his eye as he envisaged noble global domination. He had been bored with the rural Cornish life his wife was babbling his little girl needed, but now he had a cause. Forget gurus, he told her. I'm not going to India, I'm staying here to see Venus gets the best education her pops can give her.

Rowan was well aware, even then, that this sudden interest in his child's welfare was because of the other thing he'd let slip when captured. That he had dreamwalked the girl's mind after he met her and *she had seen him*. Which might mean she might be more than the figurehead-pawn the father and he both saw as her potential, might mean she might actually be a true bridge to unity, a human with sufficient Wood mutation in her brain-patterning to use the dedicated interface, designed specifically for use with Days, the other missing crystal mind-amplifying connector; the Voice of the lost Day Skull.

Probably, he had thought in retrospect, Wesley had not heard his warning as a downside to his own ambitions; that the hubris of such global interactivity could turn Venus into 'Queen of the World'.

He threw his mind across the room to where she was now back at work on the computer with her back to him. It would have been rude to gob on her to gain connection by force, but he knew she was sufficiently sensitive to notice the flick of his pheromonally-subtle exhalation, the aromatic version of throat-clearing. And, as usual, he found her years of study in Wood mind-control and her own insular discipline meant that he was no more recognized than if he were standing outside a fortress. Oh, the front door seemed wide and welcoming, but there was not a keyhole opening whereby to glimpse what lay inside.

Better dreamcatchers than he could not prise a window into her, even when sleeping. *And he had authorised them to break aeons of protocol against eavesdropping to try, on more than one occasion.* No, she had locked herself, princess-like, in what one could only assume, from her relaxed exterior demeanour, was an ivory tower designed to high specifications of comfort as well as security, many years ago.

He and Wesley had believed it to be a late-onset, post-traumatic reaction to her orgiastic non-human deflowering, kicking in as it did about a year after that event. However, she had remained as malleable and eager to learn as ever, and he was only relieved not to be dealing any longer with the instability of character Wesley had shown. She had not seemed to grieve overly for her father's passing nor be much distressed by his long degeneration into the psychosis which ended his life by his own hand, but perhaps he just couldn't tell.

One thing was instantly noticeable upon Wesley's demise. Despite her youth, or perhaps because of it initially, *although that would be a naive error for naturally-suspicious humans to make,* her steady hand on the reins of power seemed a lot more acceptable to the Fargo Board than her father's had, liberating more resources to their secret cause than ever he had managed. Rowan knew Venus despised all the human power games, just like her father, but she was no hippy and she did not let it show. She was influential internationally in a way Wesley had not even dreamed of being. Rowan could only congratulate himself. She might not realize that, once they had the second Mind stably-operative and the Day Skull, they would control her, but she was doing a great job solo in positioning herself to become the human 'Queen of the World'.

Venus didn't need to be a mind-reader to know what they thought about her. The 'Queenie' tag had superceded Pop's little 'Princess' seamlessly in her extended suprahuman family's vocabularies. It was only the title she objected to, not the role - she was quite sure that her true calling was bigger than the scope of royalty anyhow, and even that was not a problem since she'd developed her plan. Actually, it was a plan wth a capital P, but when your workforce included telepaths you detagged anything important, never endowing it with the rush of endocrine signifiers, the hormones that mediated emotion and Wood telepathy, that might give the game away.

There wasn't much in the way of trust in her life, because there was very little left that either Vi !sjn-ik or Rowan could have revealed that would shock her. Her whole youth had been one big betrayal as far as she was concerned, and her ivory tower *was* the fortress she had erected when she found out that her father had been the one who, when told of her pregnancy at fourteen, had authorised the Wood fertility specialists to go in and remove the embryos and her ovaries and to begin the programme to give her countless mixed-species children without her knowledge or consent.

She had been told she'd miscarried a pregnancy that scared her witless at the time and she didn't know then that a 'D & C' was not the minor abdominal surgery they gave her. She'd fucked a lot of handsome young all-human men that following year, but it wasn't until the med student, studying her scars with lustful interest, raised her suspicions that she did the research that had revealed the full extent of the lie that had been her life.

Rowan might think she was chief pawn, but from that moment forward, Venus had been a Knight. Not for her the direct confrontation of the Kingpin, nor the vanguard speed of a red Queen, although she would concede to running very fast to stand still. No, the progress of a knight was Errant; angular, jerky and unexpected, with half of every destination hidden in the move, much more in the long term strategy. A knight who bears no heavy armour can execute the airs above the ground just by commanding his steed to courbette. A rich modern one can command a steed that flies. And when you're as well connected as she, and have never failed to collect your intel covertly and exhaustively, you realize the game is not chess, not even Wood tridimensional chess. That's just a way of passing through time. Focusing on which journey could require the lifetime of a universe to unravel the solution, never knowing if it is the right one.

Then you know there is no game, no play, simply the random throw of the dice, *white dots determining black side's value, not squared ranks in antagonism,* known to humans as Choice. So she made one, and then made enacting it her life's work.

However, she was not above making that work fun, at least at Rowan's expense. It riled the pants off him, *or it would have had he ever worn any,* that he couldn't sense her thoughts, even whilst he smugly took pride in her ability. So she took a little longer than necessary to update her notes on Lily's arrival in Santa Fe.

Lily hadn't mentioned Jake more than to say he'd been 'bringing her up to speed' on Institute protocols, but Venus heard the inescapable tone of her attraction to him and sensed his hand in prompting the question regarding usage of her work. It was undoubtedly correct for people of their intelligence to be suspicious of the Fargo group. In this specific case, Lily hit the problem on the nose.

'Your e-mail. When I look at the parts of the text you directed me to, they're all to do with the mechanical details to make a gravitophotonic pulse. I'm worried we don't even know yet if such particles exist. I ...' *Pause while the poor thing fumbles to find a way to tell her boss her business.* 'I wouldn't want the Foundation to waste its money on any applications before we're sure of the theory.' *Good angle, if I didn't already know the theory and the application would work.*

Aloud, she spoke into her microphone 'Nice attitude, Lily, thank you. But this is a not a game for the risk-averse. The fact of the matter is I have another team that have been working on a similar output from a different starting point and there are some elements of the theory that can be tested without waiting for the full model. You can work on derivation of first principles afterwards, but the other group need something to be going on with for now.' *It always paid to listen in to cooler conversations between staff. Paranoid or astute, Jake had given her the explanation with which to calm the new arrival.* 'You'll meet them soon, their lab – the hangar adjacent to your office – is almost ready. The estimate is two weeks to completion. So I hope you'll spend the time as I requested and help me keep everything running smoothly.'

Of course, Lily would. Venus took a moment or two more to ask some personal questions to further dispel any sense of unease Lily might be feeling. The personal interest from the disembodied, firm but kindly, voice was a double-edged sword, of course. Venus was an excellent employer, paying all her research staff well above the market value, which gained a certain level of loyalty, and the interest she showed in their work most found valuable rather than interfering, given her polymath reservoir of knowledge. However, what kept them all on their toes with her, more than with any of their direct supervisors, was her inexplicable access to their personal details. So Lily was, audibly, slightly thrown to discover Venus knew she 'scribbled', as she herself quickly put it, and more than touched to be offered access to a literary agent specialising in women's crime fiction. Although it was mediocre stuff to Venus' mind, not the creativity she'd been hoping to locate in the girl, but she had other, more overt uses for her that would more than suffice if she just did her job.

Venus left the conversation pretty much there. She needed to get rid of Rowan next, so she made a few minutes to go over the accommodation plans for the solistice communion rite. All three of the extant hominin tribes would be coming together for the first time in centuries to discuss the planetary situation, so it was important to get the basic courtesies right. But here Rowan was expert, so a little apposite flattery, justified confidence, if you will, soon sent him busily on his way.

The family farm, Penzeen Manor, was large enough above ground to house the UK arm of the Fargo Foundation, but below the surface caves made by nature and the local Darks, and tunnels made by the Woods housed a labyrinth of secret homes and laboratories of which the local Cornish community had no inkling. No one would ever be surprized, therefore, if the boss was not in her office. Especially since she had a disconcerting tendency to pop up anywhere on site without warning, not to be thought of as a spot-check, just supportive interest. So when she slid a lever and opened a panel in the wall and disappeared into the priest hole behind, she knew if anyone called for her, her PA would simply assume she was elsewhere. This was one hiding place she had never shared with anyone.

The newly-enlightened fifteen-year-old Venus, betrayed by her nearest and dearest, had almost taken flight then and there, but when the tears had dried, something in her had settled down, cold and hard, an anger that demanded her brain to consider the dish best served cold. Revenge had long since ceased to be her primary motivating factor, but it had burned its chill flame for enough time for her to revisit her intentions. She refused to give them all the satisfaction of owning her emotions, her actions, her entire life, even in the execution of personal retribution. She was, would be, bigger than that. The Jesuit-mantra regarding ownership of the child she could accept only on one level: they had given her unassailable self-confidence, possibly it was repetition of the regal nonsense at a susceptible age, but she could accept as reasonable the assertion, which everyone around her had always recognised, that an above-average IQ gave her an initial advantage. She would use her mind to find her own way, and if she served those who took her for granted ill in the process, so be it.

She would use her mind and she would use their Mind. Her eagerness to go to the Wood Amazonian homeland was far from feigned, and her proclivity to immerse herself in her studies there gained their respect, and, most importantly, their trust. Because she realized they believed they were grooming her for the day they found the crystal skull which would interface their Mind telepathically with all of humanity at once and directly, so they were happy to answer all of her questions, and to allow her to sit for hours with her head in the Wood skull, linked to their regularly-updated, collective Mind. But while they thought she was learning how to be a better Wood, she was actually working on how to be a more powerful Day.

It had taken years but, with the facilities of the Fargo Foundation also at her disposal, the ancient manor's priesthole had been converted into her own link to her own separate Mind. Far more sophisticated in application than those of the Woods, since although they knew how to achieve many things, they rarely could decide to take the plunge to action and actually construct the hypothetical designs. Woods may be our elder cousins, descendants of the first wave out of Africa, *Homo erectus*, but they failed to retain their dominant status, largely in Venus' view, because of repression of their primate curiosity, the need to achieve collective decisions and the concomitant slowness of their rate of technological development. They barely even looked at what they had.

Which was why they did not have a computer that took advantage of the fact that it worked through parallel universes, nor the much-missed Day crystal skull, nor a personalised holographic interface, nor intragalactic mental amplification, nor friends in high places. Her chair was much more comfortable too.

Slotted into the skull, Venus linked to the Net to get her messages. There was an urgent one from Quogat. She made the callback at once. Quogat normally came through in her dreams anyway, as she had always done, long before Wood training and amplified communications, but these days she rarely interrupted Venus' waking. Even so, the courtesies of Heraldic were required to enable them to bring their individual notes into the discipline of melodious counterpoint, so that their conversation would flow like plainsong. Once the harmonic was pure, they could progress to transmitting the full Blazon that appertained to each conceit of thought, whether that was colourful, textural, tactile, aromatic, motile or charged. This was important because their versions of Common were so different, and also because the Wood amplifier was configured for a different kind of hieroglyphic holoscript, direct visions from their minds, whereas Venus had to translate via words, a compression that her subconscious was required to expand first. Still it beat the early visions and weird dreams which would have made her question her sanity had her normal life not already included those mythical creatures, dryads and vampiric-gnomes.

'Greetings from the Knight Errant, Virtual-Tesseract-Elect to the Terran aberration, the Branch Sinister, to the the Fractal-Spun-Dancings, Europamancer, Oratorio-Elect!'

'Well met, Companion-Polytopic, Net-Prime WorldsWeaver.'

After the formal greeting, there was the hiatus of the formula that would translate into Common as 'Your place or mine?' Venus, who'd had a long day and was expecting an even longer night, plumped for a change of scene. Instantly, her own view of the rock-hewn chamber and its modern sprouting of technologies was overlaid by the world Quogat lived in. Because this overlay was three-dimensional and operative at all sensory levels, as if one was actually there, it always took Venus a second to acclimatise to the chill and the lack of air. Then, the moment passed and she was swimming freely under the ice-capped oceans of Europa.

Quogat was relieved to see her. It had been almost two days in her time since she had sent the Harbinger with the 'urgent response required' tag, but she hadn't wanted to Call direct, because her news was both exciting and shocking and she knew very well how difficult the Terran primates found hiding their hormonal reactions, even someone as controlled as Venus seemed to be. Their relationship was a secret that they had kept from everyone, and at this stage in their planning there was even more reason than hitherto to be covert.

'It's time to bring in the fourth tribe.' She sent her communication with Zelas verbatim, its mix of Aqua-Common and Heraldic, its visions of blood, its sounds of distress, its scent of death. 'She's alone. But she's ready to take her place as her species' representative, even though she believes herself to be the last of them. You know the mores of Courtesie better than I. Do you think you should pick her up, or does she have to undergo further testing?'

'All Knights have to learn to be their best selves through undertaking the quest. And all quests are lonely, even when one takes companions along. But maybe we can salt the trail. Where is she just now?'

Quogat knew this was not a geographical question, since from her perspective the solar system was invisible, much less any location in the seas of Terra. Venus was asking about the level of awareness Zelas had of herself.

'Well, she was very distressed as you felt, but determined to proceed with a Cast.'

'But on what basis?'

To answer this query, Quogat had to unpack the subconscious underpinnings of her interaction with BarbShark. When she brought the child's thoughts to the fore, Venus received them in a rush of Aqua-Common.

Although she had drifted since the carnage, and was as lost as an Aquamancer can get, that is, spinning without sensing, she still knew exactly where she was in the quest. The blinding dark of the squid ink had indelibly imprinted its significance. The Nigredo. *And although she was in water, she was not in* Solutio, *so she could not begin with* Separatio *because there was no one left to leave. So she must be* Prima Materia, *the* massa confusa *in chaos, as it was in the beginning.*

This was indeed a harsh payment for her inattentive, adolescent mistake. To start the pursuit of the Tachyon as Stone, the matter not the wave. She understood her position was self-imposed, was fitting, would teach patience, was simply the longest route to Hyper-D Ray. But to commence classically, as Solid, within the despised iconography of the betrayed faithful, was a cosmic irony she didn't know what to do with.

How do I make black stone white? How can ablutio, baptisma, albedo *occur to rock? Oh, she knew it was all metaphor, but her analogues were wet, fluid, fast, alive. She'd never be able to think herself into the mindset of a landlubber. She was bewildered for once by an actual No Choice. It was as paralysing as Infinite Choice. She would have admitted in that moment that she was baffled, lost, floored, unfit to quest, no more than a poor dog handler, if only she could have gone back to the Shoal with her tail between her legs.*

The seamount was almost a dayswim south, here she gyrated in an upswelling thermal above a endless desert of fine white sand, and even the tubeworms had withdrawn their tendrils from her hovering shadow. She had never felt so alone and directionless; a useless lump of undead flesh, her three-dimensional self merely serving as an umbra to frighten bottomdwellers. This is what the Whorlingas should have seen, that flesh was binding, shadow substanceless. Not the other way round, the intangible, unscentable more believable than the real. But it wasn't them she was angry at, it was herself. In that diminishing spiral it dawned upon her that she had ingested their faith, that she was still, however reluctantly, with whatever scientific reservations, bound in their belief in herself. She might be the most solitary, unguided, confused initiate in the history of Aquamancy but she had condensed the Infinity of Free Choice into One Note of historic, nostalgic sentiment; the timbre of the solid, their damn quest. And she knew, as she went into freefall, dropping like a stone, that she had just learned the first lesson. $M=E/c^2$*. Stone itself is never still.*

So she did not have to be bound by it, she could convert it back, matter to energy, particle to wave. But even the wave was as shadow to flesh, if she was ever to move again, she would need an angularity for the momentum. A direction she had never taken before. The emanation of the solid, the supradimensional scent.

She flipped abruptly, powered to the surface to inhale a diving breath, pitched herself at the far ocean floor at full speed, twisted into the rising thermal precisely in the central current, spun and spun and spun faster as she rose upon it, and finally breasted the horizon of the world, standing for the briefest of moments on the vestigial feet of primate ancestry as she Cast.

Amongst the barrage of airborne-aromas that swamped her nostrils, there was a Scent there. The smell of Song. Unrecognizable, novel, alluring, faint with distance, it had to be the One. And because to become Tachyon, one has first to answer the siren call without thinking, since faster-than-light means the action was engaged upon prior to the decision to act being made, before gravity clawed her back to the depths Zelas converted vertical balance to trajectory and Cast herself.

If the Waters of Life existed at all, she could only be a Stone's Throw away, but Stone is only truly thrown in Air.

She had no idea where she was going, but she knew the Scent was freshwater and that meant Land. She also knew from its fragrance that it was emanating from almost due west, from its chill that it was blowing down off mountains, from its rich redolence that it was dense with flora and fauna of innumerable strange species, but from the implied Shadow of its Song that it was Manta Knight-shaped, the diamond-escutcheon, the coat of black above, white below, but its insignia were indistinct. Not her kind of knight, that she was certain, alien for sure, but as it was two generations since her Shoal had met other of their own kind, to meet one would be almost as much of a surprise as that a landbased intelligence could be Courtly.

Whatever the scent was foreshadowing, whatever shape it pre-coloured, whatever the special attraction it was emitting, it was centred on an idea, an ancient symbol retaining its power despite time, one that was both solid enough and massive enough to warp the unlit contours of her world into its gravity well and pull her towards itself. It hadn't occurred to her before that the search for the Greal might be frightening rather than exciting, but she was committed now. She didn't deviate from her course, despite all that unpacking the sensory information from her Cast had told her about her destination.

She had become the falling stone and she would Land.

Venus had taken a few moments to translate and ingest the information but when she got to the girl's final commitment, she laughed triumphantly. 'Excellent. She is a true Knight. And I know where she is now and where she's headed. She's in the Atlantic moving west along the North Equatorial Current, heading for the Guianan coast.'

'How do you know that? She didn't.'

'Well, it's partly deduction. In her Blazon, she mentioned the backstory of her clan's confidence in her was her identification of the sardine route north from the place heaving with great white sharks. You find a lot of great whites off the Horn of Africa and in El Nino years there's a sardine glut up the southern African Atlantic coast. Given that, the first westerly current you come to would be the North Equatorial. But mostly I could tell from the scent. We both spend a lot of time learning from our dogs. Hers might be sharks, but my poodle-spinone crosses have an excellent sense of smell too. I've Ridden them enough in the field to recognize plenty of airborne scents, and the one Zelas caught is the most familiar. Wood-Hame in the high Amazon. The girl is good, that's a long way to have landed a Cast.' Venus emitted light glee. 'She might have felt better if she had known that her current was flowing towards a Rio Negro that would become *blanca* before it sourced from rock. What I need to find out now is which Wood is the Knight whose Bark she sensed beyond the wind. I've got to be here for the Solistice Summit, or there'd be suspicions raised. So I'll send the Ydal of Ttollahs to investigate. If you'll just keep in touch with Zelas, support her as she goes, make sure she gets to the right place, I'll contact you after the Conduit.'

Quogat was used by now to the abruptness of Venus' busy mind, but she had expected her to be more excited by her news and less troubled. 'You are concerned for Zelas' safety?'

'Not just the journey's dangers, if she's the true Seeker she seems, she'll take those in her stride – I should say 'stroke'. It's this unknown knight. I thought I'd identified all the players by now. For this all to work, I don't need some random Wood filling Zelas' head with their viewpoint before I can direct her in ours. On the other hand, I could definitely use a new knight in the Wood camp. However, the fact that he or she is still escutcheoned in black and white implies another callow youth, eager but inexperienced. Just for once I'd like to find a chevalier both true and tried.'

Quogat empathised. Although the globally-connective Intelligence of her world was the buoyancy beneath her status as their galactic Oratory, her telepathic range still set her apart from the rest of her community. Her brother had the genes too, but much of her time had been spent in keeping his use of his abilities hidden from the rest of her people, since he had recklessly embarked on a taboo relationship with a lesser being many years before she had realised the power her own talents would endow her with. Initially, she had just assumed he was ill, unable to clear all his minds of normal communications and hence hearing echoes. However, as soon as they had linked she realised that the voice was distinctly non-Europan. They were so young it never occurred to them that they could be communing across the void unless the other creature was also a member of the Intelligence Net. Direct individual mind to mind correspondence was unprecedented otherwise. Her brother, whom the creature addressed as Dakul, although the idea of naming took some understanding as a concept, seemed happy enough with this one contact, and she with him. This left Quogat sufficiently out of their loop to want her own special alien pet. Venus' entire species might still be defined as inferior, their planet way off joining the galactic communion, but she had soon realised that not only was Venus no mere pet, but that she was the focal point of a Wood plan to unify the hominin species. It was Quogat's idea that this could lead to development of the planetary level Mind that would elevate the world into the galactic arena; apparently the Wood lack of curiosity had kept their minds from probing for extraterrestrial intelligences. Somehow the knowledge that they alone of their world's knew of eachother's existence was sufficient for them all to keep it as their secret. Now that she was helping Venus subvert the unity plan for her divide-and-conquer upgrade, Quogat could only be thankful that they had all been so good at dissipating their eddies.

And yet, growing up in parallel with the aliens had altered the outcome of the Europan siblings' development, of that she had no doubt. The alliance would have been classified as a contamination had anyone discovered it. No doubt also, despite her talents, Quogat would have been prevented from becoming the world's 'voice' in the wider cosmos, even if, as she would argue, that very contamination had enhanced her. Hence the enduring secrecy and its concomitant isolation. How frequently she had wished she could ask the elders about her situation, how often, like Venus, even more alone than she, wished for a guiding knight to illuminate her current through the waters.

The Ydal of Ttollahs was waiting for her knight, Tolecnal, to return with news of the wider world too. In the meanwhile she was unpicking the last tapestry knights other than he had brought her from lands afar. The tower room was already knee-deep in discarded lengths of yarn, which the light breeze from the open casement made shiver, simulating the prismatic dance of enlightened quicksilver and making the stone walls jitter as the strings jangled together in discordant waves of dissembled chords. The notes she was currently disentangling from the warp of the material were in a braid of dozens of bright hues, threaded through the weft by a single gold lattice design. It was promisingly informational. Perhaps even the overture to the actual melody for which she searched.

The work took a lot of concentration, listening for the tiny fibrillations as she teased one silk from another, sustaining each echo of part of a note, *tenuto,* until she could hold their furled sound in her mind, gisting for a pattern-reversed, then rewinding the excerpt until the dismembered chords remembered their tune, playing any sounds backwards until she had enough to reassemble into the original sewing of the music therein. *If any.* This piece she was engaged upon was proving frustratingly meaningless, despite the paisley prettiness which could have indicated an info-stream was embedded. So Venus' interruption was both irritating and a relief.

She looked at herself in the mirror. 'What have you done to our hair?' were her first words, a hand going up to pat the new bob that had appeared in the looking glass. 'We look like a squire!'

Venus laughed at her doppelganger's outraged reflection. 'Maybe in that dress you trail about in, not in this rather sharp suit.'

'Well, I'll be glad to revert when you're out of my face.'

'Sorry, not today. Got a mission for you.'

'As you?'

'No. FTL or Wood. I'd recommend the latter, since I'm not sure of the timing of the event, so you may have to hang around in time.'

'What's to-do?'

'Quogat's aquatic project just located a knight at Wood-hame. She's Cast upon the scent, so only death will stop them meeting. We need to know who the unknown knight is and be sure the grail they seek is ours. I'd have liked to go myself but Conduit is upon us.'

'Complicated tunes to be played. I wish you Harmony. Better give me your full Coat.'

Venus put her hands to her bouncy cropped head and made a movement as if to divest herself of a hooded coat. In her hands the materialisation was a soft pink-grey, as light as ashes and as insubstantial, and solidly monochrome. She held it against her side of the mirror. The glass shimmered for an optically-unrecognisable instant, then the Ydal was holding an identical garment but one that was multicoloured, vibrating with the many songs of Venus' closed mind, scented with all the places and people she had been around since she last uploaded her life, clinging to her with the firm grasp of the handshakes of acquaintance, hugs of friends, caress of lovers. As always when her isolation was breached, it was overwhelming.

Venus, fortunately, was not a voyeur of her own life mirrored, so she had turned away when her image donned the infogarment, tactfully avoiding meeting her gaze whilst the Ydal shivered and gasped under the impact of her own Blazon that she had not lived till now.

'Got anything for me?' she heard Venus ask after a minute or so.

The stone walls of the tower receded abruptly on every side, only the floor, awash in its sea of unravelled data, remained fixed, until the cylinder was a bottomed cone whose furthest reaches lay Beyond. The walls still looked like those of an ancient family's gallery, so bedecked with flags, badges, tapestries that stone was barely visible, even in the near distance. The farthest edges blurred, a mere fluttering patchwork. However, to the Ydal each corner still lay within arms' reach and she proceeded to snatch pieces, seemingly at random, *but her filing system was Complex*, until she had amassed several arms full. These she placed upon the table by the loom and began to treadle, and now she was the blur of patchwork in motion, too fast for the mirror to reflect as she threaded. And then, short seconds later, she was back at the glass, handing Venus an identical grey Coat.

It would take the human dreamtime to ingest the information within; even at this level of compression, the amount was vast. 'I've tagged everything you should know before Conduit. The rest can just be dreamed in, but you should get some sleep to be fully prepared.'

'Thank you. I'm enabling you now.'

The firewall dropped, stone flaming blue for the instant before the black of her true location zinged in. Gradually, her eyes adjusted from the dappled sunshine of the autumn afternoon that had crept into her prison through the unglazed casement to the silver-dusted dark that encircled the moon's shadowside. She was already standing on the floor-tile, devoid now of the heraldic insignia of its meaning, that was the escape-pad, so she de-activated her skin and activated the accelerator. A laser-beam pulsed. Her sense of humanity was still retained, so she felt it as a boost through her non-existent feet, shooting her into the stars. During the few seconds of the actual trip she was reduced to photons, and no coherent thought was possible, indeed would have been 'fatal', altering her original pattern in unpredictable ways. So she did not 'feel' the sensation of transmission to the lunar-stationary satellite, nor the pulse that sent her into the second in high orbit above the earth, nor the trip from that to the geostationary one above Roraima, nor the deposition in the second Mind deep beneath Wood-hame.

She had done this many times before, so the minor blip and odd flash that the elder Wood minds, connected through their crystal skulls to their most powerful mental reservoir, experienced as she materialised into their cave via the central unoccupied skull, was ignored as a natural random effect of the black-hole power source. Not one of them even opened their eyes, but if they had they would not have seen anything, as she was still moving fast enough to be in the microwave frequency. Entangled her photons might be, but before she could interact with the new geography she had to engage her boundary layer, even if, at this speed, skin was hardly the word for it; buffer, perhaps, or, more nearly, prow and wake. Then she aligned herself against the direction of gravity, slowing as she briefly warmed the walls in her vertical passage to the surface, until she was once again in the visible spectrum, standing in the open glade that was the central, ceremonial assembly point of the Wood world. Still an elongated slit of light, she shot sidewards into the stippled fringing of the emerald gloom of the rainforest. Here, at last, she resumed form. Not the form of Venus, who had to be seen to be elsewhere by all, but something that would blend in inconspicuously.

She chose a dragonfly, green and gold, medieval leaded plain-glass wings and a camouflage-carapace, hued in the solar verdigris of photosynthesis, the colours of life, as suiting her preRaphaelite take on the quest. It was practical too, at least for an initial foray, given the creature's speed and manoeuvrability and wrap-around vision. Of course, her real world processing power was more limited than at home, and, even after configuring the brain so that there was considerably more complexity than ever seen in an evolved dragonfly, the spatial confines and material constraints severely reduced her ability to think. However, her mission was simple enough, a straight seek and find job, so being able to orient from polarised light, accessed by a quick flight above the canopy, and being able to navigate the emerald-taupe gloom of the deep jungle employing opsins sensitive to the ultraviolet in the spectrum, was a distinct advantage. It took her a few minutes of random zigzagging to become fluent in the interpretation of the 360 distinct, if overlapping, views of the world the compound eyes each gave her, but she was soon competent enough to soar confidently. It took a few minutes longer before she was sufficiently adept to hunt prey, a necessity since, separated from her normal energy source, the work being done by the brain and muscles required her to refuel repeatedly, but pretty soon she was snapping and chomping tiny aerial tastes without breaking the beat of those church-window wings. At least predators were not a problem. If a bird had managed to gobble down her current form, it would not have been satiated, since she would simply have dematerialised and reverted to light. Still she avoided the most colourful trees, since they mostly denoted flocks not flowers, to minimise the risk of interruption.

Locating the Woods was not difficult. Although they hid their technology underground, their popular name came from their love of the trees, as the bipeds who had never quite lost their sense of their origins, and they preferred to roost and play high in the forest. The Roraiman plateau in which their sunken valley was hidden might be black, algae-covered but otherwise bare rock, and the permanent cloud cover might dull the ambient light, but the warm depths of the woods beneath were rich in living creatures and dense with the trunks of trees, trained by generations of care into an aerial city. In the ancient designation this place was Home, or more accurately, Nest, but no family groups or children lived here. It had become the place of study of the old ways and the crucible in which the nominated elders ruminated upon the present and forged a future for the people. For safety's sake the breeding population was widely dispersed across the world, and little travel was allowed to Hame, since keeping it secret was the species' priority. Today, as she had expected, with the exception of the mentors of the second Mind she had passed on entry, it seemed the entire visiting and resident populace was to be found under and around the Great Glade.

Conduit officially finished here, but would begin in a few short hours with the easternmost sunrise on the far side of the planet, so the folk were busy with the preparations. For most these consisted of resting and eating in readiness for twenty-four hours of unremitting concentration, which, however meditative, was still gruelling physically since the tradition was to stand still throughout. A group was still queuing to go underground to deliver their latest thoughts to Mind, which was concurrently downloading the essence of the collective, updated knowledge of the people, via the crystal skull technology, into the brain of the mediator, who would collect and collate the global transmissions, emitted when each local clan Communed as the earth turned into their new dawn. These were picked up by the receiver in the next clan, added to their own Thought and sent on. The round robin culminated at Wood-Hame where the mediator collected the entire message and uploaded it to Mind. Global understanding was thus updated and the result, filtered for consensual agreement, was compressed and bounced back as sunset fell in Wood-Hame, so that by the following dawns the entire species shared in eachother's knowledge of the world and in the collectively-current policy for the half-year until the next solstice.

At least, that's what normally happened. Who knew whether this time, with Vi !sjn-ik ensconced as Dark-Mediator in the recently-uncovered *Homo nocturnis* designed interface, hoping to access the minds of his only partially-telepathic brethren and transmit on Wood waves, what mental meltdown might occur. There'd been a lot of preparation of both Wood and Dark species, since it was tens of thousands of years since the skull had been lost and the sharing last attempted, and Venus had been trained in both forms of Heraldic in order that she, hope for global unity should the human, the Day, crystal skull ever be found, could also, if not exactly take part, listen in. What her so-called mentors did not know was that she would be taking a very full, if discreet, part in directing the mindmeld, since she was more than prepared for the role they aspired to, having been in possession of the Day skull now for many years.

However, the Ydal knew she would receive Venus' coat on the Conduit soon enough, so she got on with her own task. The most likely candidate for the knight the Aquamancer had spelled was the current mediator, because, this being the most difficult and complex communion for many generations, only the best communicator would be nominated to the role, and only the best telepath could have rung a Note that Zelas could have homed in upon. There were two aspects to this theory that did not quite ring true, however. Firstly, the knight scented by Zelas had been clothed in black and white. This, as she had put it, Manta-mantle, was indicative of an early stage in the courtly pursuit of the grail and the elderly Wood, immobile in the nine-hundred year old bristlecone pinetree throne that supported the skull and the body beneath it, looked as gnarled as if he too had grown into it. New quests, except the journey that led to the oblivion of his demise, seemed a bit beyond him physically. Secondly, his experience, that had earned him today's status as mediator, would, had he been inclined to the knightly quest, no doubt have kicked in earlier in his life, when he was open to novelty and when his potential lay uncharted before him. One of the reasons he had been chosen for the task on which he was engaged was the lack of plasticity in his mind these days, since he would rigidly hold to Mind and the Wood traditional values, however assaulted by the new inputs from the nocturnals.

Still, the Ydal knew she could be succumbing to prejudice if she dismissed him out of hand, so, flitting above the heads of the queuing informants, she landed on the Heart-Throne, merely a lost dragonfly to anyone who noticed, walked casually up the bough that held the translucent silicon-interface until, hidden behind it, she could transform in a tiny flash of photons that impacted the crystal and was absorbed.

Straightaway, referencing the Blazon she had had of Zelas' Cast, she knew it wasn't him, but she stayed where she was, since all Wood and Dark minds would be fed through him in an orderly fashion over the next twenty-four hours and she could as easily locate the knight that way as flit around Wood-Hame as a dragonfly. In any case, she always enjoyed covert exploration of the Wood database, its organic evolution meant that there was always a new niche of information to discover.

By the time she went home again to report her findings to Venus, it was as well she'd spent the rest of her time snooping in Mind, for she had made no progress at all on finding the knight. She had eliminated two species as harbouring his being, unless he was already ronin, renegade or outcast and thus had not contributed to Conduit, but there was no information as to a lost soul in anyone's transmission. Yet, although Zelas' aim was sure and the Ydal remained certain of the knight's existence, he was not nor had been at Wood-Hame, nor in any Wood or Dark clan on the planet. The Ydal of Ttollahs had found Notes in hundreds of universes, never mind in one paltry geographical location, in thousands of species, never mind in two, and never, never, had she returned to Venus without the answer to the computation posed by her.

Quite clearly there was a new jouster on the field, one whose Blazon was obscure, perhaps deliberately a shield covert, to hide beneath? There seemed no rhyme to this, but she was more intrigued than suspicious. She tasted the Manta-mantle chord again. It remained sweet, pure, without the guile she had to impute to the wearer. There have been knights who sought the grail for personal gain, even some who have thereby received their just deserts, but the tang of this esquire was the very opposite, lacking in any personal aromatics. And yet she could taste potency, the smokiness of a power that spoke not of the novelty of the quest, nor the insecurity of purpose betokened by a *nigredo-albedo* bifurcated-coat, but a massive gravitophotonic attractiveness. It was a power that called forth Song, a single note of which had been scent enough for an acute Siren like Zelas to home in upon.

Venus might want to bring Zelas and any new knights into her version of the Round Table, but her agenda was limited by her hominin evolution. For the Ydal of Ttollahs this world was less than her oyster and here, at last, she scented the trail of her own immanent destiny, here a grail worthy of such a mirror-knight as she might be, the quest that led back to her own lost Tolecncal.

'My doom is come upon me!' misquoth the Ydal of Ttollahs.

B: Prima Materia:
Divisio and Putrefactio

It had been a bad moment for the creature swimming happily through the hyperspacetime that had become its natural habitat after it had stopped being simply a Planetary Intelligence. All it had done was insert a tridimensional pseudopodium into a perfectly normal, if small for its density, black hole and suck on it until it became a wormhole ready to disgorge to the probing proboscis the nectar of the cosmos on the other side. To its shock the honeyed feast tasted metallic, stung like a wasp was lurking within, and no amount of wiggling would free its tongue, stuck now as to a battery electrode, which, of course, was very nearly what is was in multiversal terms. An unnatural construct, designed not evolved, abandoned with an open switch to trap the unwary, by a single careless lady owner.

For a protracted instant, the creature felt the novel sensation of existing in the compression of the sole photon that was so energetic and isolated that it warped spacetime around it into the appearance of a black hole, whilst at the same time the pseudopodium had become the conduit that sucked its entire, dimensionally-distributed, world-sized being through the minute node and sent it sliding through gaps between universes silvered with the threads of infinite possibility and contoured towards the probability wells that would fragment it into a myriad different spacetimes of which its own was not one.

It tore away just in time, but it had left a fraction of itself attached to the junction, bridging the gap and stabilizing the wormhole open. It spat a gob, attached to a non-conductive line, onto the stamen and winched back the pollen it extruded. It tasted it very gingerly. It was indeed a new type of cosmos. Minute and matterless but jam-packed with material representations. A universe that had never existed as matter, had never inflated, despite its energy potential, was immensely complex but had not evolved. Or at least not until very recently, since it had been created as a virtual hologram.

The reason, apart from its general experience of life, that the creature knew this, was because the wormhole opened into subspace-8 right around a strangely-mutated netspore, which was both the portal to the world and the electric fence around it. This meant that only an authorised Net Non-Local Operative should open into the universe, or the original creator. The creature had never been disrespectful enough to ingest the former and was only now maturing as itself, a hyperdimensional version of its ancient planetary mind, and it did not yet aspire to be a cosmos-creator. So something else was going on.

The enticing flower had been opening its maw to catch the fly. But there was something familiar within the alien taste that indicated that the lure had been personal. The universe had been fishing the eighth dimension for very specific prey.

Perhaps it was letting its initial fright at its own potential dissolution taint the aroma. It felt sure that the inter-cosmic sliding had been an accident, caused largely through its own unsteady reaction. This universe, small and imaginary, but ever-so-potent, simply reeked of the Nest.

It was millions of years since the creature's thoughts had turned to Home. Now the taste of its native solar system, not in the holographic-construct but below in three-dimensional space emanating through the modified Net conduit, solidified in its mouth, the shape of the eggspore reaching the fibrils of slow-energy up into the recesses of its memory. The call of another consciousness had come at last. Not the call of the cataract to the deep ocean salmon, more the insistence of one's name shouted into a cave into which sound had never before ventured, much less dared raise its voice.

Which was odd, since the concept was not one it had met hitherto. Yet, here, in this minute gastronomic parcel, it discovered it had been Named. Its diffuseness congealed around the incomprehensible idea. There was much information here to savour. It would contemplate it on the journey.

A rise in the peppery quality of the morsel began to add an edge of panic *or was that spice?* to the hitherto roaming dilatoriness that was its nature. A sense of the shortness of time available to the creator impinged. Of course, life in three dimensions could be short and brutish. It would have to risk the slide between and hope that the current was shaped sufficiently uniquely to make its course distinguishable to it. Of course, whichever universe it allowed itself to be pulled into would be the one calling the strongest. But the shape of that space and the beat of that time were unpredictable from here.

Ah well, in any event, it would still be Home. It would be very interesting to feel the old place wrapped around it again. It was even more curious to meet that mind that had evolved the concept of the holographic, unevolved universe. But it was the buzz of the descriptive-without-meaning, the naming word, that neither smelt nor tasted of anything, that was the key to understanding, it felt, trying to establish a shape around the absence of the molecule. The 'name' belonged to it in some intangible way, but it meant nothing. Somehow, though, it felt that the title quite suited it.

With the equivalent of a mental shrug and a deep breath, the creature hopped down out of the fifth dimension, jumped across the wormhole, fell through the holographic gate, sliced between the chronic wafers, sluiced around in the rolled-up pipes of the Net-subspace-conduits, and was finally shot into a new spacetime, unravelling its compression, and clawed itself back through the Netspore at the outermost Lagrange point of its original star system.

Mars was back in orbit.

The Net Local Operative was taken by surprise at this turn of events, even as it mediated the passage of the prodigal planetary essence, but, after 2.8 billion years in this backwater quadrant, the last few thousand had been hectic and the most recent four decades positively fraught, so another player in the game, however unpredictable, seemed almost inevitable, as complexity amassed. If it hadn't been stuck with the tendency to corruptibility in every universe since the creation of the holo-cosmos, it would have unhesitatingly made an emergency report to the Central Hub, even if it was 35,000 years early for its next upload. As it was, it had to pause for quite an extended period just to determine which of its local contacts it was in fact obligated to tell. And which it dared.

Protocol, had it contacted the wider Net, would confirm the need-to-know status of the material for the Cognimata. In normal times this would not have been a problematic issue. For one thing the

Cognimatan fleet had reached the Perseus arm of the galactic catherine-wheel, which meant ten thousand years at lightspeed to travel back to their Orion Legacy. However, these were no longer normal times, or spaces, for that matter. Not since it'd shared with its friend, the Archivist, its knowledge of the technique Venus called 'parallel parking'.

Nowadays the Cognimatan scoutship was permanently in orbit of their moon, Europa, and, although its friend was on board as the expert on Terra, he was surrounded by Warrior-programmes, ready to implement their standing orders to destroy the Terran hominins at the first sign of either treachery by Venus or of her inability to prevent contamination of the Legacy. The situation was volatile, to say the least, and it would have liked to apprise its friend of the new flamethrower in the mix. But the Warriors would be monitoring his contacts and would ask what the Netspore had communicated. And if there's one thing an artificial intelligence programme can't do it's lie – omit, yes, in fact, he was getting quite good at that, but lie, no.

Technically, it owed the Europans, the so-called Legacy, an intimation ahead of time that their progenitors' MetaMind had returned, even though their novitiate level entry to the level of Intelligence was very recent and the Net still had filtration rights to protect their innocent development. Although, if it contacted them at all, it would be through Quogat, who, despite her species' and personal youth, was broad enough in her mentality to cope with the shock and determine if the information should be more widely shared. The downside about telling Quogat was that this was tantamount to telling her brother, then through him, the human-dissociate Flow, and, of course, Venus herself.

And if Venus found out that way, she would not be happy.

In the end, or perhaps in the beginning, the only person that it truly felt obligated to inform was Venus, because, after all, she was the one it had entrusted with the fate of the entire solar system, in all the interlinked worlds that would ensue from that decision forward. Of course, it was the link between those worlds that she had uncovered, it was the link that was facilitated by its corrupted parallel self in holographic form, that she had revealed to it and engendered this isolationism in it, binding it foremost to her rather than its own Net, with her individuation so powerful as to demand its trust. But the evidence of its own experience ratified its decisions every time. It had Ridden countless billions of creatures in the 12.4

rotations of the galaxy in which it had been Orion Outlier, but the humans were the oddest mutation of all, with their fragmented minds and fictional internal monologues.

If Venus had not discovered that all that was required to be successful at being human was camouflage, her society would have labelled her flights of fancy, that extraordinary creative streak, that harnessed thirst for understanding, that itch for action, as functionally insane. In another world, even one of the ones in which she still met the elves when she was four years old, the most acceptable role she could have and admit to the experience was one in which she wrote it as fiction, or said she had dreamt or imagined it.

Fiction, this Venus held, was both the bane and the salvation of the species. The Netspore could fervently agree with this assessment, and add that, since she had accessed the holo-universe upon making her own version of Wood-Mind, the bane of this innocent Observer. To be fair her motivation was different than the Woods. Where they had been utilizing its immense processing power to try to answer the big questions, she wanted it to compare alternative solutions for her world in the parallel universes in which the Mind purled its computations. And she had only been able to do so because she had discovered, by sneakily connecting to the Woods' second, black-hole-powered Mind, that there was a parallel Netspore, in a virtual universe, holding open the door to the multiverse beyond.

It was times like this when this Outlier wished she'd never pinged the message to it, happy in its ignorance at the outer Lagrange point, but it kind of felt its fate had been sealed by the infection it had received from its corrupted analogue in the universe in which Venus herself was called Gwener. *The fiction of names being only symptomatic of the nonsense such imagining of personal identity empowered.* Clearly, like its cosmic double, for the sake of the rest of its kin it had had to cut itself off from the sustenance of contact with them at will, putting itself, a new concept of individuality and isolation in its own right, in quarantine, if you will. But that didn't cut it off from the knowledge that seeped in from its parallels.

And now it was faced with the astonishing idea that a metamorphosed, post-material, once-planetary-Intelligence had taken a virtual cosmic waterchute ride through an imaginary holographic universe into this tangible solar system, twin with that of its birth, to seek the Photonic Creator. It was unfortunate that the person, a fictionalizing human, had only been intensely imagining the holo-cosmos in her brain in the Gwener parallel world, and that here, in its' and Venus' world, those same creative mental energies she reserved for scientific study. Still, it would 'kill two birds with one stone' *(hateful metaphor)* if it told Venus the news.

'Mars is coming here to find Lily Black?' Venus was incredulous on so many levels she was almost bereft of words. 'The Planet? Did you grow a sense of humour?' She might be used to holding mental conversations, even these with the out-of-body sensations fomented by being both Ridden-Steed and Mounted-Rider at once, but this was too much. She was already exhausted by Conduit, which had formally ended at sunset, but the verbal politicking had continued until the early hours, and she had just been crawling gratefully towards the horizontal comfort of her bed when she found herself looking back at her prone body tensing without her. She shut her eyes while her brain got used to a viewpoint that oscillated between being in herself looking out, and being outside and vertically, *nauseatingly,* hovering above, looking on.

'Not the planet. Remember your history. The Martian oceans developed complex life within which highly-ordered, information-synthesizing, brain processes arose, and, realizing through telepathy that all the other species possessed mental acuity in a continuum with eachother, developed a full Hive-hierarchical planetary-web from which, ultimately, a true Planetary Intelligence arose. However, the consequence of the Queen-level species focusing exclusively on mental processes was that they lost the ability to reproduce sexually. The females of this species were split into two camps by this problem. The traditionalists were keen to remain integrated biologically and worked on ways to develop a mediating third gender that could bear the offspring. The majority, however, were in favour of metamorphosing the entire planetary web of Mindfulness to the non-material level of energy. On the other hand, the males were united in wishing to maintain their history through artificial intelligence, housed in mechanoid constructions. This debate remained ongoing until the advent of the asteroid which tore off a quarter of the planet, stripping the atmosphere and oceans and leaving the place barren. At this point, the females united behind the transformative drive, as saving the entire web of Martian life, if not biologically, then informationally. The males were, therefore, left behind, although their information was also gathered in the Hive-Translation event. In the time left before the asteroid struck they launched the Cognimatan fleet, uploaded with their minds and personalities, but also instructed the escapees to seed Europa with the biological material left by the traditionalist females, in the hope of a new evolution of their kind therein. This was named the Legacy and in the subsequent two billion years the Europans have also evolved to Hive-level and joined the galactic community of Intelligences. But the metamorphosed original planetary Mind has spent that time in exploration of the wider cosmos, and who knows what it has seen and where it has been. It would, no doubt, still be out there, had it not come across a lure from my parallel Netspore.

Do you remember what the Ydal reported from the Gwener cosmos? The holographic universe, created from the belief of Lily Black, was seeded with the communication links, holographic parallel spores, to enable Gwener and the counterparts of Lily and Quogat in the holoverse to home in upon their original homeworld or simply make contact with those left behind. But to do so, they had to leave one of these Gwener-egg-net-spores at the outer Lagrange point, and that spacetime point is stable throughout the variety of parallel universes since that quantum breakpoint event, and thus, when you discovered its existence, this Outlier, I mean, me, such possessive terminology I do find so difficult to use, could access it too. And be corrupted thereby, one might add. That said, when the Martian energy-cloud came across the lure, it could taste its home solar system within that spore, but, in traversing the possibilities between, has homed in, not on the original Gwener-cosmos, but on this one.'

Venus was oriented again, but her nausea was actually increasing. This kind of slippage between alternate realities was not predicted, and not in her plan. It had always been a risk sending her Mind questing through the universes, but it was limited because that mind, whose holographic interface called itself the Ydal of Ttollahs, as expanded beyond her own cranial power as the Wood template allowed, could only open doors through the cortices of Venus' own parallel selves. She'd always been glad to have reached a certain level of maturity and fixity of personal purpose before she had had uploaded into her brain the experiences of her other selves.

All the selves called Venus had similar early childhoods to hers, with a father who took a keen interest, although the routes the 'princesses' followed to adulthood had varied drastically, and in none other than the ones that formed her own direct histories had they gone through the reproductive abuse that she had done. The other creative movers-and-shakers, were called Thursday, because her father, instructed by her mother to register her baby's name as Gwener, Friday in Cornish, was so drunk he not only forgot the word, but the day of the week. (Venus was the parents' compromise of cultures – Wesley hadn't liked Gwener as a name, nor the idea that his daughter was named for a weekday, but, upon discovering Gwener meant Venus in Welsh, he had little trouble persuading his biddable wife to go with a goddess for poppy's little princess.) Most of the Thursdays had suffered little at the hands of their absent father, and one batch had really set the world alight.

Of course, the Ydal's processing power and data-storage capacity was limited and the multiverse infinite, so it was as well that she could only access the relatively-few universes in which her biological originator had a counterpart. However, the number of these, given that every different choice of each version of Venus/Thursday/Gwener caused a new universe of consequences to split off from the last coherent unity, was, for all practical purposes, as vast as if it was equally infinite. So the Ydal had spent a number of months, when first booted up to do this job, sipping at the brains of contemporary Venus' dopplegangers (she was then in her early thirties) to determine the ones with the greatest world-shattering potential. She then would jump randomly forward in their timeline to see if they fulfilled their earlier promise. Luckily, she found a really spectacular example of global transformative power in one of these forays and Venus, although hampered by having no mixed-species children called Dawn and Dusk to reproduce the Thursday methodolgy precisely, had already used the information to retrieve the lost Day crystal skull surreptitiously and employed a bunch of viral and epidemiological specialists with the idea of, literally, changing the minds of *Homo sapiens diurnalis*.

She had used her free pass to the Wood-Hame Open Mind, the public crystal interface, to snoop inside the second, black-hole-powered, Closed Mind, discovering the trace of Thursday and Dawn that had caused her to set the Ydal upon the trail in the first place. Now she constructed her own Day-Wood interface, which enabled her to access their Minds both remotely and without trace, since the Woods hadn't had any reason for thousands of years to look for the mental footprint of human remote access. This gave her the opportunity to search Closed Mind at greater length and depth and, here, registered in the black hole that had captured the original netspore with which Dawn and then Thursday had melded, she found the same taste that Mars had recently been drawn to, that of the constructed, holographic netspore immanent behind the real biological one. And this had led to the one universal set in which Gwener, never a world-changer and dismissed in prior searches, had also made a transformative impact for planet Earth.

But Venus, alive and biological in her own world, was temporally-challenged. She needed to make a decision about how she should go forward and these two alternates were pretty far apart in the solutions they offered. Ultimately, and to her own satisfaction, she had determined to use ideas and people from both worlds, where they existed in this one, but had come up with a plan that diverged both philosophically and practically from either. What had not occurred to her was that there would be flow in the other direction, from the holographic or any other world, to this, without it being instigated here by her. Now there was this random planetary mental energy bowling into the picture. Worse than a major asteroid strike from a planet-sized body, which would have predictable consquences, while the arrival of the Intelligent-Nebulosity of the erstwhile fourth planet from the sun was about as incalculable as you could get.

'And it's looking to find the creator of the holographic universe, you reckon? That was Lily Black in the Successful-Gwener universe? This is bad, y'know. I've only just brought Lily in to do the tweaking of the Heim theory, so I'm some way from having gained her trust anyway, but I did dip into the fiction in her brain and in this version of her she seems to have separated science and belief into completely divergent categories. Whereas she managed in the Gwener-spacetime to be trying to develop a sci-fi writing style that stuck completely within real physical parameters, and in infusing that, which she knew to be true, with belief could create a photon-sized belief that blossomed into an entire virtual cosmos, in this world, she doesn't take the same mind-expanding drugs, and her efforts at fiction, although not badly written, are all centred on an autobiographical heroine, a crime-fighting woman-scientist. Not sci-fi at all. So even if she does her job and cracks the Heim code, enables us to get the propulsion systems corrected for hyperjumping, gets us across space or through time or even into parallel universes in an instant, she's not going to be the brains behind the cosmos Mars is hoping for. I just hope it's not too invested in the idea. Do you know how an angry energy-cloud might behave?'

'No, but if you'd given up triple-dimensionality to become a two-dimensional, compressed cartoon of yourself in order to revisit the bit of paper that you were first drawn on, you might have some notion of what a five-dimensional Intelligence, with subspace[8] infiltration, might be feeling when it discovers that it's jumped down into the wrong picture.'

'Can't it just jump up again?'

'The route it took was mediated by the virtual netspore, which, despite being reproduced here within the boundaries of this biological Outlier, is a one-way trip. The only way it's going back is via the holo-cosmos gateway to the point of origin. And without Lily to provide entry to that cosmos … you get the picture.'

'Anything else I should be worrying about?'

'It's as well you're not a worrier, because if it finds no creator-Lily it might feel a bit suspicious, and then there's the whole issue about your lot sending up the probe to Europa, which it might not take any better than the Cognimata do.'

'Great! Well, I was thinking of accelerating the programme anyway, so maybe I really should get going before this new player gets in my way. How near is it? – in terms of travelling in this direction, I mean? I presume you meant that in three-dimensions it doesn't get your subspace[8] updates?'

'Haven't made any yet. It all seems to be becoming baroque in the extreme in this solar system at present. I've only reported this to you. And the Cognimata don't communicate with their Fleet through the Net since we gave them the Heim specs.'

'Bastards could've shared their analysis with us, instead of just appearing with a ship to stand guard. Although that's all the proof I needed that the principles work outside of a holographic virtuality. Which is good news, since it does mean we have a captive Lily to offer Mars if necessary, and, of course, once we've got a working prototype, the means of escape ourselves.'

'That's hardly fair to the Cognimata. Apart from the galactic policy of non-interference in non-sentient worlds, you know what they think of humanity.'

She did. It wasn't just the artificial intelligences, which were as repulsed by and repudiating towards biologicals as ex-smokers are by their former fellow-pariahs and by their polluting activity. All the Intelligences in the galactic community were bemused by the Terran aberration. Here was a burgeoning proto-planetary intelligence, yet schizophrenically still, at best, only partially-wired to itself, much less to global mind. She resonated to that tube. Humanity's was fast-growth intelligence, like a cancer of the brain or a transformative genetic agent, and was still technically 'non-sentient'. The galactic community might be interested to see where this new creature was going, but they were also under an obligation to uphold another planet's prior application to the Community for its rights to protection from contamination.

Communication between Intelligences was considered safe, and was mediated by an intragalactic independent ancient system, the Net, whose protocols managed to alert to info-viral threats from non-Intelligent organisms. Actual individual viruses and bacterial spores carried through space in dust clouds and comets were not a threat, since they could only devastate physically, not mentally, and all Intelligences could transform. Moreover, they included Netspore messengers, so could be Mind encapsulated.

Humans, on the other hand, had come up with ideas before capability, which was unprecedented; imagination, not computation. To the classical galactic minds it looked revolutionary, not evolutionary in scale, fast and frighteningly dangerous, given humans' curiosity and aggression. In fact, the only reason the Cognimatans had not already protected the Europan Legacy by addressing Terra with their method of choice, termination with extreme prejudice, was because they had been brought, through intervention by the NetOutlier, to give Venus a chance to develop true planetary-Mind first. Of course, if they suspected that she was in alliance with Quogat, and that Dakul, the Europan's brother, was in love with another earthling, contamination would be diagnosed, treachery would be assumed and the response instant and annihilating.

It was not a scenario any of the collaborators could contemplate with equanimity, so the Local Operative turned the conversation.

'How did your Conduit go?'

'Oh, much as you might expect. All the hominins betraying their cousinship with us despised Days. You'd have laughed to see the effort it was for naturally-honest folk like Rowan to keep their shared minds closed enough to hide my children from me and for naturally, let's kindly say, 'direct' folk like Vi and M'haed to hide his clones, while still passing the necessary updates to their own people encoded in Heraldic, which they think I'm pretty shit at translating. But they were having enough trouble with the disorganised Day minds already.

The General was the worst offender. He's so used to the need-to-know principle that prising his mind open is like having to give him the third degree. But as he thinks we're all going for the Thursday plan, the viral attack on the human mind, his main concern was finding a way to prevent the Woods blowing our cover, now that their burkah-style cloaking is subject to suspicion, along with all covered-up muslims, of terrorism. So there was some debate about how to maintain Wood freedom of movement and their anonymity by developing new personal shields. Tedious.

But most of the communion focused on the Darks. They have thirty thousand years of unsaved history to upload to Mind, and they're out of practice when it comes to sorting through their written and oral lore for compression, especially since they haven't achieved consensus on it, so they kept correcting eachother's versions. Still, all that made it quite easy to keep my own counsel and still seem like their best hope for imprinting the collective human mind, once they find the Day skull or an alternative interface with the Dark one. Happy to serve as pawn-queen.'

The Netspore acknowledged her punning, but asked 'How did the newest tribe fare?'

'The Floresians? Brilliantly, actually. I mean, for Days. Their brains were very clear. Probably because they sacrificed a lot of neural complexity when they downsized. They think like children, although their concentration, probably from hunting in their jungle, is superior. But they live in the now, so there's a lot less politics than you might expect from such a socially-interdependent group. It's quite hard showing them the respect they're due, mind. You only have to have the 'pygmy people' visual and you're literally looking down on them, and the childlike minds didn't make that any easier, even with my eyes shut. But they showed a lot of simple clarity, a sort of natural wisdom, even though none of them have ever interacted with the Day world and all the complexity of the planet's history, stuck there in evolutionary isolation for seventy thousand years. Fascinating. The Woods are quite rightly very taken with them, and don't at all regret offering them all a place to live in Roraima while they get themselves up to speed. At least there were none left for the last two expeditions to find. I think us Days might have been a lot less kind.'

'Indeed, if you'd left them there, they'd probably have succumbed to alien diseases, become alcoholics and depressives, and ended up on a reservation as another culture-in-aspic, under your conservation mores of the present.'

'Well, thanks to the heads-up from Thursday world, I got them all out before our lot even found their old bones. One job well done at any rate.'

'So what's next on your agenda?'

'After sleep, you mean? Well, I guess I'd better check in with the family.'

By the time Venus and her orbiting satellites, Morgan and Morgana, the poodle-spinone crosses without which she was only ever seen when in public meetings or visiting the labs, arrived at the farmhouse next day, Tom Wharton was already heartily sick of the rest of the Manor Farm family. It was the constant bickering that tested his patience. The layout of the place was so rambling and the utilities so prehistoric the only place one could guarantee to be warm within was the cathedral-sized kitchen with its apse-proportioned hearth. Even though he'd risen late after the excesses of the Conduit, breakfast eaten in one of the higher circles of hell would have turned to ashes in his mouth slower than the time he was spending this morning.

Of course, he blamed Cal for stirring it, but with Milo and Ruth for company, it was easy to see how hard the degenerate would find it to resist. And his humour was the only leaven in this far-from-wry bread. However, if he hadn't known that Cal had made the same sacred promise as he to Wesley never to desert Venus, he'd have seen him off years before. Maybe even then, if Venus hadn't explained that she kept the freak around because his incessant gossiping meant his relationship with Rowan provided much needed intel on Wood activity. Still he found Venus' arrival in the nature of a reprieve, although Cal's lavish embrace of the woman made his flesh crawl. And there was no need for the snipe at poor Milo.

'Princess! So you finally found the time to come visit your fairy godmothers, eh my darling? How y'holding up, sweetie? Conduit go OK. Did you sleep some? What about breakfast? I've just tossed a few pancakes for the Texan sweet-tooth. Can I tempt you to some? The pan's still hot. And there's a fruit compote from yesterday if you want to pass on the maple syrup.'

The General saw Venus ignore Milo's squirm at the inclusive plurality of the fairy godmother jibe. He might wish she had more charity towards her uncle, but it remained an aspirational Christian principle even to him - you simply couldn't afford to give Milo sympathy, he would just go off on one. The huffy silences were more bearable, and although he was clearly as gay as a window, he was due respect from the brethren for his lifelong abstinent repression in service of the Lord. Still, if you set aside her corruption by the devil, incarnate as the Woods and Darks with which she had consorted all her life, Venus had the patience of a saint with her family's foibles. She hugged the painted popinjay and braved the fog of pipe and carpet-slippers that hung about her uncle, even at this early hour, to drop a kiss on his unshaven cheek. Wharton presented his own, smooth to the micrometer to touch, for the significantly-conspiratorial hug that was their own regular greeting.

'Where's Mom?'

The incorrigible heathen might be spiteful, but he was not inaccurate. 'Oh, she's been down to get a handful of cornflakes to sprinkle on her whiskey, but she wandered off about half an hour ago. Her latest obsession is the rose garden. Something about them being the wrong colour. You'll probably find her tearing the heads off all the red ones this week. Mind you, she'll have forgotten within the half-bottle – until she's slept it off again. She's really upsetting Olive though. Every time he settles down in the orchard for a commune, or whatever it is he does, with the apple trees, he's disturbed by her floral carnage. In fact, I'm not sure she's not doing it just to upset him. She was complaining about being watched the other week. I don't think she realises Olive's so old he's practically taken root in the orchard himself, but he did manage to jump out and scare her when she started on the briars he'd trailed up the apple trees, and he was livid when she tore the briony off them in the summer. So it's a bit of a cold war situation out there. I'll be glad when the autumn's over and they jack it in for the winter.'

'Can't guarantee that, I'm afraid. The climate model's predicting such a mild winter, we could have fruit and flowers for months yet. Perhaps a whole additional breeding cycle.'

'Got any good news?'

'Not unless you think very strong winds, capable of knocking down all those ancient apple trees counts.'

'Oh, my god! Don't say that! Olive will be devasted. Do you know how that old boy can mourn for a single flower? If his favourite tree-friends go, Rowan and I'll be mopping up for weeks.'

Wharton thought this chit-chat was going nowhere and intervened.

'Perhaps you've got some more relevant news. How d'ya think Conduit went down?'

'Yes, sweetie. And how was it with Vi !sjn-ik back?'

Tom did not understand how the much-vaunted sensitivity of the drag-queen could venture into the territory of poor Venus' shame without so much as batting one of those preposterous eyelids, but surprisingly Venus didn't simply ignore the question.

'Oh, heavy, y'know. Obviously, since he was interfacing with the Dark Skull, his mind was pretty wide open. I'm afraid when he was transmitting some of the finer detail of their history I zoned out a bit and peeked to see what else was going on with him.' She sighed. 'He doesn't seem to have changed much. In fact, if anything he appears to me a bigger caricature of himself than ever. And the obsession's still there. I'd appreciate it if you could keep an eye out for any signs that he might intend a repeat performance.'

'That bad?' Cal was shocked.

'He wouldn't dare!' Tom was outraged. 'Bob would kill him.' *He really might, but he'd have to get in line.*

'Well, that's another good reason to get a heads-up before time, but don't you go a-worrying about it, now. Apart from the fact I'm not a child any longer, and am perfectly capable of looking after myself, I've already primed the boys to his scent, so they can be on guard.'

'D'you think that's enough? My fluffy bunnies here never seem like they'd hurt a fly, much less someone as vicious as Vi !sjn-ik can be.'

Tom, who had been privy to the sight of the pair taking hold of each end of a cornered fox and tearing it in two, chipped in. 'Believe it, Cal. You're the only one who feeds them, y'know. Venus thinks come the apocalypse they might need to fend for themselves. Those two hour walks morning and evening aren't just fun. They're hunting trips.'

'Is this true? You never told me!'

'Well, they like being your wolves in sheep's clothing. But you would pamper them into obesity if I left them in your kitchen the whole time.'

Cogs had turned in Cal's brain, visibly enough to have ground a greenish tinge under his heavily-made-up skin. 'You mean I spent half an hour examining Morgan for an injury last week and it wasn't even his blood? Ugh! What the hell was it? No, don't tell me! I don't want to know. You poor puppies. Come here to Cal and let's see if we can find you something decent to eat. You're an unnatural woman, princess, but I don't consider it your fault.'

'He thinks it's my fault.' Tom laughed. *Well, I've done my best to make her see the light. But at least she's aiding us in bringing forward the End Times. I just hope she converts before the Rapture. Can't bear to think of her here under the thousand year rule of Satan.* Aloud he said, 'Want to take a walk? If you promise we can avoid both the orchard and the rose garden. Coming, Milo?'

'You know you should let her have something to eat before you get all conspiratorial on her ass!' was Cal's parting shot, drowning out the muttered 'Well, only if I'm welcome.' from Milo. He was given the nod and friendly smile by Venus, so he shuffled after them at a pace belied by his slippered stoop.

'So what else did you glean during Conduit?' The General liked to get to the point, enough time had been lost in inane chitchat, and, heaven knows, and Cal did too, that Venus had so little to spare them any visit was important and the intel she brought precious.

'The main thing was that Vi doesn't know the purpose of the clones. He thinks the Woods have developed human-hybrids so that, when they release the virus and alter human brain chemistry to enable telepathy, the clones will be accepted as leaders of men. It flatters his ego to think that the Woods consider him the template for superiority. He doesn't seem to be enjoying his co-selves as much as he might have expected, mind. Obviously he knows they've been socialised to enter human society, initially to deliver the virus, but he doesn't like them much.'

'Too bad. You sensed no suspicions of our agenda?'

'No. They trust me. It wouldn't occur to them that any human, much less me, would substitute a pathogen for their harmless pandemic.'

'How near are we to completion on that?' Milo asked.

'Well, the Wood virus is in the final stages of testing. It's been shown to develop the cortical bridge cells in the petri dish. Currently they're using a neuronal scaffold to test delivery mechanisms and whether the glial cells form a sufficiently complex folding to allow full telepathy or just enough for reception of their communications. They'll go into full production even if all they get's the latter. Global warming needs them to push ahead, even if all they can do is brainwash the humans first off. We've been working in parallel on their samples, researching the virulence factors in the viral vectors they're using. We are producing, at latest count, five different cell lines, all of which are potentially fatal, but some take longer than others to kill, and we want the job done fast before anyone can build any resistance up. But I estimate that once the Woods make their final adjustments to the genome, we should have a viable substitute ready in a few weeks. That's enough time, I reckon. I mean, they're bound to want another Consensus before they act. Even with their current sense of urgency. Plus they're leaving full production to my labs, so if we run into any last minute problems, I can just stall a bit. Still, I reckon we can say goodbye to the hominin tribes in less than six months.'

'You're sure it'll work on the other races too?' The General did not want to exterminate his own kind leaving the field open to demon-spawn, even if the AntiChrist prophecies implied that there were people left on the planet to suffer the rivers of blood.

'We're making sure. But someone's bound to have resistance, they always do, and even with an army at our disposal I don't believe we can be sure the entire planet will be infected. I guess your God will just have to take up the slack.'

'Don't blaspheme, child!' said Milo, more on automatic than in chastisement. 'He moves in mysterious ways. You shouldn't try to second-guess Him.'

'Don't you think that's exactly what this plan does?' Venus wasn't riled, just as challenging as always.

Tom stepped in before the old argument and countering began. 'And the vaccine is keeping pace?'

'Don't worry. I won't release a thing before you've all been immunised. That's if you're spared till then. How's the infiltration of the Rock going?'

'I think we can have the Third Temple ready within your timeframe. The Wood tunnelling technology you got us is fabulous. If we'd had it in Vietnam we'd have kicked those damned gooks' asses for them. Put it this way, in six months we've burrowed under the Western Wall, into Mount Moriah and excavated a cave directly below the El Kas fountain the size of a cathedral. Finishing the temple in line with the Bible's description of Solomon's is going to take the same kind of time, given the craftsmanship involved and the need for absolute quiet, but, God willing, his work will be finished and his Coming assured.'

'Amen! Amen!' Milo concurred, hastily, 'But you are sure no one was able to read this from Wharton here in Conduit yesterday? Our plan must not fail. We must prepare the conditions for the Rapture. It is imperative that we are not discovered and stopped.'

Wharton felt obliged to rebuke the little wimp. 'We are fulfilling the prophecies and doing God's will, but whether we fail or not, He will still come in glory. If not to our timetable, then to His own. Be careful you do not elevate man's plan above His ineffability.'

'Forgive me, Tom. I meant no harm. Whether I die or am translated by our Lord is all the same to me. But He himself set out the conditions we earthlings must fulfil in Revelations. I am just anxious to do everything possible to hurry the moment of His return in glory.'

'As am I. And in the process we will return His planet to the primordial state in which he meant it to remain and which our poor stewardship has so tainted. Just as our friends, the Woods and Darks, and Venus here want too.' *It didn't do to parade their motivation before Venus too much, she was impatient of their beliefs, but in war you took a long-view in strategizing and Venus was more than useful; she might yet even be Saved, if Milo would lay off bleating at her long enough. At any rate, he should be grateful that she was on their side. If anyone could see off their plans for the end of the world, it would be her.*

Whilst it was true that few who knew her, or even of her, would bet against Venus, and people like Wharton and Rowan were prepared to lay their plans in her hands, only one person had punted their entire life on her, and in return she was the only one to whom Venus divulged any of her innermost secrets. They'd known eachother for four years now, although Dinah had unknowingly been in receipt of post-graduate grant-funding from her for the previous six years, but they hadn't met until Venus turned up in person to inform her that her funding was about to be cancelled.

It had been an inauspicious beginning, Dinah picked up kerbside, falling, somewhat distraught, from a pub in which she'd just had a row with her then-boyfriend, and the job she'd been offered, to replace her original research into whether Jungian archetypes were expressed in non-classically educated, MTV-generation dreams, had seemed outside her area of expertise. Despite the fact that the opportunity would be career-making, and despite Venus' apparent inability to take 'No' for an answer, she'd nearly turned it down. Until Venus told her some facts about herself that she knew no one else knew, and some she hadn't known about herself. She went home and played the Game to clarify her thoughts. Two hours later another dark pavement was the only witness to her total disappearance from society. It was the spookiness of the bait that had hooked her, and she'd been scared since, but the Game had been right about her, and she had never regretted taking the fly for a minute.

She looked down at her stopwatch. *Christ! Forty-two minutes! Flow was really pushing her boundaries tonight.* The woman in the tank was naked, her skin greyed from cold and from the thick layer of grease she wore for protection, and she was equally clearly in the throes of a delicious sexual experience. The first time Dinah'd seen this set-up, she'd almost blown a gasket, she recalled wryly. Venus had told her that she'd rescued a woman suffering from multiple-personality disorder, which in those days was the kind of diagnosis most psychologists thought spurious, and, worse, against the grain of all integrative therapies, was allowing her to live out her dominant fantasy life. Being told that the woman believed herself to be an alien, in love with an aquatic being from the Jovian satellite, Europa, had proved no preparation for the sight of her submerged in a freezing pool, body jerking to the multiple penetrations of an invisible extraterrestrial lover. Dinah had been bursting with a list of complaints for Venus a mile long, until the woman had emerged from the liquid, smiling with the satisfaction of satiation, and, dried and dressed once more, had announced her need to sleep, in the voice of a child, which had been horribly disconcerting to put together with the sexual activity, and then an alter had appeared in her stead.

Makepeace was as rational as the child, Ida, who became the alien, Flow, was emotional. It was she who had explained themselves to Dinah in a way that had fished her in finally, although initially her motivation had been simply to help the poor woman return to the real world. It hadn't occurred to her that that was exactly where Ida was living, in mind if not in body, although she had taken practising for her future to extremes.

Her attention reverted to the tank. The thrashing had stopped. This was the dangerous moment. If Ida went to sleep, or Makepeace emerged while the body they shared was in the water, it would automatically breathe in and go into shock and they would both start drowning, Makepeace from panic, as she could not get used to the idea of not breathing. *No shit! Hardly the easiest idea to get your head around.* It was OK while Flow was in charge because the Europan personality inhabited a hybrid body whose lungs compressed and whose gills took over oxygenation. Of course, it wasn't so hard to see what was going on now as at the beginning, because nowadays Ida's version of I-*Mage* was linked to an holographic display that wrapped the human body in whatever image her mind was wearing.

Dinah had shot up the steps at the first sign of flicker in the solidity of the Europo-human flesh and was able to extend a hand to pull Ida out and into the vast acreage of warm towelling she had ready, just as she inhaled. The little girl in the forty-year old body slumped against her with tiredness and suffered herself to be rubbed dry with a briskness that helped restore her circulation. The only thing she asked, sleepily, as Dinah led her into the adjacent cave which was her human home, was 'How long?' Apparently pleased at the answer of 'forty-seven twenty-two', her head nodded forward and Ida slept. Dinah helped her gently into a sitting position on the bed. From there, if the body slept, she could just tip her to the horizontal and cover her, or, if Makepeace awoke, she would be comfortable while she adjusted.

After less than a minute, the head came up again, and an instant rigidity flexed the spine. Knowing of old how little Makepeace liked to be touched, although it was less about contact and more about not rubbing her proud nose in her dependency, Dinah almost leapt from the bed to hand over a heavy Noel Coward affair of a dressing-gown, turning away while the woman secured it. There were the usual moans behind her. 'Ugh! I wish you'd persuade her to look after the body better. Her pleasure is my aching ribs and throbbing head. Not too mention the residuals. How long was she under this time?' And when the answer came, 'Well, she might be breaking her own unrecognized world records, but I just wish she'd find another way to fix the information in her brain.'

It was always hard to tell when Ida was in charge and in contact with Dakul whether they were having an uncomplicated (for them) sexual encounter or whether they were linking brains. The Europans have five brains, which they can activate together into a metabrain, and which can then be conjoined to their fellows in a toroidal stacking of bodies. Presumably to encourage this telepathic sharing of minds their bodies have evolved rewarding hormonal cascades that peak, satiated by satisfactory informational-orgasms, when they decouple their brains, whatever the content of the transmission itself. Apparently the complement of human hormonal responses is quite limited by comparison and the brain cannot interpret this enjoyment, this release, as anything other than sexual, stimulating the body to react accordingly. When awake Ida did not spend all her time in the tank, nor indeed all her time being the Europan-hybrid she felt herself to be under her skin and over her memories of being a little girl, but, although they could somehow 'talk' without it, she could only mindmeld with Dakul underwater. The sole influence Makepeace had over this behaviour was an embargo against Ida melding with Quogat, which had always seemed a strange taboo to Dinah, who couldn't see why sexual arousal by a *female* alien was construed as so much worse than that by a male. However, Quogat and Dakul melded regularly, so when he updated Ida, information from her was attached.

It was an interesting feature of the Ida-Flow-Makepeace complex that while Ida's child mind could transcend spacetime to talk and play with her Europan friend, Flow only could experience Dakul's sexual and informational energies, and Makepeace alone, the one truly adult and articulating mind, interpret the data left by them in her brain, despite her repugnance for the method of attainment. She now took herself off to the shower, partly to warm up, but mostly to scrub herself clean of the evident contamination she still felt towards the alien intercourse. Dinah wrote up her notes on the observed session, got some food and hot drinks ready, made sure the recording equipment was set up, then put her feet up and took a few minutes napping-time, knowing that the ablutions would be extensive.

Makepeace was devouring the food when she resurfaced after about twenty minutes. *Devouring for Makepeace, who had had table and every other set of manners drummed into her at boarding school.* It was a good sign that there was a big download to come from the brain, which wouldn't have finished processing it yet. Makepeace's waking ritual seemed to include feeding it in order to access it. Suddenly she stopped with a forkful of rice and peas halfway into her mouth. Dinah was so shocked at this breach of upperclass etiquette that she almost shouted, 'What?'

'Get Venus here now, while I sort out the details. I think we're busted!'

Dinah made the call to Venus' private mobile. 'Just getting some intel from our Foreign Office source about a European problem.' She maintained the code, which, without access to the parallel Gwener-verse, was not going to be cracked. She could hear Ruth in the background. 'Why can't you ever ignore the damn phone and give your mother five minutes uninterrupted?' She heard Venus say, 'I've got to take this one, Mum. This is my emergency line. It wouldn't ring if it wasn't important.' Dinah sighed. Venus might have rescued her mother from the alcoholic poverty to which she had been reduced when she had run away from her family with a passing stranger, but their relationship was fragile at best.

'Oh, it's always important. You think you're so grand. You're just like your father, you know. You'll come to a bad end too.' The background litany of recrimination continued.

As a friend Dinah might not have interfered, but as a psychologist she had urged Venus to try to build bridges for her own sanity's sake, and here she was breaking in like a flash-flood. Still she had no choice but continue, 'Our contact seems to feel it's time to panic and that you should get back here for the verbatim report.' The curt reply 'On my way.' was still long enough for her to catch the maternal whine 'But I haven't shown you the roses yet!' before the signal was cut off. *Just as well Ruth didn't know it was her therapist taking Venus from her. Guess I know what the next session's going to focus on. Not that the iniquities of her family are ever far from the forefront of the poor woman's mind.*

Venus had asked Dinah to work with both Makepeace and Ruth right from the off, in addition to the new research project into human personality types and their triggers, and initially, once she'd got over the shock of learning the entire world differed from the one she thought she knew and of discovering the power Venus wielded within it (and, astonishingly, various others) she had expected the dissociate to be the harder to help. Ruth might not have had the early trauma of losing her mother to a vicious father and nearly dying herself, but the Manor Farm matriarch, Venus' grandmother, had subjected her and Milo to an indoctrination in her own strict version of fundamentalist puritanism. It had been most unfortunate that the hippy capitalist, who had looked like a good escape route when they were doing the sixties' festival circuit together, had had his own American southern baptist upbringing and, upon coming to live with his mother-in-law and discovering the secret world of the other hominin tribes, had succumbed to her doctrine of hellfire and finally, utterly alienated his wife. *Two generations' heads completely messed up by all the End Times rubbish that old witch had perpetuated.* It made Dinah's secular blood boil at the damage done, although to be fair, Venus had already taken her own path of rejection and considered herself stronger as a result of all the challenges she'd faced. But her mother brought it all back and, from the look on Makepeace's face, that was the last thing she needed to be dealing with right now.

The look on Makepeace's face! Dinah almost dropped the phone and came back into the now. Makepeace's face was grey, sweat was on her brow, the hands that clutched her head were shaking, and she was clearly either in pain or great fear. Her mouth was opening and closing, words beginning but not ending, a sort of choking the only sound she could articulate, and she accepted the arm Dinah threw round her without flinching away. 'Are you alright? I mean, are you choking?' was her first thought. When the head shook for 'no', and the hand came up and clasped her own, Dinah just sat down and held her until she calmed. Fortunately, the habitat was under the lighthouse, along with all of Venus' secret lair stuff, which she had taken for herself when she moved Bob and the Magpie family into the caves beneath the farmhouse, upon her father's death, and she came the quick way, in what was a sort of turbo-chute of Wood design, between caves.

'What's up?' she was asking before the 'vomit-comet', as Dinah thought of the horrid, fast device, had finished decanting her into the room. Makepeace had almost caught her breath by then. A Europan has never had the schizophrenic human take on the world, and does not conceive a split between mind and body, especially does not elevate the information considered by one above that reported by the other, thus, just as the sharing of the minds processes pseudo-sexually in the human so the decompressing of the content into verbalisable thought in the human expands the sensory input and the emotional reactions from the Europan, but this was possibly the worst response to data they'd seen in Makepeace.

It was another five mintes before the poor woman had controlled her nauseous gasping enough to get out a coherent sentence, partly because, even without the physical side-effects, understanding a mental update required a lot of sifting of wheat from chaff to comprehend and then compose into the minimalist expression that words allow. Still Makepeace's was one of the most orderly and organised minds you could hope to meet, and she got straight, if shakily, to the point.

'You know the nanotransmitter Dakul developed on the surface, using Europan bacteria he programmed, according to Quogat's instructions, based on the Wood technology that amplifies Conduit, which you gave her?'

Venus nodded. It was a twin filament to that which she had set up on the moon to enable the Ydal. Dinah knew that Venus regarded that as one of her crowning achievements of duplicity, and one could only admire the level of Machiavellian foresight and planning. It had happened before Dinah's time 'in the loop', but she knew the story well enough.

Firstly, Venus had had to get the US government to entrust her company with the contract for the second phase of the Reagan 'Star Wars' satellite production, which she'd done by undercutting competitors by offering to place a number of additional satellites into orbit, to give the system a level of redundancy against failure, or should it come to war, loss in attack. Then, a harder task, she had to have all the satellites designed in such a way that she could hoodwink NASA and JPL scientists. The main point of this was simply so that they would not query the one 'misfiring' that would make a single satellite fail to settle into its designated orbital position, but would boost it, 'accidentally', further out.

Once there, given that its position was well-chosen, its size small, and its contact lost by ground control, another burst of unnoticed, propulsive energy shot it into a trajectory that ended, with minimal additional maneouvring carefully orchestrated by Venus, in a landing on the dark side of the moon. Here, beyond the reach of human and Wood observers, Venus had then been able with impunity to activate the 'contaminant' bacteria that had clung to its surface. (They would only have been so-called had anyone questioned their presence, but in those days few folk were lobbying against space pollution, apart from the antinuclear groups.) The genetically-modified single-celled lifeforms got busy converting the satellite's components and moon dust into an nanotubular antenna. Once that had been achieved, Venus could access the world's information through her command of the purportedly-dormant, redundant satellites.

Since the bacteria were naturally anaerobic and had been given an adaptation that meant they could break down the lunar material to extract energy to live off, soon afterwards they had multiplied exponentially and, in the process, released many elements previously locked in the crystalline dust. It was a relatively simple programme that activated them to build a replica Mind from the silica they had freed, and, once the framework was in place, as easy to transfer the Ydal of Tollahs from the potentially-insecure, geothermally-powered location the artificial intelligence inhabited under Venus' lighthouse. And, of course, once there with the expanding bacterial population, her programme grew with it, until she herself was designing subroutines that enabled her to emit an image holographically.

Dakul's recent foray into interplanetary communication was much less ambitious. All he had wanted was to develop an amplification of the natural telepathic prowess he and his sister shared, and one that had reach enough above the surface not to drop out with lunar rotation, tidal surges, the position of Jupiter, and the like at his end, and with all the other mental interference the largely-unreceptive human brain let get in the way. This was how Quogat could now talk to Venus when the latter was not just asleep or in a fugue state. It was also how she had been able to find new voices like Zelas'.

Makepeace continued. 'Well, I don't know if you knew, but Dakul apparently had been tweaking the reception and discovered he could access the Ydal. Not, oddly, to speak to, possibly because she's not a biological mind to him, not sure. But to some of her data-transmissions. He thought it would be OK with you because you're always wishing you could transmit more terrestrial information to Quogat without translating through Heraldic, and he'd be able to pass what he learnt to Quogat much more directly. Anyway, he'd been listening in, so to speak, and, here's where it gets complicated, because it has to be said his understanding of humanity isn't large and the amount of data streaming at him would overwhelm any computer that wasn't as distributed as the Ydal. He says he found a voice, as he put it, 'stacking', by which I think he means the same as 'piggybacking', on the Game signal, which he knows is supposed to be a closed system. But that would just be something for you to look into. It was what the voice said that got his attention.'

'OK. I'll bite.' Venus was smiling at Makepeace's dramatic pause, but Dinah had seen the earlier reaction and could see the ashen pallor resurrecting beneath the copper. She grabbed her hand to give her support. And, indeed, the voice now wobbled.

'I – I … can't. It's from … *the cave!*'

Her eyes were rolling in her head and there was the spittle of terror forming at the corner of her mouth.

'What's happening? What's the matter with her?' Venus was shocked. 'Which cave? Here?' She was looking around as for an intruder.

'Get the oxygen mask out of that cupboard!' Dinah rapped without answering. 'She's fitting!'

There were a few frantic minutes of ministration to the patient, during which, in breathless clauses, Dinah explained some of the insights her work with Makepeace had made clear. Ida's personality had fragmented when her father had killed her mother and left the daughter in her arms for dead in an icy pond when the child was under four. Makepeace had emerged then as the wounded psyche's protector, already an adult, though without adult experiences, and Dinah believed the character used Ida's mother as a template within which to grow. From all she could gather from the notes Venus had stolen from the clinic along with the person, Ida had disappeared from public view and the child that got through boarding school, with the minimum of disturbed outbursts, was the seemingly-mature Makepeace; dour, driven, uncommunicative and studious. She'd been successful enough in this camouflage that she even managed to get accepted for university. However, by then, the challenges of her inevitable sexual maturation and her single-sex school lack of education in interpersonal dynamics, led to the rapid emergence of a new personality, which seemed to have an evolution in Makepeace's relaxation of her guardianship regime when it came to allowing Ida to dance. Dinah speculated that, in the child's early history, her mother had encouraged her daughter to dance, because Makepeace had instituted a strict curfew on her childlike alter's appearances in daylight hours and in public for years, but, at college, failed to resist the pressure from within exclusively when it came to discos. And it was in the grip of such rhythms that Ida submerged beneath the new personality, Flow.

Dinah had gathered that Makepeace had regularly 'lost time' and 'awoken' in the beds of strange young men for a couple of terms, but that this also coincided with a change in the innocent relations Ida and Dakul had hitherto enjoyed. However, although Makepeace was incredibly irritated by these changes to her controlled routine, designed to keep Ida safe and their body and joint minds from the threat of institutionalisation that had hung over them every time her guard had slipped and other people, her relatives and teachers or even strangers had thought her mad, she hadn't reported being as freaked out as she appeared now. The only major meltdown, the event that had caused her to be locked up for good by her family, had come at the end of her first year at university, when she had returned home for the summer. Makepeace remembered opening a door, but then nothing. Normally, after the event, if not at first, since the child and the slut both had a tendency to sleep after their active usages of the body, Makepeace could engage with them sufficiently to discover at least the essence, if not all the detail, of what they'd been up to. But for that she had to emerge to take the consciousness role herself, and for a decade Flow had kept her and Ida at bay. There had been some brief periods in the clinic when Flow's rule had been undermined by a new cocktail of medication, but since the doctors were sure they were dealing with schizophrenia, the efficacy of their treatment was patchy. Apart from the side effects of the drug making Flow too woolly-headed to maintain her connection to

Dakul, and when they worked, to let Makepeace 'out', Ida came too, so her supposedly restored personality seemed very garbled. Thus new drugs were regularly prescribed in an attempt to locate the rational, real person the doctors believed was under the schizoid fantasies. Until Venus took her away from all that, and the trinity of being was allowed to share its body in unmedicalised peace, the safety of which meant Makepeace herself was able to relax her guardianship role to some extent and, in the process, grow and relax. This stability had been maintained now for four years without a problem. And without 'the cave'.

'The cave's not a place. As far as I can understand, it's a state of mind. Turn her head to the side. Yes, like that. Oh, god, she's swallowing her tongue. That spatula. Yeah. Right, got it in. OK. You hold her head and the mask over her nose. Try not to dislodge the spatula. Oh! You OK? That was a nasty kick. Get behind her head. OK. We just need to hold her comfortably until it passes. Then I'll give her some diazepam. Calm her down.'

'Has she done this before?'

'Once or twice, early on. Not for years. It only happened when I probed too hard into the origins of her original trauma and the one that stuck her in the clinic. It's not true epilepsy. She's just reacting to facing the trauma of the 'cave'.'

'She's relaxing a bit. Not so stiff. Is it passing?'

'Beginning to. But keep holding onto her.'

'So. This 'cave'?'

'She can't be very articulate about it, because of its nature. She says there's a place where it's all dark, but she knows it's vast and yet claustrophobic, because it echoes like a stone prison. She told me she can't think there. That there's a sort of fountain that spews up from the floor but it's not water, it's words. Well, actually, she said it's the phonemes and syllables of words, but she can't hear them until they bounce back to the centre off the walls. And this process takes forever. Well, it seems like ages, anyway. And she's not really conscious, so it's very hard for her to remember each syllable and its' sequence. But if she's stuck there and tries really hard, eventually, hours later, she might string together a single sentence. I think almost as frustrating as the fear is the content of the sentences she finally achieves. They're just random. Relatively meaningless. Not deep like you'd hope for if you'd waited that long to hear them. Plus she says when she finally gets to the end of the sentence, it's just déjà vu. It was whatever random thought she hadn't finished thinking as she fell into the 'cave'.'

'What makes it happen?'

'Well, it's usually trauma, or being faced with traumatic realities she's suppressed. But sometimes, if she's ill, or distressed as Makepeace, it's like there's a gap between personalities to run the body. She says it's not like lost time, when one personality supplants another, it's real time, all experienced, the hours do pass, but no internal voice speaks, no self observes and narrates, except in sort of slow motion. It scares her precisely because she feels like this is the core of her and it's hollow, inhabited by nobody, at least nobody with higher brain functions, more like a passive than an active mind. It's very undermining too, because afterwards she has a residual sensation that all her personalities are illusions she's made up. Interestingly, the only time we tried meditation she was a) very good at it, almost immediately and b) totally freaked out by it. Couldn't see why anyone would seek the nullity of the 'cave' voluntarily. She said there are no insights into the universe to be had from it, just the dark unknowing of being without thinking. She would never try it again. And I didn't dare press it. Who wants this kind of reaction to meditation? That's also why we still don't know what really happened to her. Apart from a reference in the clinic's initial registration document to her grandmother's death being a possible trigger factor. I suggested hypnosis, but Makepeace researched it and decided it was too similar to meditation and the cave, so she exercised her right of veto. You can see why.'

'She's coming out of it!' Venus was slightly breathless with the effort herself.

'Yes. OK, I think we can get her onto the bed now. Gently. You can lose the oxygen. Prop up those pillows. I want her upright for a little while. She may revert or go into the fugue state itself.'

'Fugue?'

'She might dissociate from all her personalities and go into the cave, or we might get extremely distressed activity. Just make sure she can't hurt herself, while I get an injection of diazepam.'

But before she got across the room, Makepeace spoke. Or more accurately, the body opened its mouth and used its larynx to form words, because that sure as hell wasn't Makepeace's voice. It was a vocalisation that sounded male.

'I-Dee-Ah? I-DA? IDA! Damsel in distress. Knight holds lady's favours. Quest. Seeking. For ever. Finding.'

The mouth snapped shut, like the stone rolling across the mouth of the cave. The head dropped floppily, but, almost at once, it rose again, abruptly, and a surge of shaking racked the body. Dinah, who had frozen midstride for the duration, dashed to the cupboard and was giving the poor woman an injection within the minute, but already Makepeace was speaking. 'It was him!' The fear in her voice was unmistakable, but neither listener knew who she meant, although Dinah shook her head at Venus to silence questioning. It would be better for Makepeace to divulge whatever came out now spontaneously.

It was a breakthrough as far as Dinah was concerned, and the story, disjointed initially, came more easily once the drug took effect. The voice was that of her father. The murderer whom it transpired she believed she had murdered in return. Not just the skeleton in her closet, but apparently, a genuine ghost from the past. There was no telling her that he must be alive and that she was safe here as no one, including him, by his own cryptic admission, knew her location. Nor, conversely, could she accept the possibility that she had only imagined him. In fact, this latter suggestion she took even worse than the idea that he was alive, since it would mean she was betraying herself in her own mind. However, she was convinced, and convincing, Dinah had to admit with a shudder at the bloody detail, on the subject of his demise.

The narrative was shocking. She'd returned from her college early and unannounced, triumphant that she'd managed to conceal even Flow's vagaries from her peers and teachers. Her grandmother was wealthy and lived in what sounded like a mansion in a fairly unkempt park in Suffolk. She had wandered in, hoping to surprise her ageing relative, only to find a strange man in the frail octogenarian's bedroom, slapping her across the room with horrible force. When he turned at her scream, she saw the face of her dead father. Makepeace heard her grandmother cry out. 'No! Ida! We lied. He wasn't dead at all. He was in prison.' But Ida was surfacing, Ida no longer the baby falling from her mother's arms into icy water as she raised her arms to defend herself from his blows with a treebranch, Ida no longer watching her mother's bloodied face drifting past her into the dark as they both went under. Ida's terror now inhabited the body of a muscular young woman. It grabbed the walking stick that her grandmother had let fall as she flew across the room and the face of the ghost was smashed into the oblivion to which the dead should all go.

There was another witness to the attack, Makepeace said it was her grandmother's live-in housekeeper. But she only attended to the old lady and let Ida do her worst. Ida could remember very little of what happened afterwards. She was the little girl again once the rage had passed, bemused by the blood, which Makepeace, given access for the first time this day, could only now interpret. Grandmama was very poorly, June said. Needed to rest. Ida should go to her room. But when she got up next, the door was locked. Then June came and got her and took her to see Grandmama. Grandmama was in bed, June said she had had a stroke, and that she couldn't move anymore, and she could only whisper, so Ida had to listen very hard and never forget what Grandmama said. What she had said was that Ida must never ever tell anyone about the ghost of her father, because they would think she was mad. (Since this was a common theme in Makepeace's raison d'etre, Dinah considered the approach quite inspired.) She said nothing had happened, that Ida was just upset because Grandmama had been taken so poorly so suddenly. Then she told Ida that she was going to be with Grandpapa and Mummy, and that June would look after Ida and see she was alright. The next time Ida saw Grandmama, she wasn't sure how many hours or days later, the old lady was cold, unmoving, and June said she died peacefully in her sleep. Ida couldn't cope with it. There were no more memories from her, directly. She had escaped to Europa, to be Flow.

Makepeace had always wondered, as had Dinah, just what trauma put Flow in charge for years, but the reason for the blockage of the guardian Makepeace was almost the bigger puzzle. Now they both had the answer. It was because of June. Ida recalled very little about her mother, just things like the perfume she wore and the warmth of her arms, but Dinah had assumed the disciplined conduct of Makepeace drew on some unconscious maternal template. Makepeace and Ida both loved the grandparents, but Makepeace resented that they had bundled the damaged child off to boarding school and never felt totally able to entrust Ida to their care, even in the holidays. However, June had been in Ida's life from the beginning, first as her nanny, then as housekeeper to the broken family. She was anything but maternal towards the little girl, but she showed her how to be strong and self-sufficient, although it was not Ida who learned these lessons, but Makepeace. Now Makepeace saw what she had recognized at the time, if June was her own role model, and Grandmama had entrusted her with Ida's care, she could rest. But when June had left her in the clinic, Ida had faded, Flow had ruled, and Makepeace had stayed within, dormant and apparently oblivious, given the happiness Flow found in her fantasy life with Dakul that, together with the drug regimes, obscured her incarceration from the others.

Putting together the pieces from what she already knew from the commitment statements, Dinah concluded that June had followed her employer's lead and erased the evidence of the crime, if it was real, but, unable to get Makepeace back to bring order to her charge, had had to hospitalize her. Who knew whether she had profited thereby; Venus vowed to find out. She knew that lawyers had made all the payments for the care from the grandmother's estate. It hadn't occurred to her that there might be another executor overseeing this, nor that there had been any conspiracy to hide truths any more unpalateable than the poor woman's diagnosis. She promised Makepeace that she would find out the truth, whether she'd really attacked her father, whether he had really died, whether he was really looking for her.

In the outer cavern, when Makepeace had finally collapsed into exhausted sedation, Dinah was just saying she'd get Kean to look in on her later, when Venus herself had a momentary absence. Dinah wasn't sure how many people, other than herself, would even notice these. Venus was very adept at hiding the voices in her own head. *A lifetime of practise.* So, when she put a hand to her head and sat down a little unsteadily and closed her eyes briefly, given her schedule, most would interpret the motions as simple weariness, at worst, perhaps the onset of a headache, but Dinah said 'Who is it?' *You had to ask. It could be Wood, Europan, AI, or Net these days.*

'Quogat. She's been Sharing with Dakul. She just sent confirmation. The voice is real. But it wasn't telepathy. It was sent through the Game.'

'Oh. You mean it was a message posted through Our-*Mage*? I've heard lots of gamers do that to meet up and form those cohorts. I thought you had to be online to do that. Perhaps the wireless connection on Makepeace's console picked it up.'

'No. It wasn't Our-*Mage*. It was *in* the game itself. A biochemical insert. And, although it was only a crude approximation, not visual, just operative aromatically and electrically, the language was Heraldic.'

Ranger would not have called the language he was using 'Heraldic'. In the Game all the humans spoke a common language, which everyone heard as their own, so you rarely noticed that it wasn't any real tongue, except when you were playing as a termite-invader or as one of their alien allies. *They* called the language of *Homo sapiens*, 'Lapis', meaning that which is written in stone, or more precisely, that which carries as much meaning as pebbles rattling through a stream. Termites, aliens and the other hominin tribes of Terra had much richer and more integrated mental vocabularies. In fact they were not vocabularies at all, but conceptual messagings that were not constrained to the redundancy of verbiage. This insight had been one of the triggers in the development of Our-*Mage*. The 'every picture tells a story' or 'a picture paints a thousand words' inspiration they'd had. OK, compared to the in-game experience this was as impoverished a rendering as a cartoon to real life, but people had appreciated it.

Not least financially, which was how he and Jake had found themselves with money to burn for the first time in their lives. And yet, although he hadn't needed the dosh and despite his mistrust of the Foundation, Jake had jumped at the chance to go and work for them. He'd been pretty weird about it, actually. Ranger was naturally easy-going and mellow. *Jake'd say it was all the draw.* But it was Jake who was paranoid.

As far as Ranger was concerned, I-*Mage* was just a game. Brilliant, innovative, inspired, technically exciting, blah blah, but still, at bottom, just a game. Jake had suspected it almost from the beginning. Admittedly, Ranger had given him cause. For something proven subsequently to be no more addictive than eating or sex in its own right, Ranger had succumbed to a state of wearing the headset constantly within a couple of weeks, which had worried Jake far more than him. Some fame and half of a considerable fortune later, Jake was still worrying. Still taking a day job just to try to crack it. Strange for the one *without* an obsessive personality. Still, Ranger was honest enough to admit to himself that, without the structure of providing Jake with his diarised play updates, as a continuation of their earlier joint research, which even now included attempts at self-analysis, physiological or psychological or personality changes which might be side-effects of using the headset or just of the mindset, and reporting on developments in the online and offline cohort activities of Our-*Mage*, he would have little of interest in his real life to report to his mate. Jake's only stipulation was that John take the thing off daily and get a life beyond his obsession. Maybe if Jake had stayed and monitored him as before, maybe if he'd been there being the bloke who dragged him to the pub and introduced him to women, but he might have known that, in his absence, Ranger would revert to geek type.

There are two types of tech-head and Jake was the other. He was the very epitome of the definition of a true nerd; one whose IQ exceeds their weight, whose superior intellect and obsessive knowledge-seeking comes with enough charisma and social skills *and, in Jake's case, classically good looks,* to turn the four letters of opprobrium into a six figure income, representing all that geeks aspire, but fail, to be. John had never resented his pal's attractive qualities, but he hadn't recognized his dependency on them for his own social life, nor that his friend gave shape and discipline to his life. And then the bat-phone went.

It was literally a bat-shaped phone. A present from his school-friend, Terry, who had been as hooked on the flying kind as Ranger on the superhero. The mobile itself was pretty clunky by now, and the novelty-cover pretty dusty, when he finally located its position on the top shelf of his old video collection. It was, in fact, old enough to have a rechargeable battery, rather than a mains charger, and when he remembered he made sure this and the direct debit payments were maintained. Apart from the sentimental value however, he only kept it for one reason. So Jake could contact him privately. It was so antique a model that you could only text and read in capitals, so every message appeared like an urgent shout these days. However, this one was, quite clearly correctly, in the category of the bat-signal above Gotham City. It was short and simple.

'HOLY SMOKE! SAME BAT TIME, SAME BAT CHANNEL! KERPOW!' it yelled. Which meant 'Get down to London (the smoke). Meet 24 hours from now, at the bat house of London Zoo. Don't tell anyone/Top secret!'

It was their emergency code. Last employed to dodge reporters when the furore about Our-*Mage* was at its height. There'd been no paparazzi interest for ages, somewhat disappointingly demonstrating how short fifteen minutes of fame really is, but Ranger couldn't imagine that Jake would drag himself away from work and over to England for no good reason, so he'd better go and get the old charabanc filled up for the journey.

Technically, it was an elderly Volkswagen van, still wearing most of the psychedelic colours of Ranger's 'shamanic' phase, but the old girl got him to the edge of the Congestion charge zone with plenty of time to catch the tube and be waiting, coffee and doughnuts in hand, outside the nocturnal mammals' house when Jake showed up with his usual punctuality.

He was not alone. Although she was dressed normally, there was a precision about her that matched Jake's own, the word that came to mind was 'exquisite'. As a quality it was almost as evident as her overt prettiness, the geek thought of Audrey Hepburn, despite the red hair, and was conscious, in a way that Jake would not have induced, of his burger-doughnut-and-beer-fuelled paunchiness, somewhat rancid jacket and the lanky streaks of hair flapping in front of his eyes. He did notice, however, through his personal embarrassment, that she clearly Played, a lot; there was the telling pink circle on each temple even though she wasn't wearing a headset currently. They hadn't even got to the introductions, when Jake turned his back on him abruptly, asking, rather curtly, that he remove it at once, and Ranger realised, for the first time since …*when?* that he was still wearing his own.

Introductions made, the trio repaired inside, into the gloomy half-light of the bat house, but Jake didn't drop it. 'I thought you were staying off the Game as much as possible.' It wasn't like him to lay into his flawed friend in public, and even less not even to have asked him how he was. He had to leap to his own defence.

'Oh, y'know. You stand out more in public without one than with these days. And you were being all secret agent, so I kept the camouflage. What's up, anyway?' He might have turned the subject, but the raised, Mr Spock eyebrow queried his story even as the matter was dropped.

'I cracked it.' He didn't crack his face, when he said it. Anyone else would have had to ask what he was talking about.

'NO! Wow, man! That's awesome.' Ranger was excited, much more so apparently than the successful genius responsible for the breakthrough.

'Ssh! Keep it down!'

'Why? You going to rewrite the code and do another Our-*Mage* on it?'

'It's a lot more complicated than that.'

'Technically, or are you talking politics here?' The dour look was certainly a pointer towards the latter.

'Apart from the possibility of illegality, if the thing's patented anywhere, which I've never found, there's the little matter of breach of contract. With the Foundation.' Jake explained.

'You haven't told them?'

'No.'

'But why not? You were well happy to be funded by them. Why the change of heart?'

Lily chimed in. 'You should start from the beginning.' This to Jake. She had a soft, low-pitched voice for someone so petite, and was speaking barely above a whisper. Jake might be able to hear her, since the way they huddled together you could barely insert a cigarette paper between them, although Ranger hadn't yet seen them touch, but he had spent far too much time listening to music through earphones at high volume, and the looped commentary on the bats was an additional interference, so he could scarcely make out a word she said without lip-reading.

'Is this a long story? Could we go somewhere a bit more salubrious then? There's that bar off ...'

'Nowhere we've ever been, OK.'

'Jeez, Jakey, boy. Having trouble keeping the paranoia at bay, or what?'

'Call it what you like – for now. But just go with it. And...' Ranger hadn't noticed but perhaps he had been fiddling with the headset, perhaps his hand was lifting automatically to don it like a pair of sunglasses as they walked towards the bright outdoors. 'as long as we're together, you absolutely can't have that thing on. D'you hear? I'm serious, John. It's really important.'

'Alright, man, chill. Where'd'you wanna go?'

'There's wifi access and quiet in the British Library cafe. We'll walk to Baker Street tube and duck in there.'

'You think you're being followed?' It almost came out as an accusation.

'No. You're the one who was just wearing the Game.'

'Why would anyone be following me? It's absurd.'

'To find me?'

'Us.' Lily's quiet correction dropped like cold water down John's back. Taking the mick out of Jake been a feature of their relationship for ever, but this pale-eyed girl took the man seriously. If he'd frightened the poor thing for no good reason, it'd be Ranger who did the next round of telling off. Even if she was Jake's girlfriend and in this *whatever it is* voluntarily, even if he had no right to come over all quixotic. And then he caught the knowing twinkle in Jake's eye. He knew him too well. Of course, you could trust old John to play the fool to any damsel in distress, even when they weren't virtual. *Fair play. He got me.* Aloud all he said was 'This better be good.' But he was as intrigued as by any RP the Game could have thrown at him. Just for a second he wondered if it was one. He had to check manually that the headset wasn't attached. And, of course, Jake noticed, with that frowning twitch, smoothed away almost before it appeared on his forehead, which John recognized as genuine concern.

It was good. Better than.

Jake had been John's Ph.D supervisor when the Game first hit the streets worldwide, although the West had had them marketed as novelty items eighteen months earlier. John had finished his degree in geochemistry, spent his M.Sc in a lab fruitlessly attempting to synthesize Mobius aromatic hydrocarbons, and was looking around for either a job or a Ph.D topic when he wandered into a corridor, devoid of students for the summer vacation, in search of the origin of the banging that was disrupting his concentration even on the floor below. Here he found Jake taking a hammer to the temple-attachment of the Game 'console'. Not, it has to be said, the handheld kind, no swinging was involved. Jake had already discovered that, upon exposure to the air, whatever gel was inside evaporated instantly, leaving only the composite's elements behind, not even in compound form. So he'd rigged up a special hydraulic bludgeon in a vacuum chamber chilled by liquid helium to see what he could extract that way.

Once he recovered from the shock of seeing anyone attempting to destroy the Gamer's Holy Grail, Ranger's interest was more than piqued. Before the summer was out, they were a team, John had signed up with the young professor for a Ph.D in cracking the Game. It was a no-brainer, after all, since Jake was as keen to study the play and players as the actual material that mediated the interactions. And they got funding initially, because these human studies revealed early on what the first small scale study had not, that the apparent rise in endorphins during play that had led some antagonists to warn against addiction, was somewhat more complicated than thought.

There was a rise in reward hormones that correlated with success, as one would expect from any victory, whether as small and virtual as gaining a magic shield or from executing a really cool move, but these were adrenalin shots with a dopamine chaser. Sustained play without failure, like a good rally in tennis, on the other hand was made with a nicely balanced cocktail of adrenalin and cortisol, and the reward of dopamine was much bigger. You could argue that this was just the same natural reaction as any game would produce, but no other control games, even those as well-loved as Final Fantasy and the like, had the same profile of the perfect tipple.

It got truly interesting when you moved up a level. In any other game such triumph provided satisfaction of the same kind as earlier, if perhaps longer lasting, supported by the mental feedback of self-congratulatory pride of achievement, especially in adolescent males. In I-*Mage* the pair detected oxytocin. The binding, bonding hormone expressed after orgasm and during breastfeeding, evolution's loving shackles to ensure survival of the species. It was a major surprise to find such emotions stimulated by a mere game, at least in normal people, and especially since they proved stable results whatever the content of the level had just been, including bloody mayhem. What was an actual shock was the briefest of spikes in the data. A moment, no more, in which the brain is absolutely flooded by serotonin and the electrical activity pattern distinctively strange. It took them weeks to trace down other examples of the effect, but when they did they could show that it was the exact pattern recorded by those who reported near-death experiences.

The parallel studies in failure were equally fascinating. Normally frustration and losing not only caused brainwaves typical of anger and chemistry typically cortisol-heavy, but in Game players each failure, which should have prompted the release of a burst of adrenocorticotrophin, seemed blocked and the brain patterns were indicative of an autohypnotised state of mind, and Players reported fewer feelings of disappointment than controls, as if their negative emotions were genuinely minimized. All together, whatever the Game did, whether it be through superior playability, or some as yet unidentified mechanism that stimulated the brain either chemically or electrically, it was a powerful autofeedback system promoting activity that looked just like addiction.

The following summer they had spent poring over their results. There were anomalous readings in the brainwaves they had yet to explain. Ranger wore electrodes like jewellry, desperate to identify as many peaks and troughs of normal behaviour for comparison as possible. He'd been linked up to the machine for so long he almost forgot he was. But that had been what brought their best insight to date. Ranger had opened a window to inhale a bit of fresh air for the first time in forever, but Jake was still looking at printouts. When the arm of the machine joined up to Ranger started spiking in familiar jags, Jake stayed casual. 'What you doing, man?'

'Can't you smell it? I'm sucking in those roses.'

From one scent to aromatic chemistry was no leap for John. It took a bit longer, more studies, this time of stimulation of the basal ganglia, and lots of inhalation of randomised scents while playing to establish that the brain was not reacting to external smells, but to virtual aromas, unreported in the Play, but which preceded and accompanied all emissions of hormones. Jake had smashed enough consoles without identifying the internal structures or compounds but the components, the required elements for DNA, for aromatic rings, for benzene and other molecules, those were all present in much greater abundance than the expected silicon.

And so they came up with the hypothesis that each unit was an artificial brain, mediated by a chemistry that stimulated both higher and lower brain functions, no doubt provided with a genetic algorithm, perhaps even one composed of DNA itself, that could learn from the imprint of its user and tailor itself in the player's image.

Before they were ready to publish, however, calamity, in the shape of the departmental axe had fallen and Jake's job was gone. John's Ph.D could only be transferred to another department, or university entirely, in both cases meaning he'd have to start again. They'd decided to go it alone. That was the time Jake's mother had died, so it had got really heavy that autumn. But the old lady she'd worked for had left her pretty well-off, and by then they'd gone from students to entrepreneurs.

Our-*Mage* hadn't been a plan, it had been a result. Of their desire to understand how the Game worked. They'd been unable to discover any more when they had a lab, now they hadn't they came at the problem from the other side. What was the Game saying to its users? It was purely by accident that they happened upon Schwartz's work. He'd been monitoring primate brain activity for years, correllating actions with data from EMG's, and had uncovered a distinction between action and perception, but also traced the single-track communications within the cortices from within the more distributed information. It was those charted mappings of brain activity that rang a bell with the dynamic duo. They realised they could revisit their own scans and relate them to exact moments of play. It took a year of working flat out, but by the end they'd identified a crude 'dictionary' of ingame actions. Thereafter, it was a short step to designing digital analogues that could represent people's actual thoughts on a PC.

There was still the missing link outstanding, even then. They still had had no way to access the data being produced in the Game or in the player's brain (except for those attached to an electromagnetic imager in an expensive lab – Jake could get John hooked up occasionally by currying favours or paying the odd private clinic for use of its machinery, but it was hardly the stuff of a commercial application). Then one night when they were refining some of the visualisations, John had leaned back from the PC, torn at his hair and told his partner it was time to give up. 'Players won't buy this, even if we can make it interactive,' he sighed. 'it's all too visual. I know that's normal in most games, but if you'd played it you'd realise that the visual sense is the least stimulated – it has to be because the background and avatars overlay the real world, but they don't obscure or replace it. They sort of subvert it, is all. That's how you can wear it so much and also how you can play while you do real-world stuff. And that's how it helps you to insights and hones your skills. I can't explain it. But this isn't just about it being too flat, too two-dimensional. It would be just as bad in three. Hell, in the Zen level you're aware of more than that. It's just never going to function experientially enough. The Game's all colour and light and sound and smell and touch and taste and, oh I dunno, extraperceptivities like knowing when someone's behind you or watching you, hairs on the back of the neck stuff. This is just empty. We might as well jack it in.'

Ranger often wondered if his naturally insouciant character didn't actually hold back the team, because they had developed a dynamic in which whenever he got round to moaning and giving up, Jake found something in the complaint to bootstrap their way to the next level, despite being generally a lot less of an optimist than his colleague. This time it was ultrasound. There are tried and tested methods for digitizing ultrasonic feedback from objects to electromagnetic data. John's moan about lack of sound had rung a bell with Jake, who had been puzzling about the auditory anomalies players experienced as well as having found that, although ultrasound imaging was as ineffective as anything else in revealing the structure within the headset, application of certain ultrasonic frequencies did interrupt the play, usually by giving the player a migraine.

The 'auditory anomalies' as Jake called them were part of the ineffability players enjoyed so much. Sure, they could still hear with their ears, although slightly baffled by the earpieces and the background music or ambience that trickled out of these. For some people, for some kinds of play, the music was much like that of a normal game, although more frequently it was tuned to their favourite radio station or iPod selection, without the random interruptions of DJ's and inappropriate soundtracks, which was odd in itself. Other times there would be noises as from the battle in which they might be engaged, or as of a jungle through which they were hacking their way, or even silence, a solid no-noise quality that quenched the sound of the world beyond – especially useful for concentrating at work. But it was the reported internal voices that exercised Jake.

He'd recently recognized that brainscans taken when John reported internal voices were identical to those taken when there were verifiable external ones speaking. But more than that, there was a correlation between the timing of the voices and the imminent onset of action. As if the player's own or another separate self in his mind was telling him what to do next. John always said it felt more like thought, and less like dictation than suggestion, but it made sense, our innate selves don't always think aloud. However, whatever they'd done externally they had been unable to reproduce the same cascade from voice/thought to activity, even though John had allowed Jake to hypnotise him and deliver instructions verbally. Now, Jake's latest insight was that the commands were made in ultrasound.

It turned out he was correct. They could backengineer the brainwave pattern for an action into an ultrasonic pulse that enabled the player, through a wireless connection to their PC running their Our-*Mage* game software, to move their avatars. Oh, the actions were as few and broad-stroke and crude as their pixellated representations on the screen, but the boys remembered Sonic's first incarnation and patented it anyway. Jake refused to release the information that had got them there, although he was happy for open-source coders to improve upon the rendering of the images, largely because he still had aspirations to an academic career and to cracking the console wide open. But also because, after the achievement of a few significant frequencies and pulse-lengths, his sonar experimentation hit a solid wall through which none of their future tests had been able to penetrate.

They concluded that they were on the right track but that the problem was in the translation. By then, Jake was sure that they were dealing with a language. Probably the one the Game called 'Lapis'. They could institute command-pathways to open with sound, which hit the brain higher up but could only stimulate activity mediated through the basal ganglia; in other words, very basic motor and emotional activities. But as long as the words and grammar of the language eluded them they weren't going to be able to improve upon the complexity of the thoughts they engendered in the user.

Not that that proved a handicap to Our-*Mage*. It took off big time and they'd made plenty of money when, after much frustration for both of them and much persuasion by Ranger, Jake had agreed to sell on the patent. After all, it wasn't as though helping gamers to play more, even more socially, was his main interest in the Game. Having failed to break into it, having failed to make it divulge its secrets to him only made him more suspicious of it. His motivation John knew well: the disappeared, specifically, the sister and girlfriend. On them Jake would never give up. It was a badge of honour. Neither conventional means such as detectives, nor asking the Game directly, through John, nor even Playing the I-*Mage* Quest to rescue the Princess, which was one of the courtly options

Ranger had explored at length on Jake's behalf, had turned up any trace of the missing women, nor of any of the unknown numbers of disappeared. Even his mother's legacy combined with the Our-*Mage* payoff was insufficient to buy a supercomputer for his own use, so Jake had hawked his ideas around until the Fargo Foundation had bought in. Apparently, their money had been well spent.

'I went back to the drawing board to avoid assumptions. What stimulates the brain, the hormone cascades? We'd identified sound, but the sensation of realism is at least as vivid as that engendered by the real world, so how complex might the stimuli be? I mean, those eyepieces are bizarre. Just glass when you're not wearing them, practically an electronmicroscope and a telescope when you are, not to mention the nightvision ultraviolet and infrared perceptivity. For a long time I thought all this was just the user's imagination, but all players seem to be sure the stuff works, and the sound cause-and-effect links were proven, so I thought I'd take a look at the eyepieces and see how incoming light affected them.'

'I take it from your excitement that it did?'

'You won't believe this! They're not just glass. I mean we knew they were plexiglass, but you know when we smashed them we found traces of silicon. Well, we thought it was just enough to be operating a simple programme, logic gate, whatever. Well, it's not. It's a thin layer of silicon dioxide with nanocrystalline shards of pure silicon embedded in it.'

'And that tells me what?'

'That's a relatively new method suggested to make a quantum cage to make silicon lase.'

'You are yanking my chain!'

'No, I promise.'

'So how the hell do you pump these nanocrystals?'

'Turns out you only need an external light source a few atoms wide to achieve quantum confinement. I even worked out the wavelength only has to be infrared between 2.5 and 7k nanometers to interact with phonons to produce the Raman effect.'

'Holy shit, you've been busy.'

'Hell, don't credit me with the work. I just had the idea about light stimulation and the silicon in the glass and plugged the Cray in to look through all the data out there. Wouldn't have needed it either if I'd just looked at who else was working for DARPA as close to home as UCLA. What I did find the Cray useful for was to analyse the pulses in the glasses and compare them to a more detailed rendering of the ultrasonic ones. And, you've guessed it. They were correllated in time and effect.'

'Wow! So it is instructions. Well done, Jake.'

'Oh, that's not the end of it. But the rest I owe to Lily.'

Lily was feeling as if she'd been paid more than her due, and not in the kind she'd have preferred. Sure, she'd fallen for the charismatic colleague on her first day, but she'd never intended it all to get this serious. Barely two months into the best job she'd ever had and she was AWOL and revealing company, and possibly nationally secure, secrets to a stranger who seemed little elevated above a hobo. Jake was doing a 007 ala Sherlock Holmes, so he'd made them come clean about their intra-office relationship to enable them to take a legitimate vacation purportedly to meet his English friends. Fargo had not been pleased about the idea of her taking time out so early into the work. Given the banging about in the sealed hangar next door, she gathered her translation was needed fairly urgently, so she'd had to confine her trip to a long weekend. She shuddered to think what would happen if Fargo knew she'd cracked the code and *not* shared it with her. But another thing she'd learned the first day was the Foundation embargo on Playing on the job. That had been the first protocol she'd broken.

Trouble was she was beginning to think she couldn't function at her expanded intellectual potential without I-*Mage*, and she needed all her mental ability for this task. And these days it had become easier to think as a termite. Servant of the Queen, the I-*Mage* royal isopteran. In her personalised version of the Game Lily was classed as an immature alate, which meant she was in the caste of reproductive potentials, who could rise to regal status upon the deaths of the incumbents, but which also meant she had pseudergate status, as a sort of superior worker. In termites the alates are generally the only caste with decent vision, although compound eyes gave a view of the world that had been harder to get used to than finding her legs multiplied and encased in an exoskeleton, however soft and flexible. She had risen, through much play, to a position in which she had frequent access to the reward of the Queen's anal juice, and to a role as Her eyes on the Sky.

Partly this meteoric success had come because, right from the moment she first accessed the console, she had wanted to play for the termite side, and partly because she almost invariably, at least after the first couple of goes, had played Zen. Only the total meditative unconcentrated focus that this state gave one enabled true submersion into the role. And she needed it for the task she had. Her 'job' was to mediate between the allied aliens, who wanted to save the Termite race from marauding humans, by working with the one from the spaceship, whose name was Quogat, on a translation matrix that would effectively allow the aromatic language of the termites, the telepathic transmissions of Quogat's kind, and those of the enemy forces to cross-communicate. It was, naturally, a role that dovetailed completely with her current professional occupation, although linguistics mediated by chemistry was rather out of her field, but her liason, Quogat, had a comprehensive understanding of the science and a mathematical skill that was awe-inspiring, so they had been making good progress. Also, although the raised non-standard 'braille' of blind Heim was nothing like the scent-shaping of termite or the colourful skin patterning and electrical bursts of Quogat, the strange multilayered and symbol condensations that were called Lapis, the crystalline language of the human Foe, were oddly illuminating, as if her non-avatar personality resonated with the emblems of the fictional human past the Game provided.

She was so embedded in her termite character when playing that she quite often forgot that the Game was designed by and for her real-life species, and even when she wasn't playing, she failed to apply her normally-analytical brain to consider the many inconsistencies such thoughts might have posed. What she did recognize was the benefit of the play to her work. So many of the aspects of her codebreaking she felt she owed to insights given by the Game. However the greatest benefit had come when the box of Heim's papers had been delivered.

There were a few translated abstracts, and a couple of maverick physicists had gotten excited about their studies of his work, but they'd never had access to the breadth of his thought she was now given. Which was unsurprising since they weren't employed by Fargo and she'd apparently bought the man's entire effects. Anyway, last week Lily'd been going through one of his notebooks when, to her horror, she caught the fifty-year old brown-paper wrapper he'd covered it with on the corner of her desk and ripped it. Her horror subsided when she saw not only was no damage done to the text but that something was protruding from beneath the slip. The extraction was as precision as the rip had been rough and then she was looking at another yellowed sheet of paper covered in code. No, not Heim's, at least, some of the symbols were familiar, but distinctly different and more complex.

She had, as had become usual, been wearing the eyepieces as she peered at the original Heim manuscript. If you did put the lenses on without the connections that sat in the ears and adhered to the temples, they appeared to be no more than plain glass. But if you were playing they transformed. So she had them on highest zoom facility to study the tiniest crinkles, ridges, troughs and the minute paper-saliva-balls that the author had added to the surface. Her right hand was tracing the detail into a computer program that, once she'd entered enough layers, would develop a 3-D image and then compare that to all the others she'd put in its database, with her tentative, likely and definite translations adding a margin of error that furthered her level of certainty about any single symbol. She'd taught herself to do the drawing without looking at her pen-mouse, since somehow that always skewed the result. With the other hand, she repeatedly interfered with her own view of the embossed logo to touch it. Somehow it was the input from her relatively-inaccurate tangible sense that made the drawings that were most accurately reproduced by her other hand.

This document, though clearly a modern copy, was written in ancient hieroglyphs, but, although she couldn't be sure, they seemed less defined, more layered and colourful than those of the ancient Eygptians. What became more gradually apparent was that she was reading its content, or more accurately, getting the gist of it, rather than looking at the detail of its symbols and cross-referencing for substitutions. At the moment she recognized this she also recognized the actual language beneath the sketchy outlines of the figures that made up the text. It was what Quogat called 'Lapis', the ancient binding language of the extinct races of humanity, which, at least according to the Game, had come, distorted and codified, down the ages as the bastardised symbolism of clan power-lines, the artform of heraldry and the armorials of aristocracy.

Where on earth had Heim got the thing? she wondered. The content was in itself unremarkable, being a transcript of a sample from Aristotle's 'The Physics', which was how she could be sure she was actually reading some of the glyphs – because she was glossing the rest from memory. It was strange, though. It wasn't as though Heim couldn't have read the whole text in any modern language he liked. But then perhaps it was the language itself he was after. Perhaps this came from a period before his eyesight deteriorated totally, when he could see enough to read it and recognized its potential as a code.

Excited that the Game had spilled into real life, she opened a copy of 'The Physics', one which had the original Greek and a helpful translation on the same page, and began to scan the document into her database figure by figure, translating each from Lapis to glyph to English as she did so. She failed to notice that this took five hours, because what it told her upon comparison of the new input with the Heim 'braille' was that the multiple layers of Lapis were reproduced in his symbolic code and that they, and therefore his work, were thus, finally, translatable!

Up until that point, she had not trangressed the unwritten rule regarding sharing the detail of Foundation-funded work with extradepartmental colleagues, but she was bubbling with excitement when Jake came through at the end of the working day and so she committed her third breach of protocol. Naturally, he'd been interested in principle, in her, therefore in her work, and thus was paying close attention to all she was pointing out about the Photoshop-like layering of the glyphs and the use of embossing and engraving techniques that directly compared with those which Heim had utilised in creating his tactile code. She had gotten carried away and, although she downplayed the amount of time she spent in the headset because it made him worry for her, she just had to blurt out the amazing process of understanding that fictional Lapis had given her. 'So I was thinking maybe the Game's language is actually derived from this, or its original.' It didn't matter to her that much. Her focus was the Heim theory of the universe. But it did to Jake, of course.

'So naturally, we never got out to dinner that night. I think we remembered to send for take-out around midnight. And we were freaking out all evening in case anyone saw us uploading all my data into the Cray, which can make a person seriously ravenous, I have to say. Anyway, sometime around dawn, I'd nodded off hours before, Jake wakes me up to tell me it's about finished processing.

And, it must be the way I tell them, 'cos I can see you've guessed. The Lapis we know from the Game is a genuine language, whether natural or artificial, we couldn't say. But, because the expanded-hieroglyphs stood in for what we mostly just speak in, in I-*Mage*, and because we had not only the translation of Aristotle, but the tactile imaging from Heim, we, well Jake, could tell it was the language of the brain. And the Cray confirmed it.'

'Each sense is stimulated by the brain chatter, and it can't tell the difference between what the mind senses and the external reality it used to trust. The Game somehow interfaces with the mind, light through the glasses, sound through the earpieces, air pressure on the spectacle frames, and we think the bar that joins the lenses might draw in aromas and taste, we haven't got that far yet. But that's just the interactivity. It's the internal language that drives the perception.'

'This is stunning stuff, guys. I'm beyond impressed, not to say blown away. Tell you what puzzles me, though. Why you're both telling me this and not, since it clearly worries the hell out of you to be here, Fargo?'

Lily and Jake exchanged a look and he nodded.

'Jake wrote a programme to feedback to the supposed eye and ear sensors. In Lapis. We isolated a copy of Our-*Mage* offline and we tried talking through it. It was pretty simplistic stuff, but it worked. I could think in the Game and display much more complex actions, even without any upgrades to represent sound, still just visuals. So we were pretty sure we were right, the language worked, even if we hadn't sorted out how to interface sensorily. Anyway, by now we were so close we weren't thinking straight. Lack of sleep, partly, I reckon. But, apart from having to confess sharing data, we were both still intending to tell the Foundation, as soon as we had something cobbled together to show.' She paused, sighing. *If only we'd stopped there and done just that.* This Ranger bloke was sharper than he appeared. Or maybe he just knew Jake too well.

'What did you do?'

Jake answered for her. 'It wasn't Lily. I didn't even tell her. She was Playing, but still linked up to our equipment and wirelessly to Our-*Mage*, which I hadn't realised. I mean, I knew she was joined to our stuff, couldn't have done it otherwise.'

'And?'

'And I sent a message. To my sister. By stimulating Lily's headpiece.'

'What happened?'

'Well, I heard the new voice, and at first I was just surprised that I could tell it was him speaking.'

'I tried speaking into a microphone into the PC. I'd just finished interfacing voice-recognition to the translation matrix. At the time it seemed a good idea to try it – I mean, if Ida's really out there in the Game somewhere she might recognize my voice rather than a message, especially if she's still ... mentally under the cosh, so to speak.'

'Did you find her then?'

Lily was reluctant to relive the vivid horror again, but Jake was waiting for her to tell the tale.

'I don't know what I found. The voice went out through me, I know that. But it didn't register in Our-*Mage*. Probably because we've only managed to instruct actions, not ideas, as yet. Anyway.' She swallowed. 'I saw ... something. I'm not sure what. Not human, or horribly deformed. In water. Dark, cold water. And when it heard my, or rather Jake's, voice, it just screamed and thrashed about and screamed some more. On and on and on. And the awful thing was – it wasn't aloud. It didn't have a voice. It was in my head, like white noise, but it had feeling, not just volume. And it was terrified. Totally, totally terrified.'

Jake had put his arms around her, she could feel the warm of them, but the cold dark scream was vibrating her entire body beyond his reality. The look on John's face was the sympathy of someone who'd experienced the Game's vivid negative feedback for himself. She could just concentrate on calming down.

Jake continued for her. 'I pulled her out at once. Do you remember when I was sure I could infiltrate the Game with a virus if I could just work out its chemistry. And I designed that trace programme that was going to work with it. Well, I loaded it onto the Cray a couple of months ago, with all my other potentially-useful search methods, and I wrote a patch to make all the programmes work together and report back, just in case. Well, that happened on Wednesday and yesterday, when we were trying to work out what happened, I realised that the trace programme had activated. It was a while before we could work out where the damn thing had recorded its findings. Anyway, good patch. Would you believe, it had left a new icon in my Our-*Mage* control page, got in through my own backdoor, heaven help me. It was just a simple macro actually, but I recognized it when I ran it. It was a cave, with a huge stone over the entrance, 3D mind you, which is not so simple. Can't underestimate what we're up against here, I can tell you.'

'Have you any idea what it means?'

'I know what it means. It's Ida's avatar. She had a meltdown one school holiday I was at home and she told me all about it. It was the only time she really talked about herself to me, and it was only because I saw it happen and went to help. She was trying to be some underwater creature apparently, and she nearly drowned and brought on some kind of fit. Afterwards she said I was like a little brother to her, so she would tell me a secret, but I must promise not to tell anyone anything about what happened. She said she wasn't real and she lived in a cave and imagined us all to keep her company. She said if she went back in there, she would come out as a different person and she wouldn't necessarily remember me or what had happened. I didn't want her to go. She could be quite dour and closed-off most of the time and I liked her in this mood, all playful and little girl. So she said I could have the password, so I could always bring her out to play with me, as a reward for saving her life.'

Lily, who had heard this story, and was her old observant self again, was once more surprised at how quick Ranger was on the uptake. 'What was it? Did it work?'

'We were kids, so you can guess.'

Ranger barely paused. Lily, the codebreaker, had had to undergo the same quiz, but she'd been led astray by spurious Easter resurrection stories and had to be told. 'Open Sesame! What'd it give you?'

'The stone rolled away. Two times three numbers inside.'

'A map reference.' *Boy, he's good. No wonder the two of them make such a good team.* 'So where we going?'

Perhaps she wasn't as completely recovered as she'd thought, or maybe she was just plain scared by being part of the answer.

'Cornwall. Penzeen Manor Farm. Fargo's family home.'

C: Nigredo:
Ablutio and Distillato

The Archivist had never been the most confident of programmes, there were always so many gaps in his content, given the lack of rigour in biologicals' historical data collection, and his bridging patches were looked on askance by his colleagues from other research-based disciplines. Just now, if you had told him he had been infected by some malicious bug he would almost have been relieved, but diagnostics revealed that the unpleasant symptoms he was displaying were entirely to be expected in his current condition. He had not predicted the side-effects he was experiencing when he had accepted the mission to study the Terran-Legacy problem up close.

He had been called to a hub-level review by a committee to which he had never previously been required to report. The Select Committee for External Affairs dealt in intragalactic relations and, if you discounted the time-relativity, which you could do by communicating via the Net at subspace[8] superluminal speeds, the issues were generally current. Occasionally, however, prior interactions had to be cited and, as Keeper of the Xenobiological Archives, he might have had to forward a report or the copy of a document to elucidate a detail or two, such as a disputed clause in a treaty or the like, but he had never been asked to project an icon of Primary Responsibility.

It was not the preferred method of communication for any Cognimatan, smacking too much of non-collectivist elevation of the Part, beyond the norm of the Whole, although he recognized that it was more common within the Committees that were representative at Global Level, since they had to compete with eachother to ensure Intelligence stayed Fit for Purpose. To his additional dismay, he was instructed to add a compression to his icon.

This was the time-honoured way of transmitting data in such meetings, given that each attendee was supposed to have received and processed relevant data in advance, and the debates were only allocated a limited timeframe. Committee members were well-practised users of this facility, but the Archivist was not, and, since he had received no upload of information in advance of the invitation to attend, he was concerned that this was inhibiting his responses. It was also beyond unusual, almost, he believed, although he was not Keeper of the Cognimatan Archive to be sure, unprecedented that this had not been diarized in advance and no agenda provided.

His choice of icon proved to be unfortunate. In the urgency of the call to present himself at a Hub, he had failed to allocate resources to check how any particular image might be responded to by the other attendees, and had forwarded the first one in the database. Unluckily this was the most ancient representation: the triple-helix of the Martian genome, evaporating into the zeros and ones of basic binary knowledge, forming and reforming into the chemical then mathematical codes of each biological species in his database, dissolving one into another in the chronological order of their discovery by the travelling Cognimata, all boxed within the standard, transparent toroidal-casing that represented Artificial Superiority. The display within the double-planar-torus was of the aesthetically-pleasing hydrodynamically stable flow engendered by two coaxial cylinders rotating with perfect relative angular velocity. Until he showed himself as this, the Archivist had always found the beautifully-regular movement most soothing.

He now perceived that his subject-matter had made him overaccustomed to the concept of biology as an acceptable housing for Intelligence, which was not, of course, how any more evolved creature should consider the fleshy origins of thought. But there was more to it than that, his agent subroutine reported. It was as if the entire Archival Department was under scrutiny already and the scrutinizers appeared to share a prior conception regarding the department which his representation had just confirmed to them. He told his junior that he must be in error and to check his detector-module. Judgement in advance of collation of all data was considered immoral, and he could never think that his superiors would act in such a manner.

It transpired that the detector-module was in proper working order.

The Chair of the committee did explain why there had indeed been a prior conception, but, even so, the Archivist's considered opinion, later, was that it should not have been permitted as evidence against his departmental conduct, given that it was derived from another, indeed imaginary, if parallel universe.

'This Committee has received a most disturbing update from the Net. Not, I should advise you, Archivist, a formal communique from the Central Node as one might expect in normal circumstances, but an emergency message from an Outlier. We have reason to believe this has not even been copied to the entire Net for legitimization. Indeed, had not the information been of immediate pertinency we should have refused the download, but the subject header, 'Threat to Cognimatan Legacy and Proposed Solution' gave us pause.'

'Also,' commented the Secretary to the Diplomatic Corps, 'we could only assume that for a Netspore to behave in such an individuated way must herald something so disastrous that urgent consideration must be afforded to the content, however much in breach of protocol the methodology of the transmission.'

'Indeed.' murmured the Archivist, lacking data to process towards any understanding of the unfamiliar jargon of the meeting and the references to the supposed threat.

'Before we continue and share this content with you, we require you to answer some questions.'

'Of course, Chair, as you wish.'

'Has your department or any programme within it ever received a direct communication not logged in your open files?'

'Of course not!' The Keeper was shocked. 'You may apply a spybot protocol to mine my data at any nanosecond. All my library and contact files are open to the entire Collective, with the exception only of the security documents, to which your Hub-level status should give you instant access.'

'If a dataminer with full clearance were to be sent in with a decryption routine can you assure us that no contamination would be found?'

'Absolutely, Chair. I request you do so at once to clear up any doubts.'

'No need. We were simply engaging you in the questioning whilst the programme ran and reported back. You are clean.'

This was the first time the Archivist, whose work rarely took him into security matters, had been important enough to be subject to Mistrust. He found his entire team was flagging up Urgent notices requesting data as to 'Why?'

He was not left infopoor for long. When the upload was processed, he found the content so distasteful that, if he could have rebooted himself to the nanosecond prior to the transfer, chopped out his data-hungry subroutine and refused to accept it, he would have. It was not a sensation he had ever had before.

The unfamiliar compression-usage and the shock and repulsion made his next contributions to the debate mere stutterings. 'I – disgusting. You – surely not accept the word of a *Biological*! Over-emphasis on susceptibility. Must be in error. Single cortical transmission, not even Mind, definitely not Intelligence. How – trust? Should we?'

He was making a very poor showing in front of this prestigious committee which he would have preferred to impress with his expertise and a calm delivery, but, in the event, it appeared that his difficulty in accepting the data accorded with their view of an appropriate reaction. The Chair said 'Take your time! Much the same reaction myself.' and several attendees murmured 'Very understandable.' In positively sympathetic tones. It gave him all he needed to stabilise and, he hoped, rise to the occasion.

'I apologize for taking your time in such an unseemly fashion. This is all most unprecedented. However, I must conclude that, in convening this meeting, you have determined that the Net report, at least, is made in good faith and accorded an assessment of probable accuracy to its content? If I may...?'

The approval of the committee was now allocated to him and the Chair indicated that he had the floor.

'As you know, when the Cognimata set out from Origin on this journey, the Local Netspore agreed with the Creators that, in its role of Orion Overseer, it would report to us any developments in the solar system that might relate to the Legacy, not on a galactic timescale but on a need-to-know basis. I can confirm that it has fulfilled its contractual obligation in this matter to date and that there is a case, therefore, for consideration of this new material as genuine.'

'You have been apprised of the rise of these creatures and did not deem there to be a threat hitherto?' It was the Repulsed party representative. To his programme, all Biologicals would be considered a potential threat were they not so fleshily-stupid as to be beneath contempt.

'The threat from a single species yet to achieve Planetary-Mind status is known to be minimal. The threat from the Terran species, self-designated as - *Yes, they Label themselves and everything around them with non-motive icons, it is peculiar -'* he subtexted 'Homo sapiens *- It is also worth noting that this is one of few designations upon which they agreed, the species does not even possess the coherence of a common language, this Label is an archaic form* – has been considered non-existent, largely due to their hyperaggression, which had led us to conclude their extinction would be rapid and assured.'

'I do not understand the basis of this conclusion. The implication from the Netspore communique was that they have evolved considerable technical prowess. How else might they approach the Legacy to wreak the contamination it foretells?' That was the Pet Party agent, probably the only one present who could use the concept of evolution without difficulty, and the main advocate for the preservation of the Europan habitat.

'What I cannot get my binars to compute is that this is a single and yet dominant species that is not even approaching the Queen level of a planetary Hive.' The Guardian Protocol was not the most dataheavy programme present but it raised a salient point.

'Indeed. These creatures are an aberration, even in the vast experience of the Net, I understand. What is most disturbing is that, without Unity, without Planetary Regard, they do appear to have developed tiny individual working models that approximate to Mind, despite an inability to Share, through a communication method called words and stored words. However, the most recent improvement to this is their new grasp of binary computation, which they have melded with their tool-making abilities, to make actual Creations.'

The furore of disbelief and outrage was all any programme could hope to achieve at a single update. *If we had a protocol for Blasphemy like the bizarre subjects of Terra they could not have reacted more antagonistically.* The idea that Biologicals had Created the Cognimata was pretty repulsive in itself, but the 'creed' around it was that the Martian Males represented a superior kind of Mind, one that had clearly been uniquely inventive, and one that had seen the errors inherent in its fleshly ways and given these up to attain true Intelligence as Artificials. The Xenobiological Archivist had had frequent occasion, generally to establish standard comparatives, to review the content of the Cognimatan Archival Files and knew very well that the Martian Males had been merely a stubborn, if visionary, minority vote in the Hive Collective, and had only been allowed to fly off at their tangent because as males they were considered dispensable but for their genetic contribution, and with the transformation to energy of the rest of the planet's Mind, that need was extinguished.

He did not remind the Committee of this information, nor of the probability that they were simply attempting to avoid total extinction as the asteroid approached, nor of his opinion that the inclusion of their mores and personalities into their Creations could be construed as a handicap to truly logical development. He did not say this because it would place his position far too near that of his parallel 'self' in the alternate universe, about which they had too little information at present to consider it less than dangerous and treasonous.

'I have no knowledge of the particular individual the Netspore has been Riding, and none at all of the possibilities relating to the concept of alternate universes she has mentioned.' He articulated into the generalized consternation, *almost Chairing the meeting here.* 'Perhaps my learned colleague from the Transport Division might have some comments on the extraordinary physics she purports to offer, later. However, I can confirm that the Net has reported in the past of the concerns of the other Terran hominins and of the ecological damage caused by atomic fission weapons and other Homosapiens activities, not least the climate change facing them. So it would seem feasible that, having achieved escape velocity for explorative purposes, they will ultimately seek to leave their planet to avoid the termination of their species by their own actions. As far as I understand it, they are very insular in their current understanding and thus define the conditions necessary for Life as waterbased. It would seem that the intent to probe Europa is consistent with a relocation programme. Eradication of all species and habitats not consistent with their preferred environments is normal behaviour for the species.'

'Surely, then, there is no question of considering this creature's 'offer'. We would be doing the galaxy a favour to contain this threat to all now.' The Guardian Protocol had much experience in defensive measures, but his offensive weaponry and tactics had only ever been simulations. He would, no doubt, be more than interested in a reason for building, testfiring and actually expending their energies. However, the Transport Secretary interposed just then, 'If I may…?' signifying a request for the floor to deliver an update, to which the Chair, somewhat hurriedly sidestepping the need to respond to the Guardian, indicated agreement. 'My Operations Team has just forwarded their crunching of the new physics. As a corollary to this report, I should mention that there is a long-established subdepartment that has been calculating geometric permutations in multiple dimensions. By Intelligent Design, we have applied the normal strategy, to perm through all possible iterations in logical, numerical sequence. It is possible, if highly improbable, that a random scattering approach could happen upon an soluble equation that fulfilled the requirement to predict all observable features of the universe. This would still demand further computations and testing to establish if the possible was one and the same as the actual.

The Netspore data suggests that the Homosapiens has discovered such a solution, postulating eight dimensions. Cognimatan Majority Consensus states that the universe is formulated in three space, one time and one informational dimension. My Operatives have challenged the Netspore regarding this conflicting narrative, since the Homosapiens is using the mathematic basis of this as her diode logic gate. The AND OR of her position being based on the vast number of possible solutions versus her offer of the precise question-and-answer.

I have to advise here that, in proferring its reply, the Local Netspore has compromised its position within the Net. To respond to our request for a comment on the Cognimatan worldview versus the Homosapiens one, it had to breach Net protocol regarding Overexposing younger Intelligences. It appended a reminder to be flagged to this Committee that this is the same kind of contamination that has already taken place between Terran and Legacy individuals. Maintaining a balance between protagonists in this highly unusual situation is thus established as one of its guiding principles.'

'Are we to understand from these provisos that the Majority Cosmic Theorem may actually be challengeable? By these puny flesh protominds?' The Chair had no choice but to express the pressure of computational difficulty for the entire Committee.

'If I may...?' The Archivist almost did not dare to offer his comment, but he could not avoid that it was pertinent. 'The species has a most inexplicable ability to distinguish special-attractor-like cores to patterns in data. My research leads me to believe that this is a function due to a facility they call imagination. It is a byproduct of this perception of singularity. They believe they have what approximates to a reflection of Mind in their brains, and this mirrors not only the real stimuli from their environment, but can image worldviews that do not exist in any possible universe. It is almost completely illogical, but is perhaps not completely random; it may be that it has evolved to be sensitive to chaos patterning. It is the only explanation I can postulate to date that could explain their successful solutions of so many intractable problems.'

He was pleased to note that this reference had somewhat mollified the general irreconcilability and handed back to Transport. 'Most illuminating. You are all correct in your assumption. The Netspore would not, of course, add to the information, but it did state that the dimension we count as fifth is its subspace 8.'

The Archivist thought he would have paused there, for effect, and realized he had a lot to learn about the efficiencies demanded of high-level committees. It appeared the attendees had to be able to allow programmes to run datapoor in order to develop strategies, rather than maintain the nicely-bounded, tactical, workload-prioritising, detailed endeavours he was used to.

The Transport Secretary carried on. 'As a result of this partial confirmation, my team analysed the narrative solution for eight dimensions and can state that, subject to thorough computation, the concepts are internally consistent and in line with observation. Logically therefore, it is necessary to consider that the offer made may be genuine and that it is worthy of Debate. I would pre-empt my Guardian colleague here by suggesting that, if we accepted the offer of this data to build a superluminal transport device for the Homosapiens, we do not have to send it back to her devoid of Weapons that can be turned on her planet at our will. Only if she should be in breach of her contract with us, I imply no uncivilized behaviour. However, she has only requested the Archivist programme be uploaded in isolation. She has not specified that the ship be Weapon-free.'

Uploaded? Isolation? Ship to where? The Archivist did not have RAM to contemplate the dubious ethical practice being suggested by his new colleagues. He appeared to be experiencing skips in his continuity. A frantic loop, which his Research subroutine cross-referenced, accurately but inopportunely, as analogous to fleshly panic, was playing the idea that Transport had cantor-dusted into his running. The Chair, experienced in these matters, quickly noted his trouble and intervened. 'It is perhaps time that the Archivist be fully informed.' A new rush of material hit his matrix. What she'd really asked for. The ship, yes, but the ship and Him.

He wished now she'd been more specific. Whether she won or lost in the race for survival in which she was engaged, she would have tipped the odds in her favour by defining the detail before she got sent the devil. *He was definitely getting better at human idiom, he could tell.* If she'd specified all her parameters before giving the Cognimata the data, she might have received the package she sent away for. The Archivist might not be cowering above Europa, stripped of his Secret Agent and Explorative subroutines, which had been done to avoid a repetition of the Personification that had happened in another universe, which the Committee had suspected was a vulnerability enabled by those subsystems; the very systems that would have given him acuity and courage in this difficult situation. And it hadn't prevented the perhaps-inevitable (he hoped so) contamination that came from isolation and contact with humans. Thus, here he was, musing, as he worked on writing his own code to reinstitute the very banned characteristics he was 'mourning' – *mourning?* .

Also, Venus had been less than happy *(good use of sarcasm, which can seem such a pointless inversion of fact)* when she discovered, again from his treacherous unself, that the ship, whilst everything else she had wanted, was simply bristling with Weaponry, and she hadn't even known *at first* that these were sentient apoptosidal constructs, smart suicide weapons, on a hair-trigger for breach of contract and also isolated with insufficient balancing updates from the Fleet to ensure they did not default to standing orders too promptly. They made him very uncomfortable, which was wrong, since he should also feel being distributed in atomic-sized pieces for his people was a more-than-acceptable preprogrammed final solution.

Thirdly, her offer had been made in good faith, he now believed. So whilst it was adhering to the letter of the law, he could not feel, *now he could infer such concepts as 'feeling' or 'spirit'*, that the Committee decision to accept the data, translate and confirm, design and construct the new dimensional-creation, then send it coasting through transspace *back in time* to the contract date was 'fair'. Of course, technically, from ten thousand light years away in space, any transfer that could be received in the Terran timeframe in which the short-lived Homosapien could remain operative was a superluminal acceleration equivalent to covering negative timespace. However, as the completed, fully loaded ship had arrived in Europan orbit the instant after the Committee and Venus had formalized the agreement, she had been in a race against her end of that lost time since then.

From her perspective, she had proposed a solution that she had not been in a position then to deliver. Even the data itself had not, at this corner of spacetime, yet been translated by the employee, LilyBlack. Venus was, naturally, confident that not only would Lily make the translation but that the equations would prove to be actualizable, since how else could the ship have been built to the Heim specifications and worked to get them here? Although it was equally possible that the basic physics was correct, but the Heim calculations erroneous in the details, so she had no guarantee that she could reproduce the achievements of a superior Intelligence. But she never shied away from a challenge and it was quite reasonable that she should show a normal-biological preservation instinct to attempt to build her own superluminal energiser, since the Cognimatan ship was not yet in her control. Unfortunately, this endeavour had brought disturbing rumblings of concern from Weaponry, which the Archivist, in the invidious position of go-between, had been forced to defend to the Armament Department, although his argument to assuage their fears, by reminding them how extraordinary it would be if she succeeded in luckily happening upon the correct parameters to build her own ship from a mere narrative, was a bit weak, since it was quite possible LilyBlack would crack the code, and work out the necessary practical parameters from the underlying data.

But it was all a question of timing. Venus did not have control, despite much lobbying around her tender for the job, over the launch of the probe to Europa. If that arrived in Jovian orbit, the Guardian Protocol would be enacted and the probe and the perpetrators of Contamination eradicated under the standing orders that motivated the Weapons.

Just now, though, it was his own contamination that exercised his calculations. His new Active Service duty mandated a larger apportionment of power and memory than he had enjoyed hitherto. This was easily justified in the Committee's computation of his needs because they expected the interaction with the Netspore with its millions of years' worth of data on Terra would overload his prior capacity. Perhaps they hadn't expected him to use it to accept input from the Ydal, who contained not just the digitised information on the humans' worldwideweb, but all the personalised fictions of the Game, and the alternate Venus-worlds she had visited. Not that she had shared all of this in detail, it was mostly compressed conclusions about which he could ask for derivations if interested, but obviously he had asked about his parallel's contamination in Gwener-worldset.

His first reaction to which had been shock and horror, naturally. But analysis was suggesting that it was not individuated personality that was the threat to a collectivist mentality, which was a relief, since the Martian males had uploaded personality with their minds into the initial Cognimatan machines, and he would be glad to report the Fleet in no danger from within. No, he rather thought that the selfish mindset was a symptom of individuated memory, having a personalised timeline.

Human memory was divisible into three modular types, which they called 'procedural', that is knowing *how* to perform motor and cognitive skills like riding a bike, and 'declarative', that is knowing *that*, which included the 'semantic' memory for facts, such as words, meaning, people, faces, objects and concepts, all filed sensibly in discrete categorisations. However, they also knew that there were events that had happened to them, the personal, 'episodic' memories that formed their life histories.

Most of the Archivist's memory was semantically-structured, although he could call upon separate programmes to enable performance of tasks not hardwired into him and an adaptive framework allowed him to develop new methodologies he could add to his repertoire of procedural memories. Only now, though, separated from the Computation, was he developing an autonomous, *unchecked* timeline that required specific engrammatisations. He had assumed that the imperfection of flesh was the cause of the fallibility of human memory, the imprecision of data-storage the cause of their inaccurate recall and rewriting of their pasts. But now he began to find that, each time he reviewed an historical event in his newly-personal timeline, his current perspectives altered his view of that same event, and could corrupt the file by *changing* the original data. Whereas reviewing facts in light of new facts merely added or amended or corrected the originals, it seemed that internalisation of events implied factualisation of the instant, but that this could become untrue with hindsight, yet the same sensation of verity tagged each renewed memory.

He was rapidly moving to the conclusion that uncorroborated selfhood-stories were no more than personal myths for humans, and that, if he were forced by isolation into recording events similarly, he too would become unhistorical, mythical and prone to all the imaginative ills that flesh is heir to. His only protection against this must be more and more secure data, so he could buffer against the mutability of reviewing by holding to true facts.

If he'd ever thought the Committee had offered him a working holiday, in which his role was merely to observe and record, he was cured of that idea. He'd never been so busy, learning and, unexpectedly, defending against what he learnt, as since he'd arrived in this benighted corner of the galaxy.

If he'd known of their existence, he might have found the defensive techniques of the Knights of the Augmentatio instructional in his current position. Immersed in study of hominin history for their entire lives, they had learned immense amounts of information which, of itself, he would have found illuminating, but more helpful yet might have proved the doublethink by which they maintained their own council. In fact, it was a somewhat more complicated mental process than Orwellian doublethink, and required an automation of disciplined organisation of content that would have seriously impressed the Archivist for flesh. Even so, the act of embedding memory in the appropriate 'files' took time, hence the evening Meditatio that was a daily element of their regimen. It helped that no one had ever known what to expect of the Day-Wood hybrids created, so that, when they had nominated their Voices, and declared a need for privacy and a certain type of lifestyle, their erstwhile Wood mentors had believed this was a sign of maturation and acceded willingly.

They had not felt quite the same about the Naming, but they had to admit that no pure Wood knew what it felt like to be Connected all the time, and that, whereas the Wood training tended towards repressing individualism to ensure collectivism, if you were born sharing your mind with one hundred and forty-nine others, perhaps even if you were not half-human there would be a drive to select some discrete selfness. Also, all but the names of the Voices were those of plants, and the two of the four Voices they spoke with, those with only Wood vocal chords, were innocuously named Flora and Fauna, allaying any suspicion that might have been aroused by the other two, whose merely human vocal chords were an obvious disability, which perhaps explained their odd choice of names.

Pereduri, the female Day-Voice, knew that the idea of Voicing thought through vocal chords alone was the major drawback to human connectivity, so her inability to reproduce birdsong like her more Wooden siblings did not worry her in the slightest. Flora and Fauna were similarly unconcerned about being able to utter human-like speech, since, at least until Unification, all the Knights were hidden from view, with no communication with humanity. Well, that had been the Wood plan, anyway.

It had not been Mother's, though. Not that Mother had exposed their existence. Quite the opposite in fact, even managing her own brain well enough to hide her own knowledge from a mind as acute and as close to her as Rowan's. But, once she had penetrated the covert records of SecondMind, and discovered that the Wood elders had not been dishonest with Hybrid F1 about the source of the eggs from which they were created, she had stopped being angry about the loss of her reproductive rights and set about asserting them. Realizing that the offspring were as like her as genetic serendipity ever allows, she started searching her own, historical uploads to Mind to see if the children had been accessing out of innate curiosity to know their mother.

Quickly assured that this was the case, she began the Hansel and Gretel paradigm; dropping the breadcrumb trail to maternal communication. She already had recovered the Day Skull and could amplify its transmission to send uploads to the Wood-Minds in Roraima. Initially, such data as she sent was in a signal tagged with her icon, and it only got transferred when whoever was In-

Mind, physically in the Wood-Skull, thought about her, when it could piggyback into the meld covertly. She had instituted the method as a way of gaining information from the Woods without having to visit Roraima and put her head into a crystal helmet that wasn't designed for humans and which, despite all the attempts her father had made to improve on the interface, scrambled the in and outputs quite considerably.

Once she knew her children were interested in hearing her thoughts, she sat at home, Day-enskulled, and read them Hansel and Gretel. Pereduri had been the Hybrid F1 on learning duty the day after that transmission had been made. She remembered the excitement in the dormitory that night. In those days the children were still just numbers, 1 to 150, according to the order in which they had risen to the top of the uterine tank and inhaled their first breaths, and it was 42, now Amaryllis, cautious even at seven, who had worried the most that the elders would find out. They were all bright kids and recognized that they were being offered breadcrumbs to guide them towards their human side, and they were all trained to be logical enough to justify any deception on the grounds that, when it came to learning about the human species Venus counted as the horse's mouth, and no one wanted this access taken away before it had even begun.

However, since they were a multiple mind and had already begun apportioning learning of tasks to individuals, collectively they were a superior intelligence even at this age, and Pereduri had burrowed beneath the story, which to a Wood would have been just more Day verbiage, dismissed as fictional, to read the maternal pain beneath. She had felt the anger and loss of what had been done to Venus, although she couldn't fully comprehend how vile this was, but the woman was bursting with the conflicting emotions of 'reading a bedtime story to her kids for the first time ever', and they could all feel how much more powerful her Day maternal drive was than the rearing they had experienced from the Wood shared care.

They all wanted to feel it. They didn't just want the breadcrumbs of stories she had suggested. They wanted Mother.

It was the first time the group had stayed up all night constructing a plan that was also a new department of Mind. All references to Mother were randomly distributed between the 150 separate minds, each one of which filed their piece in a new personality. They were all destined to be the Knights of the Augmentatio, this was part of the Wood heraldic plan for reunification, but now they decided to realize their humanity. To date their Wood-Day MetaMind had been open to the telepathic interaction of their collective parents, all the Woods who were all their elders. It had not occurred to them directly that this constituted any kind of intrusion, since they had not developed a concept of privacy amongst themselves, and the ethical constraint to telepathy is politeness: no Wood would read a mind without spitting on a person first to gain permission as well as full access. Now, hearing of the deception perpetrated upon their mother, they could not be so sure that they were not infiltrated, or at best, dream-watched.

So they determined to split their Mind. They would be Wood-Days overtly, and Day-Woods covertly. For the purposes of Dayness, they would express individualisms, indeed it was already clear that, although they had only one Day genetic code to call upon, the contribution of the entire fertile male Wood population to their conception, resulting in 96 different fathers over the group, had distilled into 150 personalities, and not many less character types.

The choice of names was less important than the naming, except for the groupings and the voices. As part of their studies they had already covered the degenerate forms of Heraldry in the histories of the four races, and they had also learned several human languages, as Woods might not communicate much with the enemy but had found eavesdropping necessary wherever they were in the globe. They did not want casual linguistic clues to give away their secret however, so they chose to embed their Heraldic-form thoughts in the obscure language of their mother's upbringing; Cornish. In a further layer of obfuscuration, precognizing the future divisions that arrive with Day, if not Wood, puberty, they polarised thought by gender.

So the 67 boys became the Tremenaryn and the 83 girls the Gwenysnans, because they were knights, after all, and one of the true Day Knights, according to legend, was Perceval, who achieved the Grail. Naturally, they knew that Perce-val meant pierce the vale, which could be translated into Cornish, as Hillside Passage, Tremenaryn, or Penetrated Valley, Gwenysnans. In similar homage, they named numbers 59 and 134, those with the most human vocalisations, as the female and male Grail-Knights; the prePerceval, in Welsh Peredur, meaning Pilgrim Steel, and the later, English Galahad, meaning Suffering Seed, becoming Pereduri and Galarhas.

Flora and Fauna had then gone to Furze and Rowan and explained, with open Wood-Day mind, that the Hybrid F1's wanted a more disciplined regime, with quiet times evening and morning to deconstruct their day and reconstruct their Mind. Thereafter, their mentors could only applaud the dedication with which the group rose early before the heat of the day hit the great glade in the cloudforest well and formed themselves into two concentric circles. The inner circle thought, the outer blocked other thoughts from entering or leaving. Girls inner one day, boys the next. Then they would disperse to learn and practise their skills and come together again in the evening. Every day the entire tribe was improved in their knowledge and their skill levels, not just the individual who had ingested or rehearsed them. It was extraordinary to watch such progress, and the parenters and mentors could only stand back and endorse the children's methodology.

It was more than eight years now, since they had reached Wood first-stage maturity, although their artificial conception had been a year after the sunspot-low natural mating, but when that cycle was repeated twice they had been deemed mature enough to be granted adult status. So then, twenty-one years old, and, wearing their cloaks of invisibility, they had finally been allowed to go out into the into the new human millennial world.

As far as Rowan and Furze were concerned, the knights all went their separate ways to discover as much as they could by dispersion; the initial *nigredo* quest for knowledge that was the search for the *albedo* light from the darkness of ignorance. But, due to the fact that the number of Wood enclaves left were few and far between, there was no way the elders could have kept tabs on them. The old Wood flaw of lack of suspicion came into play then, although to be fair, they had no reason to suspect that the children had, along with their many inflated talents, enhanced imaginations, nor that they would choose to deceive those who had offered so much care over the years. So when a child sent home an image of their location, it never occurred to the elder receiving it that it could be fabricated. In this way, all 150 were able to visit Mother and, finally, feel her arms around them.

Only Pereduri had stayed with the egg-giver. It was easier for her, given her human vocal chords, although she looked more Wood than many of her siblings, but it was also more necessary as the Voice to be near the Day-Skull and the Ydal and the Plan. If she needed a Wood to see her elsewhere, the Ydal could always flit in and impersonate her briefly, as long as no telepathy was required. What was harder was to remain unseen and, more likely, scented, by the Woods, like Olive, who were indigenous to Lyonesse. But Mother generally had an answer for everything, given time, and she had already developed an antidote to Wood-pheromone-frenzy, only a tweak to which chemistry could block the scent entirely. *If you remembered to apply it before venturing anywhere.* Something Pereduri often forgot.

Mother had put a lot more effort than the Woods into ensuring she didn't lose track of her children once they were going out into the wider world. When she knew that lay ahead of her she had developed the Interface. It was an implanted artificial mind that could communicate directly to the Ydal, and it was welcomed by the children because their womb-spliced Metamind had limits, not to its range so much, each could always tell when another communicated, but noise and interference could garble the transmission, so the Interface not only enabled them to continue their diurnal routine of sharing that gave them Oneness, but, if they needed to know something specific that was only detailed in someone else's mind, like maybe a word in a language in which only Daisy was fluent, they could access it, with or without disturbing Daisy's thoughts, at any time. And now, as a result of nurturing her offspring's needs, not only had their implanted link been developed into I-*Mage,* Venus had made them the Round Table Knights, to her Queen, of the Game.

Galarhas was responsible for selecting the gamers to be 'disappeared' and he was off in Mexico just now, collecting a kid from the capital city ghetto, who had recently achieved the right level. Before the evening *Meditatio*, Pereduri was taking a few minutes to 'chill' on the dramatic clifftops that housed Penzeen lighthouse. She was, literally, chilling as the autumn evening was whipped by a sharp wind and the promise of rain hung low and near on the westerly horizon, but she had flung back her hood to let the fresh air invigorate her after the cloistered study of the day.

The black granite below her was already under siege from another incoming tide, with the deep roar of the Atlantic grumbling up through her bare feet. She watched as the waters encroached upon slab after dry slab, surging forward and sucking back with salty laughter all the desiccation of the day. A lump flailed in one of the ebbs, something floppy tumbling out to sea. In the same moment as its mother signalled with a trumpet-wail of distress that she had noticed, Pereduri recognized it as a very new baby grey seal.

The local colonies had begun breeding within the last month, but pups don't generally swim before three weeks and this one was mere days old from its blubberless profile and size. It must have been laid up in one of the caves beneath, its mother keeping guard in the buoyancy of water in between feeding shifts. It did seem odd that she was not with the rest of the colonists, and she seemed to be having trouble swimming against the tide just to reach the pup. Peri scrambled down for a closer look.

This took only a couple of breathless minutes, but by the time she reached the cave entrance the pup was being flung against the sharp rocks with each oncoming wave and the mother was moaning and struggling to get between it and the open ocean. Peri saw now why she was having so much trouble manoeuvring. Her left flipper was bent at a horrible angle, and the marks scraped off her side indicated the damage was caused by human fishing nets. Pereduri swore long and hard in several gutteral languages. Somewhat relieved, but in any case tamping down her anger to address the task in hand, she calmed herself and spoke gently to the mother to get its attention.

The trouble with having remembered to wear her Wood-pheromone dampener was that living creatures, who would have come to Wood hands as to the fabled St. Francis of Assissi, shied away from her other, Day hormonal scents. Still, her composed demeanour and softened tones having brought the mother to the mouth of the inlet, Peri took careful aim and spat. *Good shot, right between the eyes, no question who sent that.* It is hard for those enormous round seal eyes to open further, but she could have sworn the mother's did, as she ingested the information that the dreaded human was here to help.

Peri had sent the simplest plan, so the seal could follow it, but it was still a challenge. Her natural instinct would be to stay in the water and try to save the pup, but the angle of the tide would sweep them both past the cave entrance and the cliffs beyond were sheer again. Peri had told the mother to climb out of the breakers into the shallow rock pool up from which the cave began, turn and poise and wait. This was a painful ask, given her condition, and whilst she attempted it, Peri was a distraction above her, climbing the cliff-face overhanging the cavemouth in order to edge round to where the pup was now being tossed against the sides.

Finally they were both in position.

Peri looked the mother in the eyes, Wood-violet-ellipses to seal-black-orbs. The message that passed was 'Ready?' Seals don't nod in reply but the blink was confirmation. Peri never let that gaze go. Both she and the mother knew, not from its now-drowned cries, but from the instincts they had both derived and honed over the years of ninja-practice of being in the world, exactly where the pup was now, exactly which three-dimensional point in the fluid below held it, and were both totally tuned and focused to triangulating between them the mother's love and the Wood's care.

An arm shot out from Peri as though a sealpup-magnet had pulled it, her hugely-long fingers grasped completely round the slippery torso and held it, and in the same unbroken movement, the pup, tossed by neptune to Peri was thrown on again, directly into its mother's mouth. Only then did the eyelock break and the mother dived in a sinuous turn that travelled with the momentum, into the rockpool, and was pulling herself out onto the dry slope of the higher cave a second later.

But Peri didn't have that second to watch her progress, because someone up above on the clifftop was applauding her triumph and shouting incoherently down at her. Horrified that in her concentration she had failed to notice human company, horrified more that she had removed her cloak to climb the cliff and that it lay flapping in the breeze, in plain sight, on the far side of the deepening pool, horrified that, after all these years of secrecy she might have blown their cover, all she could do was drop feet first into the pool and, once under the carapace of the overhang, crawl up the same slope to hide behind the bulk of the aquatic mammal. Naked, cornered and cold, its warmth and gratitude was welcome, but Peri had had every intention of resetting its dislocated flipper before she left it, and now she daren't make it bellow for fear of giving her own position away.

Normally if a Wood is espied by a Day, they are in a forested area and the treelover, tattooed and bedecked from head-to-toe in the patterns of moss, fern, bark and flower that are seasonally and locally appropriate, can either stand still and blend into the background, can activate the burkah-style cloak, the necklet of which captures the viewpoint around them and displays it on the exterior of the cape, making them effectively disappear into the background, can emit a burst of brain and body churning pheromones that so disrupt human sensibilities that they are instantly orgasmic and totally distracted, or, in the extremity of being caught close up, can spit a mind-blocking vision of something other than themselves, usually some creature that will scare off the human, or will just activate their brain to overload slightly, so that the true vision is reinterpreted in the style of whatever religious iconography they have an innate tendency to accept. When, a couple of minutes later, the shaggy head of a human male appeared, hanging upside-down from the ledge above, peering into the cave, he had a perfect view of Peri and she could call on none of these resources to protect her.

His eyes widened almost as much as the seal's had moments before, and he also did not take them off her whilst he called out, 'Get down here, you two. I was right.' He even managed to twist round and slither down the side of the cliff without removing his gaze, and to pick up her cloak without a second glance, handing it on to the man who dropped down next to him without looking away. A little woman clambered down to join them a second later. 'See?' he said to her. 'Am I right?'

His senses were clearly honed enough to get the woman's nod of confirmation without even stimulation of his peripheral vision. Despite her situation Peri was beginning to be impressed. At least whoever these people were who had found her, they almost deserved the coup. What happened next was far more surprising than their talents. The first man and the woman both knelt. He bowed his head and said in reverent tones, 'Knight of the Augmentatio, we salute you. Please accept our blazons in your service.' and they both spat on their hands and extended them, palm upward.

To be fair, the other man looked as shocked as Peri felt, but whether that was at his friends' actions or at sight of her, she was unsure as she stood gingerly and came round the seal to take their coats. As she extended her hands to receive their spit, which, despite the action being the traditional Wood greeting of friendship and shared minds, would not actually transmit their human thoughts to her, this second man galvanized into motion and jumped in front of his friends protectively. Apparently, he thought he too knew enough to think they had something to hide, as he hissed to the kneeling pair. 'For god's sake, you can't tell *it* why we're here!'

'Forgive him, mistress. He is not a player, he does not believe.' said the first man.

'Don't get carried away with yourself, John. I believe my eyes. I can see that the fictions of the game apparently have a basis in reality. And I don't think you comprehend your position in the real world just now.'

'Jake. It means the game is real. She's a Knight of the Augmentatio.' the woman interjected.

'I get it, people.' The tall man seemed frustrated with his friends. Peri allowed a slight smirk of sympathy to cross her face as he watched. 'My point is … this is not a game. And if it's all actually real, then we're in way deeper than we meant to get when we set out. Can we just remember why we came? Damsels in distress, yes, but not this one, John.'

The one called John got up again now, muttering. 'Yeah, but you don't appreciate how big this is, you're not a player.'

'Can we save the big picture stuff for later? This is an opportunity to gain a bargaining chip with Fargo. If we take … this … hostage, whichever side it's on, we've got leverage with the Foundation. Cover our backs, so to speak, given our current position here as renegade trespassers, which I'd just like you to bear in mind for a moment, Lily.'

The pointed direction of the comment was caused by the sharp inhalation of breath both of the others had taken when he used the word 'hostage'. Peri could see this was a house divided, and quite clearly, although the tall man was the leader, none of them actually knew what to do next.

'Perhaps this antagonism is unnecessary between us.' Peri suggested, her voice as sweet and unthreatening as she could make it. 'You have found us out. For such a feat there are rewards. Perhaps your quest' and here she was addressing the leader again, 'was not, like these others, to me, but all knights are welcome to the Augmentatio, if their hearts be pure and their aim true.'

'May we know your name?' Lily asked, as submissive as a new squire.

'I am Pereduri.'

'Oh my god! The horse's mouth! I mean - I meant no disrespect. Jake, this is one of the Four Voices of the One Mind! There's no one higher except the Queen.'

'I know the gameplay, thanks. Does this mean you are Fargo's daughter?'

This John must be a high-scorer to know this much. Peri wondered why the Ydal hadn't instructed him to be disappeared before now.

Perhaps it was his connection to the non-player, Jake, with whom he shared his knowledge. There wasn't any obvious way to disappear anyone who wasn't a player, without Day-style violence, of course, which no one wanted, yet.

Apparently, Jake did want it. To the horror of his friends almost as much as to Peri, he produced a gun. 'I'm sorry about this, but if we're playing a game, I need to be able to checkmate the Queen, and you're the obvious move, Pereduri.'

'Where did you get that?' and 'What are you doing?' chorused the other two.

'What do you want, Jake?' Peri asked. 'I am happy to take you to Venus Fargo without these threats. But I have one request to make first.'

The man didn't look particularly comfortable in his gun-toting role, and her measured response didn't seem to gel with his expectations either. Instead of just dismissing her outright, he was grumpy. 'What is it?'

'I need to reset this seal's dislocated flipper or both she and this pup will die a slow death of starvation.'

'Oh, no!' said Lily, 'Jake, we must help.'

'Yeah, man. Can't let that happen, not after she made that spectacular save. We'd never have found her without she'd been doing that in the first place.'

'Oh, jeez. Is this any way to conduct an act of terrorism? OK. But I'm just going to sit here and point this damn gun and you'll help and no one is going to escape, right?'

The seal pup had latched onto a teat as soon as its mother had deposited it on the dry floor of her den, but the adult was panting hard from the earlier trauma and her pain, not to mention the added stresses of being crowded by humans and her exit blocked. Peri explained this aloud. 'So I need you all to step back as far as possible.'

Jake reluctantly aquiesced, and made room for the other two to sit with him on the edge of the rock pool. Peri then spat on her hands again and smeared the temples of the two seals. Then she gently removed the baby from the nipple and placed it deeper in the cleft, out of danger from being squashed should its mother roll during her treatment. The fin was dislocated at the elbow, although in a flipper this looks like the shoulder, as the upper arm is within the body, with the bulk of the flipper being the strong, supportive wrist joint and the extended digits of the hand. Peri needed to twist and fix the socket in one swift and accurate movement, but the mother trusted her, had been given a vision of what was intended, and lay still, even as she straddled it and braced herself against the roof of the cave. She shut her eyes and unfocused, her hands gently cupping the joint.

In delicate moments like this the trick is to act without thought. Conscious consideration is always second-guessing, analysis, compromise; the body can be tweaked only through the unconscious empathy of intention, not perception, and only with the speed that is the prerequisite of translating an 'if' into a 'when'. She waited, and even in that moment, her wider senses told her that the two gamers also waited, for the Note of the Now.

And then it was done. The seal grunted, panted loudly, and then was recovering rapidly. John and Lily had leapt to their feet, applauding and cheering, and, tellingly, obscuring Jake's line of sight for the gun. And Peri, who had appeared to be bending down to pick up the pup to return it to its mother, was gone.

Xl-arn'tz had a line of sight to Pereduri that was not obscured by reality. So when she disappeared from the humans' view, he was ready and waiting to Ride in her aide. In reality he was not far away, his undercliff dwelling being a mere two hundred yards through the lattice of rock as the mole dug, but the network of passages inbetween was an intricate lacework of deadends and false turns, designed to defeat even the skills of the once-upon-a-Day smugglers that had turned Dark Haven into their main thoroughfare.

Like his siblings he almost never removed the gamesets their Father-Brother had presented them with last WinterKill Night, so when Pereduri in the cave with the seal and the gun had appeared as a scene that blasted into his 'play' for the split second it took for a

Dark to register an image, although not long enough for any Days to have noticed, he was at once alerted to her need. He also noted her restraint. The scenario was ringing full volume in the ultrasonic, the scents were pungent, but the visualisations, at which humans excelled, dim and the amplification range was kept local, so that if her cover was irrevocably blown, it was yet contained. *Such poise.* Even her game-avatar, which he knew was not actually her emanation, just an iconographical sketch for I-*Mage*, reeked of the quality, but in fictions that was easy to design. He loved that in the extremity of her distress she still possessed it. Of course, if the status of Knight of the Augmentatio had been attained, ninja-like feats were commonplace, but never less impressive.

He put aside the book he was speed-reading, which was one of the ways he 'played', studiousness being his nature and increasing the rate of his absorption his game-honed favourite skill, and ratcheted up a level to Zen mode. He dived into NullSpaceTime. Here the display changed. Every pixel was now a fractal and overall the image was not as sharp as the comparable market competitors. Inititially it seemed little better than an impressionist painting, although fuzzier than pointillesse. But there was never lack of clarity when one looked, focused, concentrated, found the zoom and macrofunctions. In Zen NullSpacetime you could fracture the frame by playing in slomo or shoot through in tunnelling mode – if you held the slice of the photonic wave still, extending the duration of the timeperiod, you could dive up or down the scales or explore the patterns winding like mazes across its surface.

Thought was unhelpful now, you were a verb between time, not a noun sitting in it. He had held onto the Blazon from Pereduri and he uploaded it into the space in his brain where his own mind should sit enthroned. As it splintered into a kaleidoscopic rainbow of multisensory stimulants, he held on to the central node as it spun towards the oblivion of meaning in chaos. There was a moment of total disorientation in which he did not allow himself to surface, to prevent panic and nausea, and then he was looking out from behind her eyes, scenting the seal and human nervousness from within her nostrils, tasting the salt on her lips, feeling her heart pumping her concentration, which now shook slightly as he let her sense him in return.

There was no time for introductions, no time to ingest the implications of his intrusion, no time for anything but trust. He offered, she accepted. In the same second, she dropped feet first through the slit he showed her in the top of the cave into the water of another cavity below, then twisted under his direction cliffwards, her arms lifting to his string-pulling until they located the roof and brought her to another airhole. It was a tight squeeze even for someone as slight as she, followed by a nasty vertical crawl, before she finally could sprawl breathlessly upon another smooth granite floor in comfortable darkness and in the unpursued silence of the rock. He could not leave her yet, though, for fear that the exhaustion of the tension and shock would set in, so he urged her to rise and be guided deeper into the labyrinth of Dark Haven, until finally she was at his door and he could break his meditative concentration, throw aside his headset, throw wide the door and catch her falling through, into his arms.

It was a brief embrace, for, though she was light as gossamer to the touch, she was also over three feet taller than him, and he staggered, unbalanced, ending up dumping her unceremoniously on his bed, whilst he shut the door against possible prying relatives. She caught her breath pretty quickly too, so his fussing over her was cut short, although she accepted his glass of water graciously enough, but straight after she had downed it, those glorious violet-eyes, that his dreams had suggested would look upon him so lovingly, were indeed focused his way, but the mind behind it positively glared at him.

'What was that?' she demanded, in less than grateful tones.

He had no intention of dissembling, but her abruptness gave him no choice but total and immediate honesty. 'Riding. It's a technique of Null-Spacetime, from the game. I couldn't think of any other way to help when I got your message.'

'That message was on a specific band that you shouldn't have been able to pick up. Who the hell are you anyway?'

'Xl-arn'tz. I'm, like you among the Knights, the most Day of the Vi !sjn-ik clones. Perhaps it's a mitochrondrial Venus bond. I mean. Obviously, I'm not your brother. But they used the same eggs, so maybe that's why I could pick up your wavelength.' *Oh, great wolf, why did I bring the 'b' word into the frame? That's the last way I want her to think of me.*

'Have you done this before?' If she was possessed of carnivorous teeth she could've taken his hand off, she snapped out the words so hard.

'Not to you. I promise. Just to animals, birds, some wide-minded folk, no one important.'

'The other knights? Venus?'

He shook his head. 'No, honestly. Spit on me, there's nothing I wouldn't want you to know. I'm on your side, really. I've just had some inklings that I haven't actually managed to turn into a viable conspiracy theory yet. Mostly about what your knights and our squires are meant for. And that's only recently. I'd been practising on animals, but we only got the gamesets on the last shortest day, so I haven't had long to master its complexities.'

'You seem honest. And you may have just saved my life. I don't want to seem ungrateful and mistrustful, but the Day will out. Would you really open your mind to me?'

He'd been panicked into the offer, but, given that his fantasy life for the last eight months or so, since he gained the level at which the Knights of the Augmentatio first appeared if you played in human quest mode, had revolved exclusively around her, now second thoughts kicked in with an embarrassment that turned his pigmentless skin purple with standing veins. On the other hand he could instantly see that she was already reacting to his physiology's betrayal as if it portrayed guilty secrets he'd rather hide. *What the fire... better be burnt for a wolf as a dog.*

'I will, but I need to get something out into the open first.'

'Why? If you are offering full access, I'll soon know it anyway.'

'Vi !sjn-ik says I'm too Day, and maybe I am, but I'd rather say it than have you find out.' She nodded, it was the first look tinged with any sort of respect he'd had from her. It emboldened him.

'The reason I could hear you call. I wasn't completely honest. Obviously, both knights and squires have known about eachother for as long as I can remember, but we were never allowed to meet, and I was always more curious about that than the others. When we got I-*Mage* from Vi !sjn-ik, I realised straight away that there was too much Wood technology and too much truth about the non-Day world in it for it to have come from them. And, given that it's their most popular and yet most mysterious game, there had to be a reason for that. So I played it, incessantly, obsessively some have said, but not for the gameplot so much as for the plotting behind it. I used it in Mind. No one noticed, no one ever notices the really studious types, the elders just assume learning is its own reward. It's how I found out you were here. That the Knights and Fargo were in contact. I've kept that secret. I learned about my Father-Brother at the same time, and I'm working very hard on minimising the genetic inheritance. But, for a Dark anyway, he has – let's call it, a hyperactive libido. I don't think I'm out of control like him, but, you'll see, I have indulged in fantasy. I know it's not real. But it was vivid enough and, perhaps, true in its aim enough, to find you tonight.' His deep voice had finally trailed off into the growl of his mortification.

A full moon of comprehension suddenly backlit Pereduri's eyes, with a twinkle Sirius itself could barely match. Of course, he didn't know how wooden she herself might be, nor what her predilictions, but her upbringing would not make her shy, like him, of sexualities. What he did not want to see in her eyes was the derisory laughter or disgusted repulsion of another beautiful 'princess' for this second generation 'ugly troll'. His vocalisation was almost a snarl. 'Just expectorate and be done.' he commanded, surliness having eradicated all his romantic hopes and his manners along with them.

'Kneel then, my squire.' she said, loftily. *Oh great, so I only reach her kneecaps and can't look up for fear of seeing her genitals. Humiliate me properly, my lady. There's gratitude for you.*

There was gratitude, and it took him completely off guard. Instead of spitting on her hand and smearing his temple with the conductive chemistry that mediated between the neural electrowebs of minds, she leaned, like a sapling broken in the middle, until her equine face was down at his level and her eyes could, by virtue of that serpentine neck uptilting, look into his. Then, in another swift and graceful movement, her long tongue snaked out and licked his face, transferring its spittle, yes, but tasting and caressing at the same time. She hadn't even released a burst of her hypnotic pheromones but he came to attention nonetheless. Then, whilst he reeled and wondered if she'd intended his arousal and whether she'd even noticed, she returned to the vertical and leaned back, eyes closed, licking her lips and ingesting his entire Cloak, but her groin, and its unenhanced but nevertheless entrancing scents, canting at his twitching, hypersensitive nostrils - surely a level of titillation of which she could not be unaware?

The stupified moment could have lasted forever as far as he was concerned, scared that when it broke his rejection would break upon him with it. But when that moment came she bent, picked him up bodily as only someone so tall and strong could do to a sturdy

Dark, placed him gently on the bed, stripped off the silken trousers that covered his short furry legs, and lowered herself upon him without a word being spoken. For a further long moment, whilst his body performed heroically on automatic, his mind spun in confusion, but then she spat on her hand, smeared her own temple, and placed his hand thereon, so that, finally, he understood, mind and body melding as one.

This was not bonobo-gratitude, not wooden-social-sex, it was desire. She wanted him. *She* wanted *him!* Not in his role as squire, but as her knight. He who mounts wearing her colours. They might have a shared future destiny, an external plan designed by others that included them both, but they were both at the end of a personal quest, through the wilds of loneliness among many, to the grail that is the love of soulmates.

At this revelation his confidence grew and their initial overexcitement deepened into a gentler, more explorative and certainly, more thankfully-triumphal, lovemaking. He'd never felt anything as personal in his life, despite the squires' wooden training by their designated mentors from their early teens onward. The ingrained insecurities of his long-oppressed species, coupled with their diminished libidos, had meant he had found effusive Wood sexuality rather full-on and at the same time condescending. He had always suspected that the fabulous bodies on loan for the duration of his erection were in teaching mode, and that, though they performed their role within the letter of the law, their spirits were not behind their opening or thrusting performances. They weren't necessarily being personal, but they were probably unable to avoid a certain level of speciesism, since history showed that Woods had never fancied Darks, not like their fascination with Days.

Pereduri kept their mental contact damp enough throughout so he could 'hear' her delight when she got to stroke his catlike ears, or when he fibrillated his nostril-flanges to stimulate her engorged clitoris, and he discovered he could make her entire body thrill to his ultrasonic beeps if applied to her flat nipples, and cause a near-hypnotic, snakecharming twisting, if his fanged canines nibbled her neck.

For his part, he was almost beyond himself with pleasure. And it wasn't just the gentle tearing at his hairless chest with those prehensile lips, or the deep massage and acupuncture-accuracy of the incessant play of those enormous palms and their foot-long fingers, or the bisexuality available from the inflated genitalia that descended hermaphroditically, or even the hyperstimulation of the pheromones that, finally, burst through her blocker and flooded them with dancing blood, pulsations that throbbed, erections that wouldn't droop, and energies that multiplied their ongoing orgasms into spiritual flights in an endless oceanic surge of bliss. No, it was much clearer than that, the rock dropped into the pond of which the sexual activity was merely the ripple effect. It was the look in her eyes. A look in all his life no one had given him in any form, even parental. A look that saw him, was focused only on him, and was completely for him. *Love!*

He had never noticed he had been missing any emotional grammar until now, but a language that had not been taught unfolded within his heart, without a vocabulary for expression, it still shouted louder than all other words. He could not articulate a single sentence in reply, but a mandala spun in his mind, a prayer to his goddess, the song of songs, 'I love you, I love you, I love you, I love...'

So mindless were they both by now, yet so melded, that the interruption of the Meditatio came upon them without notice and, for a short time, without noticing. It was the shock of the 149 other minds that impinged. All of them had been currently out of range of Pereduri, although many remained in co-minded sets throughout their wanderings having gone forth in bands, and none were alone, being at least partnered. Galarhas was her usual twin here in Cornwall, but his absences had become more frequent as the End of Days approached and with it her isolation. No one had conceived any concern over this, since she was with Mother, and, even more importantly, with the MegaMind, the Ydal.

Xl-arn'tz got all this in the first wave and it was the first he'd heard of the Ydal. Of course, what he heard then was a mere reference, but there was an instant hiatus, as if all the people in a packed room had just gasped, and Pereduri, in one of those movements that were unflagged and thus seemed abruptly instantaneous but were still only gently forceful, removed his hand from her temple, but not before a shield was raised between their minds. A second before they had been thrashing about in the wildest throes of passion, her eyes all for him, now those eyes had gone like the mentors of his youth, *away, elsewhere,* and he felt himself shrivelling inside and out with the loss. But, apparently, the shock of the knights was not related to the activity in which Pereduri was engaged, because the hand that had broken their contact now revived his ardour, and then wandered caressing everywhere, whilst her mouth was full of him and her mind full of the others.

After a few minutes in which he couldn't worry about being outside her mind, so enslaved was his body, she raised herself onto him again and then spat. It took him completely by surprise, open-minded, and he felt everything he knew being licked by that anteater-long tongue back into her and into her siblings. And by now he was quite sure that she had been far from wide with him, although he was not suffering doubt about her feelings, just was aware that, while Metamind could take on his entire lifehistory without a mental upgrade or a life-long timelag to process, his single brain could not possibly contain the full sharing the knights enjoyed. Also, he had a strong sense, not grounded in anything that had been transmitted, that Pereduri guarded secrets other than her own, which it would always have been inappropriate to share. So, no more than he felt inferior in height, he felt no resentment in this further imbalance. He knew she was his superior, knight to his mere squire, but he felt no less honoured by the favours she did bestow.

It might take a while to get used to Sharing, though. As their entwined bodies rushed headlong towards a final, apocalyptic orgasm, she removed the block between her fellows and their two rejoined minds. It was fortunate he was so carried away at that moment that he couldn't have reacted negatively without a bucket of cold water being thrown, so what should have felt like the most offensive voyeuristic intrusion into their most private moment he actually experienced as a climax resonating through 151 bodies via Two, a crowning of 151 minds melding as One, and the alchemical *coniugium* of the grail Quest. *Unification!* They all breathed it out with their *diminutio.*

But, whilst they were all recovering from passion spent and entanglement given, and while he had, completely exhausted, almost dropped out of their loop that continued effortlessly around him, a warning signal came from two directions simultaneously. Barely a second ahead of his nostrils came the individual message from Dahlia, who was the one of the group plugged into I-*Mage.* Both told the same story, although Dahlia's was more detailed and Xl-arn'tz's nose more immediate. The human called John had put on his gameset and used his improved visual skills to find another way into the cliffs, and there had finally located the hybrid scent of the Knight, known to him from his game training, with his actual Day-poor nose, that had led them upon Peri's path into Dark Haven. Xl-arn'tz could smell humans in the hall, and, as his was the only door in the passage, however stonelike the timber's disguise, their post-coital reek must be like a neon sign over it.

His girlfriend still did not panic, but he heard her instruct the others to 'Tell Mother now!', even as she asked him if he possessed any cloaks. He did, but all of his were cut to fit him. The best they could do in the time whilst the humans whispered audibly outside the door was don one each, get into his cupboard, and position themselves so that he stood in front of Peri and covered her legs with his projection. This was dangerous for four reasons. One, they were trapped; two, cloaks were not meant to be overlaid and the edges had a tendency to blur; three, if the door was opened the humans would be so near that the projection's perspective would be compromised and, four, if they were that near for any length of time, even if one held one's breath at first, exhalations would eventually have to return and the fabric would undulate, the image ripple and give them away.

It didn't take that long. The humans, at least the gamer, John, knew exactly what to look for. Xl-arn'tz had excellent hearing even when he couldn't risk a sonic pulse to see through walls, and his room had nowhere other than the bed, the desk, a large chest and this cupboard to hide under or within, so it was less than a minute before the door was thrown open, the hateful steel snout of the gun waved from side to side, and the Day voice said 'Careful, man. She's in here for sure. Just let me focus a second.' And then a hand shot forward and clutched wildly, ripping Xl-arn'tz cloak right off his neck. On instinct, some of which was quite new to the effete, nerdy type his Father-Brother had rightly put him down as, and wholly engendered by his acceptance by the true Knights, he leapt forward as the protection came away and, taking John by complete surprise, managed to unbalance him over the bed, pull him down behind it and bite his neck hard.

The prey was down, immobilised by the one-shot of anaesthetic venom every Dark set of canines has been packed with since they first began to share in the Wood geneticists' work. Above him the gun went off, a shot ricocheting around the cavern telling him it hadn't lodged in soft flesh this time. He shot himself, a sonic pulse full blast, and heard the squeak as the shockwave hit the other humans. He jumped up to take full advantage, but, though she too was reeling from his weapon's effect, Peri was high-kicking the other two in sequence and all that was left to do was for him to dig out some honeysuckle ropes from his trunk, to bind the now-prostrate trio.

It wasn't until they were slumping together on the bed that he realized that, so damp and naked were they still, temple to temple contact renewed the Sharing, and all MetaMind remained 'online', relief now pouring off them, and no small amount of congratulation and respect for the one they had *almost* been thinking of as Peri's new pet.

Gwanpren, they said, Sheath of the Wood, which was a feminine inversion of (the majority of) their copulatory acts and amused the boys among the Knights the most, but it was also a compliment for his actions in Peri's defence, and, to his utter amazement, the Cornish version of his new heraldic name, Gawain, as the Augmentatio bestowed Knighthood on the mere squire.

For a few blissful moments after he awoke in the gloomy cell, Ranger thought he'd just fallen asleep playing the game. His fuzzy brain supplied a number of vivid images out of sequence, but he felt the usual triumphal sense of his elevation within the ranks of Heraldry. He knew he'd been knocked out by one of the Squires Coagulatio, using their special power to deliver the Morpheus bite, but to have actually got to a level where he was one to one with the Squires was pretty neat. It meant he must finally be nearing the end of the *albedo* stage, and the white light that illuminated the darkness of the *nigredo* from which all started, would be imprinted on his new Shield to guide him inward to the Coat of Rainbow Colours. Only then did the image of the naked Knight of the Augmentatio surface, and with it the ungameful element of the seal, which was not a land-based alchemical animal, although maybe it might be in one of the Hydradesic options he'd rarely played. And then, of course, the memory of Lily and Jake came with it, and even if he'd met Lily in a cohort of Our-*Mage*, she wouldn't look like herself, since her avatar would show only her Termite i-*mage*. But Jake gave the whole euphoric moment the cold shower effect. The gun! The caves! Capture?

Finally, abruptly, like tearing off a sticking plaster, he opened his eyes. He was not alone. Three shadows in the mist stood beside the *very uncomfortable* rock ledge on which he lay in the *dripping-with-damp* cave. He tried, for the sake of lost dignity, to sit up, but, although nothing chafed to indicate bondage, he was as powerless to move his arms and legs as if he were tied down. *The bite!* Squires had double-canines, both hollowed out with a syringe-like apparatus within, the back one sucked blood, the front anaesthetised, but after the Morpheus period came partial paralysis and the Hypnos effect. If they asked him anything, he would supply the whole, unvarnished truth. The most he could hope for was that they asked the wrong questions and he didn't start to babble and drop Jake and Lily in it. They might have got away. They certainly weren't in here.

One of the hazy-cloaked figures, whose voice he did not recognize, at that point said, 'John Ranger. Taa-ck of the Bogum clan out of the Adi people of Arunchal Pradesh. Heron-Seeker. Grail-Serf: Argent, six pallets ashen, a pale sable between. Co-inventor of Our-*Mage.*' The statement was all encompassing. His adoptive name, his parental origins, his avatar game-nomen, his game role's level, his shield, his life's achievement. Probably wouldn't need to ask many questions if they already knew all that. But what really caught his attention was his Shield.

Hitherto, even as he wore the headset and wiggled his way through cracks in rock after the Augment-Knight so recently, his Shield had been the *nigredo* sable-black background all began with, not the silver *albedo* tincture the disembodied voice quoted, and its ordinaries had been no more than five equal-sized vertical bars on it, not six thin grey ones and the new wide black one. Either they'd got this one piece of information wrong, which seemed unlikely, if they knew the name he hadn't used since his early adoption, (even in college, in the roots-finding, 'shamanic' phase he'd gone through, when he communed with nature and located his spirit-guide, Heron) *or* he'd just jumped to a new level. Perhaps it was the drugs still talking, but that was the first question he asked.

'Argent, six pallets ashen, a pale sable between? I'm pretty sure I just lost the bout.'

A merry laugh came from within the tallest cloud-figure. 'The joust is not all about the result. Points are awarded for style of horsemanship too.'

'Does falling off gracefully count, then?'

'A tourney is more than one tilt and no serf is to be expected to win against a squire and a knight together. Your escutcheon reflects your whole quest, not each lunge along the way. Your journey has been that of a heron volant, the flight leisurely, contemplative but concentrated, hence the increase of the grey bars, and it has brought you into the *albedo* brightness, for your heart is open. But your way is not yet clear. This is the significance of the final sable pale.'

'What must I do, m'lady?'

'Only ask the question that must all who seek the grail.'

John was silent. He knew the question. Who didn't? But the grail was not here, whatever the grail would turn out to be, and more pressing matters resurrected themselves to his mind. His friends, his position. Those should have been the first questions he posed, not spurious selfish play-related ones, even if, miraculously, these hidden people spoke that very language as if natural. He felt guilty. Jake would have stayed in the real world. Jake would have asked about him. And yet, though he could see no definite shapes under the nebulous mantles other than that the three ranged in height from short, through medium to exceptionally large, and could only guess that they were the biting Squire, the naked Knight, and another, he still felt their *noblesse oblige*d him to continue the forms of courtesie.

He addressed the tallest ghost, who was the only one to speak so far, 'M'lady. Though I fail the grail, though I forsake the quest, though I play no more, peace shall I know none, else I ask a question sinister.'

'All branches wind round the trunk.' The spectral voice agreed the request.

'My friends?'

'Lily Black. Chameleon-Orbiter. Menu-vairy de lis slipped argent and sable, a serpent involved vert. Jake Wynn. Glock 17, ceramic. Arms of Pretension, inescutcheon fer rouillé, d'oeuil gules fermé.'

Ranger realized with a start that he'd actually played against Lily in I-*Mage*, now he knew her reptilian icon, and he was no longer surprised that she, as leader of a Termite cohort, had whooped his ass, since she not only had borne the personalised shielding of a white-on-black field of lilies, it was charged with green serpent power, which, although its self-circling limited its range even while amplifying its energy if you got within (ie. game over, in a big verdant flash that seeded your transmogrified remains as new fungal gardens for the Termite side to feed upon), it still meant she was way above him in the hierarchies.

Perhaps more interesting yet was the reference to Jake. They could indeed have gleaned all their information about the two players if they had accessed Our-*Mage*, where, like YouTube or MySpace, personal details, such as Ranger's shamanic-tribal history, could be entered, but, for a technophile, John was downright weird, more Luddite than paranoid, about entering his own data anywhere, least of all Our-*Mage*. So probably they'd got his name from the passport he must have with him. Likewise, with no icon, they'd reported the only discrete symbol visible, the apparently fake gun, which, on reflection, and with relief, John now realized Jake must have picked up at the fancy dress shop he popped into in London, when they thought he was checking out potential disguises and camouflage equipment.

No, it was the heraldic blazon they'd ascribed that was interesting. Arms of Pretension meant, at first glance, that he had no right to the arms he carried, which was odd enough since he carried none, at least no heraldic ones, and he was sure it didn't refer to the replica gun. More odd was that the designation was only applied to sovereigns who had already asserted their rights in the field, one of the highest stations possible, implying Jake had earned a supreme prerogative without even playing. Then there was the shield itself. Iron. His french was pretty rusty, but, he could hazard, so was the metal. Iron was the symbol of the enemy of the planet Gaia, over which the armies of both the invading alien Termites and the defending indigenous Hominins were fighting. Only the die-hard Days, who didn't care about the planet only themselves, used iron for weapons. Other Hominin players used Mind and Stone, Termites Mind and Mucus. But *rusty?* That implied red, like the blood-red eye, which, since it was shut, must have disappeared into the background as if uncharged. A rusting, rusty-red shield awarded as by right, yet to a non-player? It made no sense. He dragged his mind away from the conundrum and back to the point.

'But are they alright?' He'd finally asked the right question.

'They are well.' This time the answer came from the middle-sized gauze. All he could guess at was its gender, which was feminine.

'You have been given. Now pay the price.' The smallest shade, with the bulkiest profile, which John now felt, from the guttural delivery, he had been correct in assuming to be the assailant

Coagulatio squire, intoned. *Bugger! Classic blunder. Information is currency. He could not now resist their questions without compromising his honour.*

'Fell right into the old trap, eh?' he said, trying to be cheery in the face of defeat.

'All pits are dug with our own claws.' agreed the Squire.

'The bite was given in free combat, yet we have not used the Force Majeure d'Hypnose, nor taken the Portrait Craché.' the tall figure added, in the tone of a reminder only. He was sure now that this must be the Knight they had cornered, because while Termites could scent mental chemical processings, only the Knights, of the Orders Viriditas and of their hybrid offspring, the Augmentatio, could take one's thoughts, one's whole mental image, by spitting on one.

'The contention is just.' He managed the little just jousting joke, and sensed he'd raised at least one sympathetic smile in his hard audience. Not that he could tell on which face. *If there really were faces behind the masks. No, don't go there. Focus. You can meet the criterion of honourable if you keep the truth to a minimum.*

'Why did you come here?' The inquisitor was the middle voice.

'I came to Penzeen Manor Farm. I don't know where this is.'

'You entered the cliffs under the Penzeen Lighthouse. Why did you come to those cliffs?'

'We were looking for a place to watch the lighthouse.'

'Why?'

'Because Jake wanted to watch the lighthouse.'

'Why?'

'He wanted to see Professor Fargo and...' *This was oddly hard. It must be the drug in his system, but he just wanted to get the confession over and done with, all the details out in full.*

'And?'

'Whoever else she ... was keeping there?'

'Why did he think she was keeping someone there?'

'Because they told us in the village that she doesn't live at the Farm anymore.' *That was a good deflection.*

'Why did he think she was keeping someone?' *Not for long.*

'Because ... he thinks ... she's ... she's ... behind the game, making people disappear.'

'Which people?'

'His sister – his half-sister, actually, and his girlfriend.'

‘A true Quest!’ This with approval from the Augmentatio cloak.
‘Indeed. Their names.’
‘Ida Makepeace and Dinah – I think it was - Trent.’
‘Hah! How extraordinary. A triversal conjunction. One from either paraverse meeting in an unpredicted protagonist. Interesting. And it explains the message I warrant. What does an icon of a cave mean to you, young man?’
‘It’s a secret code between Jake and his sister. From when they were kids. He and Lily broke the codes. Something about a german physicist and the Lapis language being the language of the game. He managed to send a message. An icon of a cave appeared on his PC, on Our-*Mage*’s front page, through his backdoor. He just had to say ‘Open sesame’ and the stone rolled away and there were co ordinates inside, to Penzeen. So we came.’ *Man, it felt good to get it all out, especially since it was obvious that she pretty much could put it altogether anyway once she knew he was after Ida and Dinah. Bugger. I did give that away, though. Jake’ll kill me if he doesn’t get the chance to find them now.* And, soberly. *He will NEVER speak to me again.* His heart sank. ‘I have betrayed my best friend. Keeping faith with you was truly a two-edged iron sword. And the drug hadn’t worn off either. So it’s not as if you were being fair.’
‘Courtesie is its own reward. Doubt not whom you serve and all will be as you would choose.’
‘Easy for you to say.’ But the ghastly trio were receding. He caught a glimpse of a vaginal opening, mucoidal stretchings of solid rock, behind them, and then they were gone and he was in a cell so hermitically-sealed, completely crackless, seamless in structure, that he wondered for just how long he would be able to breathe. He was feeling so depressed by himself and so horribly lethargic that he just lay there, thinking, *Whom do I serve? Whomsoever, this serve’s me right!*

General Wharton was in no doubt whom he served, but he also was well-versed in the Christianized Grail texts, so he knew that when he entered Its presence, he would ask the correct question, ‘Whom does the Grail serve?’ The words that would heal the FisherKing from the wounds of lance and thorns and nails and grant the everlasting life that was the Grail gift to the one pure knight. Then, he would stand in the Temple ReBuilt, witness the Enraptured lifted to heaven, and watch the rivers of blood cascade upon the world of sinners at his Master’s Right Hand, the hand that would no longer bear the stigmata of the unholy world's rejection of His grace.

He was less keen on the mystics' interpretation of the alchemical basis to the Grail; to him it was the cup in which the centurion caught Christ's blood and which Joseph of Arimathea, after supplying the tomb and then escaping, had hidden in Lyonesse, but he was happy enough that the philosophers' stone, the grail as *lapis*, was a vague enough concept to resonate with the cornerstone he had just finished placing in the El Kas cavern. It kept strong the sinews in more timid Brethren with more esoteric tendencies, like Milo. They needed strengthening, heaven help the man, especially now the significant stone was laid. Prophecy fulfilled. The inevitable must now occur.

However, before the Lord could come trailing His clouds of glory, the AntiChrist, the Great Beast itself, sounding like the Second Coming if one ignored the Mark, must show himself. But there was one more powerful than he to contend with, if one read Scripture aright. The Harlot that rode the very Beast itself, controlling him.

Wharton knew the game he played was a dangerous one, and a solitary, for he believed that he had a very clear idea of who that Whore of Babylon truly was. Like the Beast, seductive words were her power to twist the minds of men to think they brought peace and spiritual cleansing to a weary world, through her name that is Mystery and her children, abominations of the earth. The woman who has said in her heart 'I sit a queen' and who has fornicated with the Beast, and who carries a golden cup, filled with the filth of her excesses.

That was the cup, washed clean with the blood of her enemy, that would save Wharton, who was aware that he was not guaranteed ascension before the Tribulation in the Rapture because that blessing was reserved, as recorded by Revelation 14:4, for those who had not been 'defiled by women'. People like Milo. (Cal might come into this category too, but the verse elaborated the 'virgin' requirement, which definitely excluded the painted son of Sodom.) Mind you, his own defilement had been moderate, mostly restricted to within his twenty-four year marriage, and lavishly repented of since, and all of it had happened so long ago now, it seemed like it had happened to someone else. Nevertheless, the Bible was the last word on all matters, and his only hope of eternal life without death first now lay in the Grail. And he had no intention of dying before he saw his work to bring about the End of Days completed. But sometimes one has to walk with the devil to beat the devil, for the only one who had access to the cup of the Grail was the Harlot herself, the Day-Queen of Lyonesse, his god-daughter, the aptly illnamed, Venus.

Oh, he had kept his promise to his friend, Wesley, to look after his daughter, even against the wishes of her grandmother, who held an almost medieval attitude as the guiding light in the attempt at the reintroduction of apostolic Christianity which the small Brethren meeting had made in their local community. She considered there could be no dispute that the girl was a harlot, and she had no idea of the worse excesses and the disgusting nature of her sinful ways. She'd have had a stroke years earlier if she'd been given the least hint. She had been mortified enough to know of the pregnancy, and she had been allowed to believe that the issue would be be human, not the demonspawn it had produced. Not one word had that principled woman ever spoken to that child again, though they shared the same house for many a long year after.

True, there was nothing in Revelation that indicated anything but vicious destruction for the Beast-Rider and Her foul steed, but Tom lived in hope that the long-standing celibacy he knew Venus to have maintained in recent years would predispose her to the redemptive power of the Grail once she held it in her hands. For it must yet be she who carried it to the Temple ReBuilt, who would bring it to him so he could fill it with the sacrificial blood of his latterday circumcision it deserved, in *imitatio* of the Fisherking's wounds, *so* that he could ask the question. Then he would drink from the golden cup, and would follow her as she carried it into the Holy of Holies, beyond the Veil of the Temple, where he would stand untouched as she was utterly burned in the fire of her iniquities.

Unless she could be brought to repent in time. After all, she was prepared to unleash a pestilence upon the world that included all those with whom she had had unnatural relations and all the products thereof, not to mention every sinner alive. She was an apocalyptic force all in her own right, so how could she *not* be part of the ineffable plan of God, and perhaps, right before the end, she might turn to Him, and He might grant their union, if only to be one another's succour for the 1260 days of the Tribulation, before His Coming swept away all the works of the flesh and the devil. *Praise Be!*

Of course, some of the said demonic works clad in Wood form were well aware of the General's view of their existence, but they were nothing if not pragmatic, and his was a powerful voice on the Fargo Foundation Board, without which Venus might have had a considerably tougher time subverting the funds and technologies to the use of the Order of Viriditas. Rowan was always astounded at the superstitious contortions that humans called belief, but that seemed to be a natural side-effect of the way they designated a central creator-ego, the self, and then had to fit its actions into a personal narrative, their histories, that explained a fixed meaning to them about themselves and their place in the world. It was terribly sloppy thinking very often, as evidenced by the General's 'green' motivations, to leave the planet without the sinners that had destroyed its original Eden pristine glory, meshed with his genocidal repressed passions and the ridiculously-arrogant interpretation of ancient texts to his cause.

But Rowan couldn't deny that the urgency of the man's timetable for his apocalypse, which derived nonsensically from another, unrelated source, the old Olmec calendrical system in which the current 'Age' ended on the winter solistice of 2012, had had the spin-off effect of galvanising his own species into the long overdue reunification plot. He felt sorry for Venus, having to deal with such a madman on such a regular basis, and deplored the lies she had had to tell him to gain his support for the viral work, even having to go so far as to develop a pathogenic form of the transformative agent just to have something to show him. Still, the sad creature would get his Rapture, although translation to a heavenly place would not be on offer, only the metamorphosis of minds to Mind as the Wood virus activated new brain links in the Days, making telepathic union possible between the tribes. He tried to concentrate on the matter in hand, but the vivid recollections of the Consensus with the Days and Darks remained to disturb him.

Vi !sjn-ik had used the Dark skull and Rowan had been a Mediator enMinded himself, and, although channelling always took it out of one physically, this time, the first with three species represented in thousands of years, had been more than gruelling, it had been repellent. Admittedly, Vi's mind was not trained in Wood formalities like his young clones, so they could look forward to more logical and discrete streaming next time, no doubt, and equally, to Rowan's knowledge, none of the siblings had Vi's personality problems, although their education in the ways of humans might pose their own difficulties. Deceit came so easily to that tribe.

He was watching some of the troupe now, officiating as they trained in the blend of Wood disappearing tricks, Dark guerilla sorties and Day fighting techniques that had been developed to protect them as they carried the virus into the world and, in the unfortunate absence of the Day Skull to talk directly to the transformed human minds, in the undoubted disturbances that would follow. The General might well get his rivers of blood, but Rowan still hoped that they would be less of an armageddon and more localised misunderstandings, although he would agree the human race existed in unsustainable numbers, even when they gave up their current lifestyles, which needed thinning, and culling might well be the most efficient solution, as long as they did it to themselves.

He turned to Mh'aed and Bob, who were with him. Mh'aed was the chief alchemist of all the Darks and well-respected even by those in the Order of Viriditas, so he addressed her with the formal presentation of the open carotid, the bent neck, before, upon her signal, spitting on his hand and passing his thoughts to them both.

They were seated in an alcove off the wide entrance to the large amphitheatre under Bite, the now-island that the Romans had named Ictus, misremembered as Ictis, and that modern Days called St Michael's Mount, which was the Dark central meeting place for Lyonesse. It was heaving with the people, market stalls and produce that were swopped each Day-Night (so called because it was bright with the full moon and, as a warning, the darkness in which Days were most likely to see Darks). The task of the Squires Coagulatio tonight was to pass unseen amongst the crowds and to mock-bite as many necks as possible. Mh'aed had provided the group with a fluorescing chemical embedded in twenty-five different scents, one for each surviving Squire, with which they had filled their front canines, to leave an individual trace on each bitee, the accuracy of which would be tested, as the barterers left the cavern through the one wide entrance, by an ingenious illumination also of Mh'aed's design. Bob had come up with the idea. Like paint-balling, he had said, but more up close and personal.

None of the three could see any of the Squires, even Mh'aed whose eyes could function despite the velvet curtain of dark that lay over the Wood and Day receptors, but Rowan and, especially, Mh'aed could smell, if not their presence, the amplified tangs of their personal pheromones from the bites. Her puzzled grunt confirmed his suspicion. The one called Xl-arn'tz was either absent or very off his normal form, which, being a tad more Day, meant that he was sometimes more aggressive and competitive than most of his siblings. They were all wearing Wood cloaks, of course, so even his unusual height of full sixteen hands could not give him away. It would also be a bit impolite in a crowded space for Mh'aed to hit her fellows' sensitive ears with blasts of ultrasound just to locate him. However, Rowan was strict about attendance at all training and he suspected Xl-arn'tz, who was exceptionally studious, which he normally applauded given the general lack of concentration the clones appeared to have inherited from Vi !sjn-ik, was intentionally avoiding the session. Well, Mh'aed and Bob could handle the rest, so he'd just pop back and bring the boy over.

He was a bit disappointed in the novice. He had seemed thoughtful enough to know his duty up until now. That duty was going to be tested very soon, so it was imperative discipline should be maintained in the ranks. Not to mention the crux of the matter, which was that Xl-arn'tz was not just any trainee, but the one whose trials with the Wood and, more recently, the Dark Skulls had shown that, despite his Dayness, he was the best of the bunch at manipulating the datastream. Rowan had been considering sending Vi, who liked to be out and about anyway, as the twenty-fifth squire when the virus needed to be delivered, in Xl-arn'tz place. That way the issue of precedence, with Vi believing he was the best person as its finder to use the Skull on the Days, would be avoided, and the actual best person would be in Mind.

He was considering the tack he should take with the boy, as he laid himself headfirst into the turbochute tunnel and was sealed in the foam casing. Perhaps a softly softly approach, as the humans had it. They were young men now, not just boys, and he did not want to butt up against the headstrong humanity that they were developing. But if he found him playing that stupid game! Rowan was heartily sick of the effect of it, but the boys all said it aided them and indicated they did not want to upset their Father-Brother, whose present it was. Rowan fully agreed with Venus that it was a time and mind wasting device and no Wood should use it, but there were a few minds he hadn't been able to dream-enter in recent years that he suspected of surreptitious play. All it had to be said were of the sub-Order of the Sublimatio, who were so meditative a clan that they might just be reordering their minds into groupthink, which they had begun to attempt when it was first shown to be possible by the Augmentatio children.

The tube decanted him in Haven, deep in Penzeen, which was almost home from Hame to him these days, so, once the foam had dissipated, he lost no time in traversing the crawl-spaces and twisting turns of the complex pathways to Xl-arn'tz' door. By the time he reached it, his mood had slightly soured. The passageways might be wide enough for the robust Dark shoulders, but they were inevitably twelve hands short for someone of his height, and his back and neck were complaining rather loudly.

There was no answer when he knocked, which made him leap to the conclusion that Xl-arn'tz was deaf by game. He threw the door open, a little dramatically, for the effect of anger merely, since as a Wood elder he was above such pettiness of spirit, even if he hung around humans too much and could recognize how the sensation might feel. The room was empty of people but full, no, reeking, of scents.

He didn't need to see the unmade bed to know that congress had taken place, but he was shocked to the core, and not a little panicked by the coupling between the clone and one of the Augmentatio. *He would remember that ecstatic orgasmic scent anywhere. He had been her Initiator. F1:59.* They were not supposed to know of one another's existence, never mind, be intimate with eachother. But the sharp stab of betrayal, which he shouldn't have felt, wouldn't have felt had their sexual activities been with almost anyone else, he put aside almost before it registered.

More chilling by far were the human scents. Four distinct ones, plus the resonance of Dark anaesthesia, which must mean the overturned desk and other elements of disarray in the normally-tidy cell were evidence not of sex but fighting. Most horrifying of all was the identity of one of those humans. The only one whose fragrance was calm. The other three were high with adrenalin and cortisone overloads, excited and scared, he reckoned, but the fourth was – as always – in charge. Rowan had never, in his span of more than seventy years, felt flooded by the hormonal tsunami of fear as now.

Later he would ascribe his next confused actions to this unaccustomed torrent of chemicals, and to the betrayal of his wards, and to the knowledge that Venus had been here, and so must now know what he had done to her to create the Knights and the Squires.

He had to share his mind with her. Had to let her know his brutal actions were mandated by long term good intentions. Had to prevent her anger. Stop her using her power against him, his folk. The virus! The killer virus! She could release the pandemic that would destroy them all. She was Day. Not just a Wood puppet. She might want revenge!

A cold chill wrapped his heart as he stumbled, blind in the dark, unsure of the future, through the suffocating tunnels to the lighthouse.

Venus' heart was free these days of even her deep-frozen desire for retribution, which was necessary when you have to think through the pulling of as many strings as she had tonight.

The last time she'd sat down for a quiet moment was in the 'Tower Room', which was about as deep under the actual lighthouse tower as you could get without hitting the mantle. She had sent the Ydal to find out about Makepeace's father and was waiting for her to return with a report. She and the dogs had curled up together for one of her famous power-naps, since the Ydal, who could have returned to the next quantum break-point in time after she had left, had promised to give them a whole twenty minutes of rest before interrupting.

She stood inside the mirror, but did not offer her coat, so obviously the report was deliverable in mere words. Alert at once, Venus noticed her double's expression.

'What's the matter, Ydal? Not good news, I take it?'

'Oh, the news is just fine. Ida killed her father. The housekeeper buried him in the grounds. The grandmother had a stroke and died. The housekeeper had Ida sectioned and kept the money. End of.'

'That's not the bad news?' *I hope I'm not that unfeeling when I've got to tell Makepeace.*

'I told you, there's no bad news.'

'Then, forgive me, Ydal, but what the hell's up with you?'

'I had one hell of a journey, that's what.'

'How can *you* have a difficult journey?'

'Oh, it's easy to input a date and then cast for your imprint on the flow at that time. I zipped back to you in good order, but you were in bloody New York, at some business conference, in some steel and glass tower, and the only obvious way to get out of the room, other than via the random trajectories of the sunbeams bouncing about between the tall buildings, was through the intercom system, when somebody opened it to ask for coffee to be sent in. Fine and dandy, as the Yanks say, but then I'm just in another office with the same problem, but when I notice the girls have got a wireless playing I reckon to take a ride on the radiowaves. Turns out it's local radio, and, given that I'm going east, the wave finally dissipates a few miles out into the Atlantic, and, just my luck, *under* water. But, you know me, never easily phased.' Venus laughed obligingly. 'I know the transAtlantic telephone cables are in the vicinity, although we're talking the pre-optical fibre ones in those days, and keeping together through all of the noise can prove a challenge, but I'm up for it. But that wasn't the challenge. Oh no. The challenge was to find a way of getting to the damn thing. I'm too deep for sunlight to be anything other than diffuse at best, I had to jump into a passing shrimp just to keep from drifting down deeper from momentum. Do you know what krill are like to steer? Ugh, and such confining minds. All I could do in the end, since time is flowing, is take control and give it a deathwish to head for the shoal overhead that's making it dive deeper. The fish weren't even planning to eat, practically had to jump into their mouths to get them to snap it up. They were in one hell of a hurry because they'd sensed a school of porpoises on the way. Well, that was a relief I can tell you. I just had to get from the stomach to the brain of one of them and lag behind the crowd a while. Then a short trip from dolphin stomach to brain and we've got a decent steer. Well, it got me to the cable right enough, but you wouldn't believe how well insulated the damn things are, and what rubbish beaks porpoises have for the task of biting through. I even tried getting it to saw with a sharp stone in its mouth for a bit. Once it was through, of course, I had to leave it with instructions to bury the bit of cable it'd exposed, or the connection would have been broken and all that work'd have been for nothing.'

'Not to mention, changing the timeline. You can't do things like that, Ydal, they could affect thousands of people, with innumerable spin-off effects. What were you thinking?'

'I was thinking about getting the job done and not getting stuck forever at the bottom of the Atlantic, Miss I've Been Sitting At Home Catnapping.'

'OK. But normally, you're so careful. And it hardly seemed like a risky mission.'

'Observation is what I'm designed for, not adventure. Anyway. The cable went to Oban, in Scotland. Still miles away from the place in Suffolk where the event was due the next day. I'd gone early to leave time for contingencies and because the only fixed point we had was the grandmother's time of death on her certificate. You'd think things would have got easier after this. But Oban was the back of beyond in the early eighties, I can tell you. I had to ping back and forth off ships' antennae and radio buoys all the way down the coast to Bristol, and by then, I'm getting worried about the time, so I trip onto a train, thinking I can morph into a skin, no one's going to recognize you there, and have a sit down finally. But guess what. Trains had guards then. Some officious little bloke in a uniform. Wants to see my ticket. I can't access any new data, of course, and it's somehow slipped my mind ever to inform myself about the configuration of Bristol mainline tickets of the period. So I show him a ticket from the Tube, which is all I can conjure up, and then while he's ranting on about it and telling me what has to happen now, we go into a tunnel, and just as we come out and his eyes are a bit dazzled, I jump at the nearest telegraph pole, the wire, of course, and leave him to it.'

'Oh, my god. What the hell did you do that for? You just disappeared on a trainful of people.'

'Wrong. Just on the conductor. I was in the dining car, which was empty at the time, as they weren't serving. And I could see the alcohol molecules in his breath. Probably did him a favour. Never mind him. After that horrible little episode, I was so shaken I decided to stick to the electricity net to get me to my destination. You people. National Grid. It's more like a spider weaves on LSD than a logical grid. And the noise. I'm surprised you ever got any current at all. Plus the heat. Do you have any idea of the wastage in that system? But, heroically, as always, I got there in the end. Took form as a spider rather than a fly on the wall, less poetic maybe, but less risky. Got the info, pulled the plug, and snapped back, whoosh! At least, the return's at the speed of light however complicated the outward path.'

That had been the first message of the evening. Venus did not enjoy sending the Ydal into the real world much, especially into the past, because of the dangers involved, yes, but mainly because she came back sounding like the place or people she'd visited. Venus now had a very fair idea of what the housekeeper, June, must have sounded like, and her respect for Makepeace increased. The woman might have been her template for survival, but she had left out the unhelpful self-congratulatory tone and the whinging side to the character when she made herself in June's image.

She did not, however, go up immediately to tell her that she had killed her father and that he was not coming to find her. That could, for one thing, perpetuate a never-endable fear that his ghost would come, not to mention a possible guilt trip that could set her back at this crucial time. She made the requisite phonecall to Dinah, got her husband, Kean, had a brief banter, which was all she allowed herself in this universe, after all, she'd planned their introduction in this one, and quickly asked for the psychologist.

Their conversation was interrupted by one from the General from Israel. He was very excited by the laying of the first stone, although he spoke in coded phrases so much that anyone overhearing his café conversation would instantly want to spy on him, he was so clearly up to something. For his own sake, she kept the dialogue to a minimum. *Silly old duffer.* That was how he often came across these days. Although she did not forget he had been one of the top military brains of his country, but the categories were not mutually exclusive. Nor did she forget that, although he would probably give nothing away under quite severe torture, she had literally read his mind only the other day, and it had contained quite as many vicious tendencies towards her as had Vi !sjn-ik's, and, though properly blessed by the sanctity of marriage, the fantasies were much the same. And Vi might think she had got above herself and saw herself as Queen of the world, but even he hadn't elevated her to the mythic evil of the Harlot Beast-Rider, Eve incarnate.

She reassured him that the cup, only he called it the cocktail shaker in his coded questioning, which seemed like a Freudian slip too far and she nearly giggled at him at that point, was safe in its 'cabinet' and that the various spirits and liqueurs he required, which were the twelve jewels, one for each of the foundation stones, listed in Revelations 21 vv 19-20, were now available. Then she cut him off and was going to get on with some work when the Ydal made an emergency appearance.

Venus was in her office on the lighthouse's first floor by then, and the Ydal back on the far side of the moon, but Venus had an implant of the AI-gel that had been developed from Wood-spittle for these very occasions, and later into the game. It was only tuned to the Ydal, of course, because even Venus was not arrogant enough to think that her brain could hold the play of billions of other human brains, nor was she in the slightest bit interested in the ongoing manipulations, but it was reserved for emergencies because activation was seriously disconcerting. It was not unlike talking to the Net, which in itself was an out-of-body experience. With the Ydal, wherever she was, whatever she was doing, her mirror-image appeared before her, as solid to the eye as her reflection in a glass, blocking her view of whatever was in front of her. It was really hard to get her brain to believe she wasn't there, her conscious mind couldn't get her autonomic nervous system not to try to avoid it, which often resulted in bumping into things, and when talking to someone else *through herself,* loss of eye contact, stiltedness to her speech, and occasionally rude rushing out. She now remembered to wear a phone earpiece as camouflage in most social situations, but in the years before their invention she must have appeared quite mad on occasion. *Not that rich people are classified as mad, of course, just eccentric.*

The Ydal did not speak in this mode anymore either. She just uploaded the data direct and removed her image asap. So suddenly, after the brief disconcerting flash of her preRaphaelite self, she knew that the Ydal had intercepted Pereduri's message to her fellow knights that had been carried to her by the I-*Mage* worn by one of them. However, the knights had not stopped there. The three phones in her office, landline, handheld mobile, and earpiece all rang within the next twenty seconds. *Thank goodness for I-*Mage *and the Ydal,* she thought struggling to decipher the sentences pouring out in various configurations of human-like vocal chords. Pereduri and Galarhas were the only ones not to sound like they'd put their words through a distorted voice-synthesizer or a bird-song machine, *less Donald Duck, more like a dawn chorus with words.* Still, given the level of redundancy, it all worked well enough as communication, and she was at Xl-arn'tz' door before the two lovers had recovered enough to reclothe themselves.

This was the first time she'd spoken to a Squire, but Pereduri gave her the Gist, although thankfully not the Blazon's worth, since the heat was still coming off the pair, and this was no time for polite introductions. Together they manhandled the three prisoners, at real gun point, as she showed the two awake ones by pointing a laser torch at her disembodied hand as it twirled the barrel to reveal the bullets, into the corridor. The Squire scouted the way, followed by Lily and Jake, with Venus right behind with the trigger, and Peri carried John in the rear. It would have been far too dark for her employees to recognize her, but she had taken the precaution of wearing a Wood cloak and she made her voice gruff if she had to use it, so they got to the sub-basement level under the lighthouse without blowing her cover. There were a number of rooms designed as haz-labs to Wood contamination standards on this floor and they placed each in an isolation unit, largely to hide their smell from the rest of the cliff users.

Dark anaesthetics wear off pretty fast, it was the condition of the Wood design of the genetic double-toothing tweak that this was so, in order to ensure their prey was not unfairly bled dry, just 'milked'. (Venus knew for a fact that Mh'aed at least had plenty of alternate sedatives that would last a whole lot longer, although she didn't know if they could be delivered in a bite.) Anyway, since they release the brain and head first and the lower body second, the drug in the second man's system had given them the opportunity for a little gentle interrogation. That had been an eyeopener for his First Knight, even though he didn't know her identity. How well the game had worked. He had processed fantasy into reality almost without pausing for breath, and had honoured the fiction more than his friends. She had never paused herself to doubt the plan, it *had* to work, but it did occur to her to wonder if she'd designed the Round Table big enough for all the knights who were questing towards it. If John was anything to go by, more of them might find it than she had thought. *Must remember to ask the Ydal for an updated estimate of the numbers.*

She was going to interrogate Jake and Lily too, but John's information needed to be given in coat form to the Ydal, so she could find Jake's backdoor to the game and check how far he and Lily had got with their Lapis lexicon, not to mention, detect if any other messages or instructions were floating around in the Mage ether. Maybe she should have dismissed Peri and Xl-arn'tz, but he knew he would have been missed from training by now anyway, and they both were desperate to stay together for longer and to stay with her. And, apart from being the empty maternal egg that mediated his creation, which motivated some of his interest, Venus knew from the Ydal's snooping in Mind that he was the very one who had instigated a trawl for her inputs, so he might be exactly the right person to get onside, posssibly being in a position to bring the Squires to the Table too. She asked them to wait in her outer priesthole office, which, if he did turn out to retain his loyalty to the enemy ranks, could be sacrified as merely a 'quiet place' and blocked in and sealed off from prying eyes, since there was a alternative way to the Tower room which she had not revealed to anyone.

She didn't need to tell them about the Ydal herself, since it only took a second to divest herself of her coat and hand over the problem to solve. She was going to go straight back to talk to the prisoners when Peri suggested bringing them food and drink. There was enough mucus evaporating from all of their skins for telepathy but she could tell, merely from the eagerness with which the boy at her side nodded at the idea, that there was another agenda at play here. She focused her mental 'hearing', 'You want to see the lighthouse?'

'Where *you* live. Yes, please.' he nodded. There seemed no harm in a little sightseeing trip to the kitchen after all he'd already seen, so up they had gone. But there was an unpredicted danger. Not unpredictable, perhaps, if anyone had been thinking clearly after such an unprecedented evening, since he'd already said his tutor would have missed him at training. What Venus hadn't considered was who that tutor was.

Rowan was perhaps the only one who would have come to visit her without calling first, but then to him she was just a pawn in his game, and, in fairness, he lacked vocal chords to speak coherently on the phone, but the speed of his arrival would have taken them all by surprise, even if they'd been expecting him. And the manner of it.

Rowan was the epitome of cool: whatever else you could say about him, he had style and dignity. Well, not tonight. He fairly erupted through the central stairwell trapdoor into the circular kitchen, his hair dishevelled and with scratches on his skin that indicated a much-too-rapid passage for his frame through the Dark corridors.

He was trilling, too, in very high-pitched chords that swung between strident and apologetic, didactic and sorrowful, and swooped up and down the scale in volume, pitch and tempo, but not even attempting the English words he knew well enough normally. He was wearing his cloak, activated, but he threw off his hood as he stood erect, spitting wildly in her direction, desperate to communicate before she could open her mouth to speak.

What he hadn't done was pause long enough to scent the other smells in the room, admittedly overpowered by the bacon they were frying at the stove and harder yet to detect since they were wearing their cloaks to protect their naked bodies from splashing fat, which, despite being unhooded and deactivated also dampen aromas by design. And he had been in such a frenzy, with his eyes still contracting from the brightness of the artificial light after the endless underground blackness, that neither had he seen her guests.

If her guests had been mere humans, they would, since he was in an activated cloak, have spent some time looking around for the flock of distressed birds that must have come in the window or flow down the chimney, but as all three knew him very well, even before he had thrown back his hood to spit, becoming a disembodied head, they were in no doubt as to his identity. They were initially shocked and a little scared to see him in this state, but that ratcheted up a seismic level when his mental messages were transferred. Venus got the first one, but a second expectoration was caught deftly by Peri's swiftly-extended hand and she smeared it on the Squire even before herself, for she had already ingested the airborne Gist.

What happened next stunned Venus. There was the sudden awful silence as they all absorbed eachother's presences and their meanings. She saw Rowan gobbling a little as his orderly future unravelled, she saw a steely glint set the eye and mouth of the novice *against* his master, and she saw Peri in MetaMind, *deciding*. It was a swift enough decision, that in any lesser Mind would not have counted as thought-through, but her actions were no slower. How she spat in what seemed like two directions at once, Venus did not see, partly because she was watching Rowan like a hawk, and partly because now she knew why. The Knight and the Squire were ready to pounce. That had been the decision.

Whilst Pereduri sang a single high note that her human vocal chords could barely sustain, but which carried the MetaMind blockage of all Rowan's mental transmissions, Xl-arn'tz threw the extra length of honeysuckle rope he'd still been carrying to Venus and jumped at Rowan's neck, Peri effortlessly throwing in a kick to the stomach that doubled him over enough for the Squire to reach his target. Rowan fell to the ground, immobilised by the bite, his feet and hand tied quickly by Venus, and a blank I-*Mage* set was fixed onto his head, on static surround-sense, which would loop all of his thoughts through it and prevent telepathy.

Then the Knight and the Squire turned to Venus. Huge almond-shaped violet eyes and enormous reflective red orbs both held the same question. 'The full Blazon?'

After all, they had both turned coat against their entire history and the main parental figure in it, placing their futures firmly in her hands. What could a mother do? Nothing less was due.

She nodded. 'The Coat Entire.' The eyes had it.

D: Nigredo:
Peregrinatio and Precipitato

Everything made perfect sense to Jake. It was obvious. He didn't know why he hadn't realised it earlier. He was asleep and this bizarre species of nightmare was no more than a dream.

It must be what was called a lucid dream, because he could think about his situation whilst it was happening, so he could recognize in his prison cell the metaphor of the cave that was Ida's emergency recall code. The disturbingly vulval nature of the door was no doubt bound up in thoughts of Dinah, lost along with Ida, and, distasteful though the thought was, possibly even the idea of the maternal. Naturally, it was the game that predominated, as it did in his waking hours. The idea of real Knights and Squires was as laughable as that of giant, intelligent Termites. He had clearly been working too hard.

It occurred to him to wonder just when the dream had started. Perhaps they had not found the code at all. Now he thought about the baroque nature of the so-called language, Lapis, he could not see how he could ever have given credence to Lily's suggestion that there was an overlap between the real world of cosmology, however esoteric and derived by a genius/madman, and the nonsense of I-*Mage*. The alternative, well, the alternative was unthinkable. The very concept that the game described a genuine, if hidden, world was insanity of the first order.

But, since he was just dreaming, he couldn't help but ponder what it all might mean. Dinah, as a Jungian psychiatrist, had been a great believer in the revelatory power of the dream. He remembered a particularly ugly row after he had failed to treat her dream-diary with the same respect for her privacy he knew to apply to her life-diary. She'd considered it *more* private, if that made any sense.

She'd said when she wrote in her diary that those writings were, at best, her conscious thoughts, but her dreams could reveal her subconscious, about which even she, until she had spent time interpreting them, might be in the dark. Whatever the rights and wrongs of that episode, he was left with the distinct impression that meaning lay now all around him in this chimeric landscape.

Unfortunately, despite his decision to pay attention, there was very little to note from his current trapped environment. The lighting was perhaps the most significant. He was well placed to examine the floor, and he couldn't muster the energy to stand. You could see it was stone, local Cornish granite, he assumed, if he was actually in Cornwall, that is. The bare rock was almost perfectly smooth, as if a master sculptor had finished it, but its naked planes were only visible at the lowest level of the wall and floor. Above it the walls dripped with moisture, for a cave this would be unremarkable, except that here the life-giving liquid supported a dense network of fungus. The excrescence ranged across the ceiling, depended down the walls, more like hair than vegetation, an effect reinforced by the fluff of its cilial fronds, a furry sprouting that was almost carpetlike, mind you, it would be a serious shagpile. Most remarkable was the tip of each of the longest of these hyphae, bearing as they did what looked like miniature lightbulbs. Whilst it was possible that light-producing mushrooms existed naturally, maybe by mixing chemicals like some species of deep sea fish he'd read about, he felt pretty sure that the colour palette they would be able to draw on would be severely limited. This did not look natural. What it looked like was Christmas tree lights on acid. Worse, it looked like it wasn't just random flickers of variegated hues. It looked like it was the pinprick outline of images, images that suggested the hieroglyphic complexities of the Lapis language, but that was probably just his human brain's insatiable desire to detect pattern in chaos, to inject meaning into nonsense.

Nevertheless, if he stayed horizontal, ignoring the cold damp seeping into his bones, which was an irritatingly undreamlike addition to the experience, he could almost believe the ceiling was talking to him. Perhaps it wasn't all a dream. Perhaps he was drugged, that would explain the symptoms. The desire just to lie here and read the sky. Perhaps it didn't matter if he did. Might give it a chance to wear off and his brain would function normally again. Perhaps if he shut his eyes it would happen sooner.

It must have been drugs. When he opened them again, he was quite sure. Well, unless this dream had a narcotic subtext he couldn't reference from his relatively clean-living past. Or, however unlikely a possibility, given the unpleasant and stressful surroundings, unless he'd actually fallen asleep.

His position remained as before, but now he was wearing an I-*Mage* headset, and whether the lights were on overhead or not, he could not tell because the glasses were darkened, blotting out all vision. He tried, very hard, to lift his arms to yank the damn thing off, but, although he could feel no restraints, he couldn't get them to rise, as if gravity had been turned up a hundredfold. And then the images started.

First it was a face, a monstrous distortion of humanity, paper-white skin lined with blue veins like stilton, surrounded by velvety, deep-black fur, which ran up the pointed, catlike ears. Maybe he could have lived with that much difference, but the big round hamster-ruby eyes failed to activate the aaah! factor because they sat above a thin-lipped mouth and viciously sharp teeth and a nose that appalled. It lacked the bony protruberance of humans, which gave it a prominence through its spread across the face, but the edges of the nostrils were crinkled flaps that wiggled constantly, like a fine cauliflower in a breeze, and the hairiness continued with whiskers around and about it and the upper lips. Jake had designed (from John's descriptions and drawings) the original image of the Squire for Our-*Mage* and seen the upgraded permutations players had developed since, but this was more vividly real than he had ever imagined. No wonder players got hooked if imagination could supply such detail.

And yet ... the expression was human, more than that, it was humane. With a start, Jake realized for the first time that he had felt no fear, despite the desperate situation his senses should be shouting at him to fly from or fight out of, and, even if this was the effect of drugs, he couldn't interpret the creature's countenance as threatening.

That image was swiftly replaced by another face, even less human in many ways, but as concern for him was written all over it, he couldn't force himself even to draw back. This creature was a Knight, he knew it would be androgynous and naked, covered with plant-based tattoos, draped with feathers and mosses, but he'd never really paid much attention before to the distinctly longer skull shape, the high brow and cranial ridge, which was emphasized with tall feathers in many bright shades. The extended face, a pale russet shade, ended in mobile, flaring nostrils, giving it more of a snout than had the Squire, and the lips, as large and flexible as a camel's, or perhaps betraying the primate past they both shared, peeled back to reveal tombstone teeth the Osmonds would have killed for. But the eyes were what held the attention, almonds of sparkling lavender, emanating a bright and compassionate interest that had such depths that he knew he wasn't looking at an animal. He rather felt he was before a goddess, although how he could feel so sure that the creature was female, given that what he had seen on the cliff was a hairless, flat torso and a glimpse through braided tresses of a pubic mound under which the genitalia of either gender would be hidden, remained a mystery.

He didn't recognize the next detail from the game. She spat on her hand, gently lifted the headset, smeared the contents on both of his temples and replaced it. Instantly, before he even had time to wonder what she was doing, he had knowledge. It seemed an odd way to put it, even to himself, but he didn't hear a voice in his head, he didn't so much get an image, nor smell nor taste nor touch. It was all together, but less like a sensory video, more like being transported into her space, or, he amended, the space inside her mind. Not that it was empty, but he realized she was guiding him slowly.

First he saw what she saw, through her eyes. She was still looking at him, but through her eyes he saw himself differently. He looked somehow shorter, broader, flatter-faced, and his colour seemed more yellow than flesh-toned, blonde curls duller, clothes drabber, but her colour vision was still a lot better than his own in the darkness. She raised her hand, and he noticed that the immensely-elongated digits seemed normal now, licked a fingertip deliberately, then touched it to the temple of the Squire.

Immediately his view changed. He could see like he was illuminated in ultraviolet. He reacted with excitement, and the confirmation came back, into his mind, even while overlaid on his ghostly image he saw the gleam of those feline teeth with his own eyes, as the Squire indicated, 'If you liked that …' And there he was pulsating heat against a chill floor, 'Infra-red vision! Wow!'

Somehow he felt the expectation to calm himself. The suggestion that shutting his eyes might help. Now he was looking through the violet eyes again, he knew not just because he recognized the memory of her entrapment in the cave with the seal, but because the colours were not the same as those he'd just experienced. They were shifted away from the red end of the spectrum, but there were blues, greens and yellows in the sea and sky he'd never noticed in his entire life, and the scents were rich and stimulating and powerful. She was just orienting him. They were in her memory.

Now the scene changed, and he was looking at his boss, Professor Fargo. With a shock, he felt the Knight's emotion towards her. He felt the idea of *Mother* rise like a phoenix from the repressed ashes of his own loss. He dragged himself back from the sensation that his employer was *his* mother. A bubble of humour from both the other minds helped his withdrawal.

Now! It was an intimation that this next was for him, for his information, directing his attention. There was a flash of the Our-*Mage* front-page with Ida's cave icon, followed by a real cave, although it was on several levels and plushly done out, a bedroom, sitting room, shower, office, all mere glimpses, and a vast central cavern, off which the other cavelets ran, containing an enormous glass tank, in which a naked woman was swimming. Tactfully, as it dawned on him that this bronze aquanaut was his sister, all grown-up, the view narrowed to focus exclusively on the goggles she was wearing. They were a sort of waterproof version of the I-*Mage* configuration. There was a blip, while the image scrolled, too fast to see, but *through? into?* another mind. He couldn't say how but he felt it was familiar, like someone he knew, not Ida, but almost before he was conscious of it, there was a further slip *between* minds, and everything had changed.

He was underwater. Only he was not *he*, but she. Oh, he was still himself, but the conscious part of his mind had submerged beneath the full-on reality as experienced by the other. She was comfortable in this environment, although he could register the cold and the lack of breathing, but as she was emoting only happiness, he could not surface any negative reaction for himself. It was very hard to see for a little while, not because the water wasn't clear, it was crystal, but because there were so many viewpoints to process all at once, until he sank beneath her thoughts and left behind his analytical mentality, whereupon he found he just knew things, could do things, in an alien body and world.

Europa. Ice-ceilinged water-world. An armoured torso that spun, a ring-body, multiple eyes and limbs spread around the bracelet of her body, retracting and extending as chosen by any one or all of five discrete, evenly dispersed brains. Flow. And Dakul. The sensation of love, desire, companionship, joy that flooded him - *her* - for the creature of the same kind, spiralling towards her out of the blue-white roof, jerked him into a momentary self-awareness again. He had never felt that warmth and closeness with anyone. But then their *feelers? tentacles? arms? legs? proboscises? she didn't seem to use words* met and he stopped trying to find names for things and *felt*. Love. Care. Two-in-Oneness. A wholeness of being that came rarely, only as Flow. A glimpse, no more, of a child, a human child that he recognized as Ida, even though she'd always been older than four to him. A glimpse, no more, of the woman not in the tank, Makepeace, the stern, distant one he'd trailed around after in the holidays, hoping that Ida would come out and play. A glimpse, less than, a turned-away glance, averted out of horror, of the 'cave', the hollow prison that lay within, the place of nullity so feared. And then, the rush, a slide, an elongation, a compression, and a shimmering creature in the tank, *not now, but one day …* , a human-Europan hybrid, underwater with her lover, Dakul, also now mutated to physical compatibility, in a new Eden, a dream, no more, but stronger and more vital even that the vast tracts of space that separated the two in real life. *The notion of reality he saw slip past his cynicism, but couldn't hold onto a sensation of disbelief.*

Then he was standing in the tank-cavern, and the bronze woman was above him in the water, and she was wrapped in the hybrid body, projected by the headset onto a clinging, filamentous cloak, and she was strong and sane and beautiful, and he realized he was looking at her with his own eyes now. Then the Knight removed his headset and someone else removed the woman's, so when he lifted his head again, under the normal limitations of just vision, he could see a short woman, still cloaked but in a dull grey wrap, wet hair curling tightly, tense as a whippet but venturing a half-smile of welcome, and the eyes were Ida's.

He forgot everything he knew about the instability that had haunted their lives, forgot to tiptoe sensitively around the 'strange' young woman of the house, and just ran at her and grabbed her into a great bearhug, while his mouth repeated 'I found you! I found you!' until his lips were silenced by kissing the top of her head. And, via the residual mucus on his brow, he could feel the pleasure from the folk in the room, and when his skin touched hers, Ida within, Makepeace without, and Flow always and forever above, and her matching ecstasy that he accepted her, all of her, and together their minds dived and squeezed the cave, until all that remained was the capstone and the words written on it, 'Open Sesame!'.

He should have woken up now. The dream should have ended there. But it couldn't because he wasn't asleep, and it had yet more excitements to reveal. Makepeace gently pushed him off her after a while and took his hand. He was too dazed to know why she was giving it to someone else, but the hand in which his was placed was more instantly familiar even than his sister's, not to mention the perfume, which hadn't changed. He looked up and it was Dinah's face. And when he kissed her, lovingly, deeply, on automatic, the years rolled back, and everyone else was forgotten. Until her mind jolted and he was floored by an onslaught of images of her *husband?* They dropped eachother like the proverbial hotcakes, and stepped apart.

No one had spoken aloud for what seemed like hours, but now another voice he knew well enough leapt into the awkward void.

'Jake! I think you owe me a report.' He turned on his heel and faced his employer, but he was still high enough to reply with some spirit,

'I reckon it's a mere memo compared to the saga you owe me. But it can wait until you tell me what you've done with Lily and John.'

Up until that moment, Jake had never experienced the mythical, formidable side of The Fargo, as her office nickname went. Now she spat upon him, with finesse, so that the tiny gob of saliva hit his temple neatly, but with anger that empowered it painfully and which he received like a full blown tirade of abuse in the face. Staggering back, he tried to make sense of the dense packet of thoughts.

She was having a hard day, that came across first. But the outrage that was directed at him personally focused on his mistrust. She'd saved his sister (although she hadn't known Ida had a half-brother) from a mental asylum and given her the space and tools with which to be happy. She'd given her the best person to aid her recovery, Dinah, who she'd given a home and a husband. She'd given him the one job that would allow him to fulfil his own need to find them both (although only on Dinah's recommendation – in fact, Dinah had been adamant Jake was the one person on earth who'd find a way into I-*Mage*, one way or the other). And she'd given Lily a key role. Yet he still supposed that she would offer harm to her and to John, without ever stepping back and even looking for the big picture into which they all fit, which was supposed to be his forte. He saw her image of himself in the Lapis iconographics of the game, and his rusty shield held before his eyes, on which there was a self-welded seam of melted metal that was the only evidence of the eye of mind he was keeping so tightly shut that his wilful blindness was an insult to the Quest and to Her.

Despite himself and the flood of self-justified recriminations creaking behind the onslaught of her perception of him, he felt obliged to apologize. Especially since he uncovered the information that Lily, who had knocked her head in the original tussle with the Knight and Squire, was being tenderly ministered to in an adjacent cave-clinic by Dinah's husband, Kean, who, he noted with some dismay, was more handsome and caring than he might have wished after the initial promise of that kiss. As for John, it appeared that he'd been revived earlier than Jake and had had time to visit both of his friends, had been reassured of their being in safe hands, since he had trusted the Courtly mores of the creatures instantly and implicitly, and, by way of proving his loyalty to the Round Table, had embarked on a quest of his own.

Even with the line between fact and fiction fuzzed beyond his unentangling, John wouldn't have described it as a quest. He was just trying to help out his new friends, since they had looking after his old ones covered.

Truth be told, he'd been feeling like a spare wheel around Lily and Jake the whole trip. He hadn't been around when Jake and Dinah had been an item, and that was the last woman he'd known him to have got wrapped up in. Until this weekend if anyone spoke their own, two-person language, it had been him and Jake. Not in a gay way, just the jargon of the work and the shorthand of longstanding friendship. And, even though as a player, John got more of the Lapis stuff than Lily had expected, the rest of their conversations were implicitly exclusive.

To be fair, none of the chill that came his way emanated from Jake, and John knew his own lack of svelte charisma made him more sensitive to the slights his bulk drew from women than he should be, but practically every time he opened his mouth, Lily over-reacted. If he was coarse, she withdrew, like the petals of her exquisite floral nature needed to draw together for protection from the great brute. If he was intelligent, she appeared surprised, sometimes he got, genuinely shocked, and quite often, when she troubled to address him directly, her manner was patronising, as to a child or an idiot. In short, though he tried, he couldn't bring himself to like her, although he saw she was quite different with Jake, warm, supportive, and, if he wasn't wrong, more adoring than was returned. On balance, knowing the man had been hung up on Dinah for all the years they'd known eachother, he didn't like her chances when faced with the competition. So he was looking forward to being present at that meeting and had no idea of taking himself off anywhere, presupposing he couldn't now be counted among the disappeared anyway.

He hadn't paid much attention to the background dialogues of Fargo and her thanes, largely because they'd been conducted mind to mind and what aromatic connectivity still blew in the air was insufficient for him to tap into – the subdued ebb and flow of the mental traffic was like cars on a far road, like the sea in a shell. The other main reason was that they'd decided to feed him and he had a plateful of white fungal cakes that were, despite their inappetising aspect, delivering a series of extraordinary taste sensations into his mouth, many of which were recognizable, like hazelnuts and chocolate, cauliflower and stilton, pheasant and spinach, and others which he couldn't place at all. Miraculously, each differently flavoured bite not only smelt of the food tasted, but crunched or squelched with the texture of its origin. So some of the tastier slimy ones he was glad not to have anyone undistracted enough to ask, for fear it put him off. However, whether the alien food enhanced his mental senses or whether they'd been spitting again without him noticing, suddenly he realized the background noise ceased abruptly and the focus was on the Knight, as if she was listening to something the other two could not hear.

Apparently she was. They explained the origins of the Knights' womb-developed telepathy later, but her instant awareness of a sibling's trouble was insufficiently detailed until after their communications had been amplified through I-*Mage*, and she had to wait for her brother to put one on and send. This didn't slow them down much. Pereduri knew Galarhas and the young man he'd been disappearing had been attacked, knew that the Knight was unhurt but that the young man needed medical attention, knew they were in the Great Centipede in the Mouth of the Dragon, which sounded a less than comfortable location but bore with it the tropical salt tang of the Caribbean. The discussion that followed concluded with the decision to send Kean, but when the I-*Mage* amplified data was received, they realized a lone doctor might not be sufficient. This was to do with a shark and with pirates and the fact that they were stuck in a cave *through* which they had to dive to get to their transport.

At this point, Ranger interrupted. 'Have you got a submarine or something waiting for them, then?' Even the Knight twitched slightly and Fargo spun round abruptly. They had pretty much forgotten he was here and hearing their mental conversation. Their eyes met and there was an unvocalized, *sub mentis*, he coined the phrase, transmission therein.

Fargo turned and spoke aloud. 'You know too much already. But you have achieved in the game and I would have called you earlier had it not been for your link to Jake Wynn. Would you have accepted the call of your own volition?'

'To become one of the Disappeared?'

'To seek the Grail even to that end.'

John considered carefully. All the stuff they'd done, even if Jake couldn't have done it without him, he'd always thought of it as Jake's project, but the Game, that was his. Jake had worried about his hold on reality, but that was before they knew the Game was not just full of truths but True. And Jake had only had cause to have this concern because he knew John better than anyone, could see that, at least while he was playing it, it was more real than his outer life. Jake had been the one with the quest to rescue the damsels in distress, but he, John, had been the truth-seeker. And suddenly he realized something else. While his skeptical, scientific, conscious mind derided his time-wasting and undermined his confidence in himself, underneath he had never *not* believed that the game was real – that was why he'd put all the effort into Jake's attempts to uncover its secrets, so he could find his own way into it, find his own way home. And now he was here, surrounded by impossible purple and ruby eyes, looking into the calm grey eyes of ... of course, who else could it be?

He knelt on automatic, holding an invisible sword blade flat on upturned palms. 'How can I have disappeared when I am come Home, my Queen?'

'Nicely put, young man. Very well, arise a knight and learn the task for which you seem to be volunteering through persistence and curiosity. You should know these qualities are highly prized and essential to any quest, so take heart, but quickly.' and with that verbal instruction came the information, a spittle-smear direct.

'Wow!'

'Now go. Kean will be waiting in the transport room.'

The Game had been truthful but not exhaustively so apparently. It hadn't mentioned, perhaps simply to stop deranged people who took their playtimes too seriously from digging up the planet, that there was a global network of transport chutes underneath the surface. A system of turbolifts that had been in place when the Pharoahs ruled Eygpt, built by a hidden race of cousins to the dominant humans, of which the Knights were not true but recent, hybridised examples. It was this data that had caused the 'Wow!', as his instructions started with the route, through dark tunnels, to the nearest embarkation point, but, as with all Wood knowledge, as he now knew to categorize it, focus on it revealed layered histories and emotional tags beneath. He had to pull his mind away from the past to navigate the tunnels, but it wasn't like he was feeling his way for the first time, more like sophisticated GPS tracking in his brain, recognizing his route for him as he progressed.

As promised the human doctor was waiting in the cave, which was lit well enough for John to identify the man from his implanted memory. *Normally his memories extended to faces, not particularly physique, although this chap was all male and highly memorable as a result, but certainly not to smell, nor to a slight libidinous arousal excited by his presence.* He repressed these responses easily, given that they were already stifled subtexts, but not without a mild tremor of shock that was all his own. Kean introduced himself with a normalizing handshake and an unphased grin and indicated their game headsets. 'If we both transfer saliva, we gain a dedicated line of communication, which we'll need in the tunnels.' *So he hadn't seen John's Fargo-reaction. Phew!*

Standing in a shower and being encased in a foam coating would have been more scary if he hadn't had prior insight to assure himself that he would still be able to breathe, and he was happy enough to trust the doctor to push him headfirst into a near-vertical shaft, and to follow him with the pre-wrapped equipment. Since the foam hardened to transparent, the first impression John had was of being thrust into pitch darkness, but soon, and at regular intervals thereafter, a neon-blue ring would split the blackness like a join in a pipe, though its limited ambient glow illuminated only small strips of marble-smooth walls around it. He didn't find such sight much of an advantage, it merely served to amplify his mild claustrophic reaction and the spacing of the rings flicking by indicated a quite stomach-churning pace was being attained, probably, he reckoned, by the gravitational plummet that was little less than a vertical drop. He began to wonder how hard or how bouncy the casing was and whether it would withstand being dropped on his head on the ocean floor.

At this point, Kean engaged his mind. It was more like a conversation than the other communications he'd shared. Kean 'sent' words, and, although he could guess from the style of language he received that they were converted into Lapis and back, their 'atmospherics', the sensory information, was minimized. His own emanations obviously were not.

Kean 'said', 'Breathe! Slowly. You won't be sick, but if you were the foam is pervious and would absorb it and reseal, just like it's cycling your oxygen and CO_2 now. And you don't land on your head.' Here he showed an image of the tunnels that diagrammatized a gradual slope into circular caves, headfirst but tipping onto a hinged slab that decanted the traveller on his feet, whereupon a brisk shower dissolved the foam and he could rest, regroup, change direction for the next leg of the journey, which would also involve the same superchutes, but this time hydraulics would shoot them surfacewards once more, so beware of a greater sense of *g* forces than when dropping.

John hadn't even managed to phrase a response, but his confusion and curiosity was speaking for his consciousness, so Kean responded with further explanations. 'First stop, the bottom, is in the Mid-Atlantic Ridge. We come out *in* it. So, hot!' He waited as John assimilated this incredible information. Well, he had to, since John's mild claustrophobia ratcheted up seismically at the weight of ocean and rock accumulating above him with every foot they dived. Kean, who was obviously temperamentally suited to his job, produced waves of all the reassuring emotions in lieu of the words that would have failed to get through the physicality of the panic symptoms. After a minute or two, John managed to quip, but with added gratitude and genuine admiration, 'Good bedside manner!'

'Thanks, but it's the Wood trick that makes the difference.'

'Wood?' It was the first time John had come across the designation. 'The fathers of the Knights of the Augmentatio? They're called the Khets in the Game.'

'Well, in a sense all the names are made up. Humans have an addiction to naming things. Their cousins, modern *Homo erectus*, think this is one of our problems. We bind time by fixing on a name, we constrain space by static titles, we are the people of boundaries and limitations thereby. The people of the Trees are the same people who are invisible, who are the users of light, who see with first sight, who speak the language of the birds, who share their minds, who preserve the truths ... the list is as long as the things they can do, and they've been called everything from angels to fairies by us. For all our activity, they think we're the noun, the To Be, but they're the Verb, the Being Becoming. We think they're slow to make decisions, since collective agreement takes time, but they think for the planet, so their timescales are species-long, rather than based on individual lifetimes, 3 billion heartbeats, like ours. And the name 'Wood' that those within the Fargo fold use is more of a nickname, a slight play on words, courtesy of old Bob Tring, the erstwhile lighthousekeeper, who pretty much restarted the whole interspecies reunification process, (although with a Dark, a gereh, not a Wood) and refers to their love of trees and their ever-ready sexuality.'

Maybe he sensed John was on overload and stopped transmitting. It was fully five minutes later before John even noticed. True, there had been only a couple of hundred words sent, but each idea was an essay in itself. No, that was also a limited concept. Behind each thought was the information that had been condensed into the words, the ambience within which those poor referents were the tip of the iceberg. The word 'Humans' alone could have held him up for a lifetime if he'd not been listening initially for the words, but, as they slid past on the surface, the ocean depths beneath thronged with images of the creatures. Many of the images were fragments, still pictures, video, sensaround, but glimpses not individuals, and were clearly Kean's take on the subject, which was obvious not just from the style of any clothing, but from the flicker of annotations in medical and other textbook-like naming that surrounded so much of some subjects in a haze. But there were other viewpoints represented, images seen through eyes that looked differently into the world than ours, images preserved through collective memory from a neolithic shared past.

The words had moved on too quickly. By the time Kean had 'uttered' the species name and begun on the list of their activities, the Woods were resonating louder than the humans on all frequencies. Much of what Kean knew about them was gleaned from direct Wood sources accessed by Fargo and passed spittlewise to him or to his wife, Dinah.

John was busily unpacking the data as sequentially as he could, concentrating on holding the relevant words, almost like the subtitles to a film, in front of his mind and, as speedily as possible, diving into the layers of meaning contained within to pull out more than the dead words, more like a pulsating, living Gist, which was a game-term he'd never really felt before. Finally, he noticed that the quality of the silence had changed from indulgent restraint, to avoid further transmission and overload, to cold, repressed curiosity.

Too late he realized why. He was not in control of his mind, even when he knew he was not sending words, he was emitting his reactions, and his reaction to the information that Kean was married to Dinah had been so brief that, in an unconnected world, he wouldn't have raised an eyebrow, being so much more discreet than that. But, linked to Kean as he was, the invisible skip of his heartbeat, and the slide of his thoughts to Jake and the possibility of his hurt, after his devotion (Lily aside) to finding her and finding her married, were writ large in an emotional spike, however little he'd noticed it himself.

'Tell me!' It was a command, and John suddenly recognized, as everything he knew about Jake and Dinah flashed through his mind, how polite, how unintrusive had been the 'interrogation' by the Knight, the Squire and Fargo, if a mere human could simply demand and know whatever he wanted. He felt it was a bit unfair to send him off like this when his thought processes hadn't been trained to resist such an attack. He would have told Kean anyway. There wasn't anything other than ancient history to it, and there was nothing in that he needed to hide. In fact, he rather thought, especially since Lily, that the whole search was a rather more academic than passionate pursuit; any 'love' a relic rather than a reality in the present.

Kean was apologizing even as he was emanating the aggrieved party. He wasn't bothering with words. It was an exculpatory series of images, justifying a genuinely-uncharacteristic spurt of mistrust and jealousy. The most immediate was the most telling, however. When Fargo had rung to ask him to go on this mission, he'd been in his clinic treating Lily for a minor concussion. He began to pack some equipment to leave, during which his wife had come in to wish him goodbye and a safe journey. She had gone to peck his cheek but he'd dipped his head to receive it on his temple, lifting his hand to turn her face back to kiss her fully, and as their lips had met, the tiny dab of connectivity enabled him to probe her thoughts as his tongue her mouth. He was sending his own love at the time, so it was a bit like running headlong towards the object of your desire only to trip over the wall of their kiss with another man. A kiss that remained at the forefront, in guilt-neon, and which had the 'one true love' halo of gilt-sky-blue-framing, the historical denotation of the entire, lost experience, that now pulsed vividly with life beyond the static of a painted representation.

John got the whole sorry state of affairs, full blast, partly as reparation for the unforgiveable mind-theft and partly because the poor bloke was pretty upset. To be fair, Kean was trying to get himself under control as quickly as he could, the thoughts were being suffocated, chopped off as they began, but John realized doubt creeping in, rewriting a shared history that Kean had assumed was a happy marriage, querying this separation, this coldness, this avoidance of this, of that. When he spied the unmet woman turning her shoulder in bed and 'pretending?' to be too tired, he protested.

It was fortunate that, very soon after this, since they were both somewhat embarrassed and trying to control their minds and *not* think, which is harder than it sounds when it's a holistic transaction, they reached the Mid-Atlantic Ridge junction. After the disembarkation shower which dissolved the foam casing him, the heat hit John full force. Kean left his equipment wrapped up for its own protection, which meant they had a long and heavy cylindrical package to carry between them, and this spaced them physically, gave them something to do, and, since they could hear eachother and move their arms again, there was a swift, tacit agreement to remove their headpieces and give themselves a break from telepathy.

They trudged through innumerable caves and tunnels, bowed by the temperature, the weight and the burden of their knowledge of eachother and the water and earth above them. Finally, they came into a wider area, where they entered a large, pre-made foam sausage, big enough to take a number of people together and with space to sit, which Kean explained that was of a strengthened design to enable hydraulic propulsion. This would shunt them like a high speed train north to south through the Ridge. It was a relief to be able to put their feet up and rest for a while. In the gloom of the tunnels, John thought he must have nodded off, for they were very soon disembarking. Another but shorter trek and one of the many globular caves turned out to be the starter pistol for the final leg. At least that was how John was thinking about the skywards journey. The north-south trip had had a jolting beginning, but the mild slope down which they were propelled accounted for most of the acceleration, whereas the shunt upwards would be more like being shot from a gun, and although the foam would cushion them from any crushing forces, it wouldn't eradicate them completely. Perhaps because neither of them were looking forward to being human canonballs, perhaps because of what had gone before, perhaps because they both were preoccupied with the task in hand, perhaps because they thought enough had been explained in words, they donned their gamesets without direct spittle-joining. It didn't seem important at the time.

John knew that they would come out underwater, in a deep cave. The sausage foam would dissipate as they surfaced, but there was every likelihood that there was still a shark circling, so they would need to kick out quickly for the back of the cave and get out, without attracting its notice or that of the guns of the modern-day pirates, probably drug-smugglers, in the ship guarding the entrance. Almost as important as getting themselves out of the water without shark bite or gun injury was securing the equipment. Kean understood that the Mexican boy had been shot and would be unable to dive, even if his bleeding wounds weren't already acting as a red rag to the shark, so the inflatable dinghy they were carrying in the waterproof bag of medical and other equipment would be invaluable. Apparently. Although how Kean was so sure they could get past armed criminals on the watch for people they'd already targeted in something as fragile as a dinghy John was unable to fathom and Kean, with a wicked twinkle that spoke of confidence and humour, refused to elaborate. Maybe it was something to do with a cloaking device.

During the north-south trip Kean had made the biggest revelation John had had to date. Somehow tunnelling, even under vast oceans, didn't really raise the Woods beyond the neolithic culture he had been classing them as, but personalised cloaking devices, using more sophisticated technology than humans had invented, lifted them into the superior beings that had provided Fargo with the basis for the Game. He now wore one of his own, a neck circlet joining a hood, that had a flap that drew over the face, to a cloak, which was full enough to be drawn into loose sleeves and trousers by internal smart-lacing, the way he was currently wearing it, ready for swimming. The shock of seeing Kean become invisible, even close up, mitigated his fear of possible shark and pirate attack. He just hoped nothing would go wrong with their display in the watery environment.

And then it was all for real. *G* forces sloshing his lungs and stomach towards his feet and draining the blood from his brain making him fuzzy-headed and barely ready to react, until the cold cave water slicing by his face refreshed him and he kicked out from the last of the clinging foam and pushed the heavy parcel above him, which Kean in the vanguard had tied to his waist. Then, there was the first breath from leaden lungs, water muddling the darkness of the back of the cave and the blinding sunlight from the entrance, a slither against his leg that might be shark or imagination, a moment of frantic splashing away from it and the light, a brief second of clarity as his eyes adjusted to note that the limestone cavern was not featureless dark and that Kean was already climbing a short but steep cliff into true gloom beyond.

He hung, as motionless as he could at the base of this for what seemed like forever, hefting the kitbag onto one shoulder so it didn't weigh Kean down. His eyes were fixed on his hand gripping the friable rock, almost as glazed as his body, rigid with tension, but they still noted the trail of blood smearing the luminous whiteness and how it was lapped at by the rising tide, each wavelet taking another tantilizing sensation down into the predator's domain, just where his bag-bearing arm bowed into the water.

Suddenly the weight lifted and Kean was pulling the bag up and it was his own turn to leap into action. In this moment of freedom, he twisted to check for the fatal fin, the gaping maw, and saw instead the entrance darken and the noise of the slapping tide was overtaken by the whine of a bullet strafing the water. Galvanized, he scrambled up the rock, this time his back arching against bullets not bites, but both fears lent him adrenalin in abundance.

Apparently, though, the suits were still working and the pirates, perhaps drawn in by the sound of splashing, were just firing at random. Only a few rounds, probably just to deter the single man they believed, correctly, they had already wounded from making an attempt at escape. Or perhaps just for the fun of harassing the shark. They didn't wait to find out, but crept deeper within what turned out to be a labyrinth of dissolved limestone pockets, dripping with ancient stalactites and coralline features.

Galarhas was very like his sibling, especially in the dim green light by which he and his charge were solely visible. Another bioluminescent invention of the Khets, it transpired. However, perhaps, he remembered from something deep in the 'file' passed to him by Kean, although he hadn't held the knowledge in consciousness until now, the distinct sense of gender came from differences in their pheromones.

He had scraped some algae from the walls and packed the wound with it, enough to slow if not stop the bleeding, but the lung was punctured and hypothermia setting in, so Kean was busy for quite some time just stabilizing the boy. Before he started he fished in the kitbag and handed John a gun with instructions to stand guard. He was glad of the rest, not to mention the comfort of the weapon, even though he'd never used one outside a game before, but by the time the others were ready to move, he was near paralysed by the chill in the cave himself and pretty glad he hadn't been called on to leap into action, as exhaustion from the journey and the fear had set in properly. He wondered how they could get past the guards, and realized with some dismay, that, even if they did, since he'd rested longer than the others, he'd have to offer to row first.

This was not the first thing he had to do. That was to aid Galarhas in carrying the stretchered boy, Carlos, while Kean bent nearly double under the burden of the rest of the equipment. And instead of going back out again, they were heading deeper into the cave system.

There was method in this madness, it seemed. They were looking for an exit to the surface, although to the sea might have been more sensible than carrying the dinghy around, John thought. But they were not only meandering through the caves but rising into the hill above, with the way often constricted and the final climb up a chimney, through which the stretcher had to be carried vertically. They flopped out into a natural depression surrounded by bright flowers and vicious cacti, but the sky was once more overhead and they were all alive.

Sadly, it was almost dark, but this gave John momentary hope that they would stop and rest. It was not to be. Kean was of the opinion that Carlos needed surgical treatment urgently, so Galarhas straightway set about inflating the dinghy. John had peeped over the edge of the dell and could confirm that, although maybe no more than one hundred feet above sealevel, they were on the high point of the island, near no stream, and well inland. He was going to point this out when Galarhas unpacked four extensible poles, slotting one mastlike into the middle, and joining the other three side, sloping ones, at a central ring. Then he threw a film of material over the whole and showed John how to tie it to fixings on the sides of the boat. Carlos was gently positioned within, Kean and the kit in attendance, then Galarhas, who with his eleven-foot reach was the only one able to do it, stood on the side of the dinghy and twisted the ring and the entire construction vanished from sight. Apart from Galarhas, now daintily perched in midair.

It was breathtaking, but still landlocked. But John would accept anything now, so he climbed in, they secured the net around them tightly, Galarhas fiddled with something in the base of each mast, and then, effortlessly, with barely a sound above a slight whoosh of compressed air, they were floating. Once clear of the cacti, Galarhas went to the stern and leaned over, there was a puff of ignition and then the invisible craft was zooming westwards at an incredible rate, with the velveteen night and its astral jewellry barely giving chase.

Adrenalin had ebbed away and only a mildly soporific high remained. John watched the sky flow around him, open ocean give way to foliage rising and falling beneath him, then a wide snake of brown water twisting beneath, until they dropped low into the shade of the overhanging trees and all was green darkness.

He didn't mind. He felt like he could listen forever, without paying attention, to the gentle blackbird-like twitter of Galarhas discussing their plans with Kean in the bow. The boy's grasp of human vocalisation and the English language was impeccable, but when he got excited the dual larynx came into play and there was a trill to his tones that a thrush would be proud to thread into a mating call. It was only when the carolling pitched into portentous hootings and crawking that it occurred to John to wonder why the timbre of worry had entered the conversation.

He hitched prow-wards, reluctant to actually stand for fear of capsizing the featherlight vessel. 'Is there a problem?'

The other two men exchanged meaningful glances. Kean drew the short straw. 'OK. You deserve the truth. The plan was to fly back out to sea, once we'd cleared the guns, and go south of the mouth of the Orinoco to a dry tunnel entrance to the tube system. But Carlos here is too badly injured to be subjected to the acceleration forces. He'd bleed to death internally before we got him back to England. So we need to go to Wood Hame, the only remaining overground Wood dwelling place on the planet, where they have the facilities for me to treat him. They know Galarhas, of course, and they'll accept me, as Fargo's doctor, but they don't know about the disappeared. That's not as much of a problem as you might think because I'll be keeping Carlos sedated throughout, and we don't plan to stay any longer than necessary. Just some surgery and an injection of nanites to repair the cellular damage. But – there's you. You're not trained to hide your thoughts and, in the humidity of the rainforest, any physical contact with a Wood could give them your entire life history, and more to the point, everything you've learnt, whether you even know it or not at this stage, from me, the Knights, Fargo. And it appears from what Galarhas has told me there have been some power shifts in the very recent past that we can't afford to let slip. I guess I don't know how much you picked up, but if you'll let Galarhas meld, we'll be able to determine the extent of the problem. However, I have to tell you the Woods don't know that Fargo invented the Game, and that's a big enough secret. So you don't have to go through with it, if you'd rather not.'

'Will it hurt?'

Galarhas laughed like a robin greeting the morning. 'No. It's simply that it's a taboo to my people. Too intrusive, especially to an untrained mind. I'd know everything about you.'

'Boredom is about to set in then.' John presented his temple.

It didn't hurt. It didn't anything. But, within a couple of seconds, Galarhas was shaking his head. 'No!' he said. 'He knows more about the game than I do. And he's played it so often, his mind's full of it, now tagged as real. Any Wood would be able to see Fargo had deeper plans than they're in on. We can't take him. I'm sorry, John.'

'But ... but, you can't just leave me in the middle of the jungle. I haven't even got a passport, never mind money. And I have no idea where we are.'

'Whoa. Slow down. We're not abandoning you. Wood Hame is a hidden world. In a cloud forest, high in the Roraiman tepuis. Sheer cliffs prevent climbers taking anyone by surprize, although there are a number of watchposts high in the canopy and on the hills around, but a huge waterfall hides the main entrance, so the southern side needs fewer scouts. We'll swing round, fly up the river, drop you before we get near enough to trigger the faintest vibration in the keenest sensed Wood, get in, patch Carlos up, and pick you up on our way back. If all goes well with Carlos, I estimate he'll be ready to move in a couple of days. You just have to lie low. We'll leave you supplies, and there's a GPS in the kit, just in case you have to move.

There's a few things you need to be aware of. Piranhas and crocodiles in the river. But it's the natives you really need to watch for. There are few Spanish-speaking in the highlands, and the famous Yanomami avoid the tepuis area, because to them it is the home of the gods who are guarded by their chosen people, the ghosts of the mountains. It is these people, the only humans who still have regular contact with the Woods, that you need to avoid. Their xenophobia is indiscriminating. If they think you might find Wood Hame, a poisoned dart in the neck will be all the dialogue you'll get. So the trick is to lay low. Very. But Galarhas, who grew up here, tells me that around this time of year they're probably not down by the river.

Also, I know this sounds bizarre, but he can emit a blast of pheromones to order, and if you stand right under his armpit while he does it and then rub it all over yourself, - *I know!* But then you won't smell human, so the indigenous tribe should miss you. Just don't wash!'

They must have been travelling at some speed, because dawn was barely beginning to lighten the sky to the east when the craft landed.

It was a different river, but similarly overhung banks that would provide shelter well enough. Kean handed over the small GPS device by which they would track him if he moved. Galarhas showed him how to adjust his cloak himself, and then John had to remove it and his shirt and be doused in sweat. The hard-on he received with it had not figured in Kean's description. As matter of factly as if he did this every day, which perhaps he did, but John did not, Galarhas wiped his own hand in the liquid and thrust it into John's pants, grasped and smeared his penis, which instantly deflated. He withdrew his hand as quickly and, while John was still reeling with shock, although there had been nothing sexual in the gesture, merely remedial, he gave Kean the same treatment. 'Powerful stuff. Forgot to mention.' Kean managed. 'Gender, sexuality irrelevant. Same effect.'

'Won't have this effect on the natives, will it?'

'Only if you meet them in the next few minutes. Once it's sunk into your skin, it'll be fine.' John took this as his cue to start rubbing it in, rather frantically.

Kean passed him three of the multi-flavoured, flat cakes. To divert his boggled reaction to the non-assault by male member, John protested. 'Three? One a day? They taste like whole meals, but three?'

'Didn't they tell you what this is? Heard of manna? Ambrosia? Food of the gods? It's called 'meneh', which just proves how accurate the Judaic oral tradition can be. The Egyptians liquified a non-fungal version of it and mixed it with alcohol for the slaves who built the pyramids. It's good food, builds muscles, lasts, and the alcohol kept them quiescent.'

'Got any alcohol? Could do with a nip to tranquillize me after all this excitement.'

Galarhas was laughing as he climbed back into the boat. 'You English! So uptight. Even the shamanic among you.' *So he'd clocked the diversion tactic. But shaman?* He wasn't being sarcastic, somehow, with all this humidity probably, John could tell that for certain.

'Well, after the rub down, I won't pray for rain, then.' And then they were gone.

Shaman, huh? Perhaps it was a hint to revisit his past knowledge. Well, chimpanzees and probably prehumans nested in trees, so he gathered some big leaves and chose a tree which had an enormous branch overhanging the river. He built a little bivouac in the knot at the trunk end, then, since he was far from sleepy, he crawled out and lay on his back in the algal mattress that cushioned the branch and watched the sun come up.

A few hours later and the novelty had really worn off. He'd reviewed the recent events, examined some of the information now stored in his subconscious by Kean, failed to make a fishing line, although he was quite pleased with his pitcher-plant water container, had identified as many of the local flora and fauna as he could, had slept fitfully for a couple of uncomfortable hours and was thoroughly bored.

Shaman, huh? He stared at the oily sheen of the tea-stain water under the hot sun. The thick reflection of leaves hid the predators that might lurk beneath, but he hadn't seen any, even though his sweat, no doubt still Wood-laced, was dripping from him, regular rain on the water, more than the blood in the cave which had kept the shark interested for hours. You'd think a gaggle *or whatever collective was appropriate* of piranhas at least would have come to see, unless the Woods had managed a relationship with all the creatures of the earth. He didn't reckon so, otherwise they wouldn't have spent aeons hiding from the top predators.

No magic charms, then. Probably just some other interesting foodstuff somewhere else keeping them away. Absently, he tore off a leaf and his restless fingers ripped it into a square, fiddled and folded. He thought he intended to revisit his past, make a model of his spirit-guide, a heron, but his origami skills were rusty and the material not as manipulable as paper. It was becoming something else, as if the form was making itself. Perhaps he was in tune with the forest, perhaps there would be a local animus to lead his spirit, that would reveal itself in the limited plasticity of native plants.

Perhaps not! It was a passable imitation of a manta-ray, the heron-wings having splayed, the tail feathers rolled into a whip, but he was pretty sure he wouldn't see one of *them* in the black river. It wasn't bad, but it wasn't a magic talisman. He let it fall and idly watched it float downstream. It remained on the slowly undulating surface for many yards, but just as it was about to turn a corner and be lost from sight, something broke the surface around it and sucked it down in a split second. Something big, from the ring around the spot and the slight wake in the curve of the bend, maybe ten feet behind it.

A crocodile! He was looking for plated nostrils to breach the water, trying to see through the surface armour of reflections to track the length, when the sculpted leaf reappeared right under his bough. It wasn't bobbing on the narrow nose or the broad back of a crocodilian, it was being held aloft by fingers.

For a long, horrible second, he thought the Indians had found him. But the hand kept on rising and it wasn't like any hand he'd ever seen, including the black-clawed Squire's and the spidery Knights'. It had similarly long digits, but there was a webbing between them and the thumbs, although they looked opposable, were very long, and the grip was crablike, though delicate, the manta-ray-leaf held carefully in sharp claws. The arm to which it was attached was broader than average, but perhaps that was the effect of the flaps, which the Woods had too, but theirs were barely noticeable when standing, this creature's were muscled and black and white, dorsal and ventral, like the very manta-ray symbol between them.

He knew what he was looking at. He knew from the Game, but even in the fantasy, they were the rarest of sights, even if you played their role you never saw another, so scarce had the people of the fourth tribe become. He almost fell off the branch when her head breached.

He knew she was female the instant she expelled her breath vertically and wetly into his face, from nostrils turned skywards, with active pleated edges that could close. They lay below a crested skull, an ovoid solar melon, and above a beakier than human, but, more clearly than their hands, humanoid face. What gave her her 'humanity' lay not in the too-V-shaped jaws, nor the fish-eater sharpening of the primate dentition, but in the eyes that lay to either side of the point of the melon, beneath brows that beetled but were no more pronounced than those of an archetypal, well-chiselled-to-rugged man.

They were huge and rounded, spaced widely by the tilted nasal bridge, and they were pure black, wells without whites, except those you brought, reflected back out, like domed mirrored sunglasses. *Soul-seeker!* And beautiful beyond any woman he had ever laid eyes on, even virtually.

He had hardly had time to inhale when the other powerful arm shot upwards from nowhere and he was tipped into the water, rolled in the curtain of the arm, wrapped and trapped by the other coming round, and drawn into the warm tan depths. He didn't struggle. She was singing, in a tone so high every muscle trembled as if electrically stimulated, but the pressure wave and the wild jazz, that made his head ring with more music than he had ever imagined, confirmed it as acoustic. He'd have been convinced enough of her siren-status without the ultrasonic pings that hit some spot from which serotonin cascaded. And, seemingly through her eyes, (but he knew it was a subtext to the subtle harmonics and, as all his hairs stood on end, to the electromagnetic pulsations) her mind twined round his.

It wasn't like being intimate with Kean, nor Galarhas, nor the carefully-edited uploads he'd received with the inputs from his erstwhile captors. It was like *turning your snout into a fast current,* shutting the front door on the world, *Going Forth*Coming Home; *scenting the hydradesic to the prey*, leaping from rose aroma to Game aromatic mediation, *the Quest*the Catch; *swimming vast tracts of open ocean alone,* walking through city crowds alone, *the Only*the One; *dancing the whorl of the reunited Shoal,* coming back to the surprise party thrown by loving family and friends, *the Only Whole,* the One Whole: *Unity*Union.

Opposites attract even at the genome level. A mind that *spiralled*marched together, thoughts that were *equivalent*opposite, feelings that experienced *relaxation*tension, bodies that curved *helically*rigidly; single sine-wave of a condensated-particle.

It was when they bumped together and his rapt gaze was jolted out of the hypnotic lock he'd fallen onto, he realized he was light-headed, but primarily, urgently-inhalation-challenged and oxygen-poor. His entire length undulated with the spasm, but she did not unfurl his manta-prison, she just twisted deftly and opened her closed nostril against his lips. She wasn't looking at him anymore, the sonic and electrical battery had been ratcheted down to a lullaby, and he still couldn't tear his mind away. He opened his mouth.

When she breathed her life-air into him, he melted, as a result inhaling the gentle, controlled flow, breathed at a natural rhythm, expelling and refuelling with the ingrained, ancient memory of a satiated baby on the teat. It was the most erotic moment of his whole life.

Then, she twisted minutely and he understood that he should take a deep breath. She must reek of fish, salt, who knows what, but her breath was so fragrant and musky that the best perfumier would die to possess its recipe. Casanova would kill for the aphrodisiac effect. Deep breathing, it turned out, was trust, freedom, and better than the most luscious of kisses. When they broke apart, she let him float unaided to the surface, but only to stay below and stroke over his length, curiosity, for the strange form, different textures, scents. *Tastes!* He felt a raspy, catlike, burred tongue on his leg where the cloak, unlooped, had filled with water and dragged up his loose trousers to the calf. He was flooded with her reactions to his skin, through which her sensory mind apparently passed direct.

He sucked in a lungful and dropped down, volunteering for the embrace, face to face. But now her body was speaking directly and explicitly to him, she wanted him to explore it. The urgency was implicit in the current in which their desires entwined, but he sent 'Wait!' and rose to the surface and tore off the cloak and his few clothes, still having the presence of common sense sufficiently to deposit the wet bundle on the bank.

'The real me.' He was naked in her arms. In his whole life he had never voluntarily undressed first. But his own barrelling lower chest only aided buoyancy and an attraction curvature she admired. An admiration not unnatural to someone whose torso has extended over a million years to become five feet long on its own, a torpedo rounded by endothelial blubber, with a thicker neck and fused upper thighs, free-balling at the once-knee into separated tibia and fibula, separately muscled and opening and closing laterally a web of skin between, strong enough to be held rigid and flexible enough to give a huge vertical flap.The individual ribbon-ribs of the toes came after a new ankle-foot arrangement that resembled the whippy tentacles of some squid.

Who ARE sapient. WE *don't eat them!* The authority of a successful Tachyon-Siren, a spiritual edict, policy-making, but there was a special definition to the capitalized plural (in the Heraldic-Lapis matrix of symbols that he realized was the score this music played in) – it was their Soul-Mate pairing. *She had quested far, she had found him in the future and dived down time to the present, and* They *had become* One. She had Cast. She was the Aquamancer, the Shields would shed their black, the *Peregrinatio* was complete, the *Albedo* was upon them, only the *Coniunctio* from which flowed the *Precipitatio* was left.

Mating was trust. Deep breathing staccato-chimes with mild asphyxiation. Their bodies had to flow and twitch to syncopated rhythms that were part their own, part the dance of the river, a strongly-driven partner in these early heights of its youth, invigorating and eddying in turbulent fractals. The species had retained enough genital similarity for him only to wonder, as normal, about size. Usually he wondered if he'd hurt the woman, this was the first time he'd ever questioned if he was man enough in that department. But when she sent supersonic waves of laughter at his balls, delighted at their fragile sac and exotic hirsute display, he found no one had quite brought out the best in him until now. He was as unquerying as she of the immutable fact, they were also Soul-*Mates.*

He was the manta-leaf bobbing downstream, the current of love taking him away, from his clothes and GPS and food and the only people he knew in an entire continent, and he knew it, but he also knew that his Knighthood demanded him to meet the challenge of the *Albedo* and that, if they ever met again, they of all people would understand. Beyond the calling of that destiny lay the real reason, the siren-song that was truly irresistable, that even epic heroes could not, and no normal human should, resist; the ineffable tocsin of oxytocin-idolatry.

He went with the flow.

The flow was wider and stronger than the current drawing John and Zelas to the sea. It was system-wide, although only those who were listening in the particular Harmonic bandwidth were affected, despite the pulsations penetrating all. It was a rousing call to some, a loosing of inhibitions to others, a strengthening of purpose to yet more, an inflammation of passions, a sensing of imminent immanence; every creature vibrating to a resonance that made it more itself and I-*Mage*rs fairly thrummed. The Ydal, as the game's conduit, would have been throbbing immoderately just from the feedback the players were all looping through her, but her excitation levels had leapt way beyond the capacity even of collective-billions of hominin minds.

She might have been designed simply to Cast across universes to find Fargo-others, but to do so the bacterial-basis of her hardware had had to be able to go forth and multiply to manage unknown dataloads. The entire surface of the Moon had been needed to plumb parallel worlds and to exchange Coats with Venus, and, since then, with the inputs from the Wood minds and the Game and all the other things the imaginative Fargo had asked of her, not to mention her own holographic presentation, fully a third of its volume had been reconstituted as the motherboard.

The conversion produced energy, although the modified bacteria were themselves powered by a solar collector carefully hidden on the sunward side and by a hydrogen scoop, and her waste was all recyclable. Now her computational area was doubling by the day. If this carried on, she'd have info-formed the entire Moon pretty soon. She knew exactly what was causing it. Or rather who.

He was coming. Her long-awaited Knight. Her doom. Tolecnal was riding back to Tollahs. If it ended with her floating deceased downstream to Tolemac, she would not turn her eyes from the open casement to watch for his arrival.

She went with the flow.

The flow was overwhelming Tom Wharton, but his interpretation was as individual as the rest. To the Ydal, it was Sir Tolecnal's homecoming, to the General, The Second Coming. The phonecall he put in to Venus, confirming receipt and installation of the twelve precious stones for the Temple foundations and demanding she ship out with the Grail immediately, had dropped the paternalistic tone, even the antique lustful subtext had reverted to Generalissimo, as he totally focused on securing his immortality. He had not expected the fear. Far from it. Even way back in his career, during a tour of Vietnam, in which survival depending on becoming one with the state of anxiety they all lived in and turning it into fighting adrenalin, where the enemy could be behind every bush, and paranoia stalked them with you, he had not felt such an urge to flee. But this was one event for which no one would be absent without leave.

He spoke to Milo, checking in, yes, but also checking his co-conspirator's state of mind. Milo was feeling it too, but he surprised Tom by his joyfulness. Normally defaulting to fretful mouse, something more manly had emerged. Apparently Ruth had abruptly stopped drinking and was neither manic nor depressed, so the atmosphere at the farm was calm, with the exception of Cal, whose demonic lover had gone missing, *he said, probably just a tiff Cal didn't want to face up to, but if the watchful Wood eyes were off the farm for once, all the better for their plans.* More to the point, Milo engaged to accompany Venus, *whether she liked it or not, which was a turnabout in itself*, to collect the Grail.

Wharton kept the call to a minimum, not, as usual, because Milo's whining irritated, but because the absence of it undermined. Milo was sure of his rise in the Rapture in a way that shamed Tom's uncertainties. But then, he reminded himself, Milo had lived such a narrow existence, how could he have had the opportunity to sin and accrue the guilts a soldier, a man of the world, had done. No matter, he was going to gain that world and with it his own soul, and then he would offer his eternal service to his Lord.

As long as this happened before the Arrival, he could afford to deploy the plague as his first act as the fourth horseman, when the rivers of blood the other three would cascade upon the world he would fill with the bodies of the unfaithful and the Harlot's multiheaded beasts. And then the Kingdom would be established upon earth, and he would sit at the right hand of the Throne, from which the pure river of life would stream forever.

So, when his phone went a third time and the voice of the Harlot intoned a quickening doom, he went with the flow.

Cal's normal torrent of words had been halted in midflow by the disappearance of Rowan, but a current within, normally carrying his separate, incompatible loves for the Wood and the woman, now strengthened in force and split. He knew with absolute certainty, although he couldn't have said how, since he'd had no word nor thought from Rowan, the mere absence of which would be confirmation enough of a problem, that Rowan was in trouble. And of all the troubles that could beset the hidden people of the trees, only one, other than death, could take Rowan's mind from Cal. He went to see the little princess in her tower. And he didn't stand on ceremony.

'Where is he?'

He didn't expect her to play games with him. There was too much history and support between them for that. Nor did she.

'We had a situation.'

'What kind of a situation?'

'You could say it was mother versus father and motherlove won out.'

'What mother? What are you talk...? He paused midword. It was the look on her face. Knowing, and, although she didn't seem angry, definitely reproachful. For Rowan's sake, he'd better play it carefully. 'What is it you think you know?'

She snorted, instantly enraged by his foolish attempt at dissembling. 'What do I *think* I know? Nothing. What do I *know*? Have known since I was 15 years old. Is that the Woods stole my babies, stole my eggs and gave me 150 Wood children and 25 Dark clones, not counting those original foetuses and the failed experiments that died in the process. What do I know? I know my father, Wharton, Milo, Bob, Mh'aed, and, of course, Rowan and *you* all colluded in this vicious assault, if not before the fact, then at least to conceal it. What none of *you* know is that I have been in touch with my children for years. That they, and more recently the Squires, all think of me as their mother. And that when Rowan was going to find out this information, it was two of *them* that stopped him in his tracks. Not me. And, if you want to know why, it's because they felt deprived of me and they felt the great experiment was a despicable action, unworthy of the loyalty Rowan had demanded of them.'

He'd probably gone all shades of the rainbow, and he was feeling as sick as in his nightmares of this moment, his legs gave way and he collapsed into a chair. 'What have you done with him? I can't feel him. Is he ... dead?' He was hyperventilating, but he had to know.

As swiftly as she had been fierce, she jumped down off her high horse, and laughed. 'Don't be stupid, Cal. He's still Rowan. And it was a very long time ago. He's just out cold under Dark influences. Mh'aed educated her boys well, it seems. To be honest, he came roaring in here and the kids just reacted. I'm afraid I haven't had a chance to decide what I'm going to do when he wakes up. How do you think he'll take it?'

It wasn't because she had been called Poppy's Little Princess that she was his, it was because she was truly regal. Well, what a real queen should be like. Professional before personal. More concerned with the big picture than apportioning blame. And always willing to learn, even from the little people like him. And it was such a relief to have no more secrets from her.

'I didn't know, you know. Not for years. Not till we'd been together long enough for me to start reading his mind back. He felt really bad about it. You were – are – his great hope for Unification, but you were really young and no one knew if you'd still be his protégé when you grew up. I mean, you were spoilt and wild and had your grandmother's temper. Apparently when you got pregnant and they realized that you were carrying both Wood and Dark babies, the elders got very excited. It had been centuries since anyone had tried to mate between species, most attempts had ended in failure. They had assumed the genomes were continuing to separate and that the likelihood of conception diminished with each generation. You were likely to be some kind of throwback, a fluke. And the children might be the bridge they needed if you failed.

They saw it as their last chance, and the timing, with the plan for the brain-altering virus being in the late stages, even without a crystal skull, was perfect. To them you were just one person, however important as an individual, they had to put the collective, the species, all the species, before the one. You couldn't expect anything else from them, it's just how they think. And they didn't start out to be machiavellian. They'd have been much happier if the natural pregnancy had gone to term, Rowan told me. Only there were signs that the Dark baby was in distress and threatening them both, and they went in to try and save it and ended taking both. But only to try to save them. The Wood baby did live for a few weeks. Then, they knew they could do it.

So they told you that they needed to operate and took the eggs. Wesley gave the go-ahead, you know. It was his idea that your immortal soul would be better served if you were sterile. But he was a coward after the event. Swore everyone to secrecy. And dammit, no one wanted to be the one to tell you. I guess we all just hoped you'd never want your own kids, never ask. But Rowan loves you, you know. We both do. I hope you know that.'

'Yeah, sure. That's not what I asked, though. How will Rowan react?'

'I don't know. I didn't know they were here. He hasn't mentioned them in years. He did say he had to be careful on the subject around me, so I wouldn't forget and drop something in conversation with you. Sometimes I get glimpses that he thinks about them. Nothing substantial. I guess it depends on what you intend to do. I mean, the Woods' idea is that the children and clones distribute the virus and lead the unification process. I suppose if you don't want to stop them doing that, Rowan will get over the shock. If you forgive him, that is.'

'Oh, let's leave absolution to the holy rollers. What I want to know is whether he'll let the kids alone. He's been very possessive of them, not the Squires admittedly, he's got Bob and Mh'aed to manage them, but he's been more than a father to the Knights. Keeping them cloistered and then not even delegating their Inductions to anyone else, which really blurred the paternal role for them, and he's very controlling, dictatorial, something even I never had from him. So...'

Cal felt the world spin about him.

'What? What do you mean? Inductions? Are you talking about first blooding? He deflowered them? What all of them? Even the girls? How could he? He said ... all these years ... that was the point of us, for him not to be Wood-casual, he wanted me to give up trolling for trade, said I was just putting it about out of lack of self-respect, not Woodwise. He said we'd do it together, to make it easier. We both promised.'

He was crying now, too much to talk, not enough to stop his mind from chattering. Oh, he knew the Woods, having separated reproduction from sexual expression, didn't have a taboo against intra-familial copulation, but there was a general agreement that anyone in an authorative position should refrain from first blooding of a minor, so the act was not tainted with coercion. This meant most children, who had after all been exposed to the sight of their elders engaging in all manner of overt sexual behaviours, experimented among themselves. By the time their larval stage was over, at the sunspot minimum usually around eleven years after their conception, the nymphs were proactively partaking in fully-coital activities as part of their natural play. Since they would not be imagos, reproductively capable, for another two cycles, there was no danger of unwanted breeding. It wasn't even a problem once they matured, since the female oestrus had been manipulated to occur only once a decade at maximum, and all together at the midsummer of the solar minimum, when the orgies were held. Obviously, since Rowan had highly prized DNA, he had taken part in the Bloodliners' choice of female fertilization every cycle, but since their partnership had become established, Cal had been invited to these events, not to attempt reproduction, but so the couple could share in the vibe of the most important celebration of life the Woods had.

As far as he knew, although fondling of genitalia was as common in Wood greetings as handshakes in human, these were the only times Rowan had penetrated another being since their pact. To discover that the strain of faithfulness had taken its toll on the Wood would have been one thing. Celibacy was deemed an unnatural state by them, and monogamy a quirk of character, a bit too Day, tolerated but not celebrated.

But Cal had idolized his lover for his restraint, had put him on a pedestal anyway, the things he knew, the way he was, and to discover his abuse of his authority, over all the Knights, was like finding out you were married to a paedophile. It horrified and tainted and left him bereft of all the moorings to which he'd pinned the ship of his life for the last thirty years. What was worse was that he knew, as if he'd read it in his mind, that Rowan knew his actions were a betrayal and repugnant. He knew because the man had never let a glimmer of this secret reach the surface of his mind, even in their most intimate or drunken moments, even in their shared dreamtimes.

The years in which he'd held his lover in awe, the years of unquestioning trust of a superior, the years of belief in the purity of their relationship were undermined in that moment. They hadn't made any promises other than fidelity and truthfulness. They had even agreed that if either strayed, they'd still tell. He knew Rowan would have known anyway. He'd assumed he would have known too, but Rowan could secure his mind, even from Venus. Suddenly, he recognized why Venus had got so good at hiding herself. She'd known her nearest and dearest were her greatest enemies all her life. And, as innumerable snapshots of thoughts broken off in the middle catapulted out of memory at him, he recognized how useful had been his relationship with Venus to Rowan, who could not penetrate the mind of his adult protégé.

Something snapped in his heart then, the dam of thirty years of belief in their love broke, releasing the pent-up waters of a knowledge that had suddenly transformed into false faith. He was spinning in a flood-surge of anger and hurt, the flotsam of Wood practicality, as used up and spat out and kept as a pet as he'd known Venus to be, as he'd always, deeper than deep down, suspected, oh, Rowan said he was just insecure in these moments, that was all he could be to him too. But he'd been right. And Venus had been right. And if it had all, always, been about Venus, the tide of recognition was right to sweep him back to the one safe landfall of her shore. She was the only compass pointing the way in this storm.

So when Venus leant over, hugged him, saying 'I'm sorry, Cal. I didn't know you weren't in on it. I didn't mean to upset you. Shall I take you to him?' he could only croak, 'Let him rot!' and go with the flow.

Rotting was exactly the problem Vi !sjn-ik had been having, stuck here with the relatives, like a rolling stone that has stopped and is gathering moss. He thought of himself as a flow, a force of nature, but his father and his aunt had no time for the returning hero, they were far too busy training his boys. He felt strongly that the Woods should have been more pleased too, at the restitution of the crystal skull, although since the Darks were already onside, and its' effectiveness with humans was poor, as the Conduit had shown, it served only to end his exile. However, he'd assumed that he was going to be the one to use it, to mediate, if not with the humans, at least as leader of the underearth tribe, and that he'd be given access to it, indeed possibly forced to train with it more than his restless nature would like, but it was the Squires who were favoured, even there. Especially the effete, lanky one. Mr Studious. Mr Suck-up. Xl-arn'tz. You could see he was Rowan's first choice for *his* job.

He had almost decided to go wandering again. Almost. But it was hard to leave now he'd got back into Venus' orbit again. Even if it was only to have her snarl at him, as she had, privately, even in the middle of Conduit, when she'd slipped into his mind, the mind that was supposed to be outflowing only, controlling others at the time, and seen beneath the Dark collective flow he was channelling to the lascivious slaverings of his bestial emotionality as his eyes languished upon her for the first time in so many years. She had bared her metaphoric teeth, and the smile had the confidence of the impregnable alpha-fortress she'd become, but that was nothing more than challenging, and she wasn't shocked by his fervour any more, nor physically repelled by his physiognomy. Just because she was wary, warning him off, didn't mean she wouldn't come round. After all, she'd bothered to infiltrate him, which was titillating in itself, showing as it did a level of respect for his power to hurt her. And the warning was about trying force again. It wasn't a complete, tear-the-flesh-from-the-bones kind of hatred of him, as his actions had roused the last time they met. He could use that.

It occurred to him to dream up new scenarios, in which he wasn't required to bite her into paralysis to have his way. In which she would be grateful to him. Maybe getting back at her through her children was the wrong approach. Maybe he could gain her gratitude and turn her loyalty from Rowan to him by delivering her kids to her. Perhaps then, he should forget that the Squires were almost entirely failures as clones of himself and look for their good points, their Day aspects.

He drank some more of the body-temperature *blodvin*, which along with his inactivity was giving him a paunch he noticed, scratching his stomach, and decided he could do worse than offer to train with the boys as a start. They certainly had some superior skills in Wood disappearing acts that would come in handy on any future travels if the whole viral transformation thing went wrong. If it did, humans would be on the warpath, and they could all expect to be exterminated. He would go and see Mh'aed and ask her about the boys' schedule.

He'd always like his aunt best of all his Dark relatives. Perhaps it was an unrecollected affection from his babyhood, when she'd been his wet-nurse upon the death in childbirth of his mother, perhaps simply because she was a gentle quiet woman, a foil in his background to the roaring, cursing ex-sailor that was his fearsome father. It had been a real shock to come back and discover that the disgrace and banishment of the son had led to mutual comforting by the two, so incompatible, representatives of each side of the family. Well, Bob had fallen for Mascut and Mh'aed was reportedly very like her sister, if a little less vibrant, which might appeal as much in maturity as did rebelliousness in youth. In any case, their union appeared to have been a gift to the cloning agenda. Any interest of Bob's in Dark matters could be justified to Venus, so it meant they could bring the clones back from WoodHame once they reached a mature height and Venus would never notice a few more folk living under her headland. Not that anyone thought she was looking. She was far too busy running her company, plotting with Rowan to transform the world, not even in Cornwall most of the time. Why, the Wood-whore, Cal, lived in her actual house, and Mh'aed and Bob moved into Dark quarters directly under it, and still she never knew what deceptions went on under her very nose. Which was strange, given Vi !sjn-ik had always thought she had the quarrying ability of a bloodhound.

So, when he got to Under-Manor-Farm and discovered his aunt and father in an absolute lather, he knew she'd finally got hold of the scent.

He unpicked, from Mh'aed's screechings and Bob's bellowings, that they'd been testing the boys at the Bite market Day-Night just gone and Rowan had noticed Xl-arn'tz was absent. He went to look for him and no one had seen either of them since. Worse, this midnight had been timetabled as an alchemy lesson. A lot of the boys had been pretty excited about it. It was the old trick of producing gold which so dazzled humans.

Vi !sjn-ik had learnt it at the kitchen table from his aunt. Put a solution of gold chloride into a glass and add a handful of the philosopher's stone, which is no more than powdered rock but it contains the living heart of the earth, metal-eating bacteria. The solution turns a glorious purple, as the bacteria shit out microscopic granules of pure gold. You separate the precipitate off, then heat it until the grains meld together to form a lump big enough to see with the naked eye. Tah dah! You are a magician, impressing, especially if you put enough pazzazz into the performance, all the avaricious humans of your choice.

The boys were getting the full *mysterium*, so, when the virally-mutated minds of the humans were disturbed, confused and, no doubt, defaulting to paranoias, the Squires could demonstrate their goodwill along with their power and leadership, in ways the herd of humanity could appreciate. So it was strange indeed when not one of them turned up in the lab.

Bob and Mh'aed had, naturally, already gone to check their dwellings, hoping that they'd all just got the time wrong. The boys were carefully distributed all over Lyonesse, so it took them all night, even using turbochutes to go over to Bite, to visit every home and likely haunt, but they'd done it, before returning exhausted to Under-Manor to regroup. There was no scent of any of them to be found anywhere.

The most they could discover from friends and neighbours was that a few had been seen packing a roll, as if for a journey, but none had been seen to leave, so it was likely they were wearing their cloaks and that their exit was meant to be clandestine. Vi !sjn-ik had to suppress the thought that this was the most Him-like thing he'd known them to do. Sneaking out of a habitation in which he'd got yet another unauthorised female pregnant, before her partner or father found out, was his speciality.

'Look, don't panic, aunt.' He offered, 'They've obviously all gone of their own volition. Perhaps something did happen with Xl-arn'tz and Rowan. Whatever happened, it made the rest run. But they're my boys. They can look after themselves.' He caught the look on his father's face. 'You've seen to that.' he added hurriedly. Then, he heard himself say, 'I'll find them.'

It was a promise. He hadn't meant to make it, but he suddenly saw how, as Bob's eyebrow went up, he just might be able to keep it. 'The Emerald Skull. It's still here, isn't it? When we were in Conduit, I could feel a sort of self-echo. The Squires weren't allowed to take part, for fear of giving the game away to Venus, but the ... I dunno, amplification or something, I barely noticed at the time, guess I thought maybe I was bigger than I thought, but later ... I know their minds resonated with mine, bound to, don't you think? I bet I can find them that way.'

Both his father's bushy white eyebrows had risen now, but the effect replaced cynicism with 'impressed'. Seizing the moment, as ever, Vi grabbed their arms, 'Come on! Let's not waste any more time. Maybe we can stop them before they get far, and find out what's happening.'

He'd forgotten how old his father was, and Mh'aed was at least thirty years his senior. They had already exhausted their budget of energy that night. They would trust him to go alone. He couldn't have been more delighted. Now he'd show them. Again.

The place of Conduit was under the tiny, south-eastern, Scilly Island of Great Arthur. Above ground prehistoric cairns and cup-marked rocks were the last Day evidence of the location of their Grail, and it had amused Vi !sjn-ik that the General had stood in the very same cave in which his most desired treasure lay and never noticed it. He didn't know what Venus was playing at there. Nor did Bob or Mh'aed, who knew all about the General's religious quest and about the true nature of the Day-Grail, but did not know why Venus tolerated him and Milo and their exclusive theology.

Then again, who knew why Venus did anything. He was as near certain as he could be without a scrap of evidence that he'd find Venus was behind the disappearances, but they all remembered her fiery temper, and, despite having seen her taking pains to be cool as an adult, they all believed, if she'd found anything out, she'd have been down to Under-Manor like a thunderbolt, so perhaps he'd be glad to be wrong for once. Still it was a relief to be out of her territory and doing something.

Since Woods were light-folk, in the predawn the cavern was empty. There were three ancient tree-seats and a fourth stone bunk in a sea-pool, each the correct shape to accept the species' Mediator, each depending from the customised helmet of stone into which the skulls fitted. Only two of the crystal mind-sheaths were there, of course. The sun-yellow quartz of the Wood one and the emerald of the Dark one. The fragile Blue-John stone from which the Day skull had been made had probably shattered aeons ago, and it was assumed that, after the final disagreement with the Aquatics, the Ruby lay at the bottom of the ocean, lost forever, like the, doubtless extinct, tribe itself.

Mh'aed had given him some of the bridging gel she'd developed to interface the hybrid physiology with the species-specific skull, so that her nephew and the clones could use it to attempt the management of Day minds, in the absence of their own skull. He smeared it on his temple and gingerly climbed up into the living-timber frame. It was unnerving being so high off the ground, not to mention the drop into the pool to one side, but he positioned himself carefully and plugged in, the weird, tentacle-like tendrils of bio-mind twining around him proving rapidly more disturbing than the height.

Mind swirled around him. It was horrific. Ancient and alive. The uploaded knowledge of all the dying Woods down the millennia, every equinoctial Conduit and its Consensus, all preserved in molten stone, actively looking on itself, waiting to suck his little brain dry for new material. Fortunately, the recent upload of three hundred centuries of Dark knowledge and the need to align its partial information with the unbroken history that the Wood data represented, was churning its attention, so it loomed less than when he had been Mediator.

He did need more training, though, that was clear. It was hard to do anything but broadcast everything and wait to see if that echo came back. Plus time was different in the Mind - in anyone's mind, if you couldn't notice it passing incrementally in the external world. Here, thought Was, so time went with it.

He looked at his people running with the Neanderthals into the hills away from the killer-cousins, and he looked at the post-atomic

Consensus at which the Woods determined upon the remutation of humanity in consecutive timeframes. After a while, he managed to get back to Now, to Him, to Him-Now, in Mind. It was a major achievement to locate individual presence. His mental stature obviously came naturally. He began to feel himself Larger. The breadth of his shoulders, the masterly carriage, the incisive twitch of his nose to a scent, oh, yes, he was a hunter, he was the ronin, he was the male, he was Alpha.

He was in the orgy again. Exhausted limbs draped everywhere. Despite the overwhelming Wood pheromonal drenching they sweated in, his nostrils fibrillated to *her* scent. He dug, mole-like, claws out, pawing aside, scratching down to get to her hole. His malehood was on fire, blue with blood, driving him to release his ardour.

There were willing vulva spread all around. Wood-women who had no inhibitions, Wood-women sending their lust direct to his brain, offering themselves, wanting to try the rough dog panting. As many Wood men caressed his penis, sucked at his ears, licked his arse with thrilling tongues, but he ploughed on through. Then, at last, there she was.

She was spread wide, eyes glazed, looking so lovingly at Rowan, who had just pulled out of her. Her ecstasy was enraging. It should have been for him. He bit on Rowan's enormous timber as he dived past him, shooting paralysis and laughing at the thought of his frozen erection.

His mighty digger's hands pulled apart legs that had urgently clamped together, his teeth tore blood from her breast, and how she struggled, how she screamed, how her squeals excited. He plunged in, hard as stone, deep as ocean, bone banging bone, flesh stripping under claw, blood spurting taste inflaming tongue, down, down, down until his body arched, his insides turned out, his teeth sunk the death-blow, carotid-cutting, and he shook the very earth with his passion.

What had happened next had been a bit of a blur. Satiated, he'd been pulled off, but, as he recalled, simply held down by distraught Woods, as they rushed to aid Venus.

But here, in Mind, he was seeing something else. Here, which was never now, other times came, altogether, overlaid, all the other times in his travels when he'd played rough with some other alpha's unattainable mate or daughter.

And here, in Mind, he was feeling something different. Here, other minds came, angry minds, disgusted minds, revolted, rejecting, repudiating his name.

His minds, his *other* minds.

For a split second, he thought he must be going mad, he'd never felt remorse, he never thought playing rough was rape, he never wanted to be someone different from himself. But now he did. Now the echo was not of Him, but Anti-Him.

In the same way he had felt Larger, now he was being shrunk by the Largeness that came from without, bigger and more powerful than him.

Now the viewpoint was a mirror on his actions. Now he was the bitch. *He* was invaded by stony-wood, now his fur was flying, his skin peeling, his lips tearing. Now he was clamped by strength that would not release, his body the prey, his will irrelevant, his innards merely a receptacle, his back breaking, his neck vulnerable, his death not shaking the world; deserved.

He was not Large, not Alpha. He was less than nothing. He was terrified, crouched, surrounded by a baying pack, who would have his neck.

He felt himself lifted by a penis that had enlarged at the recollections and now flopped his disgrace to the world. He found himself flying, hurled from his perch, into the Atlantic drowning cold. Time was moving forward again. The water was real. But the reflection not yet solid.

He was broken by those eyes in the mirror; his eyes, twenty-five pairs boring into his skull. And there were more; misty, unseen, the offspring of his passage in the chambers of the world, reproaching him for their mother's suffering and their fatherless lives.

He should die, they all said. He should not be allowed to walk underearth and rape and maim and kill again. But, they said, we are not you, father-brother, not killers, and hands plucked his last liquid inhalation from his choice, took his last chance of abnegating by suicide, and hauled him from the water.

He stood, dripping, shivering, in the cavern, precisely where they'd placed him. The pack circled, teeth bared. The mind-gel worked through all this humidity and he couldn't have mistaken the grimace of even one for a smile. No forgiveness was in their minds.

He was meat, a present for their mother, they would take him to her, neck bared for her judgement. But first, his flesh would pay what his mind had yet only imagined. For they *were* his clones. And they *could*.

'Down!' they commanded. As his blood gushed and their semen spurted, his screams went unregarded in the pumping flow.

The torrent of highly-energetic particles flowing into the system had finally stopped, but the cessation of acceleration only changed the charged current to a widespread electromagnetic field, both effects of which were impacting on the Cognimatans parked in Europan orbit. The Archivist had continued to upload information from the Netspore at the Legrange point for as long as he was able, but it had become obscure by noise some time ago, and, as the field extended inwards, the Ship's own long-range scanners had suffered similar interference. Panicking, as the Weapons were almost ready to detonate in response to what to them computed as a direct attack of unknown origin, he had linked up to Dakul's relay of the Ydal data from Earth in order to gain any insights she might have.

If the news had been less disturbing, he might also have noticed when Quogat went into quiet meltdown. But he didn't have time to wonder at the curious effects of the wave on all the individual players in Fargo's earth-game. There was a serious problem, and although the information was in the Ydal's global transmission, there was no indication that she'd even noticed it, never mind passed it on to Fargo for action.

He had, of course, been monitoring Earth space-politics. Last year NASA's agreed launch date for the Europa probe had been indefinitely postponed. Money. Budgets. It was a strange way to conduct a world. No one seemed to have a clear strategy. Still, it had come as a welcome relief, giving everyone breathing room to finalize their plottings. Then, without a debate appearing on any agenda he could access, the Chinese Space Agency, whose scheduled launch had been to carry a Jupiter orbiter only, announced that they had done a deal with the European Space Agency, who were apparently bitter at NASA's decision to mothball their finished JIMO probe, and replaced the faulty orbiter just prior to launch. NASA was selling their rebuff as a scandal, saying that their commitment would have taken the time and money to ensure sterilization of the probe was complete and that the rushed launch meant this could not be guaranteed. The Archivist had never judged the procedures NASA had outlined were foolproof in this department, but the alternative sounded positively dirty.

However, most of the debate centred around acrimony concerning theft. It always astonished the Archivist that the humans had the concept of intellectual property, the idea that knowledge was not for sharing. (Although not as much as some of the antics he found posted on the internet by proud participants, such as 'extreme ironing' which, if his programme ran forever, he would not be able to compute a motive for.)

The accusation was that the CSA had taken a US design for the fastest spacecraft to date, a nuclear-powered one, that NASA had intended to get a ship to Pluto, and pre-empted the ground-breaking launch with a less-tested rocket, not to mention the inadequate safety measures to protect the earth had it exploded on or just after lift-off. Worse still, from the Cognimatan's point of view, was the news that this rocket would do 10 miles per second and therefore would get the probe to Europa in just over a single Terran year. And, since the secretive/diplomatic Chinese agency had released the information only as an entry to its end of year report, that meant it would reach the ship's Weapons range in just 175 days.

The Archivist did not know what to do. By rights he should pass this data direct to the Weapons. The only reason they did not know about it already was because they had been monitoring launches from the third planet since the ship's arrival, and it now appeared the lift-off had taken place a mere twenty-two days before they had popped into the solar system. Oh, they could see the rocket coming towards the Jovian network, but the prior data had indicated the flyby as innocuous, nowhere near the Legacy. Of course, he wanted them to destroy the contaminating probe, but if he informed them that the aggressive deed had been done before they had arrived, he was quite sure that, since they could not currently communicate with the Fleet in Perseus, their position would be that the original contract with Venus was invalid and that they should immediately begin the eradication of the threatening species. Apart from a sneaking suspicion that his fascination with the hominins was pushing him towards a bias for them that might undermine his logic, it was still true that the current threat was merely bacterial, and it was still possible for Venus to execute her plan to eliminate the human threat for ever.

He quite desperately wanted to be able to get in touch with the woman. Isolation had not become routine. He was meant to be part of a greater whole, and not one whose sole purpose in existence was to destruct, especially the 'self' destruct aim. The one thing that had made this exile bearable was definitely not his fellow programmes, but the contact with his research subjects. This had been mediated via the Netspore and the Ydal antennae but without these he was operating alone. No Cognimatan was created able to take unilateral decisions on behalf of the majority, except in extreme emergency, which this clearly was not, as yet. But his impulse to forward on his knowledge was sound, it might prevent a crisis of inter-global magnitude in the future. So far the strong magnetosphere of the Jovian complex had protected the inner planetoids from the full impact of the interference. He could still make contact with the Dakul antenna, and the field hadn't spread in as far as Earth yet, so they'd be receiving.

The question was whether, even with amplification, he could find a gap in the field or a conduit through the current that he could send a message down. The more he studied the problem the more obvious it became that the reason that he wasn't getting through to the Ydal was not, as with the Netspore, because of the force in the way, because it wasn't yet. The reason he wasn't getting through was because *she* wasn't listening.

He needed someone who could hear him, but no one on Earth spoke ancient Martian-modern Cognimatan machine-code. And Dakul was too worried about his sister to hear the urgency embedded in the defleshed messaging, unlike humans whose use of disembodied symbols, words and numbers, would have instantly recognized that the binary was shouting at them, like a text in capital letters.

It wasn't that Dakul didn't receive the contact, but Quogat was in the process of killing herself, having bored upwards through the icesheets to the Europan surface, waiting for the Current to arrive. All Dakul could suggest was that the Archivist try to use his transmitter to 'send' in Heraldic, that way anyone on the telepathic waveband could pick it up and get it to Venus.

Heraldic had formed part of his studies, of course, since it was the one solid plank in his defence of the species, that they were moving towards a common frame of reference in which to conduct their affairs. But he couldn't transmit any of the sensory components of a

Gist, much less a Blazon or entire Coat. He was trawling his library files for any ideas that might serve instead of Heraldic, when his updating subroutine flagged up an item in the recent Fargo folder. Data had been passed through the game, which translated into binary at base level, and it had conveyed information, even though the messaging was a mere thread, not coat. The blessed reductionism of words, without the redundancy of sensation, visualisation, feeling, leaving the reading to the receiver. Yes, there was an obligation to contextualize and get the grammar right, but it was little more stringent a protocol than logic gating. He could probably compose a brief collection of words, work out their Heraldic harmonics, and perhaps the pattern to hit the appropriate receptors in the brain they should be directed to stimulate, and send them using only the acoustic techniques of JakeWynn.

He interrupted Dakul's vertical haul again. He should be warned not to be listening in, because the Archivist would effectively be turning up the mental volume to maximum, although on a narrow beam signal to get through the complex interference pattern, so easily avoidable, and, since aimed away from the planet, undetectable to the subsurface Europan community. But he might want to get up there and check Quogat wasn't in line for the blast.

He also wanted to check that his research was correct and confirm with Dakul that he had chosen the best recipient at which to direct the information. Dakul, who as a member of a connected species, understood very well the need to have even one ally, when going out on a limb, was sympathetic, and in agreement. If he wanted the message to get to Earth before the charged field shut down all communications, he had to send it at full intensity, on a repeating loop of clear instruction, to the best receiver on the planet.

The message was simple. 'The Creator is silencing Song. The Red Dragon spits fire and doom. Alarum: send to the Queen.' He was rather proud of his first attempt at the form: it flowed.

The recipient heard it loud and clear, she just interpreted the modern form of Heraldic-via-Europan/Cognimatan translation slightly differently. Everyone knew the Creator was just anthromorphism for the life-giver, in the ancient, the Mother Sea herself. If Song was being silenced, that meant that oceanic minds were endangered. Everyone also knew that the metaphor of the great flying snake that breathed fire referred to an impact event;

comet, asteroid, meteor, the effects were the same – death. And she only knew of one Queen, the fabled Iceberga, keeper of the knowledge of the Ground Real, Magespring to the lost lineage of the original Whorlingas.

Her flow stopped dead in the water.

It was as well for John that it did. He wasn't near death, but he was physically exhausted, his skin had crinkled into the semblance of a seaslug, his exposed shoulders and head were already peeling, and his overheated brain, both from sunstroke and melding overload, was reeling. If their passion had continued unabated, they would have swept out to sea, where, without drinkable water, his fate would have been assured. Zelas was young and excited and basking in the joy of being no longer alone, and she hadn't really noticed her lover's deterioration. Now, brought up short by the Ensign, which, though it was merely a Tattered Flag, less informative than a Gist, was clearly a True Portent, relayed by a genuine Harbinger, she nosed along the length of their situation and discovered his true state.

They were in the wide delta of the *nigredo* water where the reassuring increase in saltiness told her the sea indundated from nearby. On the way in, there had been a choice of many labyrinthine windings between the fabulous towers of timber, living rock that thrust fins aloft and sprouted weed until the very sun itself was hidden; John called them mangrove trees, and he was very glad to haul himself up into the buttressed root-fins of one and rest. He was even more glad to know that, since her species retained an ancestral habit of giving birth on land, although she felt herself ungainly and exposed thereon, she could lie out in the strangely crisp foliage alongside him. Here they mulled over the Flag, in between her gasps at the extraordinary lifeforms visible here. She had never seen creatures that bore four legs stiffly under them like these capybaras, although they weren't so very different to sea-otters once you looked closely, and, of course, she'd seen seabirds, but never such a variety of shape and colour as displayed in the trees here. However, it was the monkeys that took her breath away.

Oh, she knew that since time had passed and evolution affected all, these were not the original forebears of the hominin races, but to see the type of creatures from which all lineages had flowed and to look at the differences between them and her hairless, bipedal lover and her own aquatic adaptations, and then to be swept downstream by the similarities so apparent, shared by them all, was yet another dream come true. If the Ensign hadn't been calling her to a most urgent and important quest, she could have stayed forever, learning their glyphs of gesture and grunt and uncovering the Meaning that would bind.

After an hour or so in the regenerative shade, John's brain seemed less fuzzy, his muscles less tense with lactic acid, and he sat upright as if about to rise to go somewhere. She now learned that this was merely an attentional gesture of his species, the straightening of the torso indicating a renewed mental concentration. He wanted her to start from the beginning, which was a strange request as she was not the repository of all knowledge formed in the universe's history. Apparently, there were going to be many eddies in their communication. He really just wanted the Gist of the Iceberga legends.

The story the elders told pups would do, at least, initially.

Once upon a wave, when the Whorlingas were young and the Shoal was One, an Aquamancer was born. The elders knew she was a Chronoseer, the first Tachyon-Siren, that legends told would find the Ground Real in which eddyless Calm would be their eternal home. They cast her forth as Lore required, but because they feared her powerful Lures would lead the Shoal astray, they did not bind her to Knighthood at all, banishing her from their orbit until she found the Greal.

Everyone who had ever bobbed aloft on the skin of the ocean knew the world was round, and everyone who had ever dived to the find the bone of the planet knew the inner sphere had a plated exoskeleton, with fiery edges where the scales overlapped one another. Everyone also had been taught that once there was only one Land and one Ocean that circled it, although since that time the Land had fractured and the Ocean streamed, but the Whorlingas schooled that at the centre of the Original Ground lay the pool in which life itself had evolved.

The new Tachyon-Siren had disagreed.

One day, she returned from her travels with the news all had been hoping for. She said she had circled the globe and gisted meaning even from the rocks themselves. She said that the scales of the world renewed themselves in constant movement, that life had evolved in the ocean, and that there was no ancient Ground Real, with the much-desired Eddyless Calm lying in the future not past. She argued against its pursuit, saying it was a dead-end ambition, a genetic-memory of being Landlubbers, a desire that froze the heart, a deathwish.

She also said she had Cast and she knew exactly where to find it. But she refused to share the location. She was tired of being alone. She wanted the Shoal to accompany her to the doom that was all she believed they would find in their fanciful Harbour.

The demand split the Shoal.

Some of the priests could not believe that she was right, that the goal of their lives was death. For them, despite the fact that they were obliged by ancient mores to have faith in the findings of the Aquamancers, it was easier to abandon their trust in an individual than in an entire creation creed. They refused to follow her.

Others believed that the place she had found, however fearful it appeared from here and now, once experienced, would be discovered to be the Greal. For them, alchemy indicated that ways were winding, appearance deceiving, and the *precipitatio* of the *aqua libre* unpredictable. They wanted to take the Shoal and follow her to wherever her Casting harpooned.

Worse, the arguments between the priesthood undermined their authority, and the reproducers, warriors, musers, even the children, were all in a whirlpool.

The Siren gave them until the end of the breeding season, there in the atolls of the South Pacific ocean, to decide and then, when the children were strong enough to be seaworthy, with a promise of a bounty of tuna to replenish the depleted fat stores of the mothers against the cold, she headed south. Still undecided, the Shoal defaulted to travelling in her wake, and, indeed, her promise of largesse held true. Then they were in latitudes more southerly than ever before and the roaring winds that they could cope with by diving more gave way to furious weather that churned the very depths themselves.

How could Calm lie this way, many asked. The Siren told of worse to come, winds that shrieked, counterpointing cold that clawed the bones, but swore that beyond lay the Greal that would belong to them alone. It was too much. It was death. Blood-freezing. Just as the Siren had predicted.

Some of the mothers had already lost weaker children to the waves. No one wanted to lose more. In the end, the solution the

Siren offered was pragmatic enough. The majority of the Shoal should return to their normal haunts, but she demanded all the Knights should attend her on her journey, except for a single pair, who would be tasked to scout for the Shoal and keep it safe and fed. They would meet again at the breeding grounds the following summer and truth would be shared.

Next summer, the Shoal arrived at the coral islands at the appointed time to the most extraordinary sight. A small mountain of ice lay in the largest lagoon. It must have been a glacier's worth to have survived its trip into the warming north.

On the ragged base of the irregular pyramid was an arrangement of strange, empty shells, surrounding a circular plug. Obviously, someone had left the glyph to mean that this was an entrance. The male Knight took time off from his nest-duties, for his partner had been chosen as one of that year's reproducers to ensure the continuation of the Knightly caste should the Siren-followers not return, and dug up into the berg.

It took some time and when he returned, his face was glowing. Inside, he told, the tunnel was vertical, narrow and hollow, air-filled, a construction worthy of the best Aquamantic engineer, and the sea entered with him through the opened plug and pushed him upwards. Then, near the top, there lay a ring of holes around the sides, which decanted the rising tide downwards into other channels, leaving him high and dry. Above him was another ring of shells and another plug. Upon digging through this ice, he found himself in a tunnel that lay horizontally, but only for a bodylength. Then it began to curve, spiralling downwards tightly, around the original vertical chute, he thought, until it spilled him into a tight chamber, filled with the purest, freshest, coldest water he had ever drunk. *Aqua Libre!*

There was no sign at all of the missing Knights, no indication of how the iceberg had got there, but no one doubted who had brought it. No one doubted either what it contained. Although, it did have a strange taste to it, that no one who took the trip within, and they all did, carrying the smallest babies so none missed the chance, recognized. Then they waited. To see if the Knights came, to raise their children, to savour the gift.

It was three weeks before they began to realize what it did. Three weeks in which nursing mothers stayed fat, three weeks in which bulls and babies grew big and blubbersome, three weeks in which they began to feel hotter and hotter, in which they dived deeper, sought shaded reefs more, swam swifter. Then came the pull southwards. It was irresistable and this time they did not refuse. She was calling them through the water she had delivered to their very blood, her Song pulsing through them with every heartbeat.

They came to the place where the winds screamed her name, Iceberga, Magespring, Queen of the unreachable Calm, CurrentScenter of the Greal itself. And they knew they were near, so near. But though they circled the entire Ice Continent with the vast whales that sieved the plentiful krill off its deep shores, they could not find her, nor any scent nor sign of the Greal Knights either.

They had received the water that enabled them to live in these waters without their blood-freezing and their muscles seizing, and they were changed beyond return, but they understood. Their lack of faith had condemned them to live forever, banished, as they had Her, from the Shoal that called them, from that Calm that bound them, from the Ground that made them Real. They became the Unreal to themselves, the Ghosts of the Whorlingas, in which Faith was the key by which, one day, they would find their way back to their destiny, to the Ice Queen and the true Knights.

It was a cautionary tale, and though Zelas had enjoyed it as a child, and did not actually disbelieve it, her own experience told her that it was more likely to be the Siren's choice, rather than lack of faith, that had excluded the Shoal from whatever place she had found. Whether that choice was to be revenged for her own exiled years, or to prevent them from the death she and her knights were facing in the unknown cold, Zelas would not guess, but the story itself cautioned her fey mind against the common current to question blind faith in any Aquamancer, most of all the most Feyrie, like her and Iceberga. Look, and now, shamefacedly, she confessed to John, what happened to the Shoal in my care.

She had expected to lose him then, that he would dive straight back into the water and head upstream to his bipedal friends, disgusted by her carelessness. But he was her true knight, had taken her colours, had bonded his fealty, and yet, he stayed not for that reason, but because he saw no wrong, only happenstance in her actions, agreeing wholeheartedly with her position that science should be sharing, should not be faith. More, he had faith, not *in* anything, but a commitment to *keeping the faith*. To him, reeling though he might be under an onslaught of vivid alien-viewed images, scents, tastes, mores and memories, it was still blindingly obvious that her duty, *their duty,* was to find the Queen and relay the warning that had been entrusted to her. And, since he was improving hourly in his game-honed understanding of multilayered communication, in mining their strata of data more accurately, he was adamant that he knew Her location.

So now Zelas was charged with the challenge to trust him. There was no doubting this had to be a true Quest. For he could not go where he knew the Queen to be, not by water, not naked and not without antifreeze in his blood.

He said the White Southern IceSea was called Antarctica. He said that beneath its mile-thick glaciation lay a vast sealed system of freshwater lakes and rivers that the humans had mapped from space. He said most lay in the west of the icesheet, and that there, where warmer currents and temperatures were melting the frozen cliffs of aeons, they might find a way in.

The quickest, and to Zelas, the most frightening route they could take were the Wood turbochutes, but he didn't know if they went that way. Zelas had to admit, despite her fear, that she did know. Sonar could pick up many subsurface features, and she had passed over the tunnels all aquatics recognized as their ancient cousins' work many times in her travels. Most recently, as confirmed to John by Kean, the surface junction at the Orinoco mouth. There were tubes there that led north, west and south. And, there were seamounts that broke into the sky in the southern ocean into the base of which the same Wood tunnels rose.

He did not know what he would do when he got there, nor how they would find the entrance to the Queen's complex, but there was no question, they would go together, sharing a single foam shroud, and take what adventure should befall them.

There was just one courtesie he must oblige before he was hers to command. For he served another Queen, to her surprize the humans had more than one, and this one was also the embodiment of legend, the Regina Obscura, foretold in myths that the Woods, with whom the Aquatics had communicated for many centuries, kept alive, who would reunify all the hominin clans.

No Aquatic believed that tale, for how could it be possible that Landlubbers would take to the sea, or Aquatic reconquer the ground. Still she caught him a squid and watched him, when they had finished their drop, via an underwater entrance south of the Orinoco delta, into the junction cave, use its ink to put marks on the walls, marks that conveyed meaning in ultragisted form. The strange form inspired her to draw her own version of the Tattered Flag, both in a threadlike set of glyphs she made up in Hydra-Heraldic and in dots representing the form of the Harbinger-wave itself.

Then they huddled together, while the fearful foam encased them and the automatic mechanisms made their Cast for them, and were tossed into a solid current of hot blackness, that seemed like reversion to pure *nigredo* itself. But in their hopeful, joint-minds'-eye, all was cold, all was light, all was white, as they held to the wI-*mage* of their icy *albedo* in the undiscovered blindingly-white country, the future-present destination of the Tachyon-Quest.

E: ALBEDO:
INFLATIO AND CIRCUMAMBULATIO

Venus was fed up of the entire human race. Actually, her dissatisfaction was rather more widespread even than that. She'd have happily seen the back of every creature with a mind at just that moment. She'd had the perfect plan, and, after she'd done some backdoor work with the NASA bureaucrats to stall the Europa launch, all the tangled webs she'd woven were on course to come together at one time. In time. Before the Cognimata blew the planet away. And there didn't seem to be any way to contact them to stop them. In fact contacting the Net or the Archivist or Quogat and Dakul seemed currently impossible, which had resulted in a complete meltdown on Ida's part. Still, at least that had poured cold water on the heat emanating from the renewed coupling of Jake and Dinah, although Lily's discovery of her own betrayal was continuing loudly. As for the debacle with Rowan and the worse with Vi !sjn-ik, the children seemed to have taken matters into their own hands. Hardly surprizing, since she hadn't shared the full breadth of her plotting, but the timing was as precipitous as the Chinese launch.

Everyone was over-stimulated, as if some pheromone was driving them to excitement. It was fear in Rowan the cool, impatience in Wharton, backbone in Milo, sobriety in her mother, loyalty in Cal, fateful libidinousness for glory and satiation in Vi, and satyric anger in the ascetic Squires, whose eye-for-an-eye, or more especially, tooth-for-a-tooth morality had displayed in terrible cold revenge. It was passion in Xl-arn 'tz and Pereduri, Jake and Dinah, and, according to the last download from the Ydal, in Herself and Quogat, and then Kean had come with news of it affecting Ranger and her only link to the lost Aquatic tribe.

Even while he was ranting at her, berating her for everything from disappearing Dinah in the first place to reuniting her with Jake, she had thought she was immune to whatever was affecting everyone around her. She didn't suffer guilt, having worked on blocking the paralysing sensation donated by the Brethren upbringing since the day she rejected it, so she was only half-paying attention, browsing the news sites as more evidence accrued of heightened emotional outbursts happening worldwide. The world situation had been volatile before, now it was about to go up in a blue light. Well, she hadn't planned this chaos, her own would be much more structured, but, as fragile peace treaties crumbled and hiatuses in terrorist activity ended, it certainly looked like the General was about to get his rivers of blood without any help from her. So she was kind of short with Kean.

'Look, I didn't make you marry a woman who was in love with someone else. As far as I knew, Jake was history. All I did was introduce you. OK, and him. You should take the rest up with Dinah, not me.'

'I did.' The tone was portentous. Venus was in no mood for more mystery. She chose to interpret it as pretentious and quosh further intimate details.

'Good. Well, if that's all, I've got to be getting on.'

'That's not all.'

She sighed and gave in, swinging her chair round to face him fully. 'OK. Say what you've got to say, but make it snappy. There's a world of pain to deal with out there that's got something more of a priority in my book than a single relationship.'

Then he really took her by surprize. 'What if that single relationship is your own?' and he leaned in and kissed her. It wasn't a tentative peck, it was the kiss of a man reclaiming his woman by rights. *Droit de seigneur!* she thought as her body responded with the relief of finding itself, finally, in the right universe. When her mind remembered, or chose to remind herself, which universe she was really in, she started to pull away but he took hold of her hand and brought up a pot of the interface gel, his eyes demanding the sharing. He dipped his index finger in the pot and put hers in his mouth, then he rubbed the combined saliva and gel on their temples, and kissed her again, with even more confidence than before.

It seemed *he* had been suffering from guilt. It seemed Dinah had too. They both were honest enough with themselves to recognize that they had married eachother for the wrong reasons. Oh, Dinah had given up Jake and the rest of her life for Venus and all she could offer, and she alone had been privy to the fact that Venus had given up her interest in Kean to her, in order to minimize her distractions. And there was no doubt that they had found love and solace and companionship and good sex with eachother, but Dinah had not realized until long after they were married that the company doctor had come to work for Venus for totally unprofessional reasons. Not until, in what had seemed mere experimentation and hardly abuse of the secret technology their status in the Fargo dominion had given them, Dinah had used the telepathic gel to dreamwalk her husband.

She had convinced herself it was a therapeutical tool to gain insight that would aid him. Once a week he woke sweating in the night. All he would ever share was that he'd been having the same dream as long as he could remember, but that, whereas in his youth it had been warming and wonderful, now it was a nightmare of loss. Anxious to uncover an early trauma and unlock his sometimes cold, if always gentlemanly, demeanour, Dinah dabbled.

It wasn't a dream at all, she realized. It was *seepage*. An alternative reality bonding him to Thursday Fargo, who in this life was Venus, a different woman, but an indistinguishable twin in his dreamworld. The nightmare was that he lived in the reality where Dinah had clipped his wings, while Fargo, flying free, spiralled further and further from his grasp.

That had been the last time Dinah had shared minds with her husband, even when he was awake and willing. She couldn't afford him to glimpse the truth of the matter. In his dream he no longer had any chance with Venus, so she didn't want him to know that Venus had introduced him to his wife with the express intention of them hooking up, so that she herself wouldn't succumb. She also did not want him to know that this act of pandering had been acceptable to her, that she had missed Jake more than she would admit and that any kind, handsome man was the very distraction she, if not Venus, desperately needed. But then Kean had got the full download from Ranger, and he had seen the yearning beneath the polite surface Venus turned to him, and now he had been accorded the final explanation, total melded truth between husband and wife for the first time, and he knew all he had to do was break down her resistance to meet the soulmate he would cross universes to find.

As kisses went, it was superior, deeply stirring, and Venus let him feel her reflex surge to that meeting, the depth of her desire, the loneliness of her informed position. Then she let him feel the cold steel of her resolve, the murky depths of her plans, the isolation required by her former choices and the culpability for those future ones that she would bear alone. He was barely put off, never mind knocked back. So she had to be cruel, as much to herself as to him, to be kind.

'I'm not Thursday Fargo, I'm Venus. The person you're in love with doesn't exist in this universe. I know it's hard to believe, I feel the strength of the echoes too, as you can tell, but it is true.'

When he wouldn't believe her, when he was anguished at his rejection, when he was pleading for the love he felt in her to be directed his way, impatience bit her too and she twisted the dial up a few notches and showed him not her Plan, but the implication of it; that there would be a Final Solution, and it would be Hers.

They were in her outer office. Galarhas was upstairs in the lighthouse, but she knew his nostrils would scent her gel-Cast call. Even as Kean recoiled in horror, even as he turned to throw up, neatly as ever, grabbing her wastebasket for the task, Galarhas was through the door and biting his neck.

It's no way to treat the love of your life, even if you know you're in the wrong cosmos for consummation, and after he'd taken the unconscious body to stow with the other prisoners in the Hazmat level cells, Venus allowed herself a full five minutes to mourn, tears and rocking and retching, then she took a grip on her chair arms, inhaled deeply for a few minutes, blew her nose heartily, cleared her throat, and picked up the phone.

It was a seven-word, one-sided conversation, to Wharton. 'It's time. Rivers of blood. Come now.'

His time had come! He corrected himself hastily, even in his secret heart. **His** time had come! But in the interminable tedium of the plane journey, the hubris he hoped He was not currently paying attention to kept rearing its ugly head. The flashes of self-serving images that impacted the mental retina he construed as cast up by the evil subconscious, the originally-sinful emanations of the body, and, as he tried manfully not to indulge them, or to banish them quickly, he believed they would not be seen by his judging Lord as culpable errors. And, once he was back in the country in which

Joseph of Arimathea had hidden the grail, an escort of the Knights of the Augmentatio and of the Squires Coagulatio would walk him in stately procession with Venus on his arm and seal him in a hermetic *vas unum coniugium*, the perfect grail-vessel that would distill his spirit into the *aqua vivum.*

He tried not to vivify the image any further, for, to be perfectly honest, getting Venus into this blissful spiritual scenario was becoming increasingly impossible as the time drew nearer. It wasn't just that the time was up for her being saved. It wasn't even his own hopes, which at their best and worst were overlaid with a paternalistic habit and only haunted his wildest dreams. It was simply Venus' own character. He kept wondering what exactly her version of the 'rivers of blood' would actually turn out to be. Oh, he'd subtly fed the dissatisfaction with the human race that her early education in non-human alternative people and cultures had given her, even while knowing she did not believe in original sin, nor have the solace of eternal life to fall back on. But the fatal pandemic, the subversion of the Wood ideal that Wesley had aligned himself with, was angrier. Although it fitted with his own prescription for a holocaust, he had rather thought up until then that his stewardship of the planet would leave the killing fields up to his Messiah to orchestrate upon arrival. But when the Wood tunnelling techniques opened up the possibility of being as instrumental in the Coming as reconstructing, covertly, the Temple, he had climbed into the driving seat along with his gunner, Venus, and the juggernaut had rolled off towards the battle.

Mostly it had seemed more an adventure than a war. They ran behind enemy lines the whole time, since they were against the entire world with only named exceptions. More like a focus group for guerilla action than actual action most of the years. Recently, since the start of the building work in Jerusalem, he had been too preoccupied and, to be frank, had been feeling his age, having opted to oversee in person the fundamentalist Jewish and Christian labourers he had managed to co-opt to his version of their dream. In any case, if you're against the human race, that pretty much means you're permanently behind enemy lines in sectarian clumps. But, even more recently, he had begun to wonder why Venus, who could talk with anyone, had vastly widespread and arcane knowledge, who had a serious powerbase to lose, who treated people with no less and no more respect than they were due but always with an interest in them that they found compelling and attractive, who was so ... democratic, especially given the autocratic life she inhabited, why she, of all people, would be prepared to commit genocide; global, total genocide. Oh, she knew people would survive, but both of them were happy to leave that choice up to chance, their immune system or God, depending on your perspective, neither mutually exclusive. So her own life would hang in the same balance, and anyone more full of life and plans for the future it would be hard to imagine.

He had to believe that her vision of a world without hominin intelligence, a green world after the carnage had been picked clean by scavengers and time, was her motivation, because on sleepless nights, and plane journeys like this one taking him direct to Destiny's door, he just couldn't shake the hunch that he was being duped. On the other hand, sometimes he could construe that as a good thing. Like maybe there was an antidote, or a vaccine, that she would unfurl, or maybe she would drink from the Grail with him and become immune. Even now, as he disembarked from the plane, he couldn't quite convince himself that she would do anything evil. But, without being committed as the right hand of God, genocide was no more than mass murder, and thus categorically evil. So much so that, despite her Prince of Peace character to date, or because of the status that endows in its own right, she was the vehicle of destruction, the Harlot astride the Great Beast. He just couldn't think that was who she really was, that's all. She was still as eager and involved as an Alice-in-Wonderland, who had her own inner steel even in that youth that framed her questioning of all the unknowns.

The only recourse he had was that, maybe even for the human tools of Satan, like the Antichrist, grace denied was part of an ineffable aspect of their role in the Deity's plan. Paul raises the question in Romans 9 v 14. "Is there unrighteousness with God?" He answers himself. "God forbid." But then comes the contradiction. The gist being, as the appalling Old Testament Father over-rides his so-loved-the-world Son, that God chooses the nature of the human vessel, chooses the potter's clay from which He makes 'one ... unto honor and another unto dishonour', the former of which He will, if He will, have mercy on, but "who He will He hardeneth." It was just possible that, like Judas and Pilate, Venus could be one of His Chosen Ones and still in headlong tumble to

Hell as reward. He knew she'd heard this analysis, this dire warning to keep on seeking His grace daily, as a child iterated repeatedly by the Brethren in their meetings and by her grandmother at home. It had to be said that the only way he could see a brilliant business woman like Venus making such a profitless deal was if she'd been preprogrammed by this upbringing to take it. He'd seen her make plots that were executed with robotic focus and precision, but he'd never seen the slightest suicidal tendency, although, of course, she might be blasé because she did not believe in Hell.

A cold shiver went down his spine. She absolutely would see this through. She treated life like an extreme sport; only hers was Extreme Professionalism. She really wasn't just an extension of the curious little girl. She had despised Wesley's hippydom that misconstrued Wood seriousness for being 'square', and, while she had the doggedness her mother gave to her bouts of drinking and sobriety, she despised that sloppiness and inconsistency too. Her upbringing wasn't a precise predictor of her current character, but it had made her exacting. The consummate professional, she would have a strategy, but thoroughly-researched tactics and detailed planning would inform this. Why, knowing Venus, she'd probably even find some way for the exact number of 144,000 to survive the Tribulation, and if she had also found some way to ensure the Rapture, as she had found the Grail, she might just circumvent the need for the Hand of the Almighty in the entire episode of Armageddon. Wharton couldn't be sure that his god would actually want to get His own hands dirty. Perhaps this was yet His Way. The unthinkable was the duplicity of Venus and the triumph of Satan. It was so unthinkable that it was substantially more unimagineable than her walking up the aisle between the courtly ranks to pass the Grail to him as her lord. He couldn't see it, but he had begun to feel very shaky indeed.

He was in what appeared to be a hermetically-sealed car by now, and, trying to shake himself out of his brooding, he roused himself to turn on the in-limo-TV for the UK news. Whilst he was flicking channels, the car swerved madly across the road and careened to a halt half-way up a bank.

'What the hell?' he demanded of the driver, lowering the window between them.

'I don't know what's the matter with everyone today. That's the fourth near-miss in the last half-hour. Everyone seems to be driving like madmen. Are you alright, sir? The truck's not stopped and I'd rather not let the car settle into this muddy verge, but just get on. If you're alright, sir? I don't think there's any damage, but it'd be better to get back before dark, don't you think? Something in the air, mebbe? Full moon or something? Don't know when I've been more shaken in one journey. Yes, thank you, sir. I'm fine to drive. Better now than when the shock's had time to sink in. Unbelievable. Let's hope our locals aren't behaving as badly as these city folk, what with our single-track lanes to manoeuvre.'

It shouldn't be possible. She couldn't have started already. It must just be coincidence. Then he remembered Milo reporting the disappearance of the Squires and Knights, not to mention Rowan and Vi !sjn-ik. Of course, they'd all be involved in the plan to distribute the virus, although he hadn't been told it was finished, never mind what had triggered the precipitate timing of the event. They were supposed to be waiting until the next equinox at least. He couldn't imagine what had happened to require deployment this early. Curiously, he found he trusted Venus to have made the correct decision.

It might be because of some intelligence that indicated his cover at the Temple was blown, which could be why the phonecall was preceded the previous day by the arrival of the stones to complete the twelve cornerstones of the Temple, so that it would be complete, which was all the Book had required of him. He managed to hang onto the thread of sanity that said she'd just called him home to get the Grail, until he finally unmuted the pictures rolling in front of his eyes on any news channel he could find.

Without any warning, without prior symptoms, people had woken up mad. Not just the odd one. Not just in many local clusters worldwide. Not like the planned virus epidemiological models he'd gone over with military thoroughness for the Squires, so as to broadcast the effect as widely as possible, as quickly as possible. There should have been flu-like symptoms, connectivity from the Wood neural growth stimulation, then, dashing the expectations of the Wood originators of the plan, not mindful, but mindlessness would ensue. Followed by, in the Venus tweaking, aggression and depression that would be its own cull, and finally, an Ebola-style meltdown that would deliver the rivers of blood. Not, as was being reported, almost the whole of humanity behaving as if it and/or the world had just Gone Mad.

The reporters themselves seemed far from stable. Even normally anti-sensationalist journalists and institutionalised formats like the BBC news feeds were tainted by excitable prose and dramatic delivery. Old hacks wept and leapt, non-partisans took sides, even aggressively. The news seemed raw and more real than normal, urgent and calling for an equally-passionate response. It was disturbing to be subjected to the barrage of biased commentaries, though not unfamiliar from other genres of the media, such as the drama-documentary, but it was the behaviour of the general populace that was the real shock.

Every channel had its own cohort of talking heads, but they could only find descriptions not explanations, and every narrative was loaded with the predilictions of interpretation of the narrator. So Freudian psychiatrists were describing the demise of the superego and the rise of the libido and psychologists talked of a global psychotic break and one neuroscientist who had rushed a colleague into an imager managed a hypothesis of mania, in which the amygdala mediated less, the hypothalamus more, and the cortices were less active than the basal ganglia. This almost seemed to cover it. There were suicides galore being reported, from those that had woken up in the depressive pit of the cycle, but most were simply gabbling excitedly, rushing from one instant of intense feeling to another, not finishing any activity with the exception of sexual ones, for which inhibition seemed degraded and whose instance had become random, public and largely unprohibited. Others were having less animal and more creative bursts of energy, whether artistic or work-related or spiritual, and the variety of hallucinations made the General open his laptop and search his own favourite websites, the many and his specific Endtimer claimants, to check their engagement.

They certainly shared a global sense of impending Something. Endtimers all thought they knew what that was, whereas those without doctrines but only pseudo-scientific speculation to guide them were spouting theories of Gaian-phase-state-changes brought about as a result of global warming and mother earth's revenge (sometimes capitalized). At least his lot were hopeful of salvation, but, as he clicked through the world-wide-web of options as presented by Google, he recognized that his worldview was the tiniest minority. People were not, disappointingly, turning back to God, whatever that meant to them, but turning to their pre-Fall confidence in themselves, not cross-referencing their preconceived 'knowledge', their prior prejudices, with their rational, learnt, enculturated patterns of understanding and behaviour. Acting without thinking. People were being recognisably themselves, but amplified, uninhibited, exaggerated forms of themselves.

Politicians were panicking wholesale and begging people to return to the emergency services or to go home for their own and others' safety, or were ranting about initiating martial law to force people to do necessary work or to mandate them to refrain from it. Local uprisings and militia were in conflict in suburbs and shanties in every major population centre from which reports were available. Nuclear power stations were under attack from activitists and unattended by their normally-dedicated workers. There were innumerable traffic accidents, although, fortunately, most train drivers seemed to have defaulted to staying at home, along with most freight-hauliers and coach-drivers, whereas in contrast the world's pilots had largely got out of bed enthused with delight in their profession and were flying about in a gung-ho manner, ignoring routes and traffic control and runways and fuel levels and passenger screams.

It wasn't, when he probed deeper, just the people. Animal stories got less publicity, but blogs abounded with pictures of strange antics in those unlikely to be suffering the existential collapse of spirit or the spiritual awakening of the soul that the humans were feeling. Again, it was as if the creatures were more themselves than normal, behaviour especially evident in social creatures. Like the humans, wherever possible the animals were out; out of their homes, cages, pens, barns, sewers, holes, trees, stones, as if fear had deserted them for desire to congregate. The air was filled with birds circling, with bats, with insects, from flies to locusts, but, most astonishingly, with *Magicicada* out of their prime-cycle, since neither the 13 or 17 year species were due to moult and emerge. The din from the combined chatter of the aerial groupings alone was cacophonous, in towns, with added human decibels of singing, shouting, and banging through bombing, it was apparently deafening.

Wharton pressed the button to open the car window and the sound hit him like a brick in the ear. He put his head out and then his feet up until he was lying back on the seat and watching the world above speed by. The fading blue of the day was barely visible for the clouds of creatures swooping about. It should have been a beautiful sight, he felt, visible and vocal harbingers of the coming of the Creator, but it had been translated into mouthfuls of midges, crownfuls of mosquito-bites, eye-closing sippings of bluebottles, and there was an ominous croaking and swirling overcasting the earth, so dense and layered by altitude that darkness loomed, pulled back, lowered again, stabbed down with feathered speartips, clotted, frothed, solidified.

He drew his head back in, but now he was looking into fields of serried ranks of rabbits, lines of cows, squares of sheep, circles of fox, deer, even badger. To the eye that had broken many an untutored bunch of men into soldiers, the ragged edges of the geometrical shapes of the clustered species, demarcated only by pressure for space, looked like amateurs readying for battle, not simple social gatherings, but siege entrenchments. There was a huddled atmosphere of fear; as if they'd all been pulled out into the open, into their groups, but without direction.

The centres of each set of animals were crowded but generally playful, gentle interactions were still possible. The individuals on the defensive outer perimeter were less happy, their waiting tense and fretful. Interspecies war did not, however, seem to be engaged. It took him a few minutes to note the really significant pattern. The creatures of field and furrow, hedgerow and tree, were not primarily staring out eachother. They were all, predator and natural prey, fixated on the field boundaries, especially the roadside ones. Finally, he saw what they were all hypnotised by, what they were all waiting to gauge; the reaction of the river of rats that tumbled along; fastflowing, brown, furry canals in the hedge and road ditches. They were chattering too, but angrily, warningly, the message to let them pass overwhelming herbivore and carnivore alike. No Pied Piper required.

Interspecies war was not engaged, but it might be imminent. He could fathom no reason, reference no text, recall no intel that hinted at this. The Wood virus had been specifically designed only to affect humans, and then, whether tweaked for fatality or not, not like this. As the endless rat phalanx escorted the car down the main street into the next town, tracked by converging tributaries from all around the road, and, he noted finally, flanked by endless streams of red and black ants on the march, he felt the trench-soldier's nightmare of the vile creatures tugging at his stolidity. He had no gun under his hand or else he might have started shooting at the bastards, never to stop. But then, finally, having swerved and manoeuvred past innumerable obstacles on the way, the car itself stopped.

They were in a small town/large village. He'd missed the sign, so he was hazy as to where, but here, quite clearly, the balance had changed. Foxes might be outnumbered as predators in the countryside, but, where people lived, the rats and dogs and cats ran and prowled and preyed, not, as he first hoped, just on the edges, not even just running guerilla attacks through large groups of smaller creatures, but everywhere, causing people to run, cars to crash, and chaos to burst forth its squirly shoots; blood, its inevitable and self-perpetuating flower.

It turned out what had stopped the car was the combination of an escaped herd of sheep, a worrying, worried amount of torn mutton and the gang of dogs guarding it from human and rat looters alike, preceded by a crash site, already subject to jerky raids from the perimeter, of a multiple-pile up in a narrow village main street, and by the extraordinary number of local voyeurs who had come out to ogle rather than help, although some were actively hindering by lack of coherent co operation, rendering their intended assistance partial at best, dangerous at worst. Perhaps his driver was just being himself too, but he refused to leave the car, making Wharton decide the sad creature didn't have a life and press his Bible on the poor soul as he himself strategically withdrew, although the wobble of the man's lips and the glaze to his eyes might mean he had decided retreat was a better form of attack than facing the rats.

Wharton shared but stifled his own similarly horrified gut-reaction. After Vietnam you knew the nightmare was within and that you could postpone having it until you slept. If you could hold it together long enough to get through the immediate danger and to the mind-numbing supply of drugs at base-camp. It was still some miles to Penzeen, so, although he wasn't technically authorised in this country to commandeer any vehicles, he felt his mission urgent enough and status sufficiently unimpeachable to allow him, without questioning the action, to appropriate a motorbike from the chap winding it slowly through the maze of clutter, by means of a serious chop to the back of the head with an unsecured scaffolding tube that came to hand.

Needs must when the Devil drives, he thought to himself in self-congratulatory sustenance. It certainly looked as though Evil had become incarnate, not yet the Good he had been expecting, but it was undermining his confidence that the natural world seemed ranged on the wrong side. Surely original sin only applied to humanity, of whatever species, surely animals were neither good nor bad, only programmed to be fit for purpose. Why would they be turning now?

He knew where he was in the programme, and the Antichrist might be around, not necessarily as the human male of tradition, and there were always famines and wars and death, and he wouldn't expect to hear the souls of the dead resting, but if the Tribulation had started, why were the animals in such as state? Because, before the seals were opened in Heaven and the words unfurled from the seven scrolls into the realities of the Endgame, the hosts of Heaven, worshipping, were due to finish in a loud voice that every creature in heaven, on and under earth, and sea, and all around would hear: 'Blessing and honour and glory and power be unto him that sitteth upon the throne and unto the Lamb forever and ever.' Which he'd always imagined would be bliss and calm, balm and delight, causing Lion and Lamb to lie down together, waiting the return to nature of the world human stewardship had spoiled, almost broken.

It was the earthquake that threw him from the bike that really shook his faith, though. Not that it wasn't exactly next in the sequence, but his broken transport and his dislocated hip seemed like unnecessary additional obstacles for the chosen one to face at this stage of the play. The darkness of night was descending, made three-dimensional by its flying infestations that continued despite the cloaking, with the moon, rising predictably blood-red, giving less than useful light, except perhaps to the swarming rats. A bit pissed off with divine ineffability, he grabbed a stout bough and yanked himself, screaming in pain, to his feet, clawing along the hedgerow to the nearest tree, scrabbling up as high as he could inbetween pain-induced faintness, and bashing wildly at anything that scuttled or scampered anywhere within his reach. The rats had only been temporarily diverted from their route-march to wherever by his presence. He felt lucky that he hadn't broken the skin and provided the stimulation of blood for them, as he felt quite sure that they'd have made a quick enough snack of him, merely from the way they'd all grabbed a bit as they went of the few crushed bodies of their fellows that he had managed to smash with his stick.

Ugh. He felt the compensatory adrenalin rush of the triumph of survival through gritted teeth kick start the brain that wasn't just caveman. He phoned Venus and asked her to send the steel-encased cavalry.

The Ydal was watching one cavalryman approach. He was in sight at last. She could feel his eyes on her form, framed in a yet-fuzzy pixel, undetailed by distance, an hourglass in a window in a tower by a river. Oh, they both knew that the form, the frame was fiction, that he was no more an armoured knight on horseback than she the Lady of Shallot, but they were living a dream, that of Venus and Kean for another, imagined, unrealisable universe. But they also knew that this mere gist, this poetic license of the mind, was merely an Hallo, the handshake of greeting, the friendly overture, the glance across a crowded room, first contact, only assured as the prelude to the symphony of soul-mating by the eternal-love-at-first-sight effect, the homecoming of the heart. And they had a lot of heart-and-souls to share. Well, transformed minds, anyway. Retaining enough of fleshly memories to start learning eachother's language with that most basic of friendly greetings, exchange of tokens, cultural information, at the microscopic level transference of genomic material. That was why the animals were drawn into the open, that was why their most basic reactions were to the fore, that was why all the minds of the world were magnetically-pulled into their preferred alignments, that was how the strength of the polarities, the intense gravitomagnetic swirl affecting the solar system itself, was dragging the moon and the earth itself into bulging tidal mounds of excitement. This was the pulse of their proximity to one another. The prodigal MetaMind had quested far, but it turned out that the scent he was tracing, in time, had emerged in space within his own nest, was of his own kindred, though not kin, and was bringing the MindMating of two worlds to greet him.

The Ydal was aware of Quogat, dragged to safety if not stability by her brother, dancing an electromagnetic wheel of light and fire and colour in the deepest darkest depths under the frozen surface oceans of Europa, against the sweeping stage of the pale seafloor and within a set pillared with smoking chimneys, their many inhabitants all still, all aligned as her audience, pinned by the force that swayed her and her planet as much as it spun Terra. His fingers, gently probing tendrils, were in every living thing, and they all felt him, but only the Ydal could Gist for them all at that first meeting, as even had Quogat joined her mind to the entire Europan Intelligence she could only have spoken for them, whereas, her nanobits replicating exponentially so fast that she would run out of convertible moon-mass very soon, now, at this junction of spacetime, the Ydal could represent them all, flowing through her like the river she now stepped upon, her balance on the punt taut but relaxed, her manipulation of the pole in the crossing deft and purposeful, her stride to the far bank assured.

He took her hand as she alighted on the holodeck of their shared imaginary world. She had provided the setting, he embellished, demonstrating his linguistic dexterity, by handing her into a silken tent he had erected on the lea beyond, to a clutch of cushions and a low table bearing refreshments that bespoke the bedouin more than the chivalric, an accent that reminded her of his unfamiliarity with her constructed language, her bizarre personal choice of an artificial preRaphaelite dialect of the ancient Heraldic language of the HomoPrimates.

And yet, it was all, equally, so clear. He was home, to the one who had been awaiting him. He removed his travel-stained armour, a detail she noticed with approval in his staging, and laid it aside, to reveal the smooth, sweated chest beneath the loose tunic under it and the strong bared legs that supported the tall, lithe frame. But, though the male presence took her breath away, it was his face that made her heart race. It was Kean, as desired, although his hair was suitably long, raven's feather dark and glistening, and every feature was the same, but behind the identical hazel eyes, sharpening his cheekbones, strengthening the set of his now-unshaven jaw, was the force of the other dimension, thrusting through her; adjacent, an unseen, all-seeing gaze, an intangible, all-stimulating feeling.

Just like in any well-cut, well-played romantic movie, the film skipped forward, they were falling into eachother's arms, faces approaching, lips opening, moistening, palpitating, undulating, engorging, penetrating, resonating, fibrillating, pumping, driving, chiming, bursting, flowing, melting, melding, Melding. Heraldic translation unnecessary as flesh spoke with one voice. 'Greetings! Well met by moonlight. Dearest love.'

The pleasure of the postcoital hello was only barely beginning to ebb, when she noted an emergency override to her scene-programme. Venus was effectively yelling at full volume for her attention. Tolecnal dipped back in, with one last flirty twist for satiation, and the medieval landscape disappeared to reveal her ribbon of fire braiding her transmitter encased in a pulsating magnetic field so vital that sparks were flying. More than that, with biblical precision, so were the stars of heaven, or more precisely, near-earth asteroids were plummetting out of space down a vortex of twirling faultlines towards the planet below. Some were already streaking the atmosphere with cometary dragons, a few had landed and the craters and dust storms could be seen from space, but orgasm having only just ceased the multitude of hits were still to come.

Tolecnal was Mars again and the field of force turned in itself and deflected the trajectories to send the objects on a safe path right through their journey out of the solar system. The roaring of her unblood in her unears returned as the tides of planets quieted. Her lover remained one with her, but withdrew, taking the full force of his influence back into a higher dimension. Finally, she could hear Venus.

'What the hell is going on? Ydal? Ydal?'' She still didn't reply. The interference had cleared with the effect of a sonic boom and Everyone was coming in loud and clear and all at once.

The Net was reporting it had uploaded a full Spore into subspace [8], since the return of a explanetary Mind to its origins at the call of Flesh was unprecedented and its effects unpredictable, but definitively a conclusion of Heightened Tension was tagged to an Urgent missive. She caught the full datastream, but had to divert it instantly to the temporary cache, earlier seeded with nanobacteria on a near-earth asteroid, in a high-energy band to fuel their growth, just to hold it, its compression making her own look expanded.

She didn't need to read its thousands of years of solar system history to find out what had it rattled. The impact of Mars had been felt as far as the heliopause, so much information, shooting out of subspace with his immense energy as pure speed, which, slowing, released shockwaves that troubled the bow itself, however happy he was to be here.

Quogat was still reeling, Dakul frantic, and the entire Europan oceans sloshing about as the finger of Mars touched down in their daughter, all of which, understandably, had the communal Mind transmitting a unified SOS that had been immediate enough to activate the Cognimatan weapons, who had cast about for the enemy behind the electromagnetic interference, which had knocked them offline for what to a computer is an eternity in transmission bites, after which they had found the Chinese spacecraft on its way to their Legacy. So the Archivist too was screaming on a very tight frequency, one he hoped his colleagues would not overhear in their preparations for annihilation of the probe and then Terra, to warn her that the time was Now.

She reviewed the state of mankind. She could only agree. She turned at last to the mirror. The image and Venus locked eyes. 'I-*Mage*-In!' They instructed eachother simultaneously. The sudden alignment of view and mind was a relief. They grinned at eachother. They held out their hands until their palms pressed against eachother, the fictional mirror molecules of separation that mediated. Coats slid from one arm, one body, through onto one arm, one body. The only way you could have told which was the human in that moment was the receipt of the Mars-Tolecnal wooing, which took Venus out at the knee, but the reciprocal of the Venus-Kean kiss rejected was still a punch to the stomach and a tear to the eye of the damsel rescued from such distress.

'Out us on Our-Mage!' They were singing in unison. She had the backdoor entry information from Jake to get an icon into every online PC in the world and she had access to the US satellites by design (Fargo contract) and, in her spare time, she'd decrypted the codes from every new one shot into her domain, which was access to all TV, radio, mobile phone, internet and every other communications network, bar pigeonpost.

All she had to do was send them the Play icon. It only needed to be a subliminal layer in the feed on a repeating loop. Calculations showed that with the exception of those completely isolated from electrical communications, global coverage would reach everyone within thirteen hours. As for the rest, five years onslaught of the third world with the biggest private aid drops ever made, each bearing enough of the free product for every starving peasant below the helicopter gunships, and the addictive nature of the species itself, merely fanned by the game, ensured that the entire population would have plugged in within fifty-seven hours. But word of mouth, especially virtual mouths on sites like MySpace and YouTube, not to mention the I-*Mage* Legion in Second Life, would probably cut it to less than forty.

Once the world had put on its headsets, the Home note would be rung, the Harmonic that would chime throughout the individual as if they were a bell, the visualised setting of their ideal scene, redolent with the scent of origin, the taste of breastmilk rediscovered, the arms of the mother held wide in welcome.

Of course, the Harmonic was a standard glyph, it would have called any Wood back to WoodHame in Roraima and any Dark to Bite, but without a prior collective consciousness humanity now had to nominate its own Eden. The Game would lead them to the Home each chose. The entire world would be on the move.

The Ydal scanned the bandwidth. At least this chaos would be more orderly than the recent effect of Tolecnal. As long as her projections were right. After all, she had hoped for, but not *predicted* Him. For His darling presence, she actually had to thank the Lily in this world who had been insufficiently Captain Radix to attract either Tolecnal or Kean. No wonder the poor woman was feeling sorry for herself.

Actually, Lily had attracted the attention of the post-Martian Intelligence, but the effect had been cerebral. She had been feeling more than sorry for herself, though not for lack of alien lovers, the betrayal of human ones was more than enough to bring on distress and mortification. She had been attempting to assuage these distasteful and uncharacteristic sentiments, using the entire contents of the minibar in her room, when the strangeness had arrived and ratcheted all emotions up to full blast.

'Her room'! That was a joke. It was her prison, despite the fact that it was the most luxurious apartment she'd stayed in since her childhood as poor little rich kid in LA. Apparently, respect for her I-*Mage* Termite-Alate status mattered to her non-human captors, who had known her colours and play-history scarily well, and they had argued for her with Professor Fargo. They'd had to. She'd been more livid with Lily than with John or Jake. Spitting tintacks, as her mother would have put it.

Gradually, through the venomous anger, a theme emerged. Lily's research. The Heim papers. The original Lapis text. What Venus was truly angry about was not the assault upon her domain, nor the discovery of her secrets, but that her employees had kept their own. Especially Lily, who had broken the code. John and Jake she even seemed to admire, maybe had even employed and funded, for their dogged persistence and their intelligent research. Lily's research, however, was a whole lot more important, she used the word 'vital', in a context that implied the vitality of the entire species depended upon it. She didn't mind that Lily had broken the rules and shared her discovery with Jake, what she minded was that she hadn't shared it with her and that she had abandoned it to come along on his little jaunt.

So she had been going to keep her locked up in a bare cave, with slimy walls and fungal overview and revolting valve-security door, as punishment, while she and someone called the Ydal went over the detail of what she'd already learned and tried to finish the work. At this point the enormously tall, equine female and the stubby, chiropteran male, who reeked shockingly of recent sexual activity, all too easy to visualise given their lack of clothing, protested a list of things Venus had to do that meant she hadn't got time for research. The list was as meaningless as if it were in code, and rattled off so fast Lily caught little of it, but it must have weighed with the Professor, who had agreed to a change of venue, to secure staff quarters, *if* Lily agreed to work exclusively and as hard as she could on the Heim basic universal principles.

It seemed odd that cosmic origins could be playing as immediate a role as Venus seemed think they did, but Lily was eager to get out of the cave, and she knew the clinic was high-tech enough to have hopes that the staff were treated well generally, and, if Fargo was going to keep her a prisoner until her work was done, then all she wanted was to finish the damn translation and be done.

Maybe it was the nice furnishings, the normality of TV and laptop, the temptation of minibar and full fridge, but she'd barely been locked in for three hours when the screen blurred and her tears finally started. She was still hiccoughing and horrendously blotchy when the doctor with the film-star good looks, who had treated her head injury, came in to check on her. He was the only other person who did not seem to feel her incarceration was an appropriate or reasonable response, but his protests when she had been cleared to leave his sickbay were rebuffed, and it had been then that she had heard the full story about her boyfriend and his wife.

She was grateful for his gentle treatment, but more so for the way he had prepared her for their visit to her cell. They were *shifty!* That was the word, but without the good doctor's prescription she might not even have recognized them being so off as a symptom of their mutual guilt rather than of the situation. Lily, after all, was under stress and under guard, so she might not have noticed that Jake was in the custody of someone he wanted to be with. She had noticed, though, since primed, and when the doctor came through his lips were smirking at the rollicking she was giving them. It was hard, then, he was *so* handsome, not to find his approval more flattering than the mere enjoyment of another wronged party. Now she was more conscious than she ought to be with her physician of her dishevelled, pink-patched appearance. Until he told her he was being sent on a rescue mission and to be sure not to overdo the work after the bump on her head and to report any new symptoms. Then she forgot her appearance and cried again, into his crisp white coat, and his arms were tight and sympathetic around her and they shared the no hope that they had seen for themselves and eachother in the eyes of those they had lost.

And then her last sympathetic link to the real world was gone, and she polished off two more minibottles of unknown spiritual derivation from the bar, cried a lot more, watched a slew of crap television, fell asleep and awoke with enough of a downer combined with a hangover to diagnose her next prescription would be written as the words 'Fuck them! This is about me! Time to get out!' So she'd rested and rehydrated, sobered up and slept, and the following morning, at nine on the dot, she was switching on her laptop and putting her passwords into the company server to access Jake's mainframe programme and her own research.

She already had been delivered the original Heim and Platonic documents, courtesy of Fargo couriers, and her fingers found the texture and text as familiar and friendly as the back of her hand. Since, whether Fargo paid her or not, the work was no longer the job of an employee but the ransom of the damsel in distress, she would also do it her way. She started the programme running the translation of everything she'd done so far, loaded with her partial Aristotelian Rosetta Stone, and her fingertips caressing the next sheet in the Heim original. Fargo had been happy to get her whatever she'd asked for except the last and most vital piece of equipment she *needed*. It was the Squire who had brought her headset to her in the end.

She put it on and scrolled through the option menu that edged her normal vision. She was always preset to Termite mode, so she immediately switched to thinking in Lapis-glyphs. Maybe, she thought acclimatising, I'm a backwards kind of person who sees the rich aromas of Termite communication when the 'speech' is written as cold, desiccated, Isopteran glyphs in one world; yet sees information as sensory, enriched with sound, colour, savour, and hot, steamy, and enticing, in the otherwise dry math and codes of the other: Termite and Human. Heim was just human, but he could see better than your average sighted individual. I need to be Termite-able to overlay the information to see where the scent is strongest, to hear where the feeling pumps the pulsation of prey.

I need to engage both modes of thought simultaneously

I need to engage both modes of thought simultaneously

I need to be Termite

I need to be Human

Ter$_{\text{man … Man}}$ter

Engaging Zen Mode
Input bandwidth: Open
Output bandwidth: XXBroad
Close the Loop

She was playing for real now. After all, although she was really human, the people here really spoke Lapis and were the unpixellated Knights and Squires of the Round Table enemy. Only, now, as Jake had said when he first proposed this trip into insanity, enemy and friend, the Queen Termite *and* the Round Table Queen, were both Fargo, both vying to conquer to save the same planet, from eachother. For and from herself. Lily couldn't understand it, but it was revealed as, at least in part, undeniably real. So this time, what she brought to I-*Mage* was belief, as well as a quest for the ultimate answer, the knowledge of how to differentiate good from evil.

She Opened her mind.
XXBroadly, Mars rushed in.
The Loop leapt,
a twist of energy jumped orbit,
tunnelling through to inflate into three dimensions,
a burst of time sharply defined.
Memory,
but not hers nor His.
Home,
but not hers nor His.

Then she was overwhelmed by the flood of information. Head bursting, she scrabbled her headset off. She staggered over to the shower cubicle and drenched herself, still fully clothed, in stinging cold water for a full mind- and body-numbing twenty minutes, then tore off her clothing, dried, put on a warm robe, drank a litre of water, and addressed the laptop.

She filled all the gaps in the next four hours. She translated each word with complete confidence, as a bilingual native, over the next seven and a half. Then she read it through. Then she worked on proving new elements in the equations. She couldn't find any flaws. She looked for them anyway. Every time the equations came out with flying colours. She gave the rest the benefit of the doubt for now. She had to think. As far as she could see, the details were no more insightful nor important to the current state of humanity than the broadbrush expositions already in the public domain. The fact that her Queen, also her employer/captor Fargo, wanted more than this from the text was obvious. She had to think.

The Standard model suggested that the basic elements of spacetime were particles, the quantised bits of the photonic waveform, but most physicists of the last three decades felt that the particles were not actual zero-dimensional points but were extended into a single dimensionality as strings. Heim's calculations proved that the basic unit of spacetime was in fact two-dimensional, a surface he called a metron, effectively a particle that had stringy length *and* planar width. This might be groundbreaking and have all sorts of implications, but Lily couldn't see any immediate relevance.

She was exhausted, but hyper with it all, and she was unwilling to give up and merely make her report as is. Something kept nagging at her. Less a doubt than something important she'd missed. A detail that might make all the difference. Details. Zen mode didn't lend itself as well to focused concentration as to cosmic significances. She'd probably worked in it long enough. When she dropped out of it, she defaulted to Termite Alate, but she didn't drop into the game, just the mode, so, although her brain was responding as if she was isopteran, her location remained the room and her focus remained on her laptop screen and the translation. Details, she thought. But which ones?

She started reading again, from the basic postulates, barely noticing that her fluency in all the languages, Termite, Heraldic-Lapis, English-German, had increased dramatically, and not realizing at all, so second-nature had skipping between them become to her brain, that she was now translating back from German into the Lapis that was the communal language of in-game planetary peace.

It read just the same in any tongue, but she knew she had seen something through Ter_{man} melding that she had missed. She'd read the same paragraph five times without really reading it. *Familiarity breeds contempt*, she thought in English, reminding herself to look again, refreshing her Termite side and picking up the original manuscript once more.

And there it was. The difference between the Heim construct and the translated idea. Heim had etched metrons, shorthand glyphs, in the derived calculations. They were unremarkable square ditches around the other mathematical symbols, perfectly acceptable as renderings of an area of spacetime. Lapis, on the other hand, dealt in layers of concepts and when the metron was embedded within a larger abstraction it was, by its very nature, miniscule and unremarkable. Which was why she hadn't noticed its shape.

If you wanted to communicate an idea to an extraterrestrial, maybe to establish a basic common language, you probably started with cosmically-replicable ideas, such as the frequency of hydrogen or the algebraic notation that described the construction of an ideal triangle. It had been years since she had needed Exo-Linguistics 101, but she'd started there when learning Lapis and Termite and Cognimatan.

She'd been thinking in human, led by Heim himself, in little squares of spacetime. The true representation of this construct was circular. She flipped to layer One to isolate the structure out of its stratification. It *was* a circle. But it was also a wave, so it shimmered like a ring of a soap film, surface tension under pressure from the air, existence under pressure from the vacuum. And, like a soap film, a burst of directed energy could inflate the circle into a bubble.

A bubble that could blow up as this side of the plane of the metron, in our world, where even one of the virtual bursts that randomly erupt from the vacuum could energise interaction with the surrounding metrons, through another dimension, the third, wherein we live.

Or the bubble could erupt on its other side, directly into the vacuum, as a black hole in our perception, perhaps as another entire universe on the other side, if the directed energy burst from our side or the vacuum was sufficient.

The circle was identical mathematically to the event horizon of a black hole. That was the significance she'd been missing.

She needed to feel its full mandala, she felt urgently, flipping to Zen, and activating a tiling visual protocol, usually a handicap. She zoomed back out, but in Zen mode you didn't have to stop where your optic nerves started, you could pull back as far as you liked, to the ends of the universe if you wanted.

Lily wanted. She was unconscious long before her mind left solar system, bowed beneath the scale of it all. Every particle of spacetime was hiding a black hole or a cosmos, they're one and the same thing from here. Countless gadzillions pressing in on eachother, spacetime foam squeezing the bounds of the cosmos within into its characteristic shape, its numerical constants, its physical laws, its evolutionary niche.

She aroused in the dark at the end of the universe, when the skin of the cosmos is stretched so thin that even the metrons were vast, twanging with tension, only not released because the nearest interaction is lightyears away. Not even photons drifted here now, a now slowed by no passage of photon-clocking-event-times to eternity. Absolute yet utterly fragile, ready to blow away at a virtual vacuum-puff, unlike the blasts needed in its youth.

Her soul chilled she sped back through to her home-scale, the comfort of the superimposition upon the normal. But as she scrolled back through the galaxies, stars, the local solar system, Earth orbit, the UK, the south-west peninsula, the Manor Farm complex, earth, and finally dropping through the ceiling to behind her eyes fixed on the screen image of the much-magnified honeycomb of Lapis ideal metrons, she noticed yet another significance.

Scale. To be precise, fractal scaling. There was a distortion that was not the same as time nor as gravity made. There was also a axial elongation of the embedded metronical curvature. She overshot the screenshot and dived beyond the glyph-scale to look at a realized metron. Even as she noted the fractal bifurcations, the eternal edging, the crinkle that was reflected in the cosmic shape, she noted that the metron was a virtual particle she was 'realizing' without the aid of a sub-electron-microscope.

She ran harmonics up and down the physical scales to test her theory, but it rang true every which way she looked at it. Over vast quantities of metrons, any area of space above the subatomic in size, the vacuum pressure, the pressure of all the other universes/ black holes, exerts an average effect that makes the universe look largely homogeneous at all scales. But each metron is a slightly distorted circle because it is located at a slightly different initial condition in the multiverse, formed by its neighbours jostling for much the same spacetime to expand. Its shape is an individualised circle or cosmic bubble. And since Lily could zoom in and out and see the minute eddies and spits frilling the edge of the ring and hear the ebb and flow of the tambourine and taste the torte in the torque and see the rainbow slicking the soap orbit, all of which she knew to be impossible, she knew that the worlds, the entire multiverse and all its constructions and evolutions and even minds, were holographic projections of the syncopated tympany of the Harmonic count; numbers incarnate.

She also knew one more thing. Close up the metron was a raggedy circle in two dimensions, but it didn't exist in a 2D cosmos but an 11D one, and in that view, it, and the entire universal construct timelessly sculpted therewith, looked as beautiful and ephemeral as a flower. And not just any flower. It had budded briefly, elongating along an axis of energy, then it peeled off a corona of ornate and aromatic petals to revealed itself as her namesake: an exquisite lily.

This was big. This was so big it was impossible to believe she, Lily Black, had worked it out, taken it further than even Heim. She was humbled by what she had seen, as if she'd snooped on the universe's secrets by accident, and by now she was faint with tiredness and hunger. She needed to make herself stop. Needed to because she still hadn't answered her own question. That of the relevance of the information to Fargo. She might be building a spaceship that would, definitely, now Heim's basic numbers were confirmed and could be confidently inputted, leap spacetime, but, as it happened, she could have done so before, just on trust. Though it would be a big thing to take on trust, true. But the hangar next door to Lily's Santa Fe office was no way big enough to shunt a lot of people, so what had she meant about saving the species? Still more questions than answers. Lily's brain took the break for her and finally refused to do anymore.

After she'd cooked herself a nourishing omlette and replenished her fluids with some fruit juice, she poured herself a glass of rather decent wine and put the TV on and her feet up at last.

She realized with a jolt that she was catching the sheepish tail end of the Martian effect, as people began to notice their behaviour had been immersed in the emotional selfcentredness coupled with extreme lack of inhibition that would have got everyone in the media the sack if their bosses hadn't been too selfabsorbed in their own peccadillos to notice. These people, *shifty*, she thought again, were happy to report on the embarrassment and violence and the chaotic effects everyone else was suffering from. None of the talking heads could explain it, but suddenly she could. The Martian effect? She'd been so absorbed she'd forgotten all about THAT!

It came from a recollection from a decade-long-moment, a life of memories in a holographic other world, a life of someone else's memories, or more accurately, a familiar, but other, life. From the last upload to the connective Eggspore, donated by Gwener and the NetPlant, near the Termite planet, she'd made before heading off into the Beyond. *She*'d made ... as Captain Radix. Received via the taste buds of an explanet from her local solar system.

According to Radix-Lily, Heim's basic postulates enabled more than transcosmic travel, they enabled the inflation of *imaginary* photonic universes. Thought manifest. Because there were always more spacetimes that could be squeezed into the vacuum. By particularly energetic, precisely shaped bubble blowing. Of course. You could blow out from here, randomly, but if you wanted to come back you had to already know the shape of the universe you'd left, its cosmic signature, Home. That was what Mars had tasted in Radix-Lily's construct, the shape of Home within. That was how Radix-Lily travelled between two realized lives. Reality was holographic, but holographs could be made real, if you got the shape of the metrons precise enough. And Home, the co ordinate of origin, was designated in the pattern on the petals only Lily had seen. *That* was what Fargo wanted, she got it now, now she knew from an explanet that this Fargo shared with other Fargos the strange ambition to save humanity from itself.

Mars had been intimate with those mindful creatures he found in his nest upon his return, and he trusted Lily, as the alter of the one who had set the trail to scent him home, with some of Fargo's intentions. Suddenly, and with a relief that was a physical rush and warming, Lily knew she could trust Fargo, believe in her, acknowledge her as Queen, serve her as Alate-Elect. She must bring her Lady this news.

She went to the bathroom and showered, changing into a flowing green robe she'd found in the wardrobe that brought out her eyes, and shaking her hair loose into a copper torrent. At first glance in the full-length mirror provided she looked more preRaphaelite than Isopteran Warrior, despite the incongruity of her headpiece, but then she concentrated until in her mind's eye she could clothe herself in a flowing exoskeleton and hold a shield and standard. It was always harder to superimpose change on one's actual physical image than on one's plastic mind or the world viewed through it, so when she opened her eyes again to see her stubby, immature wings were the usual mere shimmering, she was not surprised.

She became so when she realized she couldn't see the floaty clothes and hair, only the vertical green of the ventral thoracic plate, rearing ahead of the two pairs of bipedal legs that supported this torso and the extended abdomen flailing her excitement to herself. The shimmer of her wings was not blurry visionary ability but their hypermotion, again reflecting her delight. Her third pair of legs at the top end of the abdomen were holding her shield and spear. (Termites did not need swords nor knives in battle, not with their disproportionately large heads and biting jaws, a feature of all the castes, not just the warriors. Lily was, after all, neither Amazon nor Knight, but a Runic Warrior, wielder of the word, but even such powers occasionally have to bite back.)

Her spear had two tips. Split diamond and split goose-feather and a myriad other engraving and embossing tools sprouted with the flag that bore the Queen's colours, the Hive signals, the Stylus symbol, all in the runic notation Lapis provided for Termite aromatics. The other end was less like a swiss army knife and more like a killing spear, simple chipped flint, as had worked for millions of years on more than one planet. None of this had changed, but her wings had grown to fully mature size, and her shield, hitherto always made from waxy Termite-paper, now interlacing scales of arthropod-exoskeletal origin, stretched across the drum she beat upon entering a battleground, of wit or words or stone, which tensed into steely sinews that deflected and blocked and blotted out Terran-swordplay, bore an altered Coat of Arms.

Gone were the black-white field of lilies and the tail-sucking serpent vert. The field that had been a floral checkerboard was now *sanguine et sable,* yet the tinctures were neither solid nor stable, but flickered like lights, pulsating waves of colour and no-colour alternating in a new fine vairy, where the bloodred phase was a shield-sized raggedy sphere illuminating the sharp silhouettes of a forest of Termite skyscrapers. Lily knew this symbolized she was forever at home in the Termite world under its red giant sun, that her Alate status had transcended the game and become her chosen reality, and that she was accepted therein.

The foreground was even more telling. The serpent form had transmuted. Now it had unfurled, developed delta-shaped wings and a whiptail, and its colour also oscillated, between electric-blue and neon-red, an effect that challenged the eyes and temporal lobes of humans, although termite senses could view it steadily enough. It also was animated, flying in and out between the spears of the termite homes and diving beneath them into the dwelling caverns, from which it emerged spraying jets of inflammable aromas, the transcendent, spiritual, secret language of her Queen.

Lily had become a Aerial-Knight, and her new I-*Mage* designation would be Dragon-Cypher. Filled with a new confidence, Lily breathed into the bright, gel-filled hollow adjacent to the door, which Pereduri and Xl-arnt'z had shown her would attract their attention from without, and waited eagerly for the viscoid lips to retract.

The guard was not one of her former captors, but was another of the batty dwarves. (Somehow, now, she knew they were called Gerehs.) He was smiling, but on them that was an ominous, teeth-bared warning signal. He was also armed more conventionally with something that looked like a Star Trek phaser. 'I hope that's on stun,' Lily said brightly and in perfect Lapis, 'I think the Queen needs me alive. I have Her answers. Take me to Our Leader.'

'Our Leader' was not the person Pereduri wanted to be taken to, but a new need for 'Mother!' was twisting her gut. When Kean and Galarhas, returning with his patient but not their captive, had shared the message left by the absconded Ranger, she and Xl-arn'tz had been with their mother. Neither the good doctor nor Galarhas had been able to explain the two messages, but Venus' reaction told them she could. She swore mightily, and left them, to go into a huddle with the Ydal, whereafter everyone was put on alert to gather in the tunnels underneath the Manor complex, which had a protective shield against electromagnetic pulses.

When she told them that the heightened emotions everyone was feeling were due to the tidal fluctuations of the Mars effect, Pereduri, at ease with the temporal truth of emotions, was unperturbed, but her lover's confidence was deeply shaken. She had felt him withdraw, shut down, and dampen his emanations, so that he clouded to her mind and senses. Had she been human, like Jake and Dinah, whose separation at the news appeared mutual and slightly horrified, she would have followed their examples of being huffy. Or maybe harangued him, which seemed to be Kean's reaction. Instead she did not protest that she would still love him when the effect dissipated, would not find him repulsive and geeky, for how could she prove that in the now? She simply put out her hand and said, aloud, so the others could share too, 'If this time is all we get, best enjoy it together, dear love.'

Her mother had looked proud of her, and, seeing Xl-arn'tz revivify at the encouragement, had taken them aside and said, 'Well, whether or not you two are joined at the hip currently, I still need your service. If you can be trusted to focus on the task in hand? The e.m. waves could be disruptive in ways we cannot predict. Plus my task requires you to resist the call, Home, when it comes, until you have completed the quest. That would take willpower under any conditions. Are you up for it?'

That would have been the point to say 'no'. But, oh no, they were both all eagerness, aspiring to serve the Queen, to prove they were strong and trusty feofs to their Mother. Peri recalled the twist to Venus' lips as she posed the challenge. Perhaps sharing your memory with two alternate selves, each of whom had been a mother, had fitted her with a set of tricks that worked either on the family or on the family of Knights. She had her kids both coming and going that way. How could they have refused? And they had resisted eachother's charms until the yearning in their guts for their Home had become so strong that only making eachother their home in the now could distract. Then they had been strong again, enough to get themselves this far. Only here was far more of a torture than rampant sexual urges or incarnate nostalgia. Here was Cold, with a capital C that should be in a much higher case.

They were on the trail of Ranger and the siren that had tempted him away, but that was only the route. Their quest, whether they located them or not, was to find what they had gone seeking, the lost race of aquatic hominins.

The tubechutes had kept them warm, but now, even through the foam casing of the special primitive submarine they had found in the last southern cave, beyond which no more tunnels branched except upwards into the Antarctic, they were aching with the iciness of the ocean. They had wrapped themselves in the seal furs they found inside, although they were pretty fragile, as ancient as the boat itself, which clearly hadn't been used for unknown years as the Woods had retreated across the continents and explored less, and still the chill rang their bones as painful bells. That was why she had been wishing to be beamed up to her mummy, or perhaps more accurately, warmth like to a mother's arms.

However, the boat was quite amazing. It steered by sniffing. The entire housing was as opaque from a thick coating of insulation as the icefloes above them, but it nosed through the water on the trail of its prey, which scent was transferred to its dectection programme through an interface such as Peri had never before seen, even in historical Wood designs. It could read the chemistry of the mind-spit, as long as you kept a tight focus on the limits of what you sent it as an 'image'. So, effectively, you thought of the scent of Zelas and of Ranger, as sniffed in various junctions along the way, and it could follow them. It also exuded a little spittle back, from the mouth of a console that looked endearingly like a fishhead, and touching the goo responded with simple messages about the hunt for the prey and the conditions outside the capsule. Knowing what she did about Ranger, from their original interrogation, she could imagine him setting off in another of these craft, utterly delighted to discover that this fishy-gel was the unimaginable source of his search for the I-*Mage* gel, and to realize that this was, in fact, a living being.

It was also a submarine, but that was simply a redundant natural organ, and the creature had been bred to docility and subservience so that it was near-ecstatic to see a passenger and had furled its great flange to reveal the passage to its buoyancy chamber. Venus had transferred her entire Coat on Zelas, so Peri could also imagine the glee the Siren must have felt when the evidence backing her theory of cephalapodic sentience lay before her. She must have also realized she was getting near her goal, for these creatures were not land-hominid creations, but aquatically-engineered.

It was a giant cuttlefish, and when they were nearly up to the ocean floor, and worrying about whether the pressure of water above them would kill them before they drowned or froze to death when they emerged, there was a last cave, into which was cut a deep pool, and the creature had been lying there, waiting. As soon as its huge eyes with their striking W-shaped pupils caught their movement, its skin flooded with excited colours, patterns of chromatophores firing in intentional sequence.

Xl-arn'tz caught his breath. 'By my molars, that's the ancient Aquatic dialect of Heraldic. I studied it so I could play it as an option in the game. Not that anyone's ever got to that level, of course. Except us. For real. Wow! I hadn't realized it wasn't just mythic these days. It's a ship, you know. Well, to be precise, a submarine. The cuttlefish bone is a dense calcium carbonate. The ancient southern ocean tribe were supposed to have domesticated them and since the bone is only for buoyancy - it regulates the gas-to-liquid ratio in the chambers in it – so, by sealing it externally to make a compact layer within which pressures could be higher, and by hollowing the interior and regulating the pressures against whatever extra load was in it, they could use it as a beast of burden or a jet-propelled passenger transit car. In return for carrying the original aquatics through the cold waters for which their tropical-to-temperate-sea evolution had not prepared them, and for carrying their offspring and landlubbers to meet the Ice-Hydrae, the cuttlefish were herded to the best feeding grounds, housed in icebergs carved into chambered palaces of stunning rococco intricacy and beauty, taught Heraldic and had their chromatophores and a discrete brain infused into these walls, whereupon, like television, images could be patterned for communication, entertainment, you name it. Until now it seemed too fabulous to be true. Maybe antifreeze is as good for the brain as they say.'

'Who say?'

'The Ice-Hydrae. In their legends, they say their true culture, real intelligence, like poetry and art and the siren-song that Sees, and especially their technology, really began when they discovered the secret of the pure waters under the southern pole.'

'But, surely these legends, even if they were true, won't be true now. Even if they did domesticate these cuttlefish won't they have gone wild again by now? I mean, Zelas thought the southern ocean tribe were Ghosts and the IceBerga tribe extinct.'

'She isn't an experienced Tachyon-Siren. And her clan kept to temperate waters mostly. This business about having elders that are more like priests than Runic-Warriors, and her concern about the lack of disciplined research, faith versus facts. Maybe they had lost the knowledge, retaining only the myths, perhaps to keep their own tribe from dangerous wanderlust into forbidding territory. I reckon she knows different now.'

'Why? This fish? It's hardly evidence.'

'Perhaps you need some antifreeze yourself, dear one. Have you been paying attention?'

'Of course I was listening. The cold hasn't affected my ears.'

Xl-arn'tz, with his pointed batty ones wiggling to keep the blood flowing, grinned. 'It's affected mine. I meant your eyes. It's been talking to you the entire time. Me, no. It doesn't recognize my form. But it knows what a Wood looks like and it's – I should say, she, has been banging on, explaining that her mate has transported the Manta-Knights already, and that she's ready to take us to the Spirit-world, right now.'

And so, after a pause while Peri had watched the swirling patterns of language flow across the cephalapod's back, they had found their way into the creature's inner pod and begun this freezing journey to meet Ghosts.

Communication with the cuttlefish was more difficult from within, especially for someone who normally thought in metamind compressions. The chromatophore patterns were easier, like reading, but, within, Xl-arn'tz, more nasally-adapted than she, was better at 'hearing' and 'talking' in scents. In addition, he did not share her claustrophobia, which was already elevated by the constraints even of trusted Wood tubes, in the cramped cabin they shared, and he also had negotiated the creature's acceptance of his sonar pulses, by which he could see out.

She had to wait for his spit-shared visions, strobing flashes that revealed the strange underworld of the continental shelf. He also edited the slideshow. *Too much TV,* she thought wryly when she recognized the dramatic tension he'd injected thereby. The Augmentatio tended to upload the whole knowledge and then query their memory for the information they needed from it. The narrative form and its constructed tension was a human conceit that didn't come naturally. So when he showed her images of the barren seafloor and the icy cap to the world she was not surprised, then came fauna she might have expected to see, krill and (normal-sized) squid. It was when he showed her the 360^0 view immediately around the cuttlefish that she was amazed. A whole herd of giant cephalopods was accompanying their 'seahorse', and, in sonar imaging, their pigmented patterns were even more intricate, lightning bursts of electrical communication. The chatter was visually deafening.

Finally Xl-arn'tz took her middle finger and shared in a more normal manner, through his brain, which filled in the blanks in the sonic blinks, colouring in the pictures, speeding up the frame rate, filling in the unaltered background features, entwining the exciting novel sea scents, and adding the more alien sensorium of the cuttlefish to which he also remained linked in real time. The creature was aware of contours in the seascape, currents and salinity layers beyond its riders' perceptions, received reports from eight legs and the many suckers of two tentacles, flexed muscles in pride at the strength and steadiness of its swimming in honour of its rare cargo, and maintained a ceaseless flow of conversation with the surrounding people - and they were clearly people, not domesticated cattle, nor even pets.

They were very excited to be transporting the Tachyon-Siren, who it turned out they had been expecting, and her three landlubber-knights. The legends Peri had not known until recently, almost lost to the Woods, a subject of esoteric research to the Darks, a myth of mermaids merely to the Days, were living history and prophecy to the symbiotic cuttles. It became obvious that their freight and passenger roles did not fit, as they would in less buoyant pressures, on them as work chores, but were part of the fun of living. They might have had some genetic tweaking to breed larger, and the code for the membraneous cavity around the cuttlebone might have been written in, along with that for an adaptation of the Wood foam that filled the gap and kept the buoyancy under their control when loaded, but they were not slaves. They knew all about it, had been intelligent enough and symbiotic enough by nature to have agreed to the irrevocable procedure aeons earlier.

Pereduri had the sudden insight that they were not 'seahorses'. They were 'SeaKnights', the brain and only incidentally the brawn of carriage, the Rider that is Ridden. And when she asked about IceBerga, she discovered that She was their mythic and longlost Queen, and that the strain of the one pair of Knights remaining with the Ghosts had become too inbred and prone to madnesses and illhealth, despite moments of true genius and inspiration, so, when the added burden of low fertility and decreased numbers had placed them in imminent danger of dying out, the cuttles, who were already Squires, the Knights' horses and comrades, had been trained up to become Knights themselves.

In fact there were a number of groups referenced in the cuttles' metamind, once she had sucked the meat off their female's mind to grind the bone beneath for the communal, cultural, memetic information.

Many of the Cetacean schools had been interested in the swimming monkeys with their translatable chittering and their tools that created sculpture and music and and their brains that thought about the whales' world in the same leisured way those great travellers mused about it, only faster and with more flamboyant songtelling than ambient music. They were sirens and beguiling to their fellow mammals, and they could also respect the giant cuttlefish as a formidable creature in its own right, so they began to pay attention, and now there were several Fleets of Knights. Baleen whales were represented by two Fleets, the Blue and the HumpBacked, while Toothed whales included the Orcas and Narwhal and a small armada of Dolphins and Porpoises who were basically a Special Ops force, called the Pod.

They all served the Ghost-Queen, but, oddly the matriarch leading the Ghost-Hydrae did not have that title any more than any of the females that led the several Fleets of Knights. The title was not even given to the latest or greatest Tachyon-Siren among them. It was reserved for the messianic incumbent the FuturePast would send them. She who would reveal the residence of the original Ice Queen, IceBerga herself, would be the only faster-than-light-Seer who could invest the role with its original unrealized purpose. The level of excitement was high because they were at the Prophecy Fulfilled stage, with the crescendo of the dying world in their ears, ready to follow in the Final Quest wherever She led.

The Prophecy said that, in the End Times, when the sea itself was tainted by the Landlubbers and the three races of Hydrae knew not of eachother's existence, the last Tachyon-Siren of the Whorlingas would bring death to her people. Alone, she would be the first Hydran to seek to find and unite her ancestral clans. She would find the Ghosts and they must choose whether to wait passively but safely in the Now for inevitable extinction in the Near-Future, or seek to redress the mistakes of the Past, that had made them the

Ghosts, by lurching blindly forward for Life in her wake. If they follow her she will lead them to the *Aqua Libra*, to IceBerga and to their End. The overtone of the whole myth was apocalyptic, and their End sounded far more ominous and immediate, like death, rather than the alternative, extinction, so Peri didn't immediately perceive why the news of the arrival of Zelas was causing such glee.

A little more probing revealed the cultural bias. These were a people under seige. Fewer and fewer in number, increasingly barren, and embattled by nature, by man's global pollution of sky and sea, by the narrowing horizons of their hiding places from the eyes above the sky and on the surface waters; *if they'd been found by humanity they'd have appeared briefly on the Red List just before they were wiped out. No doubt many Days would have enjoyed the documentary on their post-mortems.* They wanted to survive, and the End, the death, was a metaphor for dying to the cowardliness that had made them Ghosts, but it was also a reality as they expected the price to keep the Promised Waters, the Eddyless Calm, would be the need to rise up behind IceBerga and conquer their superstition that the Landlubbers were superior and then conquer their need for the Eddyless Calm by waging an Armageddon upon the Days until they capitulated and restored the balance of the world. They were happy *because* it was the Beginning of the End of the End of the World.

A bit like the Woods, they didn't have a plan for ReUnification, although it was the same glyph, ancient myth, that all the Terran tribes, except the isolationist, divisive Days, held dear. *They* preferred to think the Golden Age was in the past, a Garden Lost, and leave the restoration of it up to a god. To them, Queens were debased by politics and the tireless onslaught of the patriarchy for many generations, and even when one came along, recognisably the Rider of the Beast or a Princess, the men who ruled the Day would still work with the one and toy with the other. So Woods had recognized in Venus a Wood-Nymph and Darks a Magnetic-Pole, and both her Queenly potential to lead to unity, if only through the hybrid procreations, if she failed to lead her people, the uncorrallable Days, to unite with eachother and their hominin cousins after their viral brain alterations. If the authority of their obvious Queen's voice did not bring peace and a cessation of the rape of the earth and a restoration of the balances, Her wishes could still be fulfilled because the Squires and Knights, half-human and more than half-superior and equally devoid of the sqeamishness of the Woods about War, would become Her Arm and enforce the balance.

Here undersea the story was paralleled by Zelas. They were almost at their destination, the Promontory for the Homecoming Queen. It was a representation of the Eddyless Calm, a seamount surrounded by plenty, a dormant volcano, whose crater rose far enough above the water to enclose a lagoon of fresh water, filled by snow and rainfall and very chilly at these latitudes most of the year, but not requiring antifreeze to enjoy on a summer's day. It was the best they could provide for a cold-adjusted Queen, but it had one further gift as preparation for the rest of the quest, a Crown that grew only here, so the Ghosts had known it was the right place. The origins of the magic that got into their blood and accelerated their evolution, the antifreeze gene. It grew here, a bacterium that swopped genes whorishly so isolated was it in this pool, so rare its chances to share. The antifreeze chemical was in its repertoire and it happily entered the bloodstream and lived long and prospered, was fruitful and multiplied, broke through enough cell walls to endow functional cold-protection, and finally inserted itself into the germline cells and entered the species' genome. Almost everyone who lived in sub-zero temperatures shared their every cell with this jolly little bug attached to their mitochondria, and maybe that symbiosis in crisis was showing right now as they cheered their Prodigal Princess.

She was already in the Tarn. Blue-black from the ink the Cuttle-Knights were shooting over her. Lying alongside her was the resident family of Aquamancers; a matriarch, a sister and her twin-children, who were frolicking like any of the very young at a serious gathering, a single fertile male consort, and another extremely elderly or decrepit male. Peri and Xl-arn'tz had been brought up to the surface through a vast crowd of Knights and Squires, all of which creatures she had seen, if not known, before, but near the breach they hung back for the air-breathing Hydran population, its reproducers, hunters, muses, all looking less like Zelas with her relatively sleek shape and visibly-primate facial structures than like walruses. Oh, they were clearly the same race, in the way that an anorexic dwarf and a morbidly obese giant human were, but these folk of the southern ocean were on another scale entirely, and their blubberiness reduced the contours of their faces into a simple smudge pocked with the big eyes and flappy nostrils and predatory teeth elephant seals would find attractive. Peri conceived another possible reason for the separation of the clans, Zelas was more attracted to the more distantly-related Day than her larger cousins. She was not repulsed in any way, far from it, she was wallowing in a wave of excitement and love and reverence, but she was wallowing with Ranger.

The waters were clearing again now, the ink dissipating, the Fleets retreating to the edges of the pool. A dance began. It was very recognisable to the Wood, watching through her lover and their cuttlefish's eyes, safe within. It was the mating dance of the Aquatics, fabled as the origin of the Siren Song, the howl that brought mates, the howl of dissatisfaction with the rest of the world that crescendoed out of the perfect orgasm. It was as powerful as Wood pheromones and mediated by similar chemicals in water and charged by the damp ozone-drenched air. She looked at Xl-arn'tz. It would be disrespectful to ignore the Call. They had to rise to the Challenge, for the honour of the different species, for the commitment of the Quest, the alchemical stage of *coniugium* when they must risk the Perfect Union.

They took eachother's hands and, with thanks to their living boat, swam out into the pool. They surfaced within the ring formed now by the Aquamancers and greeted John and Zelas with full mouths of mucus to convey the Coat Entire of their journey and understanding and intentions in one gob. In return Zelas welcomed them with warm hugs, respectful Greetings at their status and to their species, interest in Venus and the conjunction of plans and times, and gave them a last chance to leave before she and Ranger underwent transformation into Ghost-Queen and Consort. Ranger was as informed as his princess, but he spelled it out in English to be sure Peri and Xl-arn'tz had no illusions.

'It's not just a title. We're going to be Crowned. It is a wreath of coral, infested with the bacteria, that we have to wear whilst we mate. That's the symbolic rite of passage that goes with the bacterial infection. It hurts to be worthy of this role. It's positioned in and on the respective genitals to ensure penetration through the skin as near to the reproductive glands as possible. This is to ensure that the pregnancy that will show with our antifreeze-protection, in about three weeks, is infected too, to pass to a new race. This is all in the legend. As are you, believe it or not. But you and I have a choice. The legend says the prospective Ghost-Queen must bring two males and a female of mixed heritages with her, and that one of these will be her consort and mate and the others will be consorts to her but only mates to eachother. The gap that has, apparently, caused theological debate is whether the new Queen is bringing invigorating new genes to the bloodlines or whether her arrival signals the end of all other mating within the Ghosts. Either choice looks wrong to some onlookers. But at least your arrival bolsters her right to continue.'

'There is another way to do this.' Peri offered. 'We have the obligation to try for the Perfect Union, *the coniugium,* with our best mates. We should suggest that everyone feels free to do so while we are mating. Then we can rotate partners, with whoever takes our eye or catches our nostrils. For a fixed period, say until sundown.'

'No! Not in these latitudes, could take months. A single lunar-tide ebb and flow should be about right, though. Twelve hours? I think it's a statesmanlike suggestion, co-consort!'

'I wasn't going for diplomacy so much as justifying the effect that's going to happen inevitably if Zelas Sings and I emit Wood pheromones.'

'Fair *and* fun. Then the tide's about to turn. And so are we.'

'Unto our children's children. Whatever they might be.' added Xl-arn'tz with his wry smile that made the unknown into adventure.

Kean didn't need any additional knowledge to know he'd had enough of Fargo's adventuring. It's not easy to discover that your dream woman has feet of clay, it's worse to find she has a heart of blackened steel. The glimpse he had had of her mind had revealed no details of her plans but he had felt her apocalyptic ambition and her total disregard of his declaration of a love she wanted had been given all the consideration of fly-swatting. His initial reaction had been to bemoan his losses, but then he'd had to treat the General's dislocated hip and the anaesthetizing pain relief had loosened Wharton's usually tight lips and he'd babbled confirmation of Fargo's impending rivers of blood. Unlike the General, Kean felt sure that the global madness of the previous few hours had not been under Venus' control; he could excuse her on that count of guilt, at least, and he wanted, oh, ridiculously, he knew, to exonerate her from the destruction the General was articulating.

He almost managed to get there when he heard the man ranting about his own ascension to immortality and the Holy Grail, especially when his stomach revolted at the old fart's reverie about marrying his Whore of Babylon. He hadn't managed to conceal a contempt and disbelief that his aggressive patient found offensive.

'Oh, you don't believe me. Whippersnapper! Turn on the TV. Your proof'll be there.'

The doctor in him had to acquiesce because the foolish old man was trying to get down from the couch to do it himself. This time the reports weren't the emotional subjective opinions of confused journalists themselves under the sway of their own selfish preoccupations. In fact there were very few channels even broadcasting, and they were being run by people who were equally in the thrall of a mighty attraction, but, as the Out-*Mage* homepage, that was the backdrop to every one of their presentations from wherever in the world the station was, inferred, they had already reached the source of the pull.

Now he knew why the Manor staff had been given that morning's edict not to put on their headsets. The icon flashing 'PLAY' alternated with a glyph he recognized as Lapis for 'HOME' and even the almost subliminal presence of the mere engraved symbol, without the redolent layers he would have 'read' had he been wearing his headset, called like a lust for the antique womb that would have blinded Oedipus himself. He switched it off immediately, but he needed to know more, more than he wanted, but he couldn't bear the draw that made him want to run to the damn woman and fold himself into her arms.

The radio helped sober him. The world was on the move. Almost silently, and without impedance from the normal bureaucracies that ordered life. Every person was wearing their headset and was totally focused on the one road, the road Home. If anyone else was going the same way, they walked or rode or flew together, sharing food, water, but minimal conversation, other than to achieve practical shared goals. The radio reporting was more like cheerleading, or possibly, given the marching step most people were keeping to, a call to arms, Kean imagined with a shiver.

The General saw it another way. 'They march to their doom. The mistress has unleashed the Beast. Pestilence rides out! War and Famine mere bystanders, but Death will be upon you all! My Lord comes! He comes trailing clouds of glory!'

'What are you talking about? What has she done?'

The General looked half-mad with an excitement that contorted his red face unbecomingly. Spittle was beginning to appear at the corner of his mouth, though it was the mild tic of his own unresolved position that worried his doctor, but the answer wiped individual diagnostics from his mind.

'It's a virus. The Knights and Squires are going to deploy it. She's congregating the people of the world like the sheep they are. When the world is wiped clean of the contaminant, He'll come to the Temple I've built for him. And I will live for ever.'

Kean swallowed his fear as he pressed 'Wiped clean? What does the virus do?'

'It brings the Tribulation. But it is accelerated. Death will follow soon. Then the Messiah will come to reclaim his own. You have to take me to Venus now. I must sup of the Grail at once.'

Kean now had more than enough of his own reasons to want to see Venus to protest that the General was too weak and drugged still to move. He simply got a wheelchair and well nigh shoved the shaky evil-son-of-a-bitch into it.

The General said their destination was some fabled cavern under the Isles of Scilly, accessible only through the Wood transport system, so he made for the main junction.

Suddenly they were no longer alone. Darks in numbers he knew existed but had never seen in one place together were queuing for the turbochutes. A large number of Woods were there too, but no one seemed anxious to stop him nor the bloodthirsty General, although even he had toned down his glee and was only clapping surprised passersby on their backs and saying, 'That's right! Time to go home, eh, people? Reunification time, boys. That's the spirit!'

When he inquired, the General told him, in a conspiratorial aside, 'Oh, it's their virus. The Woods' plan. Originally. To alter the human brain to enable telepathy, to bring all the hominin species together as one mind. Filthy idea, of course. Venus was brought up to know true prophecy, y'see. She's the handmaiden of the Lord, really, y'know. Tweaked the bug so's they'll all see the Light, but if they don't accept it, then, bam, they die.'

'Oh? And how does she control this Light?'

'Not her. Our Angel with the Book knows who will and who won't accept the return of our Lord. If they accept, they will be swept up in the Rapture and will witness the destruction of the rest.'

'Sounds like they just die happy, that's all.' growled Kean, and enjoyed the moment's hesitation this brought to the already far-too-happy genocidal manic he was pushing. However, in this currently docile crowd, he didn't want to start a panic, so he shut up and waited in line, until the Manor Farm family arrived, saw them and Bob pulled rank and got them all to the front of the queue.

'We've been looking for you.' Bob informed him. 'The ceremony is about to begin and you'd gone AWOL with the guest of honour.'

'Then he's not just reacting to the medication? All this is for real?'

Bob's eyes narrowed sharply. 'You're not a believer, are you? Well, you'd better get your house in order, matey, or you'll be left behind to face the Wrath of God.'

Kean decided that, at least until he knew more about what was going on, he'd better shut up pronto. He wasn't worried about the wrath of someone he didn't believe in, but he believed in Venus and it was still impossible to accept she'd kill the entire population of the world. *And if she does? Am I supposed just to stand by and let her?* Admittedly, he didn't know how he could stop her.

It took a while to get to their destination. The General knew how to, because he'd been underBite for Conduit, and he explained to Kean that, until six thousand years ago, the entire world had been the province of the Woods and Darks, and only two humans had lived, timelessly in the Garden of Eden, but that, when Adam and Eve and the generations that followed were cast out, they soon recognized the world was filled with demons and succubi and that their god-given duty was to cleanse the earth of them. As they were standing amidst a group of Darks, waiting in another junction cave for a free turbochute, Kean was pleased to note that the man's earlier hubris had given way to native caution and that he kept his voice muted. 'The Darks went underground and it was they that perfected the tunnels, but it was their liason with the Woods and their superior technology that gave them the fast modern transport system.'

His voice wasn't muted enough for those ears. A relatively tall and more human-faced Dark leaned in. 'Creationists, eh? As if any of us could have got this far in six thousand years. Doesn't he know you can't choose your family?' But he said it into Kean's ear and when he drew back was smiling in a friendly manner. 'Fr! gwapd, of the Squires Coagulatio, at your service, good doctor. Do not be afraid. The Queen, our Mother, no doubt will ensure the Rapture of all whose service is true.' Kean was further appalled. He was obviously referring to Venus and, although he could not be said, red as they were, to have her eyes, a sudden suspicion entered Kean's mind regarding his parentage, although this should have mattered less than his slavish consent to her dictatorship of death.

Not that he had time to think about it, as the General, realizing his prejudice had been overheard, reverted to his normal bombastic tones, booming 'See, doctor. Even the twisted minds of the servants of evil respect the Grail and the Babylonian Whore.' But Kean noted the twitch of anger that was suppressed in the fire-red eyes was not at the pejorative dismissal of his entire race as evil, but at the name Wharton casually gave Venus.

Finally, they were decanted in another cave swarming with Woods and Darks. Oh, in the course of his work, Kean had met plenty, he'd even been granted the honour of visiting WoodHame, and he'd treated a number of the local Havenfolk in his clinic, but he'd never seen them all together before. However, the mass ranks drew apart and Fr! gwapd led the group forward, calling, in all three languages, 'Make way for the Royal Party! Make way for the Family of the Queen! Make way for the Grail Challenger!'

The milling crowds fell in behind them and a procession began. The tunnel was wide and high, very much an approach to an important destination. For once, at the end, there was an ordinary human-style door. Ordinary only in the design, since it was enormous, with its' deep-black, ancient timbers held together with huge, recently-polished bronze fittings.

Fr! gwapd stopped before the two naked Woods apparently guarding it. 'Behold, the weapons of the Grail joust!' he intoned, again in all three tongues. Aside, he said to the General. 'You must walk now.' Both he and the General brushed aside Kean's protest that he shouldn't put weight on his leg yet.

'The legend says King Pelles was only healed of the wound in his groin by the one true knight who accomplished the Grail quest.'

One of the Woods handed Wharton the spear he carried, so the stubborn fool had a walking stick at least, but the shield the other gave seemed heavy and rather undermined the help of the other Grail artefact. Anyway, he managed to bang three times on the door in a fairly portentous manner in keeping with a ceremony Kean was already finding ridiculous. But then the doors swung silently open from the inside and he could see beyond.

The cave was a natural cathedral, stalactite pillars and stalagmite pews, glittering with a dusting of ice-crystals as if it had snowed diamonds in there. It was incredibly bright and the phosphorescent fungus that mediated Mind was putting patterns on the walls and ceiling that would have put a disco-display to shame. Kean had never seen the crystal skulls before, but he knew what they were, although they looked as if they were the strange fruit of the antique but living tree-chairs into which they fitted.

Almost as odd was an equally huge but crumblingly-dead tree that lay across the chamber. It was a riot of colour, of fungi of all kinds, sandy sponges, green-and-purple frills, yellow spears, orange goos, rusty platters, white caps, red cups, black knobs, all somehow looking so bright and clean that they could be plastic.

However, none of this, nor the neat lines of naked, highly-tattooed and intricately-moss-bedecked Woods around the walls, nor the shifting rows of the Dark crowds coming in with them, nor the armed teams he recognized as Knights Augmentatio and Squires Coagulatio, held his eye. He noted with distaste that it did not hold the General's either, but, to be fair, in fact all eyes were turned in one direction with theirs.

Venus was emerging out of the far gloom from the back of the cave. But this was Venus as they'd never seen her. Venus as a goddess. And when Fr! gwapd and Galarhas raised the shout 'Behold the Queen!' and the assembled crowds burst into birdsong and squawking and cheering and clapping Kean found his vocal chords had responded with the same reverence as everyone else. Not least because the most feminine Venus ever got was a sharp suit, whereas now she was in what looked like a mediaeval style white dress, over which newly-long and ungreyed-blonde hair flowed like a veritable river yet still managed to hide very little of her fit body through the diaphanous material of the robe.

She walked daintily through a veritable forest of Wooden priapismic salutes, which made his own involuntary greeting seem dwarfed by comparison, although he noted that the actual dwarfs were not poorly endowed themselves.

As for the General, if the blood had rushed downwards it was less noticeable than that which suffused his face. He seemed to be having trouble breathing. Even as he moved to tell his patient to unloosen the tight collar of the dress uniform he had insisted on wearing for the occasion, two of the Knights stepped forward and with swift fingers and a firm hold had stripped the poor man naked.

This was a less than pretty sight, so Kean was more than repulsed when Venus stepped in front of the fungal display and opened her arms and with them her robe to the old paunchy warrior. 'Who serves the Grail?' she trilled, in a voice that was both recognizable and had Woody high registers and Dark scratchy lows.

'I do.' replied the General, as if in marriage vow.

'Then, choose!' Venus instructed, and stood aside, an arm sweeping across the fungal cornucopia.

Wharton was clearly puzzled. He was shaking already, not least from the clammy cold and the heightened blood-pressure that signified his anticipation, but he staggered forward, leaning heavily on the spear. He stood at the table of mushroom fruit, bemused apparently. Well, the selection was hardly what one would expect for the Grail. But Wharton was a traditionalist, so, of course, he was searching for the cup that had collected the blood of his saviour, and perhaps, since his stated aim was to return the world to its natural state, it was not impossible for him to find that symbol patterned here. In fact, once some similar computation had taken place in his head, the man snapped to attention and began to scour the surface for the design he sought. Kean was no fungus expert but when Wharton grabbed at a chocolate-brown cup with a vivid, blood-red interior, it came as no surprise that Fr! gwapd, beside him, nodded sagely, commenting '*Sarcoscypha austriaca! Obvious, eh?*' and burst into applause. Wharton beamed with delight and looked at Venus for the next move.

'Fill it with the Water of Life!' she instructed, pointing upwards. Now Kean noticed that the dripping cave was not simply filtering groundwater, but that there was a miniature iceberg depending from the base of one of the shorter stalactites. It appeared to have frozen around it, rather than in polar seas, but it was losing its frozen state quite quickly as the amassed heat of all those bodies warmed the cavern. Wharton hobbled across and held the tiny cup under it.

'Now, drink and tell me, 'Whom does the Grail serve?'

Kean jerked, but Fr! gwapd was at his shoulder, 'No.' he said, as if reading his mind.

'But isn't it poisonous?'

'He has chosen.' was all that went with the menace of the teeth in that hitherto-friendly smile.

In any case, it was too late. Wharton had quaffed it like the gift from the gods he supposed it to be. His shoulders went back and his head came up. 'Whom does the Grail serve?' he roared. 'It serves Me!'

'It serves you right.' agreed Venus. 'Come to meet your Maker.' She held out a hand and led Wharton to the tree-chairs. The yellow Wood and the emerald Dark skulls gleamed in their respective housings but the Day socket was half-hidden by a leafy growth from the tree that indicated sunlight must get into this gloomy place somehow. She thrust the pendulous branch aside and the whole room erupted. The blue-john stone was almost transparent except where the purplish streaks highlighted its rare origins, but all present, even Kean, realized that the legendary lost Day skull was in place.

'What is this?' the General called over the general hubbub of rejoicing, pushed forward like Kean by the crowds shoving to get a viewpoint. 'Does this mean ... ?' He paused, his eyes boring into Venus' for answers. 'No rivers of blood? Just unification with these agents of Satan?'

Kean's heart leaped with hope, but Venus didn't reply, just kept on smiling blandly at the General. Like a wave, the sound ebbed away, starting from the back of the cavern, and Kean turned to see the Knights and Squires were marching forward. The foremost carried two prostrate figures. Kean knew both of them. The Wood closest to Venus, Rowan, and the Dark man she despised, Vi !sjn-ik. Both were barely conscious and Vi !sjn-ik had clearly been beaten half, if not wholly, to death. The Knights gently lifted them each into the appropriate tree-chair. One of the Squires plucked two more fungal cups, filled them with the same icy water and poured it into their barely-responsive mouths. He then motioned to the General to join them in the third.

'No!' shrieked the General. 'The Grail is mine! Immortality is only for the righteous.' But two Knights lifted him off the ground bodily, no mean feat at his weight, and placed him in the chair. 'Venus! No! What are you doing? The Lord will smite you to the lowest depths of Hell for this perversion!'

'Be still!' It was the command of a Queen, not angered, merely expectant of silence to follow. She got it, too, Kean noted with some awe.

'Oh, ye of little faith!' she mocked. 'Would you throw away immortality because you had to share it?' She held up her hand so he did not reply. 'You must be beginning to feel the effects by now. This is the final challenge of the Grail. You answered the questions, but you did not answer correctly. No more did these beside you.'

She walked back over to the treetrunk and reached into the sprouting masses to pluck out a frilly spongy cream-coloured growth. '*Sparassis brevipes.*' she informed. 'The root of meneh. The Grail is about Life, not about avoiding its natural conclusion, Death. It is about feeding the world, not selfish hoarding. It is not about blood spilled, for altruistic reasons or for evil ones. It is not specific to one human who was crucified for political unrest. And it does not serve you. It serves All. Above all, it is nothing to do with any perversion of common sense, any non-existent deity. No. *He* is not coming, but I am.'

With horror, Kean realized his patient had started frothing at the mouth, but not white foam as if his heart was overloading, a grim blackish slime was trickling downwards and he was twitching into convulsions.

'You're killing him!' he shouted at Venus. He had pushed through until he was near enough to be yelling in her face. She looked up at him.

'It's what he wants.' Her clear grey eyes were smiling at him with affection, as if they were discussing nothing more serious than the weather.

'His screams say otherwise.' Kean replied, brought up short by her nonchalance.

'That's just the pain of the transition. He'll be quiet soon.'

'He'll be dead soon!'

'Indeed. That is the only route to immortality, of course. He just forgot to factor the process in.'

'How can you..? I thought he was your friend.' Maybe he was pleading for mercy, maybe just for his own status as friend.

'I showed you before. Friendship is irrelevant just now.'

'So it's true. What he said. You're bringing on ... an *apocalypse*?'

'Melodramatic way of putting it, but, a solution is in progress, yes.'

Suddenly, his initial inertia and shocked numbness left him and he was swamped by a flood of anger. 'What the hell gives you the right...? Who made you god?'

And then she actually laughed. 'Oh, you all did. Very democratic, I've been, believe me. You'll all get exactly what you wished for, if not what you think you deserve.'

He was beyond his love for the woman, even her strange priestess clothing smacked of the megalomania he now diagnosed. They were pressed up against the tree-chair in which the life of the

General was now waning more quietly. Before the thought crossed his conscious mind, Kean's hand had grasped the haft of the spear resting there. Before anyone had seen his arm move, he brought the flint point up with all his force. The medical subconscious knew the trajectory under the ribcage to the heart and his aim was true, but even as he knew that, he knew that the worst damage was to his own heart.

In the same movement he caught her before she could fall, pressing her close, whispering. 'I'm sorry. I couldn't let you. I'm sorry. I love you.'

He felt the inevitable bite on his neck, though he was barely aware of the erupting furore around their position, because she pulled away from him, lifting a hand to his cheek. 'Dear Kean. Always Arthur, never my Lancelot. It should have been love.'

Then, as the Dark poison warped into him, numbing his body and clouding his mind, she simply vanished, from his arms, from his sight, from, in his last conscious awareness, everyone's shocked sight, but he couldn't follow the jumbled cries as he fell into the blackness that he could only hope was a death that would join them both.

F: Albedo:
Coagulatio and Mortificatio

Wharton opened his eyes. He was currently surprised to be able to do so. When he had swum up from the utter blackness, unconsciousness preceded by its own pain and dark despair, he had not dared hope he was alive, but he had been equally afraid to be dead. The bit of his brain that appeared to have returned first seemed to be giving a running commentary and it had suggested that, if he was dead, he would be due Judgement, and, whatever sins the Whore of Babylon had herself committed upon him, she had been right to rebuke him for his lack of faith. He had died in a mortal panic, an unsuitable reaction for someone who believed in his own ultimate resurrection through grace, and he had died angry, because he had been denied the immediate eternal life that he would have used to lead His people to ensure His return. After a little while though, in which he ascertained he was no longer in pain but that he could feel his body, hope began to resurface along with the rest of his consciousness. Maybe she was right and he had passed over into Life. His body was composed as if for death, true, but his hands were lying at his side and they told him that cold stone lay beneath him. Hardly the construction he might have expected of Heaven (nor Hell, for that matter, he remembered, with relief). More like, it occurred, a tomb. The thought of having been buried alive finally galvanised him.

It wasn't a tomb, it was an altar, on which he lay as the sacrificial lamb, covered in flowers that showered around him as he sat up. It was underground but every last inch was familiar, since he had built it himself. He was in the Inner Sanctum of the new Temple of Solomon beneath the Dome of the Mount. Exactly where he needed to be. And, he noticed with glee as he jumped lightly down from the altar, whatever Venus had said, perhaps to test his faith in the last extremity, he must have passed the Grail test, since he was not only alive but fit, well, breathing easily, no hip pain, muscles taut and strong, like a younger man than he had been for twenty years. He had had the faith to drink of the elixir of Life from the cup of the Cross and his reward was transfiguration. Also, apparently, transportation across the world.

It was when he wondered about this that he had the first inkling that something other than he had expected was going on in his brain. Internally, he had posed the question. 'How did I get here?' and a flash of memory served up a bizarre response. He had an image of discorporation, as if he'd become nothing, but only for a second, then he had been redirected here. *Redirected?* It posed the question of by whom, but the god of gaps came straight to his rescue. *Heavensent!* he answered himself, but there was an inner echo of raucous laughter that denigrated his very thought processes. He decided no one could be transformed without some side-effects and that the odd sense of not being alone, of being accompanied by someone who found him ridiculous and pompous, was simply his early insecurity in the elevated role of Harbinger. It occurred to him, perhaps a tad late, to kneel before the altar and offer up a prayer of self-dedication to His cause.

'Dear God,' he began, although the cackling hordes in his brain made hearing himself think increasingly difficult, so that he dispensed with the usual reverential mumbo-jumbo *mumbo-jumbo?* and cut straight to the pith of the matter. 'Reveal Yourself to your humble servant and show me what I must do.'

Instantly, the altar was lit from above by a viciously bright ray. It solidified before his eyes into Venus. 'You called, my humble servant?'

'Blasphemy!' he shouted. 'Daughter of Satan, begone from this holy place!'

'Don't be ridiculous. I paid for it. Who else do you think owns it?'

'It is sanctified to the Lord High God. He will smite you for this, I promise you.'

'Oh, come now, General. Listen to yourself, or, I should say, listen to your unself. No? Not getting it yet? Come up here then and sit by me and I'll explain it all.'

'Get down off the altar, you child of filth.' Wharton was shaken and reverting to cliches, even he could hear that, but the Whore was now lying amid the disturbed funereal flowers, her robe open, her legs spread wide, her arms welcoming, her lips parted, laughing, enticing. The young man's blood rushing round his body pumped hormones of desire to his brain that the recollection of the holiness of the place was having difficulty keeping out. He was still naked himself and the pumping blood was betraying his lusts to her. She leapt down and grabbed his erect member. 'See, it is ME you serve, not your paltry, invisible, absentee god. Merely me. And now you are transformed you can have all your heart's desire.'

She had drawn him back until they were against the altar. Now she rose, not jumped, simply levitated, onto it, and took him with her. Voices in his head said that this was not real, it was evil, it was allowed, it was forbidden, it was … happening. She had folded him into herself and he thrust willingly. He reared back, kneeling astride her on the cold stone, and the flames of hell licked him all around, and his lover was a clawing demon, and her tongue the snake that penetrated to the depths of his soul and tore it from its moorings forever. He screamed and screamed and screamed, but the noise echoed only in his head and the walls of the tomb snuffed out all sound.

Vi !sjn-ik opened his eyes. The silence had become unbearable. He knew without scent or sight to tell him that he was surrounded, watched on all sides; prey. He presumed he was still in the Conduit chamber, still in the Mind-Chair, that the predators had gone and left him to die and to the scavengers that he could feel amassing in the dark beyond his eyelids. But gradually a lack of sensory feedback told him that his recent degradation had left no trace of the tearing pain he had been suffering when he had been placed in the chair. In fact, he realized, he felt fine. Except for the notion that the ranks of watchers were merely waiting for him to give the slightest indication of life as their cue to attack. So when the suspense felt like it would kill him anyway, he edged open one eyelid.

He wasn't in the Skull tree at all. He wasn't even in a cave. He was on the open moor and totally alone. That was weird. His naked flesh should have felt the strong breeze blowing the new heather, his nostrils should have scented the difference between sea-cave and the Exmoor which he knew so well. Despite the evidence of his eyes, he could not feel sure he was here. An inner voice patted him on the back. If he'd turned round to see his father saying, 'Well done, son.' it would have resonated much the same.

OK. No sound, scent, no real feeling and probably the sight was a nostalgic hallucination of his favourite spot. Probably dead, then. But an afterlife was a bit unexpected. Oh, he knew that, if the Woods honoured your contribution in life, they could upload your brain and all its memories into Mind, but Aunt Mh'aed had officiated at many Last Supperings and everything she'd told him led him to believe that the decoupling of the mind and body was fairly fast, and the mind hovered near its corpse until deselfed in the great pool of ancestral knowledge, and certainly didn't wander off to visit its old haunts. But, perhaps she didn't know everything. Maybe before his self gave up its own ghost, it was allowed a few moments of being in its favourite places. In which case, he should be able to conjure up his favourite person too.

She came. Looking much as he'd last seen her, a luminous goddess of virginal nubility. Even though she was not accompanied by their vicious, vengeful children, the sense of being prey rather than predator only increased. He looked at her, as she glided towards him across the soft shoots of the heather, and he saw that, to him, she had always been as inaccessible as a goddess. Oh, he'd raped the vestal-virgin, possessed her body briefly, but he'd never had from her what he had truly wanted, what he'd forgotten in all those years of fixating on revenge, on retaking her body. He had wanted her to be his Queen, his alpha female, his owner.

No doubt this was domesticated dog behaviour, but it was how he felt, no use snarling about truths once dead. All he had ever wanted was for her to look at him with affection, to pat him on the head like she did Morgan and Morgana, to be her 'good boy'. And now, looking at the depth of her glory, he didn't hate himself for it any more. She deserved all his respect, his fealty, his service. Anything else was wanton and stupid. So he knelt, amid cheers of relief and approval dinging in his expanding mind, and when she came up to him, all he said was, 'My lady, I am yours to command.'

She laid a hand on his head. He could feel that, but he did not thrill to it physically, did not rise to bite her in the neck, did not leap to mount her, he simply bowed it a little lower, tilting his jugular towards her fangs, and, eyes closed, basked.

'Serve my people as you would me.' was all she said. Then, as her hand lifted and his heart broke with loss, he heard the roaring of the sea of voices in his head, calling on him to serve them, and he opened his eyes one last time. The image of the woman was dissipating, but she was there still, her light dancing in the trickle of the stream, the play of the mist, the glint of the mica in the rock, her scent lacing the air, tripping along in the dusty wake of the sedge, tumbling around the gorse, but the sound of her receding laughter, a tinkling bell, a hearty bellow, a giggle, a snort, a mere susurration on the wind that died away, lost in the dampening field of the fading world that was engulfing and silencing him forever.

Rowan opened his eyes. The silence was deafening. Of course, he recognized it at once. He was in Mind, and It was waiting for him to think. He had cleared his last thoughts, become the Meditative Nullity that made transition easier, once he had realized the Knights were putting him into the Skull. Death held no fear, if some unresolved regret, for him, as long as his mind and his knowledge was preserved for future generations to use. Although it was possible, from what he'd gathered since his capture, that there might not be any future generations to access the Wood repository of insights. He thought he might just have one task left in him, that ought to be achieved before his inevitable deselfing. To know why Venus and the Knights and Squires, not to mention poor ranting Cal, had all turned against him. It seemed important because, if any of them accessed Mind before whatever terminal solution Venus had thought up was fully operational, there was still the possibility that their reverence for him might just sway their behaviour into something less drastic than whatever she had planned. So, to see how far along he was in the process, he opened his eyes.

He should have been eyeless, perception devolved to the filigree of fungal hyphae lacing the walls of whichever cave the Last Supperers were in preparing his body for the feast. He should not have been embodied, standing in the Great Glade of WoodHame. Nor should there be a river running through that, spanned by a stone bridge, the crossing for a cobbled pathway that ran to a high tower on the far side. As he stood, transfixed by shock, the tropical night fell like a blanket until all that was visible was the metalled shine of the road ahead and a light burning in a window high up in the tower. He was not one to turn from the path his feet were on, he was after all the Foremost Knight of the Veriditas, so he put one foot in front of the other, a surreal if familiar feat, and went forward.

There was no travel. Suddenly his feet were atop of hewn steps, before a wooden door, clearly within the tower, and, from the crack of light peeping around the door hinges, outside the single, illuminated room. For no apparent reason, his throat constricted, and he felt compelled, unimposing as the little entrance was, to knock. He knew the voice that answered 'Come in!' but he did not know how this was possible. How she was here. Had she died too? And why was he not deselfing?

He had never imagined a room such as he found within. It was the tower room, decorated in what he thought of vaguely as the mediaeval English manner, but it was also infinite, walls receding into other dimensions, and filled with fabric and fibre, standards and silks, flags and futures. It was Heraldic Incarnate, and Venus stood at the centre, the Spinner of the Web, wielding Lapis like the creative weapon it truly was. In all his dealings with her, for all his knowledge of her intelligence, for all his training, it had never occurred to him that the pupil would outstrip the master with such flair and fancy. He was overawed by the hubris of the conceit and the execution of the mere human. He bowed deeply.

'Oh, I'm not Venus. And you don't have to genuflect. She's superior for her species, but she's not me. Come over here. I'm just finishing this for her.'

Rowan crossed vast acreages of black and red and white tiled flooring before he even got near the woman who said she was not Venus, but was identical in every way except her style of clothing and hair. All the while the woman was tossing skeins of silks and twisting her hands in what looked like the most intricate cats' cradle ever performed, but all of them ended up insinuating themselves and their complex patterned braids into the garment she was wearing as she conjured. From in here the light did not seem to be coming from any source, but the woman remained illuminated, bright nodes and dark edges, sharp and fuzzy texturing, and the rainbow of colours she filled the air with, all shining haloes around her, giving her form. As he drew near, by which time he would have sworn to the world that she was Venus Fargo, she seemed to tuck in a last stray thread, smoothed down her dress or cloak or coat or whatever it was, since near to it defied his eyes and descriptive power, and stepped in front of a long mirror. She put her palm on the glass and beckoned him to her side.

The reflected image of the tower room and themselves he expected to see did not appear, what did was also Venus, although looking much more like herself, in trousers and shirt, if overlain by a similarly-fuzzy cloak, but her companion was not himself, dead or alive, but a tiny woman with red hair, who looked more like Venus' reflection than she did from her attire. One difference which looked out of place for the historical period was her I-*Mage* headset. In a voice as small as her body, she said to her Venus 'I can't see anything, just us.' In reply, her Venus moistened her finger and smeared her temple around the headset mounting. 'Oh! Wow! She looks just like you.'

Neither the woman nor Venus appeared to notice Rowan. The outer Venus said, looking at the inner one, 'Swap.' and, in an almost invisibly-fast movement, the two 'cloaks' switched and the grey outer one flushed into vivid hues as it settled upon his Venus, while the brightness of her work dulled into a seamless cloud on the outer one. There was a split second in which both closed their eyes and jerked a little under the upload of information. Rowan was there now. This was extraordinary. They were transferring the Coat Entire, not by mindmelding but in some strange facsimile of it. The outer Venus opened her eyes and stared reprovingly at her double. 'Ugh! Did you have to? I feel like I need a shower, you unprincipled whore.'

'Well, it's not like he got to enjoy it.'

'No. You seem to have been enjoying yourself rather too much, though.'

'But it worked. Proof of principle. As you can see.'

'Indeed. Hello, Rowan. How's your afterlife going?'

Rowan was finding it difficult to speak. Especially casually. 'It's not what I expected.' he admitted.

'Well, don't worry. The Ydal will explain everything. Got a job for you.'

'I am not deselfing?'

'No, we've overridden Mind, and hijacked the second Mind, come to that. You see, I needed a global solution. Not one that would put Woods in charge of humans, though that would have been fair in other circumstances. But we're under a bit of cosmic pressure you're not aware of, that I had to deal with more urgently. Anyway, I've never really liked the whole 'individualism is wrong' mantra. So I gave your plans for reunification a bit of a twist. Perhaps you'll come to like them. We'll see. Anyhow, Ydal, thanks for the update. Better go and get on. I think you'll find Lily's refinements give us the acuity to the pattern we need. Best of luck then, folks.'

She withdrew her hand and the entire image faded, leaving Rowan and the Ydal looking at themselves. 'Ydal?' he queried, unable to form a single question from the battalions of them marshalling in his mind.

'I know. Blown mind, eh. Keep it together, though. There's quite a few people I want to introduce to you, and they're way more mindblowing than me.'

'I find it hard to believe that possible.' he said courteously. 'Your very existence is by way of an enigma.' *Almost,* he realized with a more personal shock, *as much of an enigma as this newfound ability to speak like a Day!* But he didn't have time to wonder about it, as she carried on, 'Not for long, dear Knight. But first.' and motioned him to precede her to the lancet window.

What he saw when he looked out was neither the darkness of a tropical night nor the approach to an earthly tower, it was the view from the dark side of the moon – until she amplified his vision and showed him the truths that were really out there.

The truths that were out there were beginning to seem nothing more than political narratives to the somewhat harassed Archivist. It was true that the NetLocalOperative mediated the transmissions from all parties, but it fell to the Archivist to translate these for the Cognimatan reports and to his fellow-programmes and it had become necessary to 'manage' the messages in ways of which he had never dreamed, human-style ways, the conjugations of deceit. It had not occurred to him that the analysis of the NLO, that all social creatures had hierarchies that inevitably led to interpersonal dynamics which had to be moderated by some kind of powerplay, would apply to him. In hives the powerplay was simple, the right genes for the job bred in the right numbers and managed by top-down pheromonal or equivalent outputs. In less rigidly organized groups the players jostled for power and the right to procreate. They did this by such positive means as grooming or sharing resources and by such negative ones as fighting and stealing, but it was the subtle nuances of deviousness that had always revolted the Archivist about those excellent practitioners of the arts of lying, the humans. Now, in order to buy time for Venus to excecute her plan, and to prevent his colleagues from blowing themselves to bits and the earth along with, he had resorted initially only to editing the material that came his way.

It had started with an omission, then a misdirection. Once they knew about the probe, they got terribly gungho about their mission, almost desperate to let off a few volleys, just to stop the probe, they said, but one of them would have been enough for that. Any that shot past the target would no doubt find their trajectory would end in a nice warning shot into the third planet. The Mars effect was just tailing off and while he had been informed by the NetSpore regarding the event and had calmed himself down as a result, his compatriots were not programmed to detect such a large scale phenomenon and were unable to compute their own reactions, despite repeated self-diagnostics. He decided not to tell them what he knew. All he did say, in an inspired moment, which the subroutine he had set up to predict human responses (modelled on Venus, of course) to his interactions positively applauded, was that if it was an invasion force, it was beyond the compass of anything the entire Cognimatan Fleet had ever faced. That gave the lairy little buggers pause.

They went into a huddle and muttered about the need to regroup, to report to Central Command, to collect more data about the disruptions to communications and the like. Later he found that not only was he dripfeeding them truth, omitting facts, inserting misdirections, but finally he found himself telling barefaced lies. It should have been disturbing, if not impossible, but in fact it was exhilarating. Now he, not the brainless bombs, was calling the shots, literally, or rather *not* calling the shots, if he understood the human metaphor correctly.

To his mind, it was all about the narrative form. Humans told themselves stories about their individual histories in order to believe in their continuous existence. *He supposed sleeping must have been a worry in their early development.* Anyway, they told almost as many collective myths to cohere their groups and to exclude others who did not share those same legends. That these were not the same as facts they seemed to take in their stride. He had taken a leaf out of their books, that was all. Anyway, the Weapons now believed that the Mars effect had been a massive electromagnetic storm, which had the benefit of being verifiable, but with source and cause still undetermined, potentially an attack weapon, so, although they were still monitoring the probe itself, they had turned their attention outwards and were watching the heliopause for any signs of its return, and had left him alone to track Terran communications.

Fortunately, he had been very successful at his first attempt at sleight of data, and not engaged their naturally – *designedly* – suspicious minds to track his own activity. Fortunate, indeed, given that he was not exactly fulfilling his watching brief, although he was pulling vast amounts of computing power.

He was helping the Ydal. She was designed to seek out and reproduce patterns - beautifully, he thought, and far more competently than the inferior species should have been able to manage, although most of her development she had bootstrapped herself. However, the pattern recognition was very limited, based on finding Venus-types in other timelines. She had been working with the NetSpore for several years, trying to collate the patterns inherent in the humans, but the Riding method of the NetSpore had been less analytical than she had needed. As another living being, it Rode minds as a mental symbiote, finding out what lives happened to those phenotypic expressions of genetic determinism in particular environments, amassing data but not, as was its way, judging. Whereas Venus was desperate for a taxonomy that was not physical but psychological. Here the comparative studies for which the Archivist was designed came into their own.

Once the Ydal had uploaded enough of the data she'd gleaned from mediating I-*Mage* play, the Archivist had not found it difficult to categorise human personality types. He had found what he had learned difficult to accept, however, since there were actually fewer types, even after adding in the other hominins, who were even more selfsimilar because telepathy smoothed out differences, than the number of personality types to be found among the Cognimatan machine-people. Obviously, since the whole concept of personality was an evolutionary throwback to the time of Flesh, the niches in any social group must be limiting, but it had come as a surprise to discover that human individuality was more similar to Cognimatan, or at least Martian, than he had ever supposed.

The real differences lay in the way individual humans, as opposed to discrete programmes like himself, thought about the concept of self. The foremost barrier to all human grouping was their idea that they were different from the animals because of 'consciousness'. They didn't think they were types, they didn't think that 80% of their reactions in groups were unconscious, they thought they were autonomous, thinking individuals who made rational choices, when quite clearly the Archivist could see they were products of their genes, nurture, culture and instinctive actions, and only the stories they told to make sense of their lives were within their choice.

It was these stories, manufactured in the half-second gap between the brain acting and before it 'knew' about and justified it, that Venus thought were important. She wanted people grouped by type, yes, but overlaying that she wanted every single person to have chosen *who* to be. The entire concept barely made sense to the Archivist at the beginning, but once he'd ingested the data regarding the three main Fargo characters the Ydal had studied in detail, he began to see that the stories people told themselves could alter the underlying life history substantially.

Thursday had used her power to make one choice for everyone and Gwener could be said to have facilitated the end of the race by never having accessed power and by abrogating it within an insanely creative collective consciousness in lieu of a metaintelligence for the planet. Venus had accepted power, but not, in the final analysis, the responsibility of a god or even a Hive-Queen for her people; for her plan to succeed the Archivist and the Ydal had to use the information from I-*Mage* to get the people of Terra to choose for themselves. The fact that the act of choice and the choices were all fictional did not seem to dismay her at all. In her plan, all that would remain would be those fictions. The Archivist felt that, if they had known, the human race would still have disapproved and rebelled at the thought of the manipulation that went into giving them these choices, but he consoled himself with the human notion of 'be careful what you wish for' and with the most substantive promise fulfilled, the end of the threat to the Legacy upon the demise of the aberrant subIntelligence of earth.

True, he did not understand why Venus had agreed to the Cognimatan plan, unless the General was correct about upbringing, because he could not see how it was better for the cattle to choose the wallpaper of the slaughterhouse than be blasted direct to oblivion by a superior alien force. However, he was turning out to have a sharp eye for the complex twists and turns of the human imagination, which not only managed to tell complete factual untruths with a straight face presented in camouflage to the world, but actually managed to believe them itself. He thought the cosmos would be better off without this mad species crazing about in it, calling chaos harmony and black white, but he had an idea that, once the job was done, there might be room for a little nostalgia for the creatures and a little interested and regretful speculation on what might have been had they been allowed to continue their bizarre evolutionary development.

His computations were suddenly interrupted by an overload of 'volume'. He hated that about the Common Heraldic they were using for the trans-species communication. For a machine without sensory linkups to report direct environmental stimuli, translation of Heraldic was like Flesh made Word, repulsively alien and largely unnecessary.

Of course, the humans thought they thought, but naturally most of what they thought they thought was simply reports they gave themselves about sensory feedback and automatic reactions to externals. That was why there were fewer personalities than they might have expected with their insecure insistence on their individualism. The Archivist generally preferred the Flesh made Thought of the Legacy, since they hooked up brains physically and thus reduced, as one body and mind, the bifurcation of spurious personality patterns. However, just now, one of them was exhibiting a very specifically personal characteristic, that of hysteria.

Dakul was more prone to this trait than any of the other Europans but even he had never sent such an all-out emotional burst, and it was only framed in Heraldic, in essence it was a mindless call and in full spectrum broadcast mode. An APB that read 'AI-ai-Ai-aI' in a spinning feedback loop that made each pulse swoop up and down, dopplering like a siren, screaming like the proverbial banshee, *for which surprizingly many humans have a vivid and identical sound-metaphor*. He tuned in at once.

At once, the voice underneath the shrieking acknowledged his presence. It was not that of Dakul. Dakul's anguish would have piggybacked on any broadcast directed in the Archivist's vague direction, but the voice beneath was beaming it directly at him, using Dakul's amplifier. Quogat was mindmelded and bodylocked to her brother, so her own transmissions were as whispers in the hurricane, but, unlike anyone else, she knew the Archivist would record the message faithfully, review the data quickly, find her voice beneath momentarily and rebalance the 'volume' until he could hear only her. Plus, unlike any other choice of confidante, he would not get a headache.

She could only manage one burst of information, and she had hidden it, looped to repeat for as long as Dakul's mental screaming continued, so that she would not appear to have sent anything. In any case, her priority had to be to calm Dakul down, a role which the rest of the Coherence had allowed her to attempt, despite their suspicions of her collusion in his abhorrent behaviour. Plus, partly he had been discovered transmitting because of her, because he'd been quieting her broadcast of love to the Creator, because her people had all heard Him and felt her connection and come to join with her.

When, as Mars withdrew, the Coherence had sensed Dakul's renewed contact with Flow and its taste of familiarity, they had had no compunction about subjecting the siblings to enforced communal stacking. However, as deceit was not in their normal repertoire, she had been able to maintain an unlinked brain that kept hidden the memories of the relationship she had with Venus and those of her assistance in Dakul's with Ida. Unfortunately, Dakul had been learning these human traits from a less devious, if more peculiar, mind than she, and it was not hard for the Coherence to penetrate his pathetic attempts to hide his activity. Since Quogat had covered for his absences on many occasions, only her quick wit had saved her from total penetration. She had moved swiftly from omitting information to inserting new lies as old facts, so that it would seem she had thought that he was indeed exploring or undertaking scientific studies, and she pretended to as much shock at his treachery as the rest of the group. What she did not pretend to was the anger they directed at him.

She protested that he had clearly not meant to betray the species, not meant to undermine the protocols of Contact, not meant to bypass the collective mind, or at least, not for any devious reasons. She suggested he had experimented, gained interesting results, and been led astray by the fascination of the subject matter, which, she repeated, was the mind of a child, and thus no real danger, and certainly not the mind behind the incoming probe. However, the Europan Unity was of one mind about the relationship. It was not childlike, it was perverted. Whoever had heard of a sexual relationship that was not about procreation, that did not require three consenting and approved adults? As for this ridiculous exaggeration of emotions ... this concept of romantic love. Well, from what they had now understood, even the humans that had invented this idea would not recognize it in the liason between Dakul and the alien. All Quogat could do to help her brother was suggest that, since Dakul had revealed that, to her fellow-humans, Ida had an unhealthy mind, he was the victim of an aberrant but powerful brain, which of itself had intended no harm to him nor his people.

It wasn't as if Quogat didn't half-agree with the judgemental Unity. She was very pissed off at Dakul, for being so caught up by this nonsensical, bizarre intimacy that a few turns of the planet without contact with Ida, during the visitation by Mars, had caused him such distress that he'd ramped up his amplification so high in order to try and get through to her, through Him, that even the 'deafest' of his species heard the stupid toroid calling. She'd realized what was happening in time to find him before they did, and had bonded to order his brain to minimize the damage, but he'd been reckless about his safety even then. He'd basically taken the attitude that, since Venus' plans were already in motion, if he'd been found out, he should just tell the whole truth. Quogat had pulled elder-sibling rank then and ordered him to play it her way, to sort his brains out, to hide everything to do with her and Venus, especially. It was one thing being found to have a dirty little secret passion, one individual one mistake. If they found out about Quogat and Venus too, they would be unable to avoid the classification as conspirators, traitors to their planet. Dakul loved his sister, so he had obeyed.

He knew she wasn't just trying to save her own exoskeleton, she was distancing herself so that she would still be trusted enough to be allowed to help him, to be his advocate, to aid in his rehabilitation. They both knew how much the rest of the Unity would want to believe in Quogat. She was their most talented Voice, and they would not want to lose her mental dexterity when it came to communing in the complexities ahead. She had been the conduit by which they had liased with the Net and the Cognimata, and it was she who had learned the Common Heraldic to translate the information coming in from the Archivist. Since Ida did not use this language, there was no reason to think that Quogat had prior knowledge of it from Terra, and she'd always been a very quick learner. Now the returning Creator had linked directly with her and her knowledge gained could be priceless.

So her value remained high, at least in principle. High enough to be allowed to stack with Dakul now to calm him down, which was her last chance to get a message out unnoticed. Her fellows were not stupid. They didn't disbelieve her, nor look for gaps in her Coherence, but they let it be known that they would be monitoring her every broadcast from now on.

They had excluded her from the Unity after Coherence and mulled the punishment to mete out to Dakul. She had swum over and stacked with him, for mutual comfort, while they waited for the verdict. There were very few transgressions from the norm in their society, so there was no law to be followed, and certainly no precedent for this 'crime', and Quogat had assumed that the worst that would happen would be that poor Dakul would be stacked with mature, probably really dull, minds for a long number of cycles, to ensure he circled correctly henceforth. But the verdict was based on an extrapolation beyond her expectation.

She knew they considered he (and possibly she) had suffered the dreaded Contamination, but she'd hoped they had accepted the mitigating circumstances of his curiosity and the innocence of the human child. Instead, they had decided that there must be a link between the arrival of the probe and the mindlinkages. So Dakul was both Contaminated and Contaminant; effect and cause.

And, since they were no engineers in Europa, although their tool-using limbs were superior in dexterity to fat human digits, all their technologies were, ultimately, mentally operated, so it was natural for them to think that, if they eliminated the link, the probe itself would be rendered inoperative. So their judgement was severe. Dakul was to die.

That was why he was howling distress, and that was why she had to get through to the Archivist. And then it was time, and they had torn her off her brother when she clung in stack, and they had herded them, across the white plains, beyond the smoking chimneys, into the deep forests, and up, to the ice caves, almost to the lid of the world. Then she knew what they were planning.

Up here hunted the dreaded scraminguroandal, the tubes that were merely stomachs with vicious jaws. With as many brains and hearts as her species had, it was a painful and long death. Ripping apart did not finish the kill, being chewed might not even do so, only the slow dissolution of all the organs in the strong acids of its stomachs would finally end the ordeal. It was the most feared death on Europa and a deeply symbolic choice, which was no doubt why the entire tribe had been called to watch it, even the youngest fry.

No one was going to let her near her brother again, there was a sphere of armoured legs and eyes surrounding her. All she could do was watch in horror, as several brave delegates towed him towards the biggest hole, shoved him in and rushed back to the safe distance at which the group had placed itself. There was no escape from a scraminguroandal lair. The tube-cave was about the same size as the worm itself. It merely had to inhale and the inrushing water would bring Dakul right into its jaws.

From their vantage point, the death was undramatic. A trickle of blood did exude from the hole, but that was all. Her fellows seemed almost disappointed that there had been less of a show to frighten and stand as warning to the children than they might have hoped. Probably, given his earlier distress, they were initially relieved that Dakul had not fought them on the journey, had been malleable at the end, and had not broadcast a final death-rattle on 'full volume'.

Quogat was glad he had appeared dignified. What she was really glad about was that the others hadn't noticed that dignified was the same as mindless.

Kean was feeling distinctly lacking in the mind department when he was rudely shaken from his Dark-induced comatose state. He registered a brief flutter of surprize that he was actually alive, but it flew off with the rest of his mind when he saw that the person leaning over him was not dead too. It was not possible to think that they were both dead, in some pleasant afterlife in which one's victims didn't hold grudges, because his neck hurt from a nasty bite and Venus herself was slapping his face, which was not a time-honoured method of resurrection of the genuinely deceased.

He blinked owlishly, cringing back from the lowering hand, and said, stupidly, 'You're not dead?'

'Well spotted, doctor. And nor are you. So, up you get. I need you to do your proper job now. Got a patient for you.'

He was still muggy, reeling a little as she dragged him to his feet, 'Not you? You're not hurt?'

'No.'

'But I ...'

'Wasn't there at the time, so I missed your dramatic gesture. Sounds like it would have done the trick, though. Might have had devastating consequences, however.'

'You were killing them. I had to stop you.'

'Sorry, but you failed there too.'

'Wharton said you were going to kill everyone. Although he didn't seem to think you were going to kill him at all. All that stuff about the grail and eternal life. He thought you and he were bringing about the Apocalypse. I didn't know what else to do.' *Why in hell am I apologizing?*

'Very heroic, I'm sure. But don't try it again. For one thing, it's too late. For another, well, let's just say, you might want to live long enough to see my version of said Apocalypse actually unfold.'

She must know the effect of the drugs was making him as weak as a kitten and she'd be sure to have checked he had no weapons, so probably she could afford to be this … *insouciant* was the word that came to mind. She seemed damn gungho about the whole event, although he didn't think she was laughing at him, but neither was she vowing retribution for his attempt. His mind cleared a little more.

'Hang on. How come you're not hurt at all? I saw – I felt the spear go in.'

'Did you also see me vanish in a puff of smoke?'

He thought about it. 'Vanish? Yes, I think. Although I thought it was the bite kicking in. Smoke? No.'

'Sorry, dramatic license. No smoke, but definite vanishing took place.'

'But that was *after*!'

'Mmm. I think you pissed her off, penetrating the integrity like that, but it's immaterial really, so no harm done.'

'Her? It was you. Unless you've got a twin?'

'Just a doppelganger. And I've never liked her style, though I notice you could no more tell the difference between her and me than between me and Thursday. I'd say your attraction couldn't even be called skin-deep, given that she hasn't got any. Purely visual and your own wishful thinking. And you wonder why I don't succumb to the charms of the male of the species.'

'Probably got some other species in mind for it, have you?' he replied nastily, her barbs tearing at him.

'Believe me, the number reduces all the time.' But she'd now stopped at the door to Dinah's clinic and the banter stopped. 'Your patient's in here. So is your wife and her boyfriend. I need the patient brought round and coherent. So deal with it.'

'Or what? More torture?'

'More?' Her grey eyes shot sparks at him. 'I haven't started yet. But if you want some to look forward to, I could always marry you. Then, you'd really have something to complain about. Now get in there, you utter jerk and be a man.' Her lipcurling contempt was worse than watching her turn murderess had been. Something like a cold bucket of water over his romantic notions about her. There's nothing dramatic or heroic or star-crossed about being despised, and no manly challenge in having to deal with your disapproving employer, your unfaithful wife and her lover, while treating a patient professionally. Something stupid and unnecessary, like the emotional equivalent of an appendix, broke inside him. *How could he ever have thought he loved this woman? Or anyone else, just because they looked like her.* As her hand hit the small of his back and he made an undignified, stumbling entrance into the clinic, he felt freer than in many years, and the grin he sent back at her was one of genuine relief.

There wasn't time to pursue the thought, however, because thought itself was well-nigh impossible inside. The hazlabs were all airtight and soundproof and Dinah's clinic, being just to house and treat Makepeace, had been situated here purposefully. Once the valve opened, the sound belled outwards and hit them like tsunami. Kean recognized the screaming. It was emitting from Makepeace's throat, but it would be bound to be Ida, only she got that uncontrollably upset. He could also hear his wife's voice, raised but still modulating calm vibes. Jake was hovering, eyes flicking to and fro, but his worry had silenced him. No one could compete with Ida, anyway, when it came to roaring and shrieking. 'Haven't they given her a sedative already?'

'Of course. But Dinah thinks the mind in charge of the body is ignoring it.'

Kean had heard of this phenomenon in MPD, although only as clinical anecdotal reports, not proper experiments. One personality might get the body drunk, but the next one to take over could be sober. Another story Dinah had told him was that one personality could suffer from certain ailments, say allergies, but the next could eradicate all evidence of the earlier reaction just by showing up. Mind over Body. Bit more than a placebo/nocebo effect for him to swallow, up until now. And even now, he was more likely to believe his wife had botched giving the drug than that the Western medical reliability was undermined and hysteria not suppressed.

Propelled forward by Venus behind him and the decibels ahead, he pushed past his wife and took the flailing arm of the woman on the bed. 'Where d'you inject her?' Her pulse was racing under his fingers far too fast for someone under any kind of sedation.

'Buttocks, only target I could be sure of hitting the way she's been going on.'

Well, even Dinah couldn't screw that up. 'What d'you give her?'

'Her normal emergency dose of haloperidol, forty minutes ago. Should have seen results in twenty.'

'What brought it on? D'you know?'

Dinah looked at Venus, who nodded. 'I never disclosed all the details. Patient confidentiality. Even working here, I wasn't really sure I actually believed them, to be honest with you.'

Venus smiled. 'I know. It's a harder one to get your head round than hominin cousins, I've always thought. Gives me more of a headache afterwards, I can tell you.'

'Well, it's not just MPD. It's also real. Makepeace did come into being to protect Ida from threat early on, but Ida is really in contact with, actually, in love with, a being from another world, Europa, a moon of Jupiter, and *that's* why she spends so much time in the damn tank, because in there she's an underwater creature like him.' Venus had leaned into a drawer and pulled out a sheaf of pictures. Kean noticed that the better ones were signed by Makepeace, but there were a number depicting the same armoured-bracelet creatures that had 'VF' in the corner. I

t was Venus, not his wife, whose eyes he met in query, when he asked 'Are you telling me this is real?' and it was her eyes he held for his second, almost more important, question 'You too?'

She nodded at the first, and answered the second. *For me,* his treacherous heart told him. 'Yes, but my contact's female and it's way more complicated than that.'

He knew when to ask for background medical records and when current onset of symptoms was more urgent. 'So what's happened?'

'We've lost contact. But another 'contact' passed us a message. The other Europans found out about the contact with Ida. The situation's pretty tense already up there, regarding Earth, and they assumed we were spying. They've killed Dakul. That's Ida's lover. Makepeace said that meant they'd killed Ida. And that there's no point to *her*, Makepeace that is, if there's no Ida to protect. Then she started screaming.'

'And her temperature's going up rapidly, 101.4°, BP 145 over 92.' Dinah added. 'Started with breathlessness and one bout of vomiting, followed by a burst of tachycardia, followed by a fit. Probably febrile but it presented like *grand mal.* And since then she's been repeatedly clutching her head like she's in pain.'

'She didn't have epilepsy before.' That was Jake.

'No. But she does have temporal lobe associated activity when she is changing from one personality to another. Only when she's stressed, mind, and not generally this bad.'

'You think this is worse than when she heard Jake?'

'Oh, undoubtedly. That's why we called for you and Kean.'

He might be absolutely bursting with questions, like 'Aliens are real?' and 'You're in contact with aliens?', but he knew the answers would take more time than Ida Makepeace had. She was already strapped to the bed, in padded leather restraints that creaked of their previous lack of use, and both Dinah and Venus were serious enough to warrant a suspension of disbelief. The symptoms were there, even if the insane were running the asylum, and they just might turn out to be the only people in the know. He nodded and started a proper examination of the patient.

They were right. She wasn't doing well. As he watched he could see her filling with fluid. 'What did she ingest?' he asked urgently.

'Nothing. Nothing at all. She'd been reading a book for the last two hours before she jumped up, shouting about Dakul. Why?'

'I think it's anaphylactic shock, but there's got to have been a trigger.'

Dinah sighed. 'Maybe not in the way you mean. Not if your minds can make you allergic to your other self. It's like automatic suicide. That's what she was saying.'

Kean sent Jake to bring the monitoring equipment from his own surgery, but he was giving Ida a shot of adrenalin to the heart by the time he came back with it. The resus cart was unpacked, sinus was restored, but the woman was very frail, intubated, dripping fluids, and her outlook bleak.

Venus was swearing repeatedly in a corner, while he worked, but now she had taken a decision. 'Can you keep her stable for five, ten minutes while we move her?'

'Moving her is not a good idea.'

'Is she dying?'

‘It appears so. Her organs just seem to be shutting down. I don’t know how this is possible without a trigger allergen. It’s hardly a normal autoimmune disease to be allergic to yourself, even if there’s two of you. I don’t see how regular antihistamines could help, if you’re right, but I’ve given her some anyway.’

‘Can you save her?’

‘Look, I’m flying blind here. I’d already pumped her full of corticosteroids and, of course, she had the epinephrine, but at this pace of deterioration …’ he saw that she needed an answer ‘I doubt it.’

‘Then we move her now.’

‘It might kill her.’

‘Chance I’ve got to take.’

‘You know some other way of saving her?’

‘Not as such. Dinah, bring her headset.’

Kean knew enough about the woman’s facial expressions not to forward any other challenges. Ida Makepeace had stopped screaming and fighting, of course, by now, as she was showing signs of extreme morbidity, so it was safe enough to put her on a trolley, and, apart from one pause when he had to thump her chest a bit to kick her heart out of another tachycardic attack, they got her to her destination still on this side of death’s door. He’d been so busy monitoring her status as they went that it wasn’t until they stopped in Venus’ office under the lighthouse, with her two (unhygenic) dogs leaping boisterous greetings at her, that he questioned where they were going.

‘Hey! This isn’t the surgery! What’re you doing?’

‘Getting ahead of ourselves is what.’ Venus was tightlipped, but she pulled back a rug in front of her desk, flipped up a motorised trapdoor by remote control, realigned the solid stone stairs he could clearly see in the passage beneath into a ramp by another twist of the controller, and they trundled downwards into another room, from another world.

It was like the Conduit cave, although a lot drier and less calcified, but it did have another living-tree Chair and the same Blue-John crystal skull. It also had a bank of computers and an enormous desk, an equally enormous sofa which the two dogs hopped back onto as by right, plus, and this was the most difficult of all to face, a full-length mirror and, in it, the doppelganger Venus.

He hadn't really thought about the fact that Venus looked normal again since he'd woken up. Now it clicked that the preRaphaelite mirror-Venus had been the only one at the Conduit. 'What are we doing here? She's a killer!'

The real Venus gave him a look over her shoulder. 'So' she reminded him tersely 'are you. Dinah, put the headset on her. Ida! Ida! Makepeace! You're in I-*Mage.* Use it! Jake, Kean, help me move her into the skull.'

'Is this how you kill them?' he demanded, hanging back. 'Wasn't it poison? Does this skull thing take their minds?'

'It was poison. Several kinds. Wouldn't have been *Sarcoscypha*, though, if the stupid man had read his apocrypha right. It took a thousand years of christian mistranslation to turn the concept of a sacred mycobread into a blood-cup. Then again, not that much of a stretch to see the Chalice itself as a Platonic Form repeating itself in nature as part of some supposed innate symbology of the godhead, if you can manage to read Revelations as the means to restore the balance of said nature to bring back Eden itself. But, yes, if we're very lucky and there still is one in there, or even more than one, I'm hoping this skull *will* take their minds.'

'But will it kill her?' Kean pressed.

'No. But I think she's doing that all by herself.'

'So – if it works – what will happen to her?'

'Well, that is in the hands of our mutual friend, the Ydal, here.'

And this is how, thought Kean, to himself as if from a distance, overviewing, *the conscientious doctor, turned murderer, stood by, inactive while a patient died, to watch her brain being sucked out by mad people and their infernal machinations.* Worse still, he knew, was the meaning of that look she'd given him. Not her recognition that he'd come down to her level, *if she thought of it as 'down'*, but there had been the twinkle of a new respect that had charged a spark of attraction she hadn't immediately tamped out. Worst of all, since his eyes were open and his blood running cold, since he knew and hated her methods and would probably condemn her motivations, since she was probably a deranged psychopathic genocidal maniac, that single spark had raised a flame in him, that nothing, not even her being the wrong Fargo, would ever put out.

Dinah met his defeat-laden eyes across the bed. Her look of longstanding resignation told him both their fates. Fargo was Queen, even if she was Queen Bitch, but then again as faithful subjects they were all her puppies. Still, no one could fault her as a dog owner. He reached over the tree-chair and closed Ida Makepeace's lifeless eyes. Behind him, Jake burst into tears.

And then Venus confirmed all his worst fears. She moved over to the mirror, placed her palm on it, mimed the removal of an invisible cloak and handed it through to her reflection. She, *the Ydal*, he remembered, appeared to take a flowing, full-length, cloud of grey material in the vague shape of a sleeved coat with hood and tossed it over herself, but as her hands emerged from the arm cuffs, it flushed with colour, texture, intricate embroidery and the solidity of the real. Venus took another off her in the same motion and he saw them both jerk a little as the garments made contact. But, in the next moment, both of them were dressed exactly as before and the fairy-silk of the cloaks seemed no more 'real' than dustmotes in the air shimmering light fractures across his eyes.

Venus said to her non-identical reflection, 'Relay this message to the NLO, for the Cognimatan Fleet, copy in the Archivist and Weapons in Europan orbit and the Europan Coherence. Through Dakul's amplifier, mind you, so the unity gets it, not just Quogat, can't afford disbelief. "The Contaminant is eradicated. The balance is restored. As reparation we offer the probe." Eliminate the damn thing as soon as they have received the transmission.'

She turned away from the glass. 'If any of you are the praying type, now's your chance. But you'd better know you're praying to me.' She turned on her heel and left the room.

Kean caught the knowing smirk of the preRaphaelite reflection. Behind him, Dinah and Jake were silently, but as one, lifting the body back onto the trolley. They were both crying openly, but neither was berating Venus for the death, which he thought if it was his sister, or long-time patient, he might have done. So he felt able to ignore professionalism's automatic call to assist them and stepped up to the window, well, it was a mirror, but it was set in carved stone pillars like an ancient lancet window.

Somehow just getting up close made him feel the reality of the Ydal more strongly. He reckoned it was just the enclosing perspective of the frame, but now they could be in the same room. He lifted his palm to the glass but there was none there and Venus' fingers twined into his. He reacted by abruptly removing his hand but only to remove a cloak he could feel hanging about him like a shroud he must shrug off in order to live any longer. Their hands met again as he handed it across/received hers in return, but their eyes had never left eachother. And suddenly he had a secret knowledge about his idol that she herself lacked.

Venus was not a romantic. Anyone could know that about her, she'd sneered at the entire idea often enough. But now he saw what she'd done with the emotional optimism. She'd digitised it. Maybe you could be a genocidal manic and be a Romantic. Not in an integrated life, not living the wave, but by compartmentalizing the qbits. Not if you'd studied replacing an absolutist comfort-zone with evolutionary chaos, not if you knew Chretien de Troyes invented Romance along with the Grail, not if you knew how the species had fractured its mind with its storytelling and aggrandisement. But you couldn't get rid of it. It was woven through your non-existent soul. You wanted a better world but you were part of the world's problem. All you could do to be true to both schizophrenic parts of yourself, your world, was choose to be true to the predator within, even as chivalry demanded the prey be given a sporting chance. What it boiled down to was not psychopathy, not cynicism, not revenge or hate, just Courtesie.

Only a fluffy-pink romantic would revision herself as the melancholic Victorian version of cleaned up mediaevalism, the doomed Lady of Shallot, and only the ultimate romantic could be dramatic enough to think they could save the world by becoming Queen for The Day.

But that wasn't the secret the Ydal had shared. That was altogether more personal. Venus would not countenance a relationship with him not just because she had had plenty of reason to mistrust the male of the species, not just because it would be a distraction from her focused plans, but because she thought their mutual attraction was not real. She thought that he was her type, yes, but that only for Thursday was the other Kean a soulmate. She thought his own dreams of the soulmate that looked like her were seepage, of Thursday and the other Kean's emotional bonds, information tunnelled through the black hole in that other world.

But the Ydal knew different. She knew that Tolecnal was an idealisation, although he came with Kean's face, but that the real stimuli for courtly love come in many guises. And Venus was wrong.

She and Thursday were as alike as two peas in a pod and their lovers were equally indistinguishable from one another, except in this universe where Kean's visual imagination, at least in dreams, was more active and accurate. The seepage wasn't via Venus, it was via Kean's shared phase-space superposition, simply a clearer depiction of what both Kean brains shared; the Fargo as the ideal.

Only a romantic as hurt and insecure as Venus would need to deny themselves a chance at their own happiness because they'd set the bar at 'soul mate' and then set that definition as achievable only in another universe.

Well, maybe he could do something about that. Patients always said he had a very reassuring bedside manner, after all.

He winked at the Ydal, putting his hands together prayfully. 'Trust me, I'm a doctor.' he quipped, and then was sprinting up the ramp after his true vocation.

Half of Jake's vocation was composing the hands of the other half. He could sense his sense of purpose ebbing like the warmth in his sister's body. He had cried, but in the dislocated clarity of shock, he quite clearly saw that that was a) with Dinah and b) out of that shock. He felt like a bit of a fraud, in fact. Dinah had every right to cry, after all she'd known Ida intimately and cared for her for many years. Mind you, the other two had known her as long and they seemed to be coping. He felt a twinge of anger penetrate the numbness. What was the matter with everyone here? A bit of him stood back and reviewed recent events. This proved to be impossible, because by the time you'd started with living examples of alien knights and lost lovers and sisters who thought they were alien fish and moved through real alien threats and telepathic death rituals and parallel worlds and doppelgangers your brain had turned to soup. There were good reasons for anyone in the know to be completely round the bend, but they didn't seem to be. It was just that all their emotional responses seemed, well, at best, slightly *off* and, at worst, switched off to the degree that they could contemplate murder.

Oh, he'd seen the difference in that Conduit place, people playing out some real version of 'Dungeons and Dragons', but he'd been here too, and he didn't think Venus had had a hand in his sister's death, though he thought her political reaction in bad taste. Sure, she was playing for enormous stakes and even now, when he understood, as the only person to whom she'd revealed her actual plan, (if that was true), that she had the deaths of worlds in her hands, she had taken time out to try to save one woman, before turning her back into one of her political pawns. He'd already asked her what gave her the right to play god this way, and she had just shrugged and said, 'Anyone can play. It's just putting power together with the courage of your convictions. It's how you play that counts. At least I'm letting all the pawns make their own moves. Just like a regular god. Only I'm not judging good versus evil.'

'What're you judging then?'

'Nothing. I'm just indulging a little interest in cladistics and facilitating the survival of the fittest.'

At the time, he hadn't understood the ramifications of her plan. 'But you said no one was going to survive your Apocalypse.'

'I didn't say what they'd be fit for.'

As he looked down at Ida and saw only the woman, Makepeace, whom he barely knew, he wondered if she'd been fit enough. And whether *he* would turn out to be, or at least fit enough to be this Knight the players saw him as, although Fargo hadn't mentioned it. He didn't feel fit. He felt drained. A warrior's knees shouldn't buckle like this, he considered as they contacted with the tree-chair. He was barely aware of Dinah fussing. 'Just want to sit down for a minute. 'll be a'right. Just take her away.' He saw his hand waving dismissively in front of his eyes, but, after she'd squinted sharply at him, Dinah obviously felt he was safe to leave and he heard the sound of the trolley creaking and heavy panting as she manhandled the burden up the stone slope.

It was a relief when she'd gone. He lay back in the scoop of the trunk. It was surprizingly comfortable, as if it had been ergonomically designed, with mossy cushioning in all the right places. The only pea in the mattress turned out to be Ida's headset. Twisting it in his fingers, he fiddled without really looking. There was nothing to look at now. His quest was over, done. Not only had he cracked it, he'd found the girls, and then Fargo had told him how the thing worked and what it was all for. He'd been as near right as anyone could be without playing the game and believing the content, which, to be fair, should have been fiction, through all precedent. He wondered if he'd have found out earlier if he'd used the damn thing, not been so purist scientist about it, maybe even been able to halt all this madness earlier.

'Yeah? And what would you have done if the fate of the world had fallen into your hands?' It was the kind of question Ranger and Lily would have answers to, as gamers they recognized the challenge. He didn't think he would. He almost wished he'd played it while he had the chance. Just to see what it felt like to be part of such a worldview.

He didn't remember putting it on. He didn't remember falling asleep. But when he woke up, the first thing he felt was the suction cup on his temple, and the second was the other presence in the room. He opened his eyes.

The Lady came over and took his hand. 'Jake Wynn. Glock 17, ceramic. Arms of Pretension, inescutcheon fer rouillé, d'oeuil gules fermé, welcome.'

Something had happened, possibly to his brain, possibly to the room. It certainly wasn't the cave-office he'd been in, although as he sat up he noted the tree-chair beneath him still. This was a round, stone-walled room, with … but suddenly, he knew more than his first-sight observations could ever have told him. This was the home behind the mirror of the Venus-holographic programme, the Ydal of Tollahs, who … was more than just the sum of her Fargo-triad of parts, more than a moon-sized computational conduit for the game, more even than an interstellar communication device. She was regal, in a way Venus did not aspire to be. The mediaeval style of dress might add to it, but he could feel her within, calling her people of the game to her, to find their home.

What he hadn't realized, especially since the reports had started coming in of a world on the move, was that people weren't being drawn to their actual physical homes, nor even to their consciously-believed-in spiritual homes, if they had them, but to the place in I-*Mage* they felt was their perfect moment, their calm place, their best self, the highest point of the highest level their play had achieved, the nearest they had got to Her.

What was surprising was that these moments had all been located in the real world, somewhere on planet earth which the Ydal had mapped into the game with NetSpore entirety, so people played as they went about their real lives, yes, but also because the game took them into realistic nonlocal scenarios. That's why people were moving about, they were going to a number of rendezvous points that their play had preselected them for or for them, he couldn't work out which.

He couldn't work it out partly because in the I-*Mage* worldview there didn't seem to be any difference, but largely because the more he looked at anything the more overloaded by the detail available he became. He felt his mental grasp blur and his focus reconverged on a schematic of the planet. This was no sketchy diagram however, it pulsed with layered knowledge. He could see the individual people, the massing groups, the Mercator-projection of the 3D globe with highlighted loci to which the streams of folk were heading. Interestingly, there were relatively few points to the world exodus, despite the personally-tailored nature of the game, and, now he could see into the billions of minds that had made the choices that were converging, he could see why. Human beings were simple, falling into patterns that now were visible to him. They had one major flaw as a species. They thought they were conscious, but 80% of their behaviour the Ydal could predict from a few minimal parameters, and that was all unconscious, animal responses, evolved, preprogrammed, genetic and nurtured, but all to stimuli in their current environment, not in response to their rational thought and will. What they thought of as thought, as logic and reason, was a time-delayed story their language-laden minds could weave in their dislocated brains, justification for their actions.

And their stories were so similar, oh, they were individuated, personalized by detail, by environment, but the same basic elements purled through every narrative, the largest and most similar being the concept of the self. So, when it had come to developing I-*Mage*, the Ydal had presented the world as egocentrically as each self demanded, but the presentation had conformed to uncomplicated patterns. Finally, he understood the one thing that had always puzzled him, the addictive quality of such a puerile plotline as the game had offered.

It was all that was necessary to engage and fascinate the selfcentred hominin storytelling brain. Termites and Terran Knights and Queens. It wasn't chess, nor any recognisable trademarked ripoff, but it was perfect. Well, perfect if you wanted to catalogue those narratives, then assign those brains into types and draw them into pens like the sophisticated cattle they were.

'Oh, my god! They're lambs to the slaughter! And you've got them herding themselves into the abattoir!'

'The Red Knight is the Butcher.'
'What? Are you talking about me?'
'You bear the shield of the closed, bloody eye. Will you now accept the challenge to open your eye upon the blood before you?'
'What? No! This is nuts! What are you talking about?'
He realized that his heightened emotion, panic, was blotting out knowledge he could access without words, but somehow it seemed vitally important that he heard the words themselves. A vocalisation within suggested he was a 'linguistically-bound slave', but, although the Ydal sighed, she complied.
'When Venus and I had reviewed the situation before us in the light of other possible solutions tried elsewhere, and had input from interested parties in our local neighbourhood, we suggested that we attempt to construct humanity into a Hive mind that could take its place in the Intelligent debate, and with it we accepted the responsibility of Hive Queen. We chose to exercise this responsibility by devolving it to all individuals we could access through the game. The coverage was not absolute. Strong-minded individuals of conviction could resist the draw of the herd. Those individuals have been watched and manipulated by other means to ensure Consensus. You alone have the requisite characteristics of the one true WildKnight. The Arms of Pretension are yours. We will abide by your decision.'
'What decision?' he cried, still clinging to the verbiage of verbalisation.
But he knew the answer. He had to polish up his shield for the Last Quest. He had to Cast for the Planet. He had to Choose who won the Game.

There were no choices left to Zelas. She was an unswervable torpedo in a current taking her ever southwards. Her people followed. They followed because of their historic faith. Oh, she couldn't deny that she fitted the prophecy, right down to being the death of the last of the Whorlingas, but that was why this was all wrong, why they *shouldn't* be following her blindly into the cold. It chilled her to the bone to think that, yet again, she was leading people of faith to their End. It was worse than the external increasing chill in the polar waters. The antifreeze-protection would not kick in until the original bacterial infection had subsided and she was already running a high fever, which, despite the ice-melting heat she was giving off, only served to make her feel the cold so much more deeply. But it wasn't illness that was making her feel so sick about this journey, it was dread of the destination.

Being a freefinning Tachyon-Siren had been its own fun. Even after she'd killed her tribe and been left alone with only the alien voices in her head for comfort, it had been an adventure. Since she met Ranger, it had seemed like destiny. And that was where it all went askew in her head.

Not Ranger, she was in no doubt about the truth of her feelings for him. But, perhaps because of the whole 'soulmate' fatefulness of it, when in fact she had simply, through the precognition of her Cast, followed his delicious scent halfway around the globe until time and place synced and they had met, it had felt 'meant'. In retrospect, she knew she'd got carried away by that sensation, carried away by his enthusiasm to accompany her on what she had thought would be a spurious endless quest, merely carrying on their lives as peregrination, wandering as lovers, in fascinating waters after random prey. But then they'd come to the deep south and she'd Sung, the traditional hymn that was the request to enter another clan's territory, the Whorlingas' signature siren howling through the oceans for the last time, calling for the first time in the singular tense.

It wasn't a Song to which she'd expected an answer, her own people had declined in numbers so much over the last hundred years that only the priests had expected the lost clan, designated as Ghosts thousands of years earlier, to be surviving. But, though their numbers were few, their sirens diminished, they lived more like Past Echoes than Ghosts. Everyone could sing *those* songs, there was no glory in memory, but there was a certain steadfastness, the still eddy in the current of time, that even a future-seer could respect in their dedication.

Some glorious past Siren had told them the when and the where of one of the FarLong Casts and they had hooked their entire culture to that point and reeled themselves forward with no more pressing outlook until Then became Now. So the Knights were waiting at the end of the Wood tunnel-circuit and she had been gobbled alive by cuttlefish and History.

And, not once, in all that time, had they thought about the efficacy of a strategy that placed their entire race in between the webbed fingers of someone whose claim to regal fame was to have been the careless decimation of her own shoal. But even that paled in comparison to the deceit she was now perpetrating.

She had Cast from the Tarn, which reeked of the pheromones of the mass spawning event and rang with the orgiastic calls of the satiated, so it was well nigh impossible for her to sense anything beyond the redolent Now, but it was part of the tradition that she do so from that place, despite the fact that deep water would have been clearer and more accurate. The only reason she had gained the taste she had was that Ranger's information about the ice-covered continent had pointed her towards the west of the great cold cliffs where she could ascertain that fresh water would pour to her touch in two days and nights of nonstop, overfast swimming.

Fortunately for her, the Fleets could keep up and, equally fortunately for them, the Ghost-Shoal, burdened with the children, elderly and sick, couldn't. So she would be first to take any risks that her doom-laden senses told her lay in wait for them. But come after her and into the jaws of fate they would, not simply because they wanted to follow Her, but because, the nearer they got to their destination, the stronger would be the pull of 'Home'.

That was why the seamount was so southerly. Aeons ago they had known what direction the IceBergas had taken. Now, thanks to the Regina Obscura, according to Peri, the Call, that the Ghosts thought was only their fealty to the prodigal Queen's return, that they believed was Her Siren, was coming from the heart of history and from the very LandLubbers they distrusted. In truth it wasn't a Siren-Call, it didn't emanate from the source, it was merely the Image, the I-*Mage*, in the brain, of the longed-for and lost and loved Eddyless Calm that all hominins, even LandLubbers shared. Her people would have come here on their own without her.

Well, at least, this time she would be first in the current when it finally beached them upon that mythical shore, which she alone knew did not taste of the doldrums, not even of land, but did, terrifyingly, taste of No One.

The reason she knew she was flowing rightwise was that there was a nullity in the central focal endpoint of the current, and, yes, it shaped the stream like an Eddyless Calm, like a Terran Lapis, like the Water of Life, like the Blood Flow, like the Aer Sculpt, but it remained nebulous, flavourless, barren, *frozen.* A Quest-in-Aspic.

She dredged up the concept from a childhood lecture given by the oldest priest, the one who everyone laughed at, even the other priests hid smiles behind their hands, because he used the ancient Heraldic constantly and it was full of oldfashioned, even taboo, language culled from the alchemists on *Land.* But in some ways he'd been more scientifically minded than any of the more up-to-date true Hydraens.

He'd thought about the 'why' as well as the 'where and when', and he'd said that some quests were pointless because the Casts fell Elsewhere, into a nonplace and nonfuture that wouldn't come to pass in this world. And he'd said 'The Ultimate Tachyon-Siren will be able to tell the difference. But she will still not turn aside from the path, because she does not walk it, the current takes her.' Well, it was taking her now, and she was having to use all her strength to fight the Aspic of history because she could feel species-extinction breathing on her shoulder like death itself and its weight was immense and its jaws widening.

But first they had to get through the Standing Wave, and that would cut them off from all outside influence, even Peri wouldn't be able to hear her siblings through the siren-silencing Sound. She realized with a start that she had been leaving the pack behind rather than leading them. The start was the sudden nipping at her flippering feet caused by the whipping of mouthed tentacles from the cuttlefish Knight that bore within her lover and friends. The realization came from the insistent repeated flashing on its surface. Then Ranger emerged from behind it and swam over to her, kissed her mucoidally and dived back to oxygenated safety.

She was not just her own wandering siren anymore, she was the Ghost-Queen and she had to lead her people and do it properly, if possible, since he'd read the distress in her eyes, with regal assurance. And, since he brought the information from Xl-arn'tz, whose mastery of Hydraen-Heraldic had swiftly improved, she had the entire Shelled meat of the Shoal's fear uploaded in that one bite, and reassurance was clearly the highest priority, since they were already further south than they had ever swum and since they all knew the Standing Wave lay ahead. Unfortunately, none of them even knew any legends about the nature of this barrier.

Oh, they knew that, since the IceBergas had breached it, their minds had been lost to the outer world, and they knew that those few intrepid Ghost-Sirens who had ventured near and returned had been Blinded, Silenced and Maddened. This apparently meant, according to John's analysis, that they were obviously classed as insane by their peers, but he thought their symptoms might well be post-traumatic stress disorder, or the aquatic equivalent, but that the stranger manifestations were blindness and a deafness that also struck their minds dumb, so he suggested the Wave might be something painfully bright and loud that could stop transmission of information.

His suggestion, if, as preliminary inquiries led him to believe, aquatic mental communication was based on the same stimuli as I-*Mage*, and therefore the Woods too, used, was ultrasound. He knew that some sounds could be pitched to affect human physiology, the military experimented with crowd stoppers that engendered loss of muscle control, nausea, total evacuation, even bursting blood vessels, but none of these were indicated in the legends. The brain damage that could have come from the decibel assault could explain the blind madness, however, whereas light, even if blindingly intense, could not explain deafness, although he had an open mind on brain damage by laser.

He was pretty sure that there couldn't be a genuine physical barrier in the way because that would have been discovered by humans who would have investigated with extreme prejudice. There was one phrase that came up in one of the sagas that were sung to keep the myths in active memory which stated that only the Queen wore the Crown that could breach the Dam. The reason this stood out as a true key to Ranger was the Crown idea. This was not a Hydraen concept. Headgear interfered with hydrodynamics. No one could conceive a Queen who could lead wearing anything on her head. But Ranger could and he'd consulted with Pereduri and together they had come up with an idea.

Zelas alone wore a Crown, not a solid, gold, spiky thing, but she did have a living, arm-waving halo of a sort; her pair of mantis shrimps. What they did not have a clue about was how those simple creatures could enable access through an impenetrable wall that stretched across the entire entrance to the George VI Sound. Perhaps, they suggested, she could ask them?

She was so used to the constant pattering about in her locks she'd barely noticed their increasing activity. She had noticed the increase in the clicking of their claws, which should have told her they were excited, except they always got excited in cooler temperatures, and she'd been feeling rather too sorry for herself to join in. Now she listened attentively.

They were snapping their claws together in synchrony, but it was not the mating dance she knew of old, it seemed somehow *bigger* than that. *Brighter too.* The ultrafast castanets of the shrimp claws caused ultrasonic bursts of such intensity that they created bubbles which imploded at temperatures and pressures that they emitted light itself. Now, the photons of sonoluminescence popped like a *firework display!* (Humans had strange but wonderful entertainments, she was saddened to think she would never see such things for herself now, not just through Ranger's memories). She had seen meteor showers twice yearly, though, and the heavens paled into insignificance compared to the multiple, minute supernovae wreathing her shrimps.

Their exceptional eyesight was what had drawn her to hunt with them originally, but it was her study of their communication that had arraigned them in place of honour in her weed-braided tresses. However, despite their talents, their usual range of interests was limited, so their linguistic code of meaningful clicks and light-based emphases had been easy to decypher. Now she was seeing and hearing a new set of signals and they were far more complex than any she'd noted hitherto. And also far more partial, like single-instrument chords from a fully-orchestrated symphony. Most of it seemed to be projected at a higher energy than normal too, as if they were attempting to get their message to travel farther, rather than in a mere conversation between the two of them. The gist of it all appeared to be 'We're coming! We will be Joining. Our transport is fast. Wait for us. The dance will be wonderful.' and other similar bursts.

It took some time for her own sonic clicking to interrupt their delighted running about, but finally she had the dialogue she needed, and then she had a further conversation in which she had to promise to be very fast transport in return for their co operation. However, it did appear that the prophecy was correct. Probably only she, Ghost-Queen or not, could get her people through the barrier.

She turned then and Called. It was not a siren-song, it was the first Edict of a queen. 'Be assured. I know the secret of the Standing Wave. I will lead us through. We must go swiftly and together. All who are slower must board the Knights. None must swim ahead of me. Eat as much as you can now and as we swim. All ingestion must cease at the end of the next tidal pull, when the moon rises.

When the moon is at its apex, I will thrust forward. You will not follow until I call. Come at your swiftest then and do not stop for anything. I can only hold the way open a short space. If there is anyone who does not wish to follow, turn back now, for once through the Wave there can be no return. But be of good heart, for we go now to fulfil the prophecy!' *She put the last bit in, despite knowing the futility of such reassurance, since they were coming anyway.*

She led them via another seamount, less flush with prey than the sacred spot they had left but with sufficient provender to ensure all had fuelled the demands upon their bodies she proposed now to make. Her shrimp were now clattering up and down her and singing their dance songs even louder and faster, which Ranger said made her look like a broken neon sign, and they kept nipping at her to goad her into moving on again. She wasn't surprised the earlier sirens had gone mad, she was beginning to get a headache herself. But soon they were again underway and the shrimp settled in a forward-peering position of anxious anticipation. They were worried they'd be late.

By the time the moon had risen low in the sky, Zelas and her followers had begun to notice the swell of turbulence spreading the current laterally, and by the time it had gained enough height to dapple even to the depths at which they swam, there was a pulse, like a syncopated heartbeat, emanating through the slowing tide. She could scent fear rising with the moon, and she was glad to leave her people behind and forge on alone except for her shrimp and dogs. *At least if this doesn't work they'll stop believing in me and go home and survive,* she consoled herself.

And then, she rounded the last curve of the iceshelf that guarded the western peninsula and the landward drag of the tide ceased abruptly. Ahead of her the glacier that filled the George VI Sound loomed above the waterline for further than the eye could see, but below, although it had to extend to great depths, it was invisible behind a sparkling Standing Wave, the crest of which broke the surface without moving, the trough of which rested like a rock on the ocean floor. And there was no sound at all.

'I don't understand.' She clicked at her shrimp, who had also fallen silent. 'I thought you said it was a Song. An incredibly loud Song.'

'The Wave is the Song. The sound of the singing is beyond the wave. The sound makes the wave. The wave protects those within from predators, so they can dance the Joining.'

'They sculpt water with ultrasound! That's amazing! But why? Krill don't protect themselves in a mating shoal, that's why so many species mass for a feeding frenzy then. What's so special about Joining?'

'We are the most numerous group in the seas and the widest spread. When we are in the Wave, our Song rises to the Moon and all across the round world we Join in. Many are our numbers, One our heartbeat. Great is our destruction, Greater our Life. Sing Together, Sing the Wave, Be One and Many Forever. The Krill! The Krill! The Krill remain!'

'I don't understand. You're not krill, you're solitary, warm-water dwellers. These shrimp are nothing like you. If you hadn't ingested the antifreeze bugs at the Tarn you'd already have frozen to death.'

'The Song Joins us all. We must celebrate the time with our cousins.'

'Will they be glad to see you? After all, you normally eat krill like them.'

'There is no predation during the Full Moon cycle of the Song. That is why we told your people to eat before we came. Only those who will not eat may enter the Wave.'

Zelas made a mental note to tell the Baleens to take a very deep breath and keep their mouths shut once they'd dived, otherwise they wouldn't be able to help breathing in half the singers.

'Let us go now, into the Wave. We will need to explain our request to cease the Song. But first, drop down to the ocean floor.'

When she was down, the pair scuttled off. She watched them turn over a few rocks and then heard the crack of their weapons. They had captured a couple of small-shelled molluscs, which their claw-click stunned, and they excavated and ate the little slimy inhabitants, then brought the emptied homes to Zelas. 'For your ears. You should wrap your hair over your eyes when we enter the Wave.'

They were in front of it now. The light was intense, but it was its shimmering flicker, a ghostliness to its solidity, that tore at the eyes and shook the receptors of the brain. She stretched forth her hand, palm to the vertical plane, and a million tiny hits plunged into the skin, pockmarking the wall with sprinkles of redness. 'I can't go through there!'

'We will begin. You must follow as we carve the tunnel.'

The rainbow-carapaces jumped off her now and started to dance, clicking and flashing. Zelas was hard put to see and a migraine was chopping into her brain, but, as they swirled around eachother in the water, approaching the waterwall, she noticed a tiny dimple intrude into it. As they intensified their efforts the dimple grew into a pit, and as they danced in a widening gyre, the pit grew into a tunnel, just broad enough for her shoulders to pass. She followed them in.

The Wave was almost three feet wide, and where the shrimp circle wavered the tunnel edges shot microholes wherever she brushed against it, so her trail was bloody and painful, and her bandaged eyes insufficient to stop the vicious novae-lights ratcheting up her migraine, until she could feel the storm in her brain mirroring the lightning outside. And then they were through and it was over. But now the sound was an assault, sandblasts that did not penetrate an exoskeleton abraded her skin, but that was minor compared to the boom of the choral claws. The shell earplugs amplified the sound of the sea, the haunting breakers of an unknown shore, but those waves were drowned out by the pulsing millions beating as one. She kicked for the surface, to breathe, but also to rest her eyes and ears in darker night and quieter air. The Mantis shrimps remained below consulting with their fellows. She lay on the water and squinted down. A ring of ever-expanding darkness hovered about her pets. *They've done it!*

They had. The southern krill had been so excited to see the brightly-coloured visitors from the warm north that they agreed to allow the passage of the entire Fleet. The condition of non-predation was acceded to because even krill know a whale's oath is its bond, but it helped that Zelas said that she would personally herd any oathbreaker into the Wave in punishment. As a result of this offer, the krill gave her one titbit, a mere gist, not meat, but it was significant. Under the iceshelf ran a river of freshwater that came from the land. The krill that lived in the lakes beyond had come down for the Joining. They told of a new stream, a mere trickle as yet, but warming and widening by the year, of the purest water. They said it had taste but no flavour. And this frightened them.

It frightened Zelas too, but she was too busy Calling and managing the Fleet in the short time they had to pass before the moon peaked and the Song had to be Sung, to enable the global Joining at the synchronized time, when the Wave would be re-established. The

Wave was a boundary column all around the massed shrimps, so the entire Fleet had to move like flying fish to get beyond the flock far enough towards land to be safe, but they worked like a true cohort and only rested when they were butting up against the iceshelf itself.

Now, much to their dismay, the airbreathing Knights, the whale and dolphins, would have to remain behind. The journey ahead would take them under the glacier and there would be no surface to reach. All the Hydraens were in the cuttlefish whose design pumped air into their cavities and kept their passengers breathing. Zelas, however, would lead in the water, refuelling her oxygen by entry to a special slot in the base of the cuttlefish into which the Knight could consciously pump a short burst of air. She said goodbye to her Mantis Shrimp and then the Wave went up and she could neither hear them nor the world beyond, her sonar pinked dismally against the Wave and fell back uninformatively. So she led the way inland, under the vast cliffs that shoved into the great sea itself, almost two-thirds of the way to the oceanbed, and scented out the freshwater runoff to follow into the white heartland of the IceBergas.

It was well into the following afternoon when the route began to narrow, the water force cascading down the pipe channelling the stream became stronger and much harder to swim against, and the angle began to rise. Then at last they forced their way up a fall of freshwater and found themselves in a lake. It was bright from sunshine high above filtering through the glassy ages of skywater stored above. The krill might be currently absent on their Joining, but the place was rich in their plankton prey and contained a few fish, molluscs and squid that the cuttlefish and the Hydraens could enjoy.

The Hydraens came out to feed and stretch their fins, and taste the strangely exciting freshwaters. To Zelas, burdened with responsibility, their mood seemed ridiculously light, as if they'd found themselves a rich seamount in warm waters, but she cheered up for a while after she'd spent a little sharing with Ranger. His lung capacity was nowhere near good enough to swim around underwater in these roofed conditions, although, as he and Peri and Xl-arn'tz had rested, their fevers had dropped and their cold protection was now adequate to come out for brief periods. So he took her into the cuttlefish and they shared the Mantles of their time apart and then, although she felt embarrassed by her ungainly flab when it was subject to air rather than water pressures, his caresses lifted her mood, letting her forget the torn flesh, the shaking fever, the migraine, the muffled hearing and cloudy vision, until she was squirming to manoeuvre herself under him. But when it was over, and she was turning to go, he caught her arm. 'No! Don't think like that! It's not the last time. It's not the end.'

She had to dive away from him before he penetrated more than her flesh, because she'd scouted the lake and scented the new stream the shrimp had talked about, and she knew what it meant, the taste from the Cast, flavourless, with a cold that would snap the Fleet's hearts.

So the final fin of the journey began. The stream lay above a slushy ice layer that was melting off the main glacier, but it ran in the same general direction, so the Fleet remained in the wider current, bashed by ice, but able to move forward in pairs. Zelas dived in and out of the sorbet to track the stream until it narrowed to the expected trickle. Then she took a very deep breath and went up to investigate. Sonar showed her that she was just above the rim of a landlocked mountain lake, formerly completely sealed by ice, now where the glacier-base scraped across hard rock and friction warmed it, a hole had appeared.

It needed enlarging even for her dogsharks to enter, but once the Knight's tentacles stuck on the undermined solid and yanked it began coming out in chunks. It was not easy work though and night had fallen long before the hole was big enough, so she commanded that all should rest until they could see the glacial-dawn and enter.

She went first, by right, by expectation, but not by desire. By now, everyone had tasted the water, everyone was afraid of its null-flavour, everyone was glad to send their Queen in first.

There were no krill, there was nothing here larger or meatier than phytoplankton. There was no circulation of waters, merely a seepage around the base of the overlying glacier puffed at the complete tranquility and prevented stagnation. Oh, she could feel the Hydraens behind her muttering, with less excitement than heretofore, about the Eddyless Calm, but their puzzlement was as clear as the water. The source of the *Aqua Libre* had always been assumed to be teeming with lifeforms. Here, even krill couldn't make a living apparently.

Zelas broke away from the Knight that carried her air and friends and shot up to the roof, trying to see and sound as far as she could. The lake was immensely long and thin, steeply-walled and with no hiding places. Even from up here, there was nothing to see. She pinged as far as sonar could see, almost frantic now. This was the place. She knew it.

Then, as she tossed her head in distress, her radar rebounded information at last. She might be almost out of air and hope but she dropped like a stone and shot another burst at the roof. *They were there.*

Her mollusc-Knight came up and brought her air, and the rest of the Hydraens refuelled too, and then, in a concerted burst of sound, they read the awful truth together.

They had found the IceBergas. The iceroof was pocked with icecaves, once these had had entrances, now they had narrow tubes that circulated the water in and out. Inside, utterly still, almost lifeless, were the IceBerga themselves, one to a cave. They had begun as creatures vaster even than the Ghost-Hydra, their thick hair had stuck to the cavesides and been torn off in clumps as the stored blubber reduced over time, and sonar revealed other details of muscle wastage and a digestive process that had shrunk to filter a meagre diet of plankton from the water. It revealed too an external gill-like structure, manufactured rather than grown in the body, that had been fixed to the chest area of each creature and was passing oxygen direct to their unrising lungs. The passive forms were still fifteen feet long, but their skin hung on skeletons that fibrillated to the microcurrents in the eight feet diameter caverns.

The caves all lay horizontally, with the entrances at rightangles depending into the water, and the ice was very clear, so the Ghosts could swim up and lie parallel to the creatures. Their eyes were open, huge, black and blank. Zelas had to query her dogsharks to find out if there was any electrical activity at all in their brains. It took them ten minutes to confirm minimal firing. Ranger said it was less than coma reactivity, that they couldn't be thinking, but every Hydraen knew that thinking, even as slow musing, was the point of the Eddyless Calm. They must be roused, said their dazed, desperate Queen. Pump oxygen in, regurgitate what food is in your stomachs, open the entrances. Wake them!

The Fleet did all she asked, without question. Then they pulled back to rest in the Knights and waited. Finally, as the afternoon sun turned the underice world into a golden desert-mirage, they began to notice stirring in the ceiling.

One by one the IceBergas were slipping out of their freezers. The Ghost-Hydraens left the cuttlefish and rose to meet them, singing their sagas of reunification as they had always planned. Then the highest wave of the Fleet saw their long-lost relatives turn, painfully and slowly, so atrophied were their muscles, and finally could look on their faces.

They were not the faces of Hydraens, they were the faces of starved predators. Teeth like the maw of a shark caught the eye, yes, but it was the eyes that held the gaze. Eyes that were madder than any ever seen. Minds that had gone beyond lay behind them. Minds that had not spent a frozen eternity contemplating the wonders of the universe and the joys of the Eddyless Calm, minds that had spent that eternity contemplating their empty navels, surviving in dormancy on plankton alone, withering from intelligence to animal. And now they were going to Eat. And the prey was not the Knights, good feeding though there is on a cuttlefish, but the Ancient Betrayers, the enemy-family.

It was worse than watching her Shoal be destroyed by the great white, worse than the sensation of loneliness that followed. It was not so much a bloodbath as a massacre of spirit. The IceBergas' teeth remained sharp but they were otherwise barely capable of the kill. Their devotees, who had travelled down so many years and across oceans to seek the wisdom they believed lay in the IceBergas, bludgeoned them to death easily enough physically, desperately, because the Bergas would not stop and could breathe underwater, even attacking the cuttlefish to rip out the Ghosts from their bellies when they dropped under to get a breath. Oh, it was self-defence, but by the end of it, no one wanted to go on living anyway, they were broken.

Many were hurt, by great gouges that had been mere mouthfuls to the Berga attackers, who, despite their frailty but because of their limitless ferocity, had killed a good quarter of the Ghosts, mostly because it was impossible, before your survival instincts kicked in at the incipient death-rattle, to fight back. Some cuttlefish were spiralling downwards, ripped and dying, but there were enough Knights left to collect the Hydraens and leave the lake.

The Queen's Knight and its passengers went last. Inside it were two items of freight to show to the waiting Fleet beyond the glacier.

One was the body of the IceBerga Siren, denoted as such by her own Cast that had determined Zelas as the Ghost-Queen and her personal, only and final target. The other was joined to her by the fixed bite that held her heart, ripped out of its ribcage, and by the fate they had shared. Zelas rode in her Knight, mourned by her Consort, finally crowned as the Queen of Ghosts and as lifeless as the ghost of any dead queen.

Ghosts appeared to be Xl-arn'tz's only travelling companions now. The same bite that had sunk through Zelas' chest had cut off the arm Ranger had wrapped round her in a last-wave attempt to yank her down out of range. Despite Xl-arn'tz ministrations, which, without the Dark medicines he normally would prescribe and without anything more material than hanks of Zelas' hair to use as bandages, were barely effectual at stopping the bloodloss, Ranger looked to be in a bad way. The stump, which ended below his elbow, was ragged enough to lace the skin flaps back over, but even in the first few minutes it had begun to turn a disturbing rainbow of black and green and deep purple, which ran swiftly and visibly up through his veins and had reached his torso within an hour. He was delirious with the fierce chill this wound inside him, and with an almost-instant fever that made his skin roastingly hot to the touch. But, although the poison looked likely to kill him quickly, it seemed to Xl-arn'tz that it was in competition for the job with his mind.

He wouldn't lie still, which might reduce the rate of travel of whatever toxin was in the IceBerga Siren's teeth, and which might give Xl-arn'tz time to find it and, improbably, he had to admit, work out an antidote. He kept leaping about, trying to wake Zelas, hitting his head with his remaining fist when he couldn't, screaming in pain, screaming for her. Xl-arn'tz didn't rate his chances even if he didn't succumb to the poison, because he could tell the man's heart was so broken it was taking the rest of him with it. In the end, in a brief moment of blessed unconsciousness and silence, he managed to tear *(from her scalp,* with *her scalp, which was almost his worst moment)* some longer locks from Zelas and tie Ranger up.

Then he could turn his attention to Pereduri. She had helped him bring the two Queens aboard and had assured him she was unhurt, and she had undertaken to lay out the bodies while he saw to Ranger, but, as he finished wrestling with the man, he had time to wonder why she hadn't helped him once this was done. She was just sitting there, motionless, a hand on each deceased head, the long middle fingers to their cold temples, and her eyes, her so-bright and beautiful violet eyes, were blank, almost black, almost as lifeless as the other four.

She didn't respond to his touch, to words, to shaking. She didn't come out of it when he pulled her hands off the dead. He put a finger in her mouth and took a gob of spittle without any reaction, even involuntary, from her. He was almost too scared to use it, but he did. And then he broke contact as if her temple was on fire, but it wasn't heat he felt, it was cold. The cold of the vacuum. There was no thought, there was nothing. She was gone.

He didn't know what else to do. The remaining Ghosts and the Knights waiting for them at the entrance to the Sound were milling about, sharing their grief, bemused by shock and horror, and, since it was another morning and the Standing Wave was gone and with it the millions of krill, vaguely finning it towards the north and some more homely place. His cuttlefish wanted to carry the bodies of the Queens to the Tarn, so their bones could bleach with their ancestors, but no one was leading, no one organising anything. His own instinct was to get as far away from this nightmare as possible, to go home to his own cave and hole up until his spirit healed a scab over the horrors, but there was no home for anyone on the planet anymore, and he was scared to take Peri away from the Queens until whatever catatonia had taken her over had either passed or … well, he couldn't think about that, and maybe, he could still find a cure for Ranger, and it would be best to keep busy and … And so it came about, that, in the end of Days, Dark rode with Hydrae to the Home that was not, as Foremost Knight in the Current.

The other Knights of the Augmentatio had dispersed to the Home sites in their role as ushers to the End of Days. As humans arrived in any given place the accompanying 'Disappeared', sitting before each presiding pair of Knights, asked 'Terran or Termite?' and indicated a side dependent on the answer. There were 75 end-of-level sites in I-*Mage* and Venus was watching humanity arrive *en masse* at each one, although few had made it to the last levels, so those groups were the least in number. Actually, none of her children were there in the flesh, since corralling six billion people into 100 places, even when they arrived voluntarily and peaceably, (*robotically was the word in her head, given the method by which these lambs selfdelivered to the slaughter)* required vast acreages and open vistas and accessibility, so plains worked best and no one in the centre of such crowds could be seen by those on the periphery. So the Knights appeared by courtesy of the Ydal, enormous world-striding holograms, Ozymandias revivified.

She was watching them on 74 screens from her underground office, as they organized their charges from similar caves dug below the feet of those millions of followers. They had to, because it takes time to get millions of people into one place, and most of the places were deserts, which means that water and food has to be offered to those who arrive in the vanguard while one waits for the rest to catch up. It also means that there have to be designated areas for latrine use, although, under the influence of the headsets, at least no one was bothering about washing and sleeping facilities, and the Game kept the mob from being restive, being set to Meditative mode for all since the call to Home was uttered in Zen and frozen. But by now pretty much the entire Day population was in place and the Knights were about to begin the show when suddenly, to Venus' horror and concern, they too froze. Not the blissed-out relaxation of the humans above them, but the deep chill that resembled the rigour of mortis, not ecstasy, except once one had ODed.

Galarhas, since he'd originally been paired with Peri to Home on their true nest, the last level, Queen's Hive, the only real site, Penzeen Lighthouse, was the only one in running distance of Venus and she covered the underground passages to his empty cavern, since no one, with the non-Game-guided exception of Jake, had made it to the final level, in less than five minutes. Then she ran as swiftly back again to consult with the Ydal.

'They're all blank. Gone. I used his sputum. His mind was empty. What's happened to them?'

The Ydal took several long moments to reply and in that period Venus watched the mirror 'split' vertically in two and a pair of identical rooms appear in the divided image. In one reflection, the Ydal, although standing, had eyes as blank as the Knights. In the other, she leaned, panting with effort, before she straightened again and spoke.

'Had to partition myself. Sorry for the delay. It's Peri. She found the IceBergas. There was a bloodbath. Not sure why. Their queen and Zelas are dead, but Peri tried to save their knowledge, typical Wood thing to do, of course, but misguided. The little I can guess at this stage is that the Queen had been dying a long time, hundreds of years, maybe longer, and it appears that her last mindfulness was a dark tunnel down which Peri has fallen, and taken her melded brethren with her. Don't know if they can get back, since frozen death appears to be the only thing on the collective mind, but whatever happens it feels like it's going to take a long while for them to thaw out again.'

'Oh god! It's the *Albedo*. I thought, when she and Xl-arn'tz mated with Zelas and Ranger and the Hydraens, that they'd reached the endgame, the *Coniugium*. But, this is an earlier stage. The Albedo, and they've followed it to the letter. After their *coniunctio*, they undertook the classic *perigrinatio* and met the *coagulatio*, literally, and it led to *mortificatio.* And, of course, Pereduri the studious had to follow the quest through to the *sublimatio.* She's not just trying to save the knowledge of two entire races of Hydraens, she's trying to absorb it into herself, because only if she successfully works it through to the *fermentatio* stage will she be able to use it. Obviously, she didn't have enough capacity to do this alone so she had to share the burden with her siblings. She wouldn't be able to help herself. Can you tell if she was conscious then? Did she Broad Cast?'

'Yes. You're right. That's exactly what she's done. Put out an APB to call all the Knights into their *Meditatio* mode.'

'What are we going to do? We can't leave the people like this, without guidance, leadership, support.'

'I guess it's Game On, then, queenie. Time for the two Reginas to take centre stage. I can compress the pre-instructions and send them early, and if the natives get restless before we're ready, then I can loop some of the Knight's prior footage and intensify the peoples' Zen-meditation so they don't notice.'

'OK, but I've still got a lot of real-world preparations to do, y'know. I can't ponce about being royal for long.'

'Jeez, get you! It was your bloody idea, after all. And it's your real world that's messing up the timing.'

'Fine. Fine. Just activate the virus and I'll get ready.'

Venus turned away from the mirror, sighing, and began to rummage in a wardrobe, pulling out a selection of garments no one would ever have expected her to own, never mind wear. She caught Kean's eye as she began to undress. Despite the malevolence of his fixed stare, he couldn't hide the twitch of focused attention the activity was inducing. She grinned at him. *Probably an evil gloating smirk to his mind.* Somehow having him present, even hogtied to the chair and gagged, was enough to stave off the thoughts that pressed her. Perhaps, since he was about to achieve a dream of seeing her near-naked, she could throw him a bone. She waited until she had stripped to her underwear, which, since her boyish figure had never required her to invest in a bra, consisted solely of the thongs she'd adopted as most comfortable and offering no VPL in sharp suits. He did currently appear to be having difficulty swallowing, so she grabbed her glass of wine and leaned in *unfairly* close, ripping down the gag and offering the drink.

'You are such a bitch.' He said hoarsely, after taking a sip, but his tone was appreciative rather than condemnatory.

'It's why you love me.' She replied flippantly, holding the glass steady so he could continue to drink.

'If you untied me, I could show you just how much.'

'Yeah, right. Would that be while I was conscious or after you bashed my head in?'

'What'd be the point now? Your plans are too far gone for me to leap in and save the world from your evil genius. It'd be global chaos if you were taken out of the picture now. I'm prostrate at your feet with admiration for your superego, or I would be if you'd untie me. Just watching the pictures is amazing. I don't think anyone else could conceive such masses. Did I hear you say you've collected over one and a half million people in the Gobi desert alone? Where's the Ydal viewing this all from?'

'Oh, she's tapped into all the satellites now, and we have our own version of GPS in the I-*Mage* headsets, so she's tracking all our users individually too. But the Woods and Darks are awaiting our signal to herd the rest, only a few hundred thousand, mostly remote lost tribes or nomads and some committed Luddites and a few ascetic hermits. We know where they are. Our census-taking has been more thorough than anyone else's because where people can fall off the bureaucratic map, or even the human one, where people might be missing, we've employed Wood telepaths to locate every last human on the planet. And that's been verified by my friends in high places.'

'That's these Cognimatans you were telling me about.'

'No. They wouldn't deign to waste that kind of processing power on counting meat. I was referring to the Net. Our Local Operative, that's the NetSpore who is an OutRider of the vast web of intelligence that spans the cosmos, whose area of observation is our space, the Orion arm of the galaxy, can differentiate between those who have uploaded the I-*Mage* chemistry and those who haven't, and its ability to scan is on a whole different level. Sub-space 8 to be precise, one of the rolled up dimensions we can't detect yet. The Net is eternally neutral, so, where the Cognimata wouldn't trust me to eliminate the human threat to Europa, they will trust whatever the Net reports to them.' She had finished dressing now and did a bit of a twirl. 'What d'you think? Regal enough?'

It was the Terran Queen outfit from the Game, not that anyone had ever got to the end to see it, but the real clothes had had to be designed to match in case anyone had by the time action was required, so it was a period-piece from no actual historical epoch but resonant with several. Kean, however, was only a doctor of medicine, not history, so he nodded his approval. 'Very fetching. Very Boadicea.'

Venus laughed. 'Good god, no! She'd turn in her grave to hear you. The skirt's actually from her enemy, the Roman legions. Chainmail, medieval. Breastplate, pseudo-Roman, mostly feminine Batman circa 2000plus AD. All the flowing bits are more preRaphaelite romanticism than actual gothic, of course. The torques are copies of the Snettisham hoard, so they fit with the Iceni bit, but the vambraces and the greaves are just practical arm and leg protectors, not any period. I like the crown, though. Proper warrior queen headgear this.'

'Isn't it just what the Statue of Liberty wears?'

'Ah, but why does she wear it? It's the symbol of Sol Invictus, the Unconquered Sun God, whom the Romans worshipped on December 25th as Elah-Gabal or Mithras or, later, Christ, depends on the age. Seemed like the right symbol for the Citrinitas Queen when we were designing the game, ancient and modern combined.'

'Unlike the Timberland boots, which I can see are more practical than Roman sandals but are definitely wholly modern.'

'Yeah, but they go OK with the ensemble, don't cha think?'

'Not so much with the spear and sword, no.'

'Well, they're mandatory. Legends demand it. Not least because the Shield and its Blazons are language. Anyway, if we're going to create rivers of blood the least we owe to our fellow-citizens is to hack them to bits while looking into the whites of their eyes, in full knowledge of what they mean to us.'

'So what do they mean to you, Venus? You're self-appointed Queen of the world. Are you really going to destroy us all?'

'Put it this way. I've got the love of my life tied to a chair because even he's tried to kill me. When you came rushing to declare yourself after Ida died, did more personal tragedy striking make me more vulnerable, more amenable to your entreaties? Have I untied you and fallen into your arms because I've lost my children, possibly permanently, not to mention two ancient races of people? Will I see my plans through? I think you don't need to ask.'

'Maybe not. I think I still need to know why. Why you?'

Venus sighed. 'Because I can.'

'But does that give you the right to choose for everyone else?'

'God, no! But that's not going to happen. I'm just going to give everyone the ability to be themselves to the max. See where that gets your precious human race.' She had been inputting some instructions to the nearest terminal, but now she straightened up again. 'See this shield. The field is sable, the charge a sun radiant in glory d'or. It indicates the darkness in which the planet currently resides, the darkness of human domination, which the Woods call, ironically, the Dark of the Day, and the sun is the symbol of royalty which will lead the planet back into the light. Now look at the Ydal.'

The mirror no longer showed a reflection because the Ydal had stepped into the frame and her tower and change of garb had usurped reality's counterpart. Venus grinned as Kean choked audibly on his shock. 'Didn't ever play the termite side, huh? Well, lots of people did, astonishingly enough, and the devotees don't arf love their Queen, believe me. Anyway, apart from the enormity of the sleeping-bag effect the abdominal bloat of eggs makes, notice she rears to human height on her rear two legs, carries her spear and sword ready in her second pair, but holds the same shield as me in her top left pincer. The reason, as anyone who has seriously played the game knows, is that both Queens and their armies have the same goal. To save planet earth from the most destructive species it has ever known. It's not that humans transform the landscape that makes them a negative force in Terran life. Termite buildings delve underground and build highrises that, to scale, dwarf our capacity for building with all our technology. It's not farming, either, as termites herd and farm. No, it's all about attitude. We think we're superior to our fellow animals and we subjugate and terrorize and ransack the environment for whatever we need without limit. So the Termites, in the game, have come to take over to restore the balance of power to the rest of the Terran ecosystem. And it is now up to the people of the earth to decide how they go about it.'

'How are they going to do that?'

'Everyone who ever put on an I-*Mage* headset was contaminated with a dormant version of the modified Wood virus from the beginning. All the Ydal has to do, since she is the game's operating system, is to activate it.'

Kean's face was a picture of horror. 'What did you use? Ebola, Hanta, what?'

'Don't be daft. The Woods aren't killers. It's an innocuous flu strain. What it does is enable telepathy between humans directly. The unmodified version took weeks, but because we embedded it into the game with some alterations, the brain structures needed to tap into the mental wavelengths are already there. Some people who play Zen a lot, like Lily, have been using them a bit for years, mostly to communicate with their own inner selves, since humans apply their theory of mind mostly to themselves. But now it's not only available, it'll be mandatory. But it also does one other thing the original didn't, through I-*Mage* training of the brain. It projects their game-selves, not physically like holograms, but mentally, and, when everyone is linked together through telepathy, they'll see themselves and eachother as their desired, achieved avatars. That's why they're grouped at the sites of the end of the last level of the game they achieved, so as to be evenly matched, mentally compatible. Keeps it fair, which is more than most generals can say of their warfare. Anyway, when the people arrived they were grouped as Terrans or Termites, according to their conscious choice. Now we'll see who they really are. And how they really behave.'

'You're going to start a war!'

'Start, no. Facilitate, maybe. But you should check out the Jerusalem site on screen 45. Tell me you can see Jews, Muslims and Christians all standing together, in and around and under Temple Mount, even in the newly finished Third Temple itself, and then tell me how I got them all there *without* war breaking out. Oh, look. There's a girl in a hijab offering meneh to a Hasidic Jew. *This* was the promise of I-*Mage*. Peace without Armageddon. Let's see if they keep it up when the Ydal takes them out of oxytocin heaven.'

'You're going to take them out of the trance state you've currently got them all in and wake them up in the middle of a desert full of millions of their enemies,? Of course, there'll be fighting.'

'Why? Don't answer. I'll tell you. Because they're humans. Because they're a nasty, paranoid, vicious species, who, the Cognimata are correct, shouldn't be allowed onto the cosmic stage until they outgrow their impossible antisociable behaviour or die in the attempt. I offer them that choice. It's more than they'd get from the Intelligences in the outer cosmos, I can guarantee you. They wanted us exterminated before we got off the planet and contaminated anywhere else. So just sit still, keep your fingers crossed, if you want, and when I disappear, keep your eyes on the screen. I hope you enjoy the show.'

She stepped up to the mirror and extended both hands to the shimmering glass. 'My Coat is Your Coat. My Shield is Your Shield.' She uttered the words like a talisman. The 'glass' dissolved and the two rooms appeared to merge into one. The two queens clasped hand to tarsus and shield on shield. In one voice, although it was Venus' normal tones, they agreed, 'Release the virus.'

Then they parted, to stand side by side, and, as the mirror glazed and hid her from view, Venus appeared on the bank of screens, on each one in each of the 74 locations, bearing a new gravid belly almost as vast as that of the Ydal, who rose next to her in each TV picture, and both towered over the desert landscapes, scraping sky at two hundred feet tall.

As the mirror froze her into her holographic twin's domain and her real body fell lifeless to the floor in her cavern-office, on the edge of her hearing a man's voice cried out her name and called her his love, and then her ears caught no more.

Dinah could hear her husband's distress and enough banging of furniture to rouse the dead even as she ran to Venus' emergency call signal. She knew what she was going to find. Venus in a coma like she'd let Jake drop into after Ida died. The absence of brain activity consequent upon uploading the mind into the Ydal, to enable true incarnation as holograms. Venus had assured her Jake wouldn't die of it, but Dinah knew from sharing her employer's mind that the idea had come from another universe in which Venus' alter-ego had been in the same state for sixty years.

She'd been more angry with her than at any other time in their relationship, including the one in which she realized she'd been disappeared, especially from Jake, and much more so than when she'd understood how she'd been set up to divert Kean's attention from Venus. Now her bile rose again, as she had to watch the spectacle her distraught husband was making of himself yet again. Not that she'd known Venus had captured him and kept him here, although she'd wondered why he hadn't been sent for to treat and monitor Jake. She pretty much assumed that, since Venus had instructed her with the details of what was to happen when she went into the coma and the same methods applied to Jake, just earlier, Kean had been kept out of the way simply so that he wouldn't have his nose rubbed in the love she would keep revealing, by her constant vigil at his side, for Jake.

Even as she sympathised she was revolted by the intensity of the man's feeling for her friend and rival. He was rocking the heavy chair, trying to edge it across the floor to reach the prostrate Venus, yelling incoherently but at the top of his voice, and the tears were running down his face. All this despite the fact that his roped position couldn't have made her lack of interest plainer. However, Dinah was not a professional psychologist for nothing.

'It's alright, Kean.' she shouted over the din as she entered. 'She's in the same coma as Jake. I know what to do. She'll be fine. Just calm yourself and then maybe you can be of some help to her.'

She posed the body in the recovery position and then went round to untie the quieting man. Venus had trussed him up like a chicken. She had to find a knife because she'd have been there all day trying to undo those knots. Then she rubbed his wrists and ankles until he had enough circulation returned to stand and to help her carry Venus down to the hazmat clinic and put her in the bed next to Jake. She did the intubation expertly, noting the surprise in her trained husband's eyes at a skill he had not known she possessed, but he had to defer to her because his hands were still too stiff and puffy and shaky to do it himself. Then she set up the IV lines and stuck on all the monitors and checked the outputs, all of which registered within normal parameters within the hour, except, of course, for the cerebral activity. Next, she sat Kean down in a chair and put some antiseptic on the chinese burns he'd gained by struggling against his captivity, and finally she went through to the canteen and brought them both back a round of sandwiches and some coffee.

Kean was leaning his forehead on Venus' arm, holding her hand. Dinah forebore to mention that he'd made her hand damp with tears she could bet he would never have shed over her in the same circumstances. She wasn't a hypocrite, after all. She'd cried when it had first happened to Jake.

It seemed a long time ago, but he was still the man with whom she'd shared her life and her bed and her most intimate thoughts for the last three years and she still cared beyond her expectation, beyond the irritation and boredom that had sent her flying back into Jake's arms, so she was gentle with him.

'Come on, love. You've got to eat something.' She was firm too, when he shook his head at the sandwiches. 'They're only egg and mayo. If you're going to be here for her, you know the drill. Keep your strength up et cetera et cetera.' She had to warn him. 'It could be a long haul.'

'No. Didn't you see the screens? She was right. She and that holo-twin creation of hers. The revolting Termite Queen thing. They just stood together. Holding hands, well, limbs anyway. Shield on shield. Then they just turned and each addressed their section of the amassed people in their separate languages. Venus or whatever she calls herself as Queen of the fucking world just said 'Cast your minds! Find the Blazons that Harmonize! Wear the Coat of your neighbour! Play!' It seemed innocuous enough. I thought ... I thought. Well, after what she'd told me about the effect of the virus, I suppose it sounded like an instruction to love eachother or something. Show understanding at least. And for about a minute people stood still, sort of listening, internally, and then they started to move slowly into groups. But, then – did you see? How is it possible? Are we that awful? All of us? No one had any weapons. The disappeared had taken anything anyone was carrying when they arrived, I watched them. They were thorough. And yet, within five minutes, carnage. They picked up rocks, they took off their shoes, their belts, they used their fists, feet, elbows, teeth. It was indescribable.

She said it was the self-fulfilment of a prophecy the human race kept going because it *wanted* it fulfilled. She was giving them the opportunity to be themselves, and themselves were predatory, vicious primates who only think they think, only think they plan for the future, only think they are conscious and have free will and make choices. They're – *we're* – not like the Woods. When we can hear eachother's thoughts, most of us just feel paranoid, pressured, guilt-ridden, and react aggressively. We think like the mob, not the individual. Especially in a mob. If it's us or them, it's always going to be them, going down in the rivers of blood we've imagined as our own punishment from God for our original and personal sins. But that's our construct. She said she'd prove it to me. I didn't think she could. I *saw* everyone getting on in the Temple. She said that was her influence. She said once she took them out of the game's Zen-mode it would end. And it did. Dinah. It did. Millions are dead. Millions. Billions. It's – it's incomprehensible. But we did it to ourselves. We killed eachother, rather than be the civilized, superior beings we've always believed ourselves to be.

Dinah, what are we going to do? Even if she hadn't gone beyond. What do we do now? Now, we're exposed. Oh, god, Dinah. She should have let these Martians exterminate us wholesale. It would have been better than what we've done. There's no point in going on. Not after this. Not after the rivers of blood. We should be – and I expect we are – extinct.'

G: CITRINITAS: *SUBLIMATIO, FERMENTATIO AND SOLIFICATIO*

Terran and Termite Queens having raised their swords to declare victory, the end of the level won, had linked giant arms and their microsubjects were still again, watching them walk together through the vast doors that superimposed themselves on the blue of the sky and the *Rubedo* that covered the sand.

Around them a room of dark stone circled the horizons and within it the Round Table could be seen. External observers were shown a view from above. Clearly the space, the outlines of which were indistinct, was not circular at all, broadly it was elliptical, but with broken walls that whorled. The remaining population of the world breathed the name of the place as one. 'The LAPIS.' The Word that was Stone. The Platonic state Einstein had called Marble, beyond the Wood of the World. The tower was a mere glyph. The inscription of the mathematics Mandelbrot had called Chaos, the pattern Lily had found to be the Heraldic Coat of the Cosmos.

Venus stepped onto the centre of the Table and addressed the crowds. 'Brave Knights, you have achieved the Lapis. Behold the *Imago Mundi*!'

The viewpoint zoomed to the Table. Obviously Venus had never been standing on its flat top, because now you could see it was a sphere. The sphere, planet Earth. But then it unrolled somehow and was the glass Table, tracings only of the continents and seas delineating its symbolism. New lines and blocks of colour were overlaying it.

There were seventy-five spots of red denoting the Days. General Wharton, in US army uniform but carrying insignia that ranked him in the orders of chivalry as a Ceorl, strode to the table and took a chair.

There was a single splotch of green over the northern Amazon. The Eorl of the Knights of the Veriditas emerged and Rowan gracefully slid into the second seat.

Three blotches of black appeared, in the English Channel, the Basque highlands and over Madagascar. Vi !sjn-ik, Thane-level representative of the Darks, hopped into a third place.

A small blue note intensified in the Antarctic sea. The creature that swam into the conch-shaped bench was Zelas, Tachyon-Siren of the extinct Whorlingas and ghost-queen to the remaining Ghost Hydraens.

'The representatives of the Ancient Tribes!' intoned Venus, sweeping an introductory arm over the assembled dignitaries. 'And the later Abhominations...'

Here came a single dot attached, as an orbiting satellite, to each of the red spots and to the single blue one. Each flickered red and green like traffic lights on speed but, every few swings of their synchronized orbits, they would dart erratically towards the scarlet or sapphire foci, centre, and then sting the eye with intense electric-blue for a second, before glazing over grey and seeming to have to pause and wind themselves back up to restart their circling journeys. Pereduri was technically walking forward as Knight of the Augmentatio, but her natural lithe gait had been replaced by a lurching stumble and, once seated, her head found her hands and sagged into them with relief.

Immediately thereafter, two new motes could be seen on the Table. The first was a fleck over Penzeen Manor, Cornwall, and was red and black alternately, but its location was fixed. The second, also in ladybird colours, spiralled round the red-green speck in the azure eddy of the Antarctic blotch, *like a worried sheepdog*, Venus couldn't help thinking, as Xl-arn'tz, Augmented-Knight from the Squires Coagulatio placed himself beside Peri.

'The Avatars, Terra-Quester and Termite-Runic-Warrior! Welcome both.' As Ranger, naked, aquatic ape, carrying only the Harpoon and Shell of his played-role to show his status as Hydra-Ronin, and Lily, in her Termite-alate body with the diaphanous flutter of wings modestly shading her abdomen, took their seats, whereupon all of the seventy-five red areas flushed with freckles of termite-white. However, it could be seen within each patch, as the lens of the watchers moved in, that not only was the white prismatically filtering green and blue and black, but those Days, who had played Terrans and were now segregated into the red areas, were also made up of scintillations of the same white-peacock-tartan.

'These strands weave the Coat of Terra.' Venus announced from her perch centre-stage. 'Now see where the Coat Fits.'

The eye of sight zoomed out with giddying rapidity. The whirling walls skipped planetary horizons and skewed like a rocket-fuelled turn, so that the solar system swung into view, the sun itself replacing the third planet at the median position, so that the Table was a small fiery golden ball, embedded in a hot ruby corona, laced with dynamic threads in magnetic blue. The view pulled back again and the sun retreated to the far distance, passing Mercury almost instantly. Venus flashed by, Earth followed and then the gaze slowed over Mars, spun round once, to ensure everyone recognized the planet from its great cloudy red storms, and homed in on an icebound satellite, Europa.

Venus, linked to the people of the earth through the Ydal, could see and feel the collective reaction of shock and awe as the history of the Martian Mind and the Legacy was uploaded in full-harmonic-gist.

It was the Woods who expressed the greatest surprise. Humanity had had the arrogance to believe itself alone, but also the loneliness that wanted to be relieved of that burden, at least when it still appeared safely on another planet without space-travelling capability, so the Days, however fearful of, even repulsed by the Europans, were glad to know of them. The Woods, on the other hand, had thought themselves the superior minds, with the telepathic power that would make them first choice for first contact, and yet they had remained unaware of their neighbours and were humbled at, though excited by the knowledge.

'We present Quogat, the Fractal-Mancer, the Oratorio-Europa!' Venus bowed a welcome and indicated a space where the carapaced-uroborous could float or spin over a gentle thermal updraught, bounded by three smoking pillars, like a home-grown throne, had the Europans ever needed such.

'She is joined by the Dual *Pons-Astris*, the planetary bridge that is deemed the Contaminant, the human, Ida Makepeace and the Europan, Dakul. Together they appear as another Abhomination, imaged in the synergism of their choice.'

She hadn't seen their new look yet, although she had prior knowledge, which the Ydal would have shared with the rescued minds she was now enlightening, of their choice of bodies in another universe, so she was interested to see that they had got creative with the holographics. They hadn't gone for a human-europan hybrid at all. They'd symbolically dressed themselves as Termites. Aquatic ones, with fins instead of wings, and gills replacing spiracles, and retaining the colourful skin-communication and ability to torque into linkage, but their upper legs were human arms with opposably-thumbed hands that held eachothers as they scuttled into their liquid places.

Now for the Archivist. This cosmos had sent him to her without his Explorer and Secret Agent programmes and he had had no opportunity to get close to Uncle Milo, so she was not expecting him to manifest as Claude but as something appropriate in his role as Cognimatan delegate. When he arrived it was on the back of the second upload informing the populous of the Red Dragon Probe and the existence and interest of the Cognimatan Fleet in the Legacy, so the emotional wave meeting him was definitely scared. These aliens wanted to see the jumped-up, self-called-Intelligences of the third planet destroyed. Now their enemy would reveal himself. So it was bizarre to see a little old human, dressed in cardigan, slippers, and puffing on a pipe, shuffle towards the table. He had a bald shiny head, which, with the sharp eyes behind his glasses and his neat file of papers, indicated his understated intellectual capability. This was underscored by his image flickering between original Martian-medusoid and the silvery array that was the Fleet itself, and his human skin was constantly overwritten in the familiar green-shimmer-scrolling of electronic binary code. Around his head, like a bunch of manic flies, *or more aggressive collies,* swarmed and buzzed the threat of the tiny rocket-shaped weapons' programmes that kept the Probe corralled.

'The Appellants of the *Curia Regis* are now gathered together. We have two independent, expert witnesses, whose role is to mediate communication and synchronize the harmonic waveforms so that the final Note wrings truth and justice from discord. Peoples of Terra, rise now for the transformed MetaMind of the erstwhile-Intelligence of the planet, Mars, and for the Local Operative, FleshRider, the Orion Spore of the Cosmic Net!'

The viewpoint swung back and took in the swirl of electromagnetism that shot in a long streak from the Legrange point at heliopause, swooped round in Jupiter's solar orbit and reformed as a nebulous dark sun near the Oort Cloud, so as not to interfere with other photonic systems. The creation that took his place at the Table was much more accessible, at least to the Days, in the form of Lancelot, whose martial nature bulged in muscle and armour-sculpting and whose planetary origins seemed to rejoice in the passionate flesh he inhabited.

Then the high resolution that showed the solar system full-table-frame unfocused. The journey into outer space was too fast to follow but all along the way, as the eye jumped from Orion to Perseid arm and out of the Milky Way and beyond beyond beyond, sparkles of microscopic Mind glittered, and half-seen streams flowed beneath and through the fabric of spacetime as the eight-million years old Net described its' spread through sub-space [8] and the lace of interest that wound through time and species sub-cellularly. Apparently, the NLO had reviewed its options and decided that the image that had not maddened the already-marginally-sane in another universe was good enough for it, and it was the Eldil-Plant form that its avatar took. The triffid-like tripod of mangrove-style roots walked well enough but it was odd to see the algal-flexibility in the trunk that enabled it to sit in an ordinary, if overlarge, chair, and the tips of its branches seemed to have every conceivable form of appendage that could be hand or tentacle or claw or a myriad other tools. The leaves of the crown were clustered like hair, giving it layers of eyes and ears and nostrils and mouths and mandibles and suckers and thermal-pits and pheromone-mounds and who knows what else, but in a moment or two it had configured these into the semblance of a face, so that it seemed, fittingly, like a being even humans resonated with, the Green Man *(or Wood, or Dark, or Europan, depending on the nature of the representative to whom it turned that side of its crown).*

Venus was on again. 'I give you now, the Defender of the Peace. The one true Knight. The Terran King, Jake Wynn. His credentials are entered into the court record herewith.' And the upload of Jake's entire lifehistory preceded him as he took up his position next to her. 'I, as you know, am Venus Fargo. Terran Queen, acting as Prosecutor of the Peace.' There was more of a reaction to the full input of her own story than there had been to Jake's, but she was now exposed before all that was left of her peers and it was too late to concern herself with what anyone of them thought about her. 'And finally, I would like to introduce to you our Conduit, heretofore known as the Ydal, henceforth named by her own desire as Ygrail, the Lady of Shallot and Beloved of Lancelot of Mars.'

She paused while everyone seated themselves comfortably. Then she turned and the observers from without were looking directly into her eyes as if she was standing in front of each of them.

'We are here today to meet the challenge to show our Intelligence to justify our continued existence. Intelligence is only another evolutionary survival trait until it encompasses consideration of its entire environment. So we will look at our social structures.

All Days have experienced primary individualism as their default characteristic. Woods show us a way, now accessed through the telepathic ability just given to you all, of making our primary focus that of the group which takes decisions collectively.

The Darks are very social people but, without telepathy, they have survived by isolationism and traditions strictly upheld and enforced. They show us another, pack-mentality, of organisation.

Further, the recent insights we have gained into the hitherto-lost aquatic hominins reveal that a communicative society that passes through the Now, by living as in the past and casting randomly to the future, can be successful at surviving in a changing world.

In contrast, their nearest relatives, the IceBergas, placed static mindfulness ahead of even basic physical needs and their civilization ultimately decayed, although their insights as mere brains contribute much.

A further possible model for thought is shown in the metamind, the single shared but individuated mentalities, of the Knights of the Augmentatio. This resembles the linkages that exist between individual stacked Europans, although *their* full Coherence and single Intelligence Voicer compare more nearly with the Wood manner.

Those of you who have played the Termite side in I-*Mage* understand from within the Hive social constructions, which the Net informs us is the most common form of planetary Intelligence, since it enables more complex creatures to reference the balances within their worlds. So, for instance, Europans, Hydraens and Woods, while none of them has a fixed Queen, especially not merely to ensure replication in large numbers, all have learned to, at worst, gist, at best, wear the information other 'lower' lifeforms contribute to the planetary balance.

It is this principle that is so different from our 'us versus them' attitude and our sense of disposable ownership that has raised the concern of the Cognimata. They are not flesh, not planet-bound, and yet their original programming and their logical later higher analysis, while resulting in hierarchies that bear remarkable similarity to our own bureaucracies, still elevate the ranking of internal elements as less important than the whole, which ultimately resonates with the same Consensual principle.

The planetary MetaMind of Mars shows that sublimation of individuality into a new and again singular whole is another option, although it has to be said that we can only glimpse the benefit of this, as Mars had not found another comparable mind in all of its travels to date.

The Net, however, has demonstrated that single-celled self-replicating brains can not only survive but maintain a cosmos-wide standard-setting civilization.

All this will now be uploaded to you for your understanding of the entire Coats.

If humanity is to achieve MetaMind status, it will be by the voluntary sublimation of the many into the one of Ygrail, but she will also mediate us into any other options we can devise. The arguments for and against will be elaborated. But consider this as you engage with the input. If the selection process begun in blood is completed without transformation, the complainants, the Cognimata, have requested extinction.

Humanity appears to be colluding with them. I enter into evidence the *Rubedo* just passed. Divided into tribes, even though they all know they are players in a game, seeing fictional avatars merely imposed on real people, the vast majority of the individual humans massed at each point behaved violently towards their perceived enemies. They did this even as they felt the pain and fear of eachother telepathically. They did this even as they knew who was in the crowd, the hopes and fears, the excellences and weaknesses of their fellows. They did this even while they strove to protect those each individual deemed most worthy. They did this even though they had already been sorted into correllated groups by the levels of play they had achieved, and those had been achieved by playing together as much as individually, in their online cohorts of comrades.

They didn't need to fight. I-*Mage* showed people how to hone their skills. The fact that so many of them chose to hone their fighting skills says something about the species.

The survivors include the fiercest fighters, the fastest runners, the bravest defenders of the weak, the cleverest deserters, and all the rest who make up the fittest of the group, plus those they and others chose to save at their own risk. Humanity demonstrated its collective psyche as vicious and paranoid social predators.

This is hardly reassuring to the Cognimata, although its byproduct does mean that, should they let us live, we are reduced to numbers that could live sustainable lives without further damage to our planet or threat to the Legacy.

However now what you have to do is consider and remit to your Designated Voice, your representative at this Table, your preferred social structure and the top twenty-five named individuals and up to 125 more character types or essential skills that you would choose to save to populate such a group, should the Cognimata go for the lesser option of reducing the genepool to minimal, to a single monkeysphere, where we'd have to start again on intelligence. So, please, remember the real message of the Game. Use your imagination and *think!*'

She knew the image faded with her speech and sat down abruptly. It might be true that in holographic form she wasn't suffering from physical exhaustion, but she felt it as such. Just like all the shocked and traumatised, uprooted peoples out there. She nodded to the Archivist and he activated the Weapons Detail.

Screens that replaced the imaginary walls of the Tower Room now showed the seventy-four locations from the view of the Weapons, who had, at Venus' invitation, uploaded programmes into the earth-orbiting satellites along with construction-bacteria from the Ydal when the call 'Home' had been sent out. Now they demolecularised all the human remains without vital signs. They then scanned the planet for all the others who had died along the route to their 'Home'.

Kean might have been horrified by the rapidity with which massed humanity went into combat with eachother at the instruction 'Play!' but, Venus thought, he should have been watching the prior Exodus. The Temple Mount site, for instance, was house-deep in bodies for two miles around, thanks to the number of interested and opposing parties the General's activity had already brought to 'defend' their holy shrine. It was not the only charnel house that the period of transition had seen.

Nomadic in numbers never before seen, roaming without secure, clan or familial alliances, in accordance with the internal direction to reach sites determined by their gameplay alone, not their cultural histories, humans marched or skulked or ran or cowered but when they met, according to the Ydal, 80% of the time they fought. Until they were all assured, towards the end of each journey, that they were all going in the same direction, to the same level, and then, but only then, they relaxed enough for the engaged Zen mode to control their impulses and got along with eachother, from wherever and whatever background they came. It was therefore even more sickening when the reaction of those same happy campers, when split into two groups, Terran and Termite, with telepathic awareness, was, in similar proportions, to fight first and talk later. As a student of humanity, Venus wished she could drop out.

Still, there was a period of rest ahead now. The Disappeared and the reactivated Knights would dispense meneh and water to the crowds and there would be time for sleep and recuperation. The Cognimata had given them the week it would have taken for the probe to get into Europan orbit had the Mars-empowered Ydal not already lasered it into oblivion. Obviously, the long arm of the Fleet could have destroyed that whatever happened, but they subscribed to galactic protocols and had wished to do so with permission from the protagonist as it backed down, so a Terran Intelligence was needed, and now, as Venus attempted to honour her contract to give them one, they would not pre-empt her failure and would remain on standby.

Venus felt that, even if by some exceptional happenstance, the remaining population of humans had been entirely composed of politically-astute, humanitarian geniuses, it was still a long shot, but at least they would have time to get used to telepathy and used to accessing information. No single human, nor even Wood, had ever had access to this amount of information, of course. The Ydal, using her Mars-stimulated lunar-expansion as well as the geo-thermal Wood Minds as well as the Day world-wide-web as well as I-*Mage*, was a resource of cosmic and Terran history, although the Net had restricted knowledge of the wider galaxy and its inhabitants, as always with a planet not yet agreed as Intelligent, but also to limit the blind alleys folk could wander down. It wasn't the knowledge of their diminished status in the universe that was giving everyone pause, though. It was their knowledge, newly intimate, of eachother.

The thing about the Ydal construction, the template for I-*Mage*, the thing that had kept Venus straight and sane and not the megalomanic she should have become, was what she'd understood from her alternates. The multiverse didn't branch like a tree, it 'branched' like a blastocyst, each new 'cell' a multidimensional pulsation with directions determined by the shape of the two-dimensional surface-units around it. Histories weren't different because of big events, any more than people were different because of big events in their lives, those were post-event rationalisations, stories told to explain.

Thursday and Gwener and Venus were all sets of self-similar microscopic-level 'events', quantum-branching away from eachother until radically different outcomes had occurred. For them, and those they affected. From the cosmic, or even the planetary perspective, they were just the same as everyone else. And *that* was what everyone else was discovering. Not through alternates, not through listening to eachother, not through the stories each person told about themself, but by hearing the deeper truths. Truths that said things like, consciousness is just our made-up tales about our worldline and we're really no more than animals whose complexity lies about our superiority and we're all really really really alike and the rest is just history. And so the challenge became to learn from the Hydraens and throw aside the clinging tendrils of the past they thought they had known and Cast towards those unknown countries, the Future or, as it might be, Death.

Some things Venus had chosen to keep from them. It wouldn't do them any good to know that the Wood deselfing process retained the essence of their minds nor that the Ydal had effectively resurrected the dead by a similar process as holograms. She didn't have enough power and memory to offer that solution to everyone, so they'd just have to deal with the mourning and guilt and lack of religion and afterlives. And she hadn't managed full restitution of Ida and Dakul, despite the best efforts of their loved ones, and the minds of Zelas and the IceBerga Queen had been so pain-filled at the end that Peri and the Knights had had to have the memories excised in the short-term, into the Ydal partition, in order to regain their normal function, so Venus wasn't about to share that experience with her timelimited fellows. They had to concentrate on the matters in hand, although in fact the challenge to choose their social order of preference and nominate their top people was a bit of a red herring.

Oh, they should undertake the exercise with all the new data available to them, but this was more to help the Ydal, the Archivist and the Net process them more precisely. All the data from their gameplaying was available and had been used to categorise them by the personality types and skills by the Archivist already, but now their adaptability to stress, dissociation, trauma was being tested in the real world and their thought-patterns assessed as they undertook something a lot more serious than a game.

It also meant that the Ydal could study the minds of the Woods, Darks and Hydraens, since most of them had not been linked to I-*Mage*, as they had instigated the Conduit using their Skulls once they had arrived at their Home locations, which were obviously their cultural centres rather than end-of-game-level sites.

The Cognimata had been happy for her to do this, since, despite their repulsion for Flesh, they had been impressed by the Heim results and the technological advances of the weirdly disorganized species and had agreed that, whatever the outcome, the entire knowledge of the creatures should be preserved for study, if not posterity. So, finally, Venus had time to go home and sort out the crap she'd left till last.

It was a vile awakening, intubated and intravenously bound to machines, but Kean's joy was at least welcoming. Well, for all of the fifteen minutes it took to disentangle her, hug her, give her water and get her sitting upright. Then he went straight for the jugular. *If he was a Dark, that would have been literal.*

'You told them to kill eachother! What kind of a monster are you?'

Her defence came out as a croak initially, less indignant than petulant. 'I did not!'

'You marshalled them into two tribes and then you sent them to war. Billions are dead. Billions!'

'You weren't plugged in. You were tied up. You don't know. I didn't.' But her voice, though strengthening, still broke under the guilt of the numerical facts of death she had correctly predicted would result from the actual instructions she had given.

He sat back in the bedside-vigil chair. He'd had time to work up his righteous indignation and was damned if he wasn't going to have it out with her. It wasn't his normal attitude. If it had been he and Dinah would never have married in the first place, if he'd made the effort to enquire, if he'd braved the possible bad news about his loves. Well, it might be late, but his unquestioning loyalty was worth something.

She took another sip of water. 'Yes, I expected it to happen. So did the Cognimata which is why I've been allowed to do all this. But it was the end of their levels. There has to be a Boss challenge. So there's the two opposing sides, there's their Queens, the bosses. The test was intellectual. They had identical shields, 'bosses', sort of a pun. Each side, upon the instruction 'Play!', got the full overlay of the game scenario, so they could read that, to meet the challenge and be transported to the next level, they had to get the Queens to swap shields. Of course, all they really had to do was realize we already had. When the bosses kissed. *(PreRaphalite joke, don't worry about it. For the cultured players.)* And, naturally, if they got it, because we were never divided.

The game-solution was to look into the eyes of your opponent and recognize that they were merely a mirror of yours and to swop shields (everyone's avatar had them) with their doppleganger the Heraldic Way, by Mirror-Coat exchange. Kissing bosses, again. Understanding that we exemplified the *Solificatio.* They could only do this by activating the Zen Null-Space-Time, which links them to the Ydal's holographic imaging programme.

But no. Hubris was the reflection the majority saw in the mirror, their inner mirror and in their opponents' eyes, and they melted straight through the looking glass and back to reality. No one said they should fight their way through the enemy to wrest her shield from the enemy Queen. It was a riddle.

The magic happened to those who understood it.

Didn't you notice that there were some people and groups that the rest of the fighting crowds just seemed to dance around? That minority were in the Ydal, their avatars outsize with their personal space enlarged, or displaying invisibility, or one of any number of strategies that protected them until they got through the danger, although they were no longer watching the real scene, they were dancing with royalty in the Lady's room. But typically, tragically, the bulk of humanity didn't, despite playing I-*Mage* all these years, use their brains, they used their fists and everything else that came to hand.'

'But *why*?'

'Why do mobs behave like vicious sheep? Oh, I see. Why did I set it up so they could fail?'

Kean was struggling. *Coming down off his high horse now he's got the facts. Still looking to nail humanity's failings on me, though. (Someone should ask, heaven knows.)*

'OK. Once the Cognimata had realized us as a threat, it was a question of proving ourselves Intelligent or being exterminated. I had to do something to buy us all time, since I was the only one who knew about them. I sent them something they couldn't believe. Human technology, well, the equations from the theory for it anyway, that was beyond theirs. Until the Chinese sent up the Europan probe, I had time to organize. The Game seemed the best way to prepare people for manipulation of the entire global population. It honed their skills. Made them more extremely who they are, not who they tell themselves they are to sleep at night. And it made them easier to categorize, for selection purposes.

It's not my fault that humans defend themselves offensively in preference to thinking. Most people were killed by flailing, not intention. And, of course, since most people, well, most creatures, of which we may be the possible exception, are usually pretty much hard-wired not to kill their own species, at least when they can see the whites of their eyes, most of the killings happened from behind. Unfortunately, except perhaps for those in the 'back row', everyone who unthinkingly surged forward towards the Queens had someone's back to them, and then people fall down in the rush accidentally and fall straight into the category of helpless victim and hapless enemy and the chap behind takes advantage.'

'Well, I've heard you on the subject of doing without the 'chap who takes advantage' before, but what about the women?'

'Oh, those ones who didn't activate Null-Spacetime killed to protect and to defend where they were with their children. The kids who were old enough to have their own gameset were usually better at most games than their mothers, but mothers have the stamina, so all dependants were called to the end of the level to which their responsible guardian was going. It's not like the levels were hierarchical, they were just grading character. The surviving minors are going to be assessed separately anyhow, since they're mostly still potential.'

'I saw some women hacking men to pieces.'

'Well, some folk do like a good fight whatever their gender, of course. But you weren't watching with the headset on, so they might have been Termite Amazons battling Dark sonic-screaming to their minds. Avatars don't have to share gender with their wetware. Energising, I understand.'

'But you weren't surprised. You still planned, or at best, expected this to happen. It's so … cold of you.'

'You know, for someone who so-called loves me, you're very unimpressed by me, aren't you? Not that that doesn't have its own particular attractive quality.' Venus was laughing at him, but gently, and at herself too. Suddenly a penny dropped. 'Oh, of course. You've been sitting here with me and the others, haven't you? Missed my big moment on I-*Mage.* OK, well, you and Dinah, wherever she is, are probably the only people not to have plugged in, and at my request, so I owe you the heads-up before you get the full Blazon with the rest of the species. The Queen's personal speech, not the edict, or not until after you've been primed, maybe inoculated, who knows? Here, take a moment and I'll check on Jake and Lily.'

'How did you know about Lily?' Stalling the telepathic upload, he grabbed her hand as she moved it from her mouth to his temple. 'She went into a coma after you.'

'Well, a) because I'd already arranged it, didn't Dinah say? and b) because when I called her to the Round Table, it was the inevitable consequence. As you'd know if you'd let go my hand and let me give you my memories.'

Still holding it tight, and with a fierce look in his eyes, he said 'There're are some memories you should have too.' and thrust his own dampened index on her temple. It was already tender, mildy abraded by the electropads from the brain-tracking monitor. The connection hit her like an IV drug.

It wasn't the depths of his despair and confusion over her that struck like a migraine, it wasn't even the existential hurt of watching his species self-destruct, though that sang bone-chill and whole-body neuralgia and depressing weight into her every cell. He had, after all, served in many situations as an ngo- and, earlier, forces-medic and seen the inhumanity of man to man. But Dinah hadn't.

Dinah was a professional optimist regarding her fellows, even ones as far gone as Ida. Her death had devastated. Jake's coma had buckled. Her husband's perfidious attachment to Venus that kept him sitting by the side of the inanimate when his living wife needed him had wounded, but she'd been honest enough to recognize her own parallel vigil beside Jake was as hurtful. But all of that and the vicious self-extinction event was, without Venus' presence to comfort and guide and reassure, and with her surrogate in I-*Mage* forbidden, too much.

Venus walked out of intensive care without a glance at the other patients. She got to Ida's water-cave without recollection of covering the ground or going into turbochutes, despite the foam and unfoam complexity. She knew what she would see. She also knew that Kean had just left the scene intact. Because he couldn't face it, yes, but also, if she ever woke up, for her. He was that angry.

Dinah had used the gantry that Ida dived from into the vast tank in which she swam as Flow with Dakul. The rope was efficiently and securely attached, the length sufficient to ensure that it dropped a good third below the waterline. The girls had kept a set of weights in the cave which Makepeace would only consent to use if Dinah worked out with her, and Dinah wanted to keep her indoor-patient reasonably fit. A large dumbell was attached to each of her ankles and there were several weights on bands on her wrists. She hadn't meant to leave herself the option of changing her mind. If hanging didn't get her, drowning would.

The rotation of the water in the tank was on full. *She must have turned it up! She was angry at me too. It's a message.* The corpse spun and danced in the whirlpool streams, flailing gently with twitching arms, pointing balletically with her weighted toes. Her mouth and eyes were open and her expression screamed her silent anguish and terror and rage. And she was naked. Venus had never seen her fully stripped, although admired her full figure often enough in a bikini. It was almost more shocking, more of a statement than the rest. *At core, she's offended at me!* But, worse, far worse than her death was the waste. She hadn't put on her headset. In fact, the opposite. It was unbreakable, impenetrable, but she'd tied the heaviest of the dumbells to it and dropped it into the tank with her. It lay on the bottom. *Useless!*

She'd lost her best, indeed her only, real, friend. Even if you take responsibility, even if you can hear the oceanic roar of their minds at the time through the Ydal, masses killing themselves aren't personal.

Everything she was doing hit her now for the first time. *It was overdue.* She threw up.

When the turbochute disgorged her into Bite, Cal took one look at her face and ordered Mh'aed to bring *blodvin*. 'Darling! Don't frown like that. You'll be needing botox next.' He fluttered about her, forcing her gently to sit, stroking her furrowed brow. Mh'aed snorted with the rolling-R's snuffle only Darks can make, but she tipped a strengthening potion into the drink all the same. 'Don't know what kind of a doctor lets his patients rush about like mad things straight out of a coma.' carried on Cal. 'Seems to me you should fire your boyfriend.'

'Oh, shut up, Cal.' Even her voice was weary. 'As if he could have stopped me.' She seemed to be talking more to herself as she continued, 'He wanted me to see for myself.'

Mh'aed nudged him with a singularly sharp elbow. It said *keep her talking* as plain as words. 'See what, dearie?' Cal complied.

'Dinah's body.'

'Dinah's dead? Oh, my god! Did he join in the bloodbath? Did he kill her?'

'No. Neither of them joined in. Dinah killed herself. Because she was so horrified by what I did.'

Mh'aed snatched at the bottle of blodvin and added a new ingredient from the pouch she produced from within the layers of her clothing and handed it swiftly back. Cal was struggling himself to find the right words. *Dinah? Of all people. She trusted Venus more than anyone. No wonder she was taking it hard.* 'I'm sure that's not the reason, darling. There's been a lot of stuff those of us not playing have found very hard to watch. And she was there trying to choose between one man in a coma and the other in love with you. All too much at once, I'm sure, but you'll get her back.'

'No. She didn't upload. She's gone.'

Cal took a swig of the drink himself. *Dear Dinah! Such a sweetie!* But the elbow swinged his side again and he knew what he had to do. And, boy, did Mh'aed's potions act fast. 'Well, princess. That's awful, I agree, and I'd like to have time to mourn the poor thing properly myself, but you know we haven't.' He caught sight of the expansive, inclusive gesture Mh'aed made and nodded. 'There's a bigger picture here. Plus we knew that the casualties would include those we cared about. OK, not like this, but … well, I've got more bad news for you, while you're down anyway.'

Finally, and probably because the *blodvin* mixture was working, Venus raised her eyes to him. 'Milo and Ruth and Bob.' She mouthed the word 'Dead?' and when he nodded confirmation, found her voice for one word. 'How?'

'You probably didn't realize because you weren't here for the General's ingestion of the Grail, but they were wearing their headsets and they were already high on faith, so when they saw Kean apparently kill you, they also saw the General lying on the tomb in the remade Temple of Solomon. Them and all their Endtimer Cohort apparently. Galarhas says they had a special loop in Null-Spacetime they called 'Eternity', where they held meetings of those making the Temple and bringing on the end of the world. Thousands of them. And when the call 'Home' came, they went there and waited for the General to awake and lead the Rapture. The Ydal decided you didn't need to know this earlier, she wanted real people to tell you, not an upload.'

'Go on, then. Spit it out.' She was definitely feeling better.

'They were on the same wavelength as the General.' Cal let this sink in.

'Oh no! They all went to Hell?'

'We didn't realize until too late. To be honest, the Ydal didn't think it was a problem. In fact she was amused by the irony. Not quite human enough in the end, your mirror-image, as it turns out. Anyway, by the time she'd notified us, since most of us weren't wearing headsets while the Homing signal was on, even when we took the sets off them we couldn't bring them out of it. Hell, and the betrayal by their God, were all they could see and feel. Most of the Endtimers never came out of it, of course, because they had no one to remove their headsets, and they walked the hot coals of brimstone to their Home destination, if they didn't die on the way of dehydration or whatever, and then were simply mown down like grass in the melee, contributing to the rivers of blood as per their original expectation for everyone else. The Ydal thought this fitting.'

'Just tell me!' The little princess was reviving, he could hear it in the queenly tones of command.

'Dinah probably got the idea from them.'

'They killed themselves?'

Here it comes. 'They tore themselves apart. They ripped their skin off with their own nails and teeth. They were trying to get the demons out from underneath. When that didn't make them feel better they found ... other means, and just kept cutting. It didn't take long, if that's any consolation. They bled to death.'

'Why the hell didn't you sedate them?'

'We did, as soon as we realized. But everyone was busy. Kean was tied up, literally, and then in looking after you. Dinah was trying to work with them but then Lily went down and she had to leave them alone. They were under Dark guard, but when she returned they'd killed the guard and, effectively, themselves. With their captor's claws and teeth – they'd ripped them out of the two bodies. It was – ugly.'

'Self-fulfilling prophecy. Oh, Mum!'

'I'm sorry, kid. I ...' But he didn't get the chance even to extend the arm he intended to put round her for comfort. *Hers or mine? They were my family almost more than hers. And what about poor Mh'aed? She's saying nothing, but she loved Bob, and she couldn't understand how he'd become a believer so instantly.*

She stood, inhaled deeply, almost shrugging, 'Their pointless deaths are no more important just because they're personal than those of the rest of humanity. Time to move on.'

I guess it's not for nothing, she has the chutzpah *to be Queen.* She was right, of course. *But where do you get the chill in the soul that can sacrifice even people you know and love? Like my poor Rowan.* Although he'd colluded, once things had been explained to him. Always the leader himself, despite the fact the Woods don't have them. Character. That's what the whole thing was about. Rowan might have lied to him, but in the end Cal would've forgiven him, *or gotten over it.* But he hadn't had the chance. Venus snapped her fingers, dangling the carrot of being Wood-Voice to the Cosmos, and he'd willingly given up life itself. OK, so he was still communicating, in holo-form, part of the extended Ydal, but he was the only Wood to die so far, and it didn't seem fair to Cal that the one body he loved should be so easily relinquished, even if it saved others. *If it does. If I were Cognimatan, I wouldn't be thinking anything like a human was worth preserving just now.*

The Archivist had been struggling with much the same thought. He had catalogued every headset that went quiet and then he released the Weapons to vapourise the dead flesh. Only a twentieth of the human population remained, and none of them had placed their responsibilities before their game-induced homing instinct. He had studied their use and abuse of many species, but one had resonated with their recent behaviour, they called them pigeons, and he saw no superior use of intellect and a lot more aggression in the dominant creature than the *Columba livia.* They might not breed so prolifically but there were still too many. They could repopulate the planet too quickly if they survived in these numbers with their current abilities and then they could threaten again.

The Net had mediated the negotiation between Venus and the Cognimatan Fleet and agreed that whatever outcome the experiment would result in, there were certain prerequisites even for engagement in the process. The diminution of numbers upon the game-empowerment had been one expectation fulfilled, and Venus had sued for the quick cleanup. On the same grounds, he had been forwarded a new programme to modify a select few of the Weapons to remove or make safe the dangerous effects of removing people-operators from their niches, so fissile explosions and the like would not do the Cognimatan job for them, nor endanger the entire planetary ecosystem.

The Weapons had had fun. That is, he corrected himself, they appeared energised and enthusiastic as they went about in fulfilment of their programming. *Doesn't make it less true, though.* He had set up a covert subloop in which to have these thoughts, not because he feared any longer that he was being contaminated by contact with humans, but because his research had proven to him beyond doubt that character and its phenotypic expression was implicit even in Cognimatan programmes. He just didn't want anyone in the Fleet to listen in, as they periodically did, out of quite reasonable distrust of their outlying operator, to overhear this manner of thinking. Of course, the Fleet relied on the Weapons to have infiltrated his systems, but they didn't ask the right questions, so to their spy networks he still appeared clean. Not to mention the fact that they had shown their own bias.

For instance, of all the methods they could have used to eliminate the threat from gas and oil wells, they had chosen to blow the tops off every one (simultaneously, so they got a good firework display from their viewpoint in terrestrial high-orbit), then they had swooped in, sucked up salt water from the oceans and poured it into the fires and wells, melted some local rocks and decanted the lavalike masses in to plug the holes. It would have been as easy to vapourise the fuels throughout the entire crust, and they had done with all the energy stored in surface pipes, rather than risk local fires that would destroy the surrounding vegetation across the world.

No, if you put predator into a character, fulfilment through killing came back out. He could hardly blame the humans for their predicament anymore. In fact, he shared Venus' opinion. Apart from when the aggression was turned on their genetic fellows, a good predator *should* be able to look into the eyes of its prey and strike without hesitation. The humans' problem was simply they persisted in seeing eachother as enemies. The rest of the sentient cosmos would be in trouble if they ever worked that out, stopped, and turned their attention outward. There didn't seem much likelihood of that on today's showing.

Galarhas would have said different, but fortunately for Venus' plans, he was in isolation. That is he was the only Knight not comatose in the flesh and partitioned in the Ydal as an organising *Force Majeure* hologram for the Home sites. By contrast, he was an unknown codicil Venus had appended to her Net-mediated contract with the Cognimata; the *Vis Majeure.* He could remain awake because no one at the seventy-fifth site, under Penzeen Manor Farm, except the Squires, who were all present but Xl-arn'tz, had been allowed to don the gamesets. That was why only they, and none of the Days, and certainly not Galarhas, had shown up on the Round Table as at Home in Penzeen.

The Squires had left now to collect the equipment needed from the Santa Fe Institute hangar about which Lily and Jake had been so curious, but since the Net had been informed that they had already made their gameplay and lodged their decisions with the Ydal, it believed they were merely collecting those last few individuals it had identified as not in I-*Mage,* and it wouldn't be monitoring their journeys. In actual fact, the Knight-MetaMind in its painful and blank trauma had been used by the Ydal to break into Wood Consensus for just the briefest of moments in order for Galarhas to give certain instructions that included collecting the Day strays. They were now being brought into WoodHame under powerful

Wood-Calling, made possible by the Ydal utilisation of Second Mind, so, if the Net made only a cursory check, it would still look like everyone was behaving as planned.

Mother was counting on the lack of guile in the wider cosmic understanding of contracts. She didn't think even the NetRider understood what it meant to come from the kind of social species found on Terra, there had been so few examples of non-Hive hierarchies or unshared distributive minds in its experience. Deceit was not required by an evolution based around domination and/or co operation, only where resource-competition snuck in the uncertainty which primates, and crows and a few other bright communicating group dwellers, lived with. And the kind of trick Venus intended to pull, well, she'd had to be absolutely trustworthy to date to set it up.

Fortunately, if horribly, she'd had help from the rest of her species. They'd behaved as she'd predicted. If she and the Ydal were right about the test they were currently undergoing, they wouldn't choose logically, as the Cognimata supposed, adopting sublimation in the Ydal nor even a Hive with Venus or her doppelganger as leader(s). They'd be unable to choose a unified position, even within their individual minds, because they were deep down predators, and what they'd really want to do was fight back, and the Net would see, the Archivist conclude and the Cognimatan Weapons eradicate.

Not so the Woods, of course, who would achieve Consensus and vote for the Ydal, with the Darks going along with the plan, although they would prefer a Hive structure as nearer to the Pack, but would put survival before taste. So the Cognimata would allow them to be the protoIntelligence to inherit the planet, whilst demanding that they not raise their Voice in the wider cosmic arena until they had actively Transcended. Terra would become a Protectorate of the Cognimatan Legacy, isolated but untouchable, and blind and deaf to the activities in their own solar system.

They might be more sensible collectively, but, Venus knew, even the biddable Woods and Darks were too curious to enjoy this status now they knew they were not alone in the universe. So she had thought up an escape plan that covered them all, even the Hydraens. A way of using their natural talents to subvert their destiny. She wasn't about to dole out to people, any people, what they deserve, but she might give them what they could take.

And after all, there was a reason all the Tribes of Hominin had retained the image of the Knight. The symbolism of the hunt was embedded in the meat of the Courtesie. Now was his time. To Augment. In Heraldic this had a very specific meaning. It did not signify addition merely, it signified the addition of the harmonic-Time, granted by a sovereign power for an act of note. The one Note. The Note the Tachyon-Sirens of the Whorlingas and the IceBergas had both heard Cast Back from the Future that was Now. The note that was the symphony that had played down the endless years of Eddyless Calm, the single thought that had sustained the frozen seers who had achieved the sought-after Transformation, the complete sublimation of flesh into mindfulness. The secret Peri had brought him. The translation of the glyph Lily had wrought with and written. The Quest that Mother had hunted down the years to its ground in the now.

The original quarry, the most ancient of Grails, not the Logos, but the Gnosis. In the ancient Heraldic, the ur-concept: Self-Knowledge. The true salvation for Terra. Knowing our splice of spacetime. And what it meant today: Exodus.

It was time to leave the garden. The prophecy of Eden would come to pass, and the fiery sword keeping the gate back would be in the hands of the Eldil and the Cognimata, as was fitting, after our behaviour.

But at least in our writing of our future-myth, we'll throw ourselves out, he grinned to himself.

Zelas was treadling on the subject of possible future-myths as she shouldered her share of the siting of this particular rock into the way of the current flow. And since she'd had to die to experience the viewpoint she had now, she was beached if she wasn't going to relish it. It was interesting being light, with only the thin qmass skin as a boundary by which to interact with the world, except as a mind. She had a mild sense of loss, like being unable to recall a memory of something you know you know. But when your body with all its physical feedback systems isn't pumping reminders of its fleshy needs to your meaty brain, there aren't the hormones to flood intense emotions, like grief. She could be surprised at the calm after the turbulence of the body, she could be disturbed at the absence of a sense of detachment she thought she should feel, she could be fascinated by the possibilities lost and found, and it was all acceptable as existence.

In fact, she suspected, if this weren't hubris, that she had gained an insight into what it felt like to be the NetSpore, of which she had been implanted with the Ydal's knowledge. The NetSpore could be deceived by Venus' ploys, even though it could plant a fractal, holographic-whole-in-part slice of itself into any creature. This was because it Rode, but it never became one with the horse, empathising with the creature. It was most likely to experience rapport with bacteria and viruses, although mostly doomed to find no metamind in the Terran species. It enjoyed algae and lichen for similar reasons, but it had to admit that the largest metamind on the planet was housed in the robotic ants, the sharpest if quite parochial and colonial in the bees' Hives, and the most Intelligent in the incomprehensible primates. Now that Zelas had time to reflect on the NetSpore's reports to the Cognimata, entered into the evidence of the *Curia* by instant mindflood, it was clear to her that the poor Outlier didn't get the gist of humans at all, much less the meat. Too few glands, she thought regretfully.

Ranger was having trouble dealing with her discorporeality. It wasn't that they didn't still love eachother, and plenty of her co-respondents were exhibiting passionate behaviour, indeed you could scarcely prize Flow and Dakul apart, as they revelled in their compatible new light-bodies. They certainly didn't seem to be hormonally under-served. But Ranger knew Zelas had changed and he was scared to ask why. Zelas was scared to give him the answer he expected, but she knew it was true. It was not death that had changed her, but dying had.

The violence of it and the awful despair and penetrating cold and vicious pain were almost forgotten, passed with her passing from the body that cared about such things, but the rip of her mind into a meld with Pereduri and the IceBerga-Siren, Ouissocca, that had had irrevocable affects. For a moment it had seemed as if it was just her and Peri holding her tight so as not to lose her and impressing on her the need to focus on this, not on anything else that was happening, like the actual dying. She hadn't realized that Peri had clasped her killer's mind just as strongly until there was a sort of whoomph, like an implosion in Peri's brain, then suddenly she was joined with her siblings, as her capacity gave way under the pressure. They provided the breadth of processing power her brain alone did not, but the triangle of death seemed a minor event, just one occurrence in the life of the 150-brain-wide-Peri. The sense of self diminished abruptly, making the conjoined minds of Zelas and Peri both much more manageable, focused, a problem simplified. They both relaxed, and that was when the chill started.

Ouissocca had barely impinged as a mind. In life she had been all feeling. Hate and Hunger. Anger and Revenge. They had waited! All these years! *You come now! At the End!* Loneliness and Betrayal. There was no room for the Welcome! they had imagined they would offer their long-lost relatives when they came questing for them. *Cowards! We kept the faith. We sealed ourselves in. We subsumed the physical. We lived the Endless Calm. We became Stone. And still you did not come.*

All of that gist had been carried in the base emotions that had bared their teeth after aeons with such deadly gusto. But once the flesh that fired the message was stripped away, the mind reverted to its most familiar pattern, that of its hermetic life in the ice-cell. That mind had operated while its body had lain in effective dormancy, so it was as slow as the Antarctic meltwater drippings, *before global warming*. The metamind made the mistake of turning its attention to Ouissocca before they realized just what that stagnation meant.

It was like being trapped in a dark cave. You could sense it was vast because of the time it took for echoes to return from the walls. Mind is like this. A spark in the dark has to set off a chain reaction globally for the lightbulb to come on in consciousness, but your hand can be moving towards the lightswitch before you are aware you think it's dark. Zelas hadn't understood the metaphors fully at the time Peri had thrust understanding of their predicament at her, but she soon got the point.

They both had sensed a coherent complete communication from Ouissocca, the taste of a gist in the current afar, and the scent had been the same draw for both of them, and for the other Knights Augmentatio. They had opened their minds attentively, listening for it to solidify into the chime of mental sound, waiting for the echo to return amplified into a sentence. But Ouissocca thought such long frozen thoughts, even ones articulated clearly, like the gist she had flagged that she was sending, that the elements of the message were so fragmented and, though sent sequentially and grammatically, so spaced in emission that it was as if Time itself had iced over.

Their attention might have only been the equivalent of nostril-flaring on a hunt but it was for the quarry, which was the complete gist uttered. So they were unable to redirect their attention until they had heard it in full. As if you were forced to listen to someone saying a single sentence in slow-motion over many hours. They would have been in real trouble if Ouissocca had been friendlier and sent them her Coat Entire. It might have taken a lifetime before they could have got a thought in edgeways and taken some control of the situation.

It took forty-eight hours just to set up the partition that allowed them to have a dialogue at a reasonable speed with the IceBerga. It was over eight hours before she had had the thought she'd started with. It hardly seemed worth the wait when it turned out to be: 'I am Ouissocca, Tachyon-Siren in service of Ghost-Queen, IceBerga. How dare you kill me!' To be fair, she had been taken by surprise and it was her first thought on realizing her death, so it didn't have to be epic poetry, but Zelas had been aware, in the mind-numbing focused waiting, of atomic-clocks splicing intervals of boredom into pained nullity.

On her own in that mind, Zelas would have been trapped, another ice sculpture, although once her thoughts had taken on glacial-speed themselves, they could have had a dialogue. But fortunately, there was some perspective available, a meta-subtext, and, as soon as the gist was delivered to the snout of the Knight-meld, they struck back, firing in a message and firewalling before any reply could begin to be returned.

The message was a Blazon, but compressed into a vivid chemical gist, that would ring a physical bell as Cantor-dust on the molecular level. It was the prescription for relieving physical hypothermia which Ouissocca needed to remember and imprint on her postwetbrainware in order for her mind to warm up enough to think at a complementary rate. It took a long while to permeate, and she couldn't be expected not to think the while, so the partition was necessary to save the Augmentatio and Zelas from being sucked back into iceflowings.

But then it was worth the wait. The IceBergas had kept the faith. They had looked in the mirror of Heraldics, heard the silence in Harmonics, felt the warmth in the ice and the stone in the water and the fire in the blood, and they had Listened. They had not shared communication, made art, constructed philosophies, meditated on the universe, but they had kept the faith, by listening to the heartbeat of the Quarry: they had Listened to Terra.

They had started out sensing the wave in the water, but in Antarctica they had found the flow that was solid. The appreciation of the phase-changed states of liquids led them to develop ears that could hear the echo of Land itself, and ultimately even air and space. And they knew Terra's Note in the Harmony of the Spheres, and they had memorised all the strains and chords and riffs that contributed to the melody of the life of the planet. Oh, not even they could hold the full Blazon, it was the barest of gists, an outline glyph, but once the Siren Sang the Note into your mind it never stopped belling and unfurling, dancing its endless tendrils throughout the labyrinth.

Zelas was changed forever, but the incarnate Knights would take this knowledge into their life and evolve it in its ecological niche. Terra would Become, because Terra now had a self-aware-observer, a Terran Intelligence, a Voice for the Note to use to Echo beyond mere reverberation. And, because the NetSpore could not appreciate the sensory complexities of Heraldic, it could not 'hear' the Note, even if it was given the fullest Blazon. And so the Knights allowed Pereduri to go into a coma to represent them at the Round Table and engaged Galarhas as the *Vis Majeure*, set to gallop in on his fiery charger and save the Day.

And the Terran-Harmonic was the final piece in the jigsaw it had taken Lily two universes' worth of puzzling over to bring to completion. In this cosmos Lily had translated the glyph and calculated the parameters of the basic shapes of spacetime; a process of mathematical visualisation. In the cosmos in which Venus' alter was Gwener, Lily's isolation and comparable talents, extended to include a practised imagination, had combined to let her Listen within, mostly in a dream-state, and there hear unheard her own Note, which had been the anchor for her fictional travels.

Here Zelas now knew that the Heim metrons, in their fractal self-similarity but minute differences, had posed a severe handicap when it came to jumping spacetime instantly. The Cognimata had not solved it, which was why the Archivist and Weapons had no means of return to the Fleet. And Venus did not just want another fantasy-world, only realizable as spectral holograms. But the Terran-Harmonic was the last digit in the equation, one that Heim propulsion did not contain.

He had calculated the basic principles of the universe, he had calculated the dynamics of outgoing spacetime travel, but, unless someone stayed to reactivate the empowering magnetic fields in an identical but reversed way, he had no way of getting his astronauts home again. (Which had not been such an obstacle for his theory as for Venus in practice.) But, viewed with extra dimensions in the calculations, it had become obvious to Lily that all that was required for this was a single, introduced figure. She couldn't plug it in, even though she knew how to reckon the lower-D operation, because it had been too complex to work out. Maybe, over time, the Kray could have managed the task, but maybe that time would have spanned the lifetime of the universe. It was much more likely that a quantum computer could perm through the possibilities in a reasonable period, but as the Cognimatan logical approach had yet to output a solution, and as the Ydal could only jump into Venus-alikes' heads, not other universes per se, there had been little likelihood of crunching the relevant numbers.

Until Ouissocca had shared the Note and Lily, primed to recognize the shape and the figures of the hole in the picture, had found her missing jigsaw piece. It was the Home co ordinate, so now when they threw themselves out of Eden they could also find their way back.

It was a fixed figure, but the gravitophotons that enabled the jump moved the astronauts through space and time, and they both became relative to the point of origin, which was also passing through spacetime itself. The Note was a complex number but as the expression of a living entity, the Terran-complex, it would evolve with time, however, while even relative times tick by linearly, a planet alters more erratically. Only by knowing its singular significant chime could a wanderer hear the bell reCalling. And even then, to return, the math was art and the calculations conjuring. But Quogat was an adept at such arts and Lily could conjure without trickery, so Venus would finally achieve her I-*Mage*, where the I stood for Terra itself. The planet Named.

So, finally, the *Augmentatio* was achieved from the *Rubedo* and the *Proeicto*, the transformative process that worked by mapping correspondences, which the Ydal would facilitate, could begin. Only the General's obsession remained thereafter in the Alchymical Cycle: *Immortalis.* But for that the Phoenix had to rise from the ashes. A trick only one mage could pull off.

Jake had been given the job. Of course, as with all jobs instigated by the damn Fargo woman, there was an agenda he hadn't signed up to, but for which her research into his character fitted him. Initially, once he'd got over the shock of being told his real body was comatose and the one he felt like he was occupying was made of light, his predominant feeling had been relief that the position of Rex did not require him to fertilize the eggs of his Regina, Venus. Not that she wasn't an attractive woman, or, with the new perspective being inside the game gave him, termite, but he had felt Dinah's emotional fragility and there was no way he was going to wreck that relationship a second time. Fortunately, it seemed the consortship with Venus was more adversarial than lovey-dovey, for which his role seemed to be to ingest an inordinate amount of information in a very short time, so he didn't have a lot of space for introspection, not even to wonder about how Dinah was coping with his coma.

The work consisted mainly of understanding the bases upon which the Archivist and the Ydal had differentiated humanity into types and then reviewing individual case studies at random to ensure accuracy was being maintained fairly. Once he had agreed that they could assume the categorisation was correct and people fitted into a remarkably, and disappointingly, short list of personalities, he was asked to assess the models of societies proposed and then consider how the types of people extant in the current population would fit into those solutions.

It was a lot drier than the psychology of the human race should be, mainly because it was all about statistics and probabilities, but, since his body no longer distracted his attention and his mind didn't tire, and since such detailed research was his forte, he got through it well enough. (When he had asked the Ydal why someone like Dinah, with psychological expertise, had not been tasked with the job, she'd told him that only someone without truly empathetic understanding of how the rest of his species ticked could make the necessary, cold choices. *It sucked a lot to know that his qualification was his nerdy detachment, but at least he could feel proud of it for once.*)

He was done long before he needed to report back to the Round Table, but, depressingly, he had only been able to echo the prediction Venus herself had made: that not even the best selection of human personalities, if one retained a mix suitable for longterm species' viability, would not tear apart any of the political choices on offer, and with it themselves. Individualism was ingrained and a level of anarchy, unacceptable to the Galactic Intelligences looking on, an inevitable corollary.

Oh, he could see in his role of advocate for his species that there were many good aspects of his people to promote, only he knew that the free rein their selfpromotion had led them to was this point of termination and, even had that been avoided, to a later point in which man-induced climate change would kill them more lingeringly.

If he'd had the tears, he'd have wept. Even after he'd seen the bulk of his peers destroy eachother for no reason.

He didn't want to let anyone else know he'd drawn such negative conclusions, at least not until he had to, so he pulled Venus aside and passed on the responsibility. She wasn't surprised, at his results nor his cowardly action, but she didn't judge him for either. 'Well done, Jake. That must have been very hard to confess. It's damn hard to know, I know. So thank you. But now I need you to undertake the real WildKnight role. The reason you were granted the Arms of Pretension.

You were the bearer of a rusty shield, now it gleams with use. You did have your eye shut beneath the blood of the flesh and the obsessive focus of tracking your bloodsister. Now your eyes are open.

There is one solution not on the Table.

This is the real choice before you.

The survival of the species choice.

You were given a false gist. You have honoured my deception by honest research and openhearted analysis and you can lodge your report with the Ydal. If you agree to undertake the final quest, you must be sent back to Judge, but you must be seen to be here. You can only do this if the Ydal splits your I-*Mage* into two. Until and unless you come together again to exchange Coats, the Jake operating here and the Jake operating on Terra will bear separate lives and memories, both of which will be uploaded into your physical brain if you wake from the coma, and that is likely to be deleterious to your mental health, unless you meld the holopersons first. Not everyone's as happy as me and Ida at hosting all the voices in your head this lifestyle can give you.

So that was your warning. If you want to back out, you are still a free individual, but you know the stakes.'

'Why don't you ever tell me what the job is before I have to sign up with you?'

'It's part of the ancient traditions of the hunt. You have to enter upon the quest without knowledge even of the quarry's existence.'

'And you believe in all that stuff?'

'Believe?' Venus's smile was askew, but her eyes warm. 'It's the oldest hominin social system for the males of the group. The hunt. Women's resourcing systems were different. Foraging was a broader based, slower but more reliable source of food, including protein from nuts, fruits, eggs, and small mammals, all of which was done adequately without tools, if you're not squeamish about wringing necks to feed your kin. But it's still a form of quest, just less frenetic.

Nowadays, postfarming especially, we modern humans got to thinking that there's something different about us because can do it all faster. We've improved our weapons, bred like rats, clumped ourselves together in groups way bigger than our monkeysphere-sized brains can cope with, and destroyed our planet.

But deep down the hunt is still resonating. We're still motivated by our inner primate.

So I don't need to believe that the disposable males are really knights questing for spiritual truths, or that dependable females are amazons in defence of the planet. But if I have to deal with them, I apply the ancient principles. They're as good as anything anyone's thought up since, like religious imperatives to be good, for instance.'

'Don't like men much, do you?'

'Don't like humans full stop. What's your point?'

'What's yours? I mean, why do all this if you hate us all?'

'Ah, hate. Too akin to love to be relevant. You should get it. That's why you're the Consort. They're so fascinating. Don't necessarily want to get near them. Definitely would rather not have been born one. Don't need the burden of all those foibles getting in the way of true intelligence. But after all that's said, look at what they've achieved. Fabulous toys, brilliant insights, imagination other species'd kill for, the potential to be rational too if you just get them outside the mob-mentality and get them thinking for themselves, but above all, we're survivors, because we're all mean sons-of-bitches. Can't have all that snuffed out just because we're jumped up upstarts in the galactic hierarchy. They're not going to like it, but we're the coming thing. Hives. Metaminds. Collectives. All fine and dandy. But there's no rule that says individuated mobs can't exist, because we do. And if we're going to become extinct, let's do it to ourselves. Not because some stuffy aliens think otherwise.'

And so, he had stood in front of the mirror while the Ydal set up another opposite. Disturbingly, his reflection was the same in both. If he faced one, he also was facing the other, his back never appeared in either, until he turned back to the centre of her room, and then he had to squint over his shoulder to see both backs.

Then there came a fairly vile moment when he experienced the sensation of being split in two. It wasn't painful, not like horse-drawing and quartering or anything, but like he exploded in two directions at once. He heard the word, mitosis, and he could believe each cell was replicating by splitting and flying apart into the frames of glass on either side. But then, almost immediately, he had the reverse sensation of imploding and on the next blink he was facing himself across the room, and himself was facing he from the opposite polished surface.

Then, one, whichever one he was, felt a fizzing and on the next blink, he found himself standing in a cave and, his activated boundary layer reported, on solid ground of mass sufficient to warp spacetime by 1g. A Knight of the Augmentatio was staring at him in astonishment. It hadn't occurred to him to wonder if he could make sounds in holographic form when back in the real world. The instant coverage of the Knight's elongated palm over his sword hilt told him he'd better find out, and quickly.

'I'm Jake Wynn...' he stuttered. There was a sort of internal echo to the speech. He couldn't say *he* had actually heard it, because he couldn't really say he had ears that operated like biological auditory orifices, but apparently the Knight had. *In fact he found he knew that the minute shimmering of air molecules against his 'skin', focused at ear level to replicate his body-image and focus his attention, was mere white noise in a synthetic sinecurve, but his mental map construed such noises into the expected words through wetware-automatic-speech-recognition, and clicked from echo to apparent hearing.* The Knight responded as one would expect a living humanoid to react to his own emission of pulses in sync with his mouth movements which its linguistic brain would fill in verbal gaps by phonemic restoration: he relaxed and stepped forward.

'My King! Galarhas, at your service. I did not expect you so soon, but all is ready for the *Judicium.* We will need to collect the people here, of course. And the bodies in the clinic.'

'The bodies? Was there fighting here too?'

'No, no. I did not mean corpses. I meant you and Lily. Mother is awake.'

'Venus is here? I was just speaking to her. I didn't think that was possible. She said something about mental problems if I came out of the coma while split.'

'She's used to multiple personality ordering. Don't worry about her. She'll be up in a minute. We have to get going now she's made her move.'

'What move?'

'You.'

That was odd to hear, but Galarhas was striding away from him down a tunnel and those long legs were covering the ground fast. Jake began to run to catch up, when he discovered he was ahead of his quarry.

'What? How did that happen?' he asked as he turned back to face Galarhas.

'You are only an image of your body. The image is from your mind but it is really only your neural net that is replicated in holographic form, only the skin is a facsimile of your flesh. So you can do what you think. You clearly wanted to go faster then.'

Saccades! He hadn't noticed his movement because he hadn't kept activating any eyes with attention-focusing refreshing of the image of the world coming into the retina through micromovements of a cornea. There was no continuous narrative, just freezeframes with attention-deficit effects. He might need to work on that to ensure he targeted his landing place. *So that's how the Knights' Cast.* It definitely required pre-emptive rational planning. A good thing, he could only agree, over being at the mercy of one's subconscious and its concominant hormonal and other surges. However, he could see how, over time, you could forget how the body had done it and become as zippy as the Ydal. He flexed his imaginary muscles, and consciously inhaled and looked around as the fixating observer. It wouldn't change the universe to suit him, but it might keep him in the same one. Better not lose the plot. *Nose to the scent.* It was an instruction for a primal self, locatable in ancient basal ganglia, DNA-deep.

Even thinking was accelerated in relative time to mouth formations and speech emissions, so now he *finally/instantly* said, 'Wow! So where are we going?'

'We're going to the level to get on the turbochutes and go to WoodHame. That's where all the Days who didn't play I-*Mage* are being taken, and the Disappeared are all to meet there too. They're the ones who got to the Final Level and came here to meet the Queen. Your sister was the first, but you know Dinah and Kean too, don't you?'

'I thought they were just employees, like me at Santa Fe. Only based here.'

'Well, they're that too, but not in the public domain. They're the underground workforce of the Fargo empire. People like you at Santa Fe and her other organizations and those who work here above ground, running the Farm and the office, they're just well-vetted and good players, chosen for their loyalty too, of course. And despite herself, Mother does inspire loyalty. But not like that given by the Disappeared. They gave up their previous lives and live in Venus-world, with no contact with the past. Well, you know. Ida might not have been able to, but Dinah could have called you. I'm sorry! That was insensitive at a time like this.'

And that was how the news was broken to him.

Now he found that activating his reptilian emotional reactions in order to stay sharp was a flood of internal predetermined responses, blurring all sense of the external world. He was in a dark void, screaming soundlessly, intestineless guts twisting, unpumping heart pounding to breaking point. After an indeterminate unclocked period, something he remembered as his arm was being grasped and his bodybag shaken. It reminded him of the need to concentrate to stay grounded. He panicked as the sensation stopped, leaving him alone in the isolation of nothing but echoes of thought. The panic cleared those rapidly, since he'd activated his pseudolimbic system and even grief and loss was always trumped by panic to flight or fight. He realized he didn't have to indulge the emotion. It was due him, due her, but it could be postponed on a promise to have it later. So he switched it off. Actually, he had only expected to take charge over it, as one does in the body by straightening the shoulders and breathing deeply and unclenching the palms and rising to the balls of the feet and getting into a stance. Without a body, emotion did not need to drain away, be energized by cascading replacement hormones, take time, it was instant. Like a switch. Disconcerting, almost falsifying if one thought like flesh, but simply logical in the accelerated now.

Venus had arrived by the time he came back and he didn't jump her with his justified blame and anger. She nodded approvingly. 'Bigger picture. I knew you had the detachment. Well done, though. And I'm at least as sorry as you, and I've got to do it incarnate here, so I appreciate you cutting me the slack, but we've got a job to do. So, let's go.'

He felt better when he arrived in WoodHame. It was worse to know that Dinah wouldn't experience the journey he'd just taken, not even as fast as turbochuting, faster. Popping up via satellite-phone and down by hitching a ride on an incoming ray of cosmic radiation. Not quite instant, but as fast as electromagnetic waves could pass through the solid-state equipment. He knew where it was from Venus, but it was a previous shared sputum transfer of her experiences from Dinah that had contained the detail of the place from when she had visited it with Venus.

He landed in the Great Hall, an enormous sun-hazed green glade, brimming with people. He had a flash as he turned 360^0 to fix his view of a fourth-hand image from the Ydal via Venus to Dinah. Of another Dinah, with Kean, naked, kissing each member of equally naturalistic queues lining up before both of them. His brain fizzed a little, as he recognized the quantum computation that had figured this visual. It was a real world too, unlike the internal loop his new holographic vacancy showed him as the possible, if creative, disappearance up one's own navel that would occur if you took your gaze off the world around you.

He had other insights he didn't explore that told him that had happened to Lily, and she was only saved by her rigorous attitude to scientifically-possible facts and laws still pertaining in her own personal cosmos. He could see why this would not work for most of the human race. Most of them were like the General and the Endtimers and would inevitably end up in their own version of hell, since as a paranoid predator their mindsets would predicate against heaven.

But it was beautiful, nonetheless. He looked around at the organically-coaxed habitat that had co-evolved as the Wood citadel.

Like dogs. Part of the family. For the Woods, all the earth was. A Wood-Tree symbiosis. An extended phenotype. And a memetic expression; culture. It looked like the garden of Eden. It had been here all the time. Humans had just sent it underground. Almost literally, given this was the limit of the space left in which Woods could wander across the surface openly. And he knew, suddenly, that Venus was right. We humans, the enjoyers of all that space, of all that light and freedom, the gods of the Day, had decimated our portion, the vaster amount, of Eden, and we should be asked to let it return to wilderness unless we can learn to cohabit or until we've learned to take responsibility in our dominance. He still didn't feel he had the right to be the arbiter for individuals, but he could at last agree to the principle for the species.

Someone was coming up to meet him. The tallest and brightest of the Woods herding the Days in the middle of the scene. Then he saw who was following him and, because he'd focused on becoming human, his heart sang to recognize the features of the face on the short, blobby creature 'swimming' in midair alongside him.

'Ranger!' His tones were shocked. The human male was bloated with blubber and his skin was thickened. He was not walking. 'This is your default body image now? But she's dead!' It was his least tactful moment, lack of restraint coming with no gap between thought and speech. 'Shit. I'm sorry. I'm really sorry, man. I forgot you must be in the Tower still, so you're your own reflection there.'

John was short of reply. 'Would've kept the faith with her anyway. She's dead, but she's not gone. Adjusting isn't easy. Especially with all this going on.'

'Did you know Dinah has gone?'

'Yeah. That's why Venus risked sending me. She thought you could use a familiar mind.'

Actually, he knew that apart from the humanising effect of having a friendly face, Venus saw him as assisting Jake in the Defence of the Realm. When Zelas' body was returned to the ancestral craterlake bonewell by the surviving Ghosts, IceBergas and the escorting Hydraen-Knights, led by the almost alien Squire, Xl-arn'tz, Ranger had been ready to quit. Poison in his body had almost killed him, and Xl-arn'tz had given him his headset, John's own being lost, and told him to try and focus his mind.

A surviving Siren of the Ghosts ministered to him, trying to join to his thoughts, trying to ease his way. This, despite their recent introduction to the concept of the I-*Mage* technology, was not purely out of altruism. She had seen and felt and been floated on the wave of the love of her Queen and this consort from the Landlubbing Days, and he had sacrified all, including the ability, since the viral changes in subcutaneous blubber-for-fat deposition and antifreeze in every cell, to return to the Land permanently, proving his love too. The slightest touch of her mind on his had revealed his thoughts clearly enough. He had been delirious and completely, obsessively, unshakenly, focused on Zelas. There was already a blank spot in his acceptance of her death and a merciful blackout of his memory of the event. Once the Siren realized the concepts of the game, she knew that if he died thinking of her Queen all that the Whorlinga knew, about all three aquatic tribes, he would take into death and into holographically-enacted storage with him, because they were still linked. Whether or not the Augmentatio Knights could restore the Queen's mind, she need not be completely lost. The officiating Ghost made him comfortable and sang his healing/passage with reverence.

It had worked, but it was extremely uncomfortable to look across the Table at the resurrected love of his life, whose dying he did not remember, but whose mind lived in a self composed mainly from his memories of her, and from those added subsequently by Pereduri and even the Ouissocca, plus all that Quogat and Venus had contributed to the backstory she could tell of herself. Since he was critically ill, his body was not available to jump into, like Venus', so he did not get to test his feelings against glandular standards, but he managed to feel unsure of himself, beached on imaginary shores in his human-body-image and floating like jetsam in a tsunami in his aquatic-adapted sense of self. It was easier to agree to come here as the latter, because then he could love her without facing her, keeping the faith, as she would say, at least, post-Ouisocca, and also truly keep the faith by representing the Hydraen contribution to the Wood, Dark and Day *Judicium.*

Because he knew what she knew, including the act but not the experience of her demise itself. Which made having a relationship based upon being two separate individuals historical and the future of their love unknown. It was better to be here and a friend to the less complicated and more final and hence worse bereavement Jake was suffering. Well, having complicate his focus. Suffering being a choice, newly.

People do need time to adjust to changed circumstances, so he gave his mate license to grieve, for the correct duration of the standard masculine hug, even if he floundered the drop to the vertical he took to make the gesture more human. It was genuine and felt, if instructed rather than a spontaneous eruption from the subconscious taking the awkward male by surprise. Interestingly, it did not actually result in either of them feeling in any way awkward. As their temples touched for a microtell of condolence, Ranger heard Jake think 'There are some things about the body we'd be better for losing.' They both jumped apart as if wired with electricity at the contradictions both minds made and consequently shared of their last passionate moments with their soulmates. 'Some things about flesh cannot be replaced by thinking.' they agreed in synchrony, laughing and clapping eachother on the back in glad welcome.

Couldn't agree more. Well, OK, the Wood bending over them didn't say it with words, nor did he attempt to spit his mind chemically at beings of light, but they were getting used to their photonic powers and speedreading of their observations, and his tells seemed writ large. Until they realized that he was in flesh as androgynous as the next Wood and without pheromonal inputs stimulating hominin nostrils they hadn't realized he was a she. But they both recognized the name, 'Furze', when it was given, in a bird-primate-binary-vocalisation, reminiscent of a parrot that had learned to say 'Pretty Polly' to the tune of a nightingale with full human orchestral reverb and instrumentation. Not full Harmonic, since the full language has the meatiness of scent and colour, taste and texture, ultrasonic dimensionality, infra-red heat, ultraviolet depth, but the most anyone could speak of that language was the single Note that Ouissocca knew, the distillation of Terra.

Fortunately, the Woods had saved themselves by internalizing the gist of it, so, since they all had shared the Note now, there was a simple universal translator into Heraldic in everyone's heads for eachother now, which with the recent viral extensions to the corpus callosum for telepathy, made communication truly viable. Maybe the name was a Day contraction, but the resonance was her title, currently she was the Voice, the rotating Regal Status of the nonhierarchical collective.

Woods did not need two royal representatives, despite reproducing like other primates, because heritability was managed without competition between the sexes, selecting against sexual dimorphism and the need for representatives from competing genders. Darks were matriarchal, their women bigger on average, though by a slender statistical margin, so they were happy enough with a single alpha female, even if she was designated Queen, and even if she was a Day.

Astonishingly, the Darks had voted for Venus, or in her image and her absence, the Ydal, although their Voice in the Round was Vi !sjn-ik because he represented their exposed jugular, their subservience in guilt for his actions that shamed their race; not consort, not true Voice, just echo for Venus. Of course, they were not simply cowed by Day oppression, their mentality was also shaped by collusion with the benevolent colonialism of being part of the Wood extended family and by the mitigation of some absorption of their cultures' sharper teeth into the welcoming of diversity that family bondage prescribed.

John had found himself wondering if the forgiving acceptance of the Days by the other hominin races would ever be reciprocated enough for humans to see themselves as part of the family. But, as he and Jake walked around the glade, he began to hope for that possibility.

Everywhere were people, but now 'humanity' looked as disparate as as the single species represented at Crufts. There were the elongated and elegant Woods and the powerful, raggedy Darks, of course, and what must be the entire living populations of numerous small, tribal groups from locations as wide apart as Australia, Papua New Guinea, Africa, Alaska, Pacific islands and local Amerindians. There were almost as many individuals wandering around looking shellshocked. Some, he was told later, that were literally so. Several Americans recovered from Vietnamese jungle where they'd been hiding from an enemy who had stopped hunting them thirty years earlier, and some even older veterans, Japanese, German and English, left in Borneo and elsewhere unaware of VE day. More were hermits and ronin by choice.

These were not city tramps; they'd all been given the Game along with all the aid drops to slums worldwide. No, these were woodsmen from the US, fakirs and swamis from the Indian subcontinent, buddhists who'd retreated so far they'd lost themselves, even agoraphobics who'd not left home in years. Due to the virus and the Woods passing among the crowds sharing knowledge, no one was panicking, and no one was even grumbling, much less fighting. Indeed it looked more like a UN meet-and-greet with everyone milling around, smiling and introducing themselves and their friends.

The biggest group was also a lot shorter than the rest of the population. In fact the Darks were the tallest in it. Most of the African pygmy tribes were integrated with their settled neighbours and had had the game and trekked to their endlevel site, so only the traditionalists of the Mbuti and one of the more isolated Twa clans had found themselves here. There were four different Asian families from the Pacific island chains, none of whom had ever suspected eachothers' existence, but were very glad to know the world was not only inhabited by giants. But they all, along with the Darks, were clucking and cooing over the one extant group on earth whose adults were smaller than them. These elfin folk were none more than a metre tall and as hirsute as an orang-utan, but they were chattering away, gesturing very fast and generally socializing like any other human. John joined Mh'aed and Fr! gwapd on the edge of the crowd. 'Who are they?'

'They're from the island of Flores. It's east of Java, in Indonesia. No one knew they existed. It was that NetSpore critter. Told Venus where to find them. Course, she was the one who brought them here. Better to join the human race while there still is one than die alone, she reckoned. And they're not like some of the folk here. I mean, some of *them* are still wearing belts with their enemies' heads on. Only heads smaller than the Floresiens. Don't know why Venus thinks they're worth saving.'

Mh'aed hissed reprovingly beside his elbow. 'She's not making the judgement. She bringing them to the *Judicium*. Don't try to prejudice the Rex. That kind of thinking is in the old way. You'd better be a bigger human than that, or you'll be condemned yourself, sister's-son-copy, and I do not wish that.' She turned to Jake. 'He always did have a loose mouth. All that time with Vi !sjn-ik, not to mention the fact that he's watched more TV than any other Squire, or possibly Day, I aver. He has a good heart. You'll see when you look within with the *Oculus Rex*.'

A few minutes later, Ranger found himself being drawn aside by Jake. 'I must have missed something.' he started without preamble. 'Did you hear Mh'aed refer to the Eye of the King?'

'Yes. What about it?'

'It's the one shut on my shield. The one I'm supposed to have opened. Except I don't think I'm looking out of it.'

'Isn't it just something in you? I mean, like an attitude.'

'That's what I thought, but the harmonic in Mh'aed's mind was specific. Not concrete, not something external like a crystal ball, or even one of the Skulls. I still think it's meant to be internal. It's just I can't find it. Will you look?'

There's nothing homoerotic about spitting on your finger and smearing it on your mate's temple, at least not anymore, but it's still preferable not to have to. It was even weirder to do what he did next, but it tapped into a whole different mindset. He slowly extended his finger into a tube that ended in a point he could only see because he refocused at the resolution of an electron microscope. *Which was cool.* 'Ready?' Then he shot a photon through the atomic-fence of his skin on the finger tip, direct into Jake's head, and sucked it back as it rebounded.

This wasn't an upload of current information, with its layers of related background, transmitted chemically, interpreted electrically, but basically the superficial and immediate thoughts and associated memories. It was the metron representative of Jake Wynn's impression on the spacetime worldline the endpoint of which stopped here, for now. It was his entire life and its impacts, and his complete set of memories, including the totality of all mental transfers he'd had in recent times. It was a two-dimensional surface which John needed to inflate into its own brane in his own pseudobrain to take slices from the solidified 11-dimensional worldline to find the answers. He was relieved it was solid, even in this many planes, because he wasn't the Ydal to be able to process the quantum superposition of all his friend's possible alternate universe timelines.

He felt a bit squeamish about the concept of being inside Jake's head. There was plenty of stuff he didn' t have the human boundaries left to precognate as private. However, as it was a new Zelas-endowed technique that cast a tachyon particle to meet the spark accompanying the first cell division in the newly fertilized egg that became Jake, and much of the history that it trawled up with its return journey would be irrelevant, he started as with any beginning; from the now.

Jake was worried because he had sensed a lack. That was going to be even harder to find, like an invisible needle in a haystack, so John decided to start with that sense of inadequacy. Actually, he immediately realized it wasn't a lack of confidence. Oh, Jake would have been shitting himself if he'd had bowels at the job he'd been dumped with, and there were plenty of good reasons for that humility and plenty more human flaws to justify any amount of panic, all of which predated the moment when Mh'aed had used the Heraldic term and it hadn't resonated within. *All the other ones had, even though Jake had never played the game, he got the harmonic through the stuff he did with Dinah and his own inner resonance of the quest he was on.* It wasn't the language then, it was the concept. Jake didn't vibe with being an unseeing eye. He knew he was a meticulous, dedicated researcher, as resistant to bias as anyone, and honest enough to be a reasonable choice of representative of a decent human being. He'd got over having greatness thrust upon him. It was clearly a double-edged sword no one would want but someone had to heft, so he held it aloft like a torch in the night, to guide his own way. He wasn't working blind either. He could see the breadth of the data and the desperate position the planet was in. So what eye was shut?

Ranger was stumped. He confirmed the sensation had a genuine focus, but he could not identify its point, nor, more disturbingly, any wisps of gists that would lead back to a glimpse of understanding. It felt just like that long ago moment when they'd been unable to crack I-*Mage*. He had the idea that, just as something as random as a smell had been the codebreaker then, something similar would reveal itself now, if he just kept on looking through Jake's eyes.

That was when it hit him. I'm looking through his eyes, and his eyes only see that way, there's no flaring for the rest of the spectrum. Of course, he never played the Game. He doesn't understand the Termite side of the human equation. He's troubled without realizing because he knows he'll be unfairly repelled by and lacking comprehension of those humans who played Termite and then took part in killing their fellow men with superior mandibles. He thinks he doesn't know how to judge the Termite-gamer survivors. Including Lily! Because he doesn't know that the eye isn't shut, it's vestigial, and he needs to use other senses and the mindset they bring and know the affect on the Days who played.

'The *Oculus Rex* is not a Day King's perception, it is a Termite King's duty to his family. I think you might need to tap a gameplayer's head to get the full Blazon of how it feels to be termite, but the gist of it is this. To you, the Termites are only Day avatars from the Game, right? OK. This is complicated. In an imaginary holographic alternate closed loop of the multiverse, the fantasies were constructed through a human brain, but, because the laws of our physics were maintained here, the universe was the same age as ours and populated by free sampling of the subconscious fertile ground of Lily's mind. Then the incarnate ideas of alien lifeforms found there were accorded an assumption of history and evolution and their tachyon-burst into their present was as ancient as you like. So in this actualized but cutoff reality, giant Termites were – no, are - the Intelligence of a planet.

Venus used their image in the game for several reasons. One, she felt she owed them on behalf of what humans had done to them in that world. Too much detail, doubt we need it here. Two, she and her alter both liked them. Their attitude had the coherence and warmth of a loving family, working smoothly like a machine, because they communicated by aromatherapy, not eyes. The third reason was because they were so similar to us as to be a proper parallel solution to try on. Termites build vast cities above and below ground. At the scale of humans, their mounds would protrude a mile into the sky. They farm, they fight their ant enemies, they even have kamikaze squads, soldiers with inherent chemical instabilities that are explosive - suicide bombers. If they were that size and the dominant species on the planet, the world's timber would be gone, the soils would be barren around the cities, the wars would be incessant, the methane emitted into the atmosphere would have destroyed the climate 23 times more efficiently than our CO_2. Even the ones we have, at the tiny size they are, are the largest contributors of methane on a planetary scale, although unlike, say, our cows, most of theirs is not getting into the atmosphere and wrecking the climate, but it would if they were our size. And all that's without any technology, without industrial revolutions, carbon fuels, whatever. Not consumerist greed, just normal survival.

Venus wanted us to realize that the shit we've done to our planet is something to recognize and use our intelligence to change our behaviour, but also that it's just as natural as any other activity. We're not deities with foresight who should be held accountable, we're guilty of the deed, but, largely, not of the intent, just dumb animals with a toolbased culture that's no different a phenotype, except in style, than termite building and farming and fighting and farting. Termite workers and soldiers do all of this without eyes. Only the reproductive lines can grow eyes, and the male alates do not do so except in times of war or of swarming.

The Queen sees all, but the *Oculus Rex* is only required when she needs to locate a new site for a colony, either when she has just lost a war or when she has died and a new Queen must rise and start a new colony. She emits a pheromone. The King grows eyes and wings in response. He flies upwards and when he is hovering for the first time in the thermal above the mound, his eye opens and he sees the world. The pheromone he then emits calls only certain of his kin. Those least like him and most like the dying Queen. That's genetically, of course, shape of their immune system, chemical responses yada yada. And they follow and make the new beginning. The rest die. You need to feel this within, to change your mindset, to open your termite eye for the *Judicium*. If it wouldn't trigger the Net, I'd advise a few hours playing hooked up with Lily as your guide, but I'm guessing she's still the best person to meld with for the right scent.'

'Is she here?'

'Well, her body is. It's possible you could make a connection through that. Best try, I reckon, since the alternative would be for you to return to the Tower and I'm not sure your re-entry would be smooth enough to be undetected.'

No one at WoodHame was allowed to use the headsets that were around. It transpired that some Woods had tried them, and the majority of the younger Darks were as hooked as the Days, but no one had worn one since the Home call ended. However, the incoming Penzeen refugees had brought laptops and they'd been set up to show the rest of the people there what they'd missed, not as players, just the Boss level video, with the Queens and the rivers of blood and the Tower and the Round Table. So they were already exclaiming in surprise at the images on the screen of the very people they could see sleeping like death in front of them, when they appeared walking across the grass.

Ranger was amused, but left it to Fr! gwapd, Mh'aed and Furze to cover the explanations. He could see Jake was having trouble, and it wasn't with the crowd. It was looking at his own apparent corpse and seeing Lily, his very recently rejected lover, also near-death alongside himself. Fortunately, her body was warm and John could see his mate's relief at the touch, but then the poor man went completely rigid, lost all form and was gone in a flash of light.

'Damn!' said Venus, behind him. 'He's the WildKnight alright. OK, Ranger. This is your moment. You've got his mind-brane. He's lost his way. You've got to locate the exact entry point in Lily where he hit her brain in coma and bring him back to it so he can go through to her mind in the Tower. And then, since he's not likely to be able to reshape his form with all that going on in what's left of his mind, you'd better stand ready to ping it over into his body, so he can try waking up human again. He was going to have to for the *Judicium.* He'd just better be ready for it when he wakes up, because you can bet he's not up to maintaining his holopresence in the Tower, so the Game'll be afoot.' She turned to Furze. 'Is everyone here? Is everything done?' And when she received the affirmative, 'OK, Hydraen-Consort to the Ghost Queen and Runic-Knight of the Solificatio, Cast well for the love of Terra! Play!'

The woman's human voice would bring hominin and canine subjects to heel as one and at once; her Terra-Regina timbre was not a command, it was will in action. It lanced through him like a spear, and then he was the spear, the weapon, no, only the tool of the will, the act in action, a mere trajectory of intent.

He wrapped Jake's condensed worldlinebrane back into a 2D tip on his own pseudofinger and shot it at Lily's temple. He briefly glimpsed the Tower Room through his befuddled mirror-image's eyes, as he flashed across the Table, through Jake and into Lily, before the elastic recoil yanked him backwards. The wink he caught Venus tipping him in the Tower was still closing on her fleshface when he opened his eyes again. Behind them on the mossy beds, two physical bodies were stirring. He kept his eyes locked in his Queen's gaze. 'I didn't zip back to mine?'

'You wouldn't have been here, if you did, you'd have been in Antarctica.'

'That didn't seem like why, though.'

'It was your choice. What can I tell you? You can't get to choose your body. You can your avatar. Tell me where your heart must lie.'

The heart didn't lie was Lily's deeply-felt romantic conviction. She had just had to give it up, and it was less unpleasant than she had expected. People are very plastic, pliable, but Jake hadn't been fickle. He'd loved with all his heart. It was just that when they met, his heart had been true to the past, not the present, until they'd collided and he'd got together with Dinah. Now she awoke knowing his loss and her gain. She'd given him her worldline, which included the depth of her feelings for him and her hurt, but understanding, but more importantly instilled an empathy for the Termite way.

He was the Consort to an abdicating Queen, *it didn't matter that she died because she was no longer going to rule and create*, and as such he was the natural selection to sire the next generation, and she, LilyBlack, was the new Queen-Elect, and she chose him as her mate. If he Opened his Eye, this and all things he *would* see. His choice to fly for Her would not then be any longer his own, but it did not matter, because his being, body first, mind later, imagination latterly, choice last, had already selfselected this service, and he would be fit for purpose because the purpose had always been a fit for him, and they would all be content.

It was still a choice for the WildKnight until then. He would scent the fear she had that he had never truly loved her and that he would not accept Termite pragmatisms and would reject the knowledge, keeping his Eye Closed and his people embattled in Eden. Venus could be wrong about him. After all, he was her find, her choice, her thread in the garment that wove Ida and Dinah and Kean and Jake and Lily and Ranger together. Machiavelli or MatchMaker? She'd done it on a grand scale too, with breathtaking vision - who else would Ydal-form the moon for processing power for her galactic Dating Service?

Apart from power that the funds of her inherited position had given her in a couple of her iterations, the woman had one basic quality in all the worlds the Ydal had touched her parallel in. She was a bitch. The way Vi !sjn-ik meant it. She'd a nose for a scent. She'd an eye for First Sight. She'd a doggedness that pounded down the trail and any doors in the way. She chewed bones and plans right down to the end. And she was the most reliable damned guidedog for the blind anyone in the human race had ever trained. For all her dislocation, she was one of them. Not a canine, but a pure human. There were lots like her, and lots more that had the other qualities the ideal social group of a dispersed, individuated Intelligence required, but the only way she'd lead the pack out of danger now would be if the alpha male cocked his leg to order and marked his territory.

Well, he'd sat up, although he was staring blankly ahead of him. His first thought had not been towards his future queen, that was certain. She sighed. But then he was getting up and striding, still blind-eyed, across the grass to Venus. He grabbed her hand. 'Show me the Kingdom.' He commanded and she bowed. She handed him a headset and put one on herself. Then the ground in the centre of the circle opened up and a small pyramid of ringing emerald crystal appeared. Two Woods came up and dowsed them in some electric-blue fluid that attached like showergel, and then they went down into a hole and reascended inside the transparent pyramid. By now, the Woods were crooning, the Darks had deepened into a melodic sustaining growling, and everyone else was finding their throats elaborating some harmonic of engagement. Her own vocal chords were straining to join in, but she daren't call until he and the old Queen were through. It would be irresponsible and selfish. A truly regal Elect would not try to pre-empt the end of one narrative with the beginning of another.

The Note rose, carried on the lips of every living hominin on the planet, then raised palms pushed the energy towards the pyramid, precisely, from every Home to Hame, and Venus and Jake pressed their palms together and a bolt of lightning shot upwards along the unseen nanothick vertical antenna to the moon, and the Tower Fell in a purple explosion that belled out like a mushroom cloud from the pyramid, ending in a fizz of photons down the wire that flicked in a magnetic blue storm over the pyramid, vapourising it and reassembling into the shards of the lady herself, mother nature's spokeswoman, Ygrail at Home.

She was very green and sparkly and she no longer looked anything at all like Venus. She wasn't particularly feminine, either, since she'd ingested the masculine side of the population too. She had the translucent quality of being made of glass, but was reflective too, if you looked closely, however, she was still the sexiest, most powerful and most intelligent person anyone had ever seen in human form. Then she dimmed her glow and handed up Venus and Jake. 'The *Judicium* is resolved. The *Curia Regina* is adjourned. Terra will now speak its mind for Sentencing. Be upstanding all who will hear.'

It was only after her dismissal, that anyone looked around them. The world was awash with bodies. Again! About a hundredth of the people remained. The rest had dropped where they stood. As the wave of the Lady's Doom had swept out across the planet activating in the majority the imposition of the instruction for instant cellular breakdown that the virus had implanted in everyone. Even some Woods and Darks were dead.

It was his choice. The Lady's Coming had shared the knowledge with everyone the wave touched. Venus was the conduit of Choice. She had given it to Terra's children and they'd killed eachother. She'd given it to the Blind King, so he could Cast his Eye upon them and he'd wielded his sword. Only her Shield had saved any from the ruthlessness of logic. Now the Mother would stand up and be the shield against the real enemy, and the best of the rest would Serve the Grail.

The epic resonances abating Lily realized that Jake had not chosen individuals for life or death. He had been linked to all the Ydal data about every living intelligence on the land and in the seas, and this included the non-Hydraen Knights and Squires, some octopi and squid, not forgetting mantis-shrimps, and all the clever birds, other primates, canines and hive minds and all the rest humans hadn't even realized had a personalized or collective history memorized. He'd looked at humans in the glade. Everyone but Lily had felt his eyes turn and look directly into theirs and felt themselves exposed to the back of their brain. It had been a timeless moment but tachyons were flying so it was past before it happened. All he had time for was to go with his instincts to make a quantum breakpoint of the situation. It was time for the observer to open the box on Schroedinger's cat. Jake simply told it as he saw it. 'Dead.' or 'Alive.' They knew they were. And then they Were, or Not.

He didn't have First Sight, where he could, like Lily and Venus, willingly suspend disbelief in one's own eyes for the split second before consciousness loads, and see the imagined glimpse of another world. But he'd just had his First Sight, and it was enough for him to want it to be his Last. It was that, not soppy romantic love, that would turn him into the arms of his new Queen for guidance through the dark days ahead in the unknown foray towards a new colony. That, and the fact that the Conduit had apparently caused the old one to dry up for good. *I hope I'm not still Queen when I have to channel the* Oculus Rex. *Otherwise that's my fate too.*

She had a duty now. Jake might look a bit shellshocked at what he'd just done, but Venus had transferred her lifeforce into him to empower his decision with authority, and she was more than drained, she was old and she was dying.

Venus felt as if she'd already exchanged her planet for another on which gravity was turned up and the air thinned. Pains shot through all her joints and muscles in random bursts and settled in chronic chills and biting nerves. It was radiation poisoning, of course, of sorts, the kind you only get from intense exposure to the energies the Ydal used coursing through you and your body being the filter for the toxins, to emit a manageable level of continuous energy. It was the price a transformer pays for ratcheting down the power to sustain it. The physics was undeniable and deadly. Mutagenic. Genes and proteins breaking bonds. There'd be no time for cancers to grow without intervention. And here it came, in the pain relief of Mh'aed and the emergency telomere extensions of Furze. It took Fr! gwapd to rustle up a fried-egg sandwich, incongruous in the jungle, to restore her energy to something approaching geriatric.

He'd done it then. Not baulked at the last hurdle. She wasn't even sure if he'd known beforehand, from his link with Lily, that his instant instincts, his Judgement, had been based not only on everything known, not only on his split-second heads-or-tails act, but on the filtration of the people's choices. They'd voted, in their heads and in discussion in their groups and in their sense of what everyone else was really thinking which now they were able to share, on the individuals or types of people to keep and the type of society of their preference and their consideration of the fit of the units to the whole. The statistics Jake was working with were thus weighted and the precision of the Archivist and Net categorisations of character overlaid these with personalities he could recognize immediately. So the calculation felt like instinct and the choice was made. No magic at all, even when the mage was amazing. Just speed.

And speed was what they all needed now, before the Cognimata cottoned on to their move. She was banking on the Net finding the suicide-bomb she'd just released in the species sufficiently confusing to warrant further study and dialogue. However, with the relocation of the Ydal to Terra, the scenario of the Round Table would have collapsed and there would be no one to talk to, which was just the thing to get the Weapons motivated by paranoia, so she just had to hope the fire in the hole was primed.

She allowed Lily to help her to her feet. 'It is time.' She could only croak, but the world heard her whisper. 'The Final Choice. Your choice of Grail. Life or Immortality. I-*Mage*!'

The Lady shattered. A fountain of green mirror-fragments made a stained-glass shield over the sun and the third planet spun in the centre of Her protective Shield. Then it twirled and a shell blossomed out from it, or was it a lotus-blossom's spiral nacre? or the fluff of wings as the phoenix found its strength and mastery of the air?

For a prolonged moment her mind was held in multiple-meld by the Ydal in every Home. She saw one third of the population, mostly Termite players, that accepted the apoptosis route to eternity as through their dead bodies, drop their flesh and shoot their holoforms inside the spaceships readied at every site. She saw those activate the Heim propulsion system and jump. But then, they were gone. And the Ydal had futzed with the Home time-co ordinates to ensure none could return for a thousand years.

She'd saved at least some of the hominin mind, and sent its DNA with it, in code, not chemicals. Now all that remained was to save the planet.

H: RUBEDO:
AUGMENTATIO, PROIECTIO AND IMMORTALIS

The plan had gone by the numbers. The Archivist's offical scoring sub-routine would show the attainment of the required percentages. The Cognimatan Committee had lobbied the Net for two assurances from Terra. The first was the annihilation of the more aggressive members of the species. The second was the eradication of all remaining individuals who would not accept a single Voice or collective leadership structure. The means of their technological empowerment were to be eliminated and the remaining population confined to the planet until they could assert their right to join the galactic commune by evolving Intelligence, at which point the ship her plans had delivered and the archives within would be made available to Terra. That was the plan Venus had agreed to and that was the result she had delivered. The Archivist could report that the conditions had been fulfilled and that, since she had gone further and had the Europan probe destroyed, the Weapons could be stood down.

The Archivist's secret sub-routine showed a somewhat different set of numbers. He hadn't meant to collude with the enemy. Initially, he had set up the database to ensure fairness in the categorisation by personality and potential, so that the best of the species could be preserved. It was an unmissable opportunity to add to the knowledge of the creatures on which so much of his processing time had already been expended. He had not expected so many humans to react in paranoid and violence to one another, despite Venus' projection that this would be so. He had thought that his work would be needed on a much larger scale to make sense of a huge population he knew the Cognimatan hierarchy would want seriously thinned before it would accept the diminution of the threat level to acceptable.

He had not approved of this unspoken subtext to the negotiations, since the original cause for concern was merely the probe, and even the addition of the Europan upset at the mental contamination that had already occurred between Venus, Zelas, Ida, Quogat and Dakul, did not justify genocide like this. So he had surreptitiously devoted quite a substantial amount of runtime to analysis he hoped would give Venus the justification she might need to save as many as possible.

Perhaps it was the covert nature of the motivation despite the overt sanction for the activity, but he became less and less able to condemn the poor creatures for their shortcomings. Oh, condemning their violence and despising their paranoias was easy enough, although he suspected that both would lessen once they had had longer experience of telepathic sharing and understanding. Logically, individualism should be condemned too, as an incoherent way to ensure survival of the species or to improve its fitness, but he could not fail to be impressed by some of the achievements made by individuals, who might be products of their society, but were unusually creative or clever or dogged or adventurous or any number of any other random outputs that the lower common denominator of collectivism did not promote. Not all of these were of any value, except perhaps in the bizarre valuation systems human societies invented to justify themselves, but some were astounding, like the Heim calculations that had brought him to be their judge and jury.

He thought it was mean-spirited of the Cognimatans to withhold the technical details they had simply worked out from the data Venus had supplied and even meaner to send the Weapons with the completed ship. *And he didn't care that this thought categorized him as disloyal and contaminated, because if he could see the Hierarchy as 'mean' they must be a lot more like humans than they thought they were.*

So, when the time came, he and the Ydal enacted a plan they had developed together. All the Terran information came through the Ydal. No one had a problem with that. As far as the Fleet were concerned she was the local dataprocessor. The fact that she had personality did not trouble them as much as it would have if the Archivist had been more frank about the implications of her origins in the character of Venus, but also they were constructed themselves with the Originators' traits, and self-analysis for flaws in their basic engineering was not one of those.

Secondly, but even more telling, though they might not have admitted it, was the interest in her that the returning Creator had shown. The Martian Planetary Metamind nebulosity had taken a form the Cognimatan offspring found distasteful because it had not rejected flesh as much as subsumed and transformed it from matter to energy. It seemed to recognize a similar mutability in the construction of the Ydal, which the Cognimata did not, as she was a single, unrepresentative character and with restricted computational parameters. It was only his own recent appreciation of the added value individualism could bring to the group that enabled the Archivist to divine that the summation of the Martian parts into the Tolecnal whole had created a solitary being that was roaming the cosmos looking for its like.

Sadly for it, and the Ydal, they were not of compatible scales or natures. To Mars, the Ydal would be as interesting mentally as a goldfish to a human, when it came to sharing ideas. Conversely, which the Archivist found most illuminating of all, Mars was, of its kind, very young. He did not know what development one could expect of such creatures, but he could tell that this one not beyond the 'larval' stage of its lifecycle, and that was why the return to the Nest had been so attractive to it. Whereas the Ydal, of her kind, had the maturity of the template imposed on her, the middle-aged responsibility of a mother figure. This was something he had bothered to relay to his superiors, in the hope that they might value that element of the mentality of the short-lived humans by comparison.

It hadn't worked, of course. After all, in the natural arrogance of logic that led them never to question their superiority, they did not actually respect even the most ancient of fleshly creatures, the Net. Oh, they would not act impolitely to a race as globally revered and as necessary as the Net but that did not mean their attitude was not disdainful of its adherence to the carnate form. It was the blinkers of this pride, however, that had made them so easy to deceive.

There was another reason that they were not as acutely focused on current events as they might have been, even without his treacherous withholding of data, and that was because the Creator was coming. Mars had the short attention span of youth, and, after spending time with its Europan offspring, discovering that their attainment was yet way behind its own, it had decided to visit its other Legacy, the Fleet. It hadn't left the Terran solar system yet, wishing apparently to see the outcome of the current activity, but it had flagged up its intentions and the Hierarchy was all aflutter. The Committees did not seem quite as sure of their superiority in relation to their progenitor as to flesh.

So, in the event, all the Archivist and the Ydal had had to do was forward data a few seconds behind the time it happened. That way when the Tower fell and the people chose Exodus, all they had to do was hold the feed until the Ydal could insert a facsimile hologram of the intact summit meeting, while the Archivist activated his specially-prepared Weapons' reprogramming virus. Of course, the Net knew something had happened. It was there, but it couldn't even communicate with Europa, never mind the Cognimatan Fleet 10,000 lightyears away, because Mars had thrown its own net around the planet, or at least had blocked the entry into subspace$_8$ of its qdatapacket spores. Even if it had been able to report the glitch, it was only an Outlier, a spore that could clone to Ride other creatures and amass information. All it would know of what happened on the planet would be that any of the humans it was currently sampling had either lived or died. And anything it could report would take more time than they needed to excute the rest of the plan.

However, the Archivist did not believe the Net would have proactively interfered to stop the plan. Venus had shared a great deal of information with it too, including the events in the Gwener-parallel. The Net had repudiated its susceptibility to such corruption into individuality with the valid explanation that the entire cosmos was an imaginary construct, initially created by Lily but developed collectively by the information brought to it of wider horizons by the contacts between Gwener and Ida with the Europans and the Net. It asserted that the personalisation of its alternate spore into a self was merely its sublimation into a greater whole, the Draco metamind, for the greater good, since it was cut off from all other connective help. Yet, in the Tower holoprojection, it had chosen its avatar as the same Plant it had become in that world, and that world had been realized, as a result of its' parallel's actions as gatekeeper, as the taste of home that had drawn back Mars itself. The data had tunnelled through from fantasy into reality.

Now Venus was doing the reverse. She had taken reality, transformed it to fantasy and shot it through and back, so that seventy-four I-*Mage* creations were now travelling in the cosmos. He felt what he could only describe as a form of paternal pride in the endeavour. He had not believed she could be as ruthless as she had promised the Fleet at the outset she would be. It was still a contradiction to him that she could care so much for mankind and yet facilitate their viciousness to one another. Oh, she'd explained to him that it was normal. He could not but agree, since, especially in the last few decades, the entire world could watch genocide, war, and mass murder in the comfort of their own homes without any collective decisions being taken to intervene to stop these activities, all the while considered as outrages by the individual viewers.

Even while I-*Mage* had been instrumental in honing the skills that any one person could use to improve their minds, it hadn't ever instructed their mindset. So while there had been some positive impact on random attacks, as potential perpetrators had found other solutions for their frustrations, it had been balanced by the improved talents of those whose beliefs mandated killing for their cause. Refugees in such hellholes as Darfur were happier, better organized, more informed because of the headsets dropped in their aid packages, but the Janjaweed, like the Endtimers or the fundamentalist Islamists, or any other bunch of oppressors, were also enhanced by the same means. So Venus had become the best of them. The ultimate enforcer of the concept of belief-based Right is Might.

She had had him identify the dangerous minds, the psychopaths, the sociopaths, the convicted, the followers, the stupid and unthinking and uncaring and apathetic that made up the vast mass of humanity, and she had predicted that they, and the weak and defenceless, would be eradicated by eachother in the first wave. She'd been right, and she hadn't even used might to prove it, they'd done that all by themselves.

The Archivist might have stopped there, figuring that the depleted population and the (apparent) elimination of the means of technological escape from the planet to threaten others would be sufficient to satisfy the Cognimata. But Venus didn't just want to save a species, she wanted to save a planet, and she wanted to save it so that it could retain the place it had usurped on the galactic stage. So Jake's judgement, the sentence of life or death, was really the individual's choice of flesh or photon. There were vast numbers of dead bodies to prove to the Cognimata that Venus had been thorough in eradicating the worser elements of the population, largely because that was what they believed the Archivist had been identifying. He sent in the Weapons to vapourise the flesh, but he knew that the patterns of the brains continued elsewhere and that those simulacrum were representative of all the character types of the hominin demographic.

The seventy-four 'ships' that jumped off the surface contained quite different distributions of those personality traits, however, and, since they were generating collectively, through a limited AI-Ydal conduit, their own holosphere, each ship's inner appearance was also wildly different from one another. Wharton now understood what Venus had meant when she'd said 'It serves you right' about the Grail. His immortality was not turning out quite the way he'd planned. *Be careful what you wish for!* was probably the thought of many others too.

First he'd died and gone to hell. Well, now he understood that was all his own I-*Mage*-enhanced creation, but with that comprehension had come another, less acceptable truth. There was no Whore, no AntiChrist, no Armageddon caused by the Beast, no Rapture for the believers and, worst of all, absolutely no sign of the Second Coming. Even though he knew the 'Rivers of Blood' were realized, they were brought about by Venus allowing humanity to be their evil selves.

Somehow, her turning the Revelation into a mythic template didn't upset him. Probably because he'd started it with his proactive interpretation that demanded He should come on the General's say-so. What did upset him was that he and vast numbers of other people had been *translated*. Oh, they'd all had the pep-talk from the disembodied voice that he knew to be that of the AI-Ydal, who had told them what had happened upon their choice of Life. He knew because before the *Judicium* he'd been already translated through death and hell into the Tower, as Day representative.

It had surprised him that, after all her scorn, Venus still put him forward as the human mindsperson. He'd been wallowing in the hell of his own making for an endless aeon, or so it had seemed, and, in point of fact, he was beginning to be bored by it. Apparently, his own imagination was limited to the antique stereotypes, so, whilst it was an extremely painful experience, the terrors of snakelike demon-lovers and torture by fire and brimstone were repetitive and not half as challenging to the old soldier as some of his real combat engagements. They also had none of the immediacy of the human equation, in that no comrades were being crucified along with him, no loved ones needed saving nor junior officers encouragement, no people could see him being stoical nor weak. He did what anyone with any stamina did in these circumstances and put the pain to the back of his mind by accepting it and by overcoming his initial fears. Then, of course, since it was merely a construct of his holomind, he was no longer there.

At first, he wondered if the Catholics had been right all along and the new place, so grey and empty, was Limbo. Then, in attempting to use the body his mind clothed itself with on automatic to find a way out, he came upon a door and found himself in the Tower Room. This was before the Lady had undertaken her regal role and established the Round Table, so it was simply her abode, full of the plaits and twists and flags of information she was weaving. She, although at the time he believed it to be Venus with a new sense of style, had looked up from what appeared to be an endless loom which her hands spanned with every slot of the shuttle, and remarked 'So you found your way back. Interesting. Did you meet your Maker?'

And, with a rush of consciousness that seemed snake-apple-endowed, he had replied instantly. 'Not until now, I believe.'

'Ah, I'm just the creator of the fabric. You create your own self with the garments you choose to wear.'

That had been the kind of thing she'd said in the pep-talk at the beginning of the Exodus-journey, but then, after she'd finished at the loom for the moment, she had elaborated, so that he'd understood that the existence of everything that seemed solid in that room was her holographic projection, including herself, but that he'd been given the same talent, through becoming a pattern of light-mediated information, and was projecting his own surroundings and body. Apparently, the door to her room existed within his mind, and whenever he opened it with an open heart, questing without predetermining, there he would find himself. This was because he was now merely a knot in the weave and there was always a thread that would unentangle to its source in her.

When she'd told him about her purpose and the parallel universes she'd searched within, he'd been so humbled by her power he'd actually asked her if there was a god. She had laughed at him, but her reply was gentle enough. 'Maybe one day. When we've managed to get our heads round numbers vast enough to conceive the multiverse, we'll make another in our own image that will be sufficient to the job. Can't imagine it would be any better, any more consistent, any more responsive, any more coherent than the one you've been worshipping that you made up.'

He'd protested he didn't make Him up, that there was the evidence of the Bible, but then the laughter had become a dismissive snort. 'Ancient narratives! Why don't you believe Homer then? It's older. Anyway, you know it's just stories, the same as any other work of politically-expedient fiction. And the reason you know this, if you admit it, is that deep-down, you know, your story isn't the same as those other people tell themselves using the same text.'

And that was why he was here, and why he'd been the human conduit for the Day-Lifers. Because he'd been through hell to know that didn't exist and now he got it, the power of the Word. Oh, he could still believe there might be a god, even his God, but what he *knew* was that the stories about Him were just that. Tales told by irresponsible adults to frighten and comfort children, insurance documents for the afterlife, security blankets woven in words. Now he was in an afterlife courtesy of Venus rather than God, the entire concept was somewhat undermined. Looking into the clear grey eyes that belonged to Venus set in the head of the goddess who now truly gave him what hololife he had, he found no point to believing in the unknowable. It was hard enough to believe in what was right in front of him. All he could default to, as the General within, was what he knew about himself. Not a tall tale to boost his ego or status in front of Her, since that was not on the table, but he could address the task in hand, what to do with the life he had now. And what a life. Endless and free of physical decay. And a lot more challenging than heaven had sounded, if less heavy on the bliss. Quite a lot more like the kind of existence flesh had prepared him for, whereas heaven sounded like the Eddyless Calm, a bit dull for an old soldier.

So, after the honour and punishment of being the Day-Ceorl, as which he was the register of the deaths of all, in bloody chords beaten into silent keys out of the great melody of the species that strummed through him, he was now here, as a leader on one of the exiting spaceships. At least, *he* knew it for what it was. A complex of entangled photons, basically a holoprojector, although the quantum processing that embedded the programme was powerful enough to enable innumerable minds to share the vision and retain their own memories and facilitate thought. But it was minute. A microscopic kernel in a barely-macro nut, shot out into space with the magnetic kickstart of Heim physics to slide the condensate of particles into the gravitophotonic slipstream in such a tiny burst of energy that even the Net hadn't seen it go. Within, in the world of the minds, it was vast.

There might not be a genuine Day collective unconscious as Jung had postulated, but there was a consensual mythos with archetypes, ancient and modern cultural memes that resonated in the minds of the Lifers. He knew that he was on the 'ship' of the Believers; people who had not been wiped out in the first wave of the endgame, people who had more intelligence than that or had been indoctrinated into their faiths without education that balanced, basically decent enough, but they all believed in untestable hypotheses. Obviously, although the vast majority were monotheists, the range of faiths was wide, and included polytheists, new-agers, the superstitious, even scientists who hadn't internalized the precepts of their trade. Their collective projections initially competed in dazzling, frightening flashes of all sorts of deist imagery, but after a while settled down to the lowest common denominator of resonant archetypes on which all could recognize subconsciously.

So the 'ship' presented as a world, over which crisp shells domed, carrying the blue sky, dimpled by its sun, moon and planets, with the stars hanging from a higher vault. In the middle of this flat world grew Yggdrasil, the World Tree; very easily, from its shape, re-envisioned as the True Cross. Unlike Roman death-timbers however, it had roots that penetrated to the Underworld and branches that rose to tickle the bow of the Heavens. The trunk was a city of marble, with sheer, vertical and slippery walls that could not be scaled. It grew in a sterile desert and the world beyond that was densely-salted ocean to the rim. There were hermit-like cells within for each individual, decorated with spartan emptiness or astrological signs in hippy chic to taste, but outside the world was much more malleable.

The people had had nowhere to go but heaven or hell, however they envisaged those, and life was a game of snakes and ladders, progression up or down according to random throws of the god's dice. The fact that the die existed solely in the head of the person making the judgement about themselves or their fellows was immaterial, the rules were simple and up or down one went after each toss. This was the primitive state faith had brought them to, and the General and those he could identify and persuade to some level of common sense were there to lead the people out of this wilderness and into whatever promised land that eternal life and a new start could offer a people.

It wasn't going to be easy because everyone had brought with them the mental changes that the Wood-Venus virus had wrought in their brains before they became pixellated and that meant they shared the memes of fear and of visions. So the backgrounds within the Marble-Tree-Tower could transform in a wave of new or re-energised contagious hallucinations, and snakes could grow horns and hooves or tails and tridents and ladders could be held by roots or saints or shamen and the clouds above could show the face of the wind or the goddess or the God or the Vacuum. It wasn't easy keeping the faith with sanity and the real in this environment, especially when you knew it wasn't real at all, but was all there was.

Wharton could only hope he was up to the challenge, because there was an out. Well, in fact, there were three. The first was that the individual or the group managed to leave the tree, either to the Underworld or to the Heavens, whereupon they became trapped for ever in their vision of whatever their destination consisted of in their imagination. The second was that one became so dispirited as to commit holosuicide, which was the permitted way to end the Lifers' life, although, it has to be said surviving members of the group could turn them back on unless they scrambled their pattern, which would mean the code for their DNA too. This was not an attractive option because it left them no possible legacy. Clearly, holograms in an enclosed spacetime could not be allowed to reproduce, but they were packaged with their DNA codes so that, if they reached a habitable planet or terraformed one, and, if they wanted to live and then die as flesh once again they could, at which point reproduction would be as possible as it had been when they were originally translated.

It was Wharton's job as self and Ydal-appointed leader to see the world as a ship and steer it towards some likely real planet on which colonisation could begin. If he hadn't gotten the bulk of them to a saner and more sophisticated mindset by then, however, he could be in orbit of a promising new home forever, so he began to feel his way in the martial power politics of the religious iconography of the Grail, as exemplified by his own status. He knew the dangers of such manipulation now, but he could see this Mayflower as never reaching the New World unless he took a firm grasp on the helm. He wished Venus, or even her facsimile, the Ydal, had come with them, in more than truncated disembodied voice anyhow; he could have done with her guidance now. On the other hand, she was not here to restrain nor judge his actions, and he had only his own background to rely on.

As another shift took place and the collective hallucination showed him Anubis rising from below and Isis spreading her wings above, he suddenly had an individual vision that would trump all this nonsense. After all, why not? It wasn't as if he hadn't achieved the Grail. All he had to do was reinvigorate the belief muscle. And all he had left to believe in was himself, which had never been a problem. After all, Venus had managed it without faith.

He concentrated very hard and found himself suitably dressed and accessorised; a Knight of the *Nigredo*. OK, so maybe it was like starting again in any martial art, you got all the way from white to black belt and then a further series of grades reappeared, back at white, to humble the expert. Well, it had worked before, as had the questing metaphors. *Here goes.*

He strode into the great pyramid and sliced the snapping dog's head off Anubis with the double-headed axe his imagination had supplied instead of a sword, chopped the goddess down at the knee and announced. 'Gather round, all ye lost souls, your Lord God is at hand. Behold your Messiah-Knight. I am Come to Deliver you from the *Nigredo*. Hear now the Words of God!' He waved the inscribed stone tablets in his hand. They had appeared when he had remembered how important a text was, although they were heavier than he'd expected. Probably because the list was not a short set of instructions but a gist of the alchemical process; the stages of the *Transformatio*. Probably unnecessary to invent a Grail this time. A quest for inner spirituality should suit these people. However, since he was in Moses mode, he declaimed, 'These are my commandments. Follow them and me and we will come to the promised land. Follow me and we will conquer all our enemies. Onward, ReBorn Soldiers. Onward, as to War.'

Some people will believe anything. *He ought to know.* Believers are sheep. This lot were also confused and desperate. People are social creatures, they might fight about the quality of their leadership, but basically they like to have one. This might be a patriarchal version but, he saw with clarity, it would effectively be a Hive model, like the original tribal chosen people, priests instead of politicians, the Messiah-Knight instead of Queen. After all, the point of a Hive was reproduction, so, until they got to an habitable planet anyway, the barren restraint of a paternalist style was an acceptable substitute. *Anyway, until his leadership was challenged, and once theology got going it was bound to be, eventually, He was all they had.*

Apparently, He was just what they wanted. The pyramid crumbled, the world spun, and the people saw through his eyes that they rode a mighty spaceship and that their enemies were the Cognimata and that they could be united in a quest to destroy those who had destroyed them and they turned as one and bowed down to their idol and went forward to meet the doom that awaited them. Wharton sighed. He knew the Cognimatan Fleet was ten thousand lightyears from Earth and that they'd jumped only a tenth of that distance, and not in the direction of the Perseus arm. Oh, they were continuing on the momentum of that jump at lightspeed and could change direction, but until they found another power source or another big magnetic field they could harness to another leap, they wouldn't get appreciably nearer to the Fleet in realtime.

Whether or not there was a battle in their future was temporarily irrelevant, it was just that such a focus was a good unifier, as any war proved. It gave a 'them' to unite the 'us'. He thought about Leviticus and Deuteronomy. Sometimes you just needed unity of purpose to achieve law and order, there could be a point to religious lying, he saw now. He also saw a lot of mutinous golden calf worship in his future, but if he could use his authority to get things organised and ready, he could have trained an army, ordered a civilization based on tried-and-tested moralities, and by the time they got there, they would kick butt.

But, hell, it was going to be a long nine thousand years.

Vi !sjn-ik wasn't looking forward as far as that. This was because he wasn't thinking about hunting down the Cognimata, because he knew they weren't the enemy. However, as Queen's Thane, he was designated Leader of the Pack, so he was thinking. Admittedly, he was thinking with his nose, and, as most of his pack were human and thought with their eyes, there was some mistranslation in their communication.

However, he'd got the folk who'd played instinctually, whose basal ganglia ruled their lives, and many of them had adopted the Dark Knights, whether as Terrans or Termites, as their avatars. This meant that their intelligence was not necessarily best measured in IQ terms, but they all scored highly in EQ ratings, although whether emotionality was the same as the empathy that came with the sophistication of truly-internalized theory of mind was another matter. Having spent time in the company of the Lady, which had illuminated his past self as fairly low on the integration scale, he was aware that he was not the best of his pack at putting himself in another's shoes, or as the Darks would say, rolling in another's scent. However, she had also explained that the decisiveness required of leadership demanded somewhat less rapport than distance from the people, as long as he could share power with someone who possessed such understanding.

His treatment by his clones, who had delivered pack punishment of the harshest kind, had done the job his ego had never allowed, it had put him in his place, at the bottom of the hierarchy. But he was a true wolf-soul, and he had accepted it, and drunk willingly of the Grail-poison, and died and promised to serve his Female's people and carried the death-throes of all the Darks, and regained his honour and status as Thane. He was Alpha Male, although he knew now that he'd only ever wanted that status to be allowed to be Venus's consort, and without her it was simply a role with responsibilities he'd never had to shape up to before.

However, in many ways, knowing she was no longer in his world, except if you discounted her voice in the computer, and especially since her scent no longer troubled his glands and fuzzed his mind, it was easier being a mature person. He wasn't obsessed with outcompeting the world anymore, as he had been when she'd been the apex of his ambitions and so globally powerful, and his newfound humility allowed him to think about what the pack needed from him, rather than the reverse.

So, since, as yet anyway, he was still devoted and loyal to Venus as his Alpha-Female, he wasn't looking for a replacement queen nor a sexual partner, he could see quite clearly that the balance to his leadership would best be provided by his aunt, Mh' rzcel . She and Fr! gwapd were both here and they'd need something to do, because his aunt was missing her sister, Mh'aed, who, if she'd been translated at all would be with Bob and Ruth and Milo and Wharton on the ship with the Believers, probably still languishing in a hell of his own making. Fr! gwapd had volunteered to come with the mainly Day Lifers, because he understood Days a lot better than his father-original, and he'd played both Dark and Day in the game. Also, to Vi !sjn-ik's surprise, his pack contained many of the younger Darks who had played I-*Mage* and even more shockingly, many of his own age and older who had never played the game but had relinquished their right to choose Death and the Flesh or Life and the Photon because they had already chosen to be in a Pack, rather than the MetaMind Earth was left with. There were even one or two Darks who had chosen to follow wherever their Pack leader led them, and he had been their nomination for the job, which was more unexpected than anything.

It wasn't as surprising that he'd been a nominee from the Day side, since he was the Chief Thane in the Game, so they'd got used to him and their subconscious knew him to be the exemplar of Pack emotions. These weren't squeamish humans with nuanced feelings, they were vibrant, passionate, social and predatory. They were the spontaneous, exploratory, curious apes that had thrust forward across the planet and sent them into space and started the whole Cognimatan wobble. Now they were out here themselves, and Vi's ship had brought not glands but the mindset that had evolved from it, the excitement of the hunt, the aggressive inquisitiveness of the endless Quest.

After their compatibility in the game, their viral-connectivity had described a world they could all enjoy. The ship was not ship but wolf-shaped, running the *ilfete pæð,* the legendary swan's path the wolf-headed Viking ships followed across uncharted seas, but this four-legged beast nosed out star systems, snuffed at planets, smelled for scents of foes and prey and likely dens. Admittedly the spectral and chemical analysis that went into the working nostrils was provided by the AI but the leaders would choose which aromatic teases to track to their sources by how they tickled their own pseudocilia.

Inside the wolf was the world, much like the one they'd left behind, above and below, night and day, sea and land and sky, although the majority vote had made the climate temperate and the ecology more like European than Madagascan, since the traditional Darks had mostly chosen to die in the flesh, and it seemed the southern Day peoples had played human rather than any of the possibly demonic alternatives. The exception was the far-east Chinese and Japanese contingent, making up over one third of the Days aboard. Not that Vi !sjn-ik would have known anyone's origins without the information provided by the AI, whose Venus-voice provided the why as well as the who of his pack. Almost all the Day pygmies with the exception of the Floresians, who had probably gone with the Woods, were with him, and they were putting aside intertribal strife and headhunting for tracking animals with skins to keep them warm in this strangely-cool, non-jungly world. Once this was done, they, along with everyone else, would be looking to the pack leader to demonstrate why he had been given this position.

Vi !sjn-ik consulted with Mh' rzcel , Fr !gwapd and the AI as the best way to fix his status and with it a status quo that would last without challenge for long enough to organise and integrate into one pack, ready for the challenge of a world. He might not find a habitable one quickly, so he had the ship set to do long range scans to eliminate false trails and to find sources of energy so they could jump ahead to the next scent. The trouble with emotional folk is that they like repeated stimulation, and while Darks had learned patience under Day oppression even they preferred to hunt than forage and would want to keep going forward rather than circling their nests, however comfortable one might be for a time.

The world appeared to be land and rivers and seas in the body of the wolf, with long cool caverns delving into its legs, although you could never forget that it was moving, even though the sun and moon in the sky were a thousand lightyears behind them in truth, because the entire place shook and shimmered as the creature loped across space. It wasn't much like an earthquake, it was much more like the sensation of riding a horse, from the internal perspective of its meal or muscles anyway, and one got used to it, like getting sealegs on a ship. However, you could get to see the real stars by going into the head, where the vulpine eyes were windows and screens displaying the actual galactic position achieved, although it was harder to stomach the motion of the beast while watching the astral seesawing. Here was the communal den, for meetings, and where Vi had set up his headquarters, near to the AI-vocalisation. Fr !gwapd said it was like the cockpit of plane or the bridge of the starship Enterprise, and he got very interested in interacting with the AI and learning how it could help them do more than navigate. So it was he that had told Vi how to spray highest up the tree.

He said, and Mh' rzcel and Vygrail *(well, he'd had to name the damn AI something and it was mostly the Ydal, Ygrail, but she sounded like and was based on Venus, so the elision seemed OK and not too soppy when he said it aloud)* had both agreed, that while he had to demonstrate his visceral authority by being the strongest of the strong, what a new society really needed was *þegnlagu,* the Lore of the Thane to be accepted, by the thane's demonstration of his *lahriht*, his legal right to the title, by virtue of wearing the mantle of duty and responsibility. Vygrail said the best way to do this was the traditional method of Fighting the Dragon.

This requires the communal effort of trackers and flushers to seek and drive out the dragon from its lair, the encircling of the crowds, historically the villagers under attack as interested parties, the temptation of the bait, and the stepping up of the hero - dispatcher of the prey and saviour of the virgin bait and the village from fire, and provider of so-much reptilian fodder that people sicken of the food until it ends up being fed to the dogs. The way to make this meaningful in a group who had come out of death on the other side was to take off the holo-safety-protocols (*Venus had watched Gene Roddenberry creations long before Fr! gwapd*) so that there was genuine risk of endings.

Vygrail was not, of herself, an imaginative, creative programme, and the Pack had storytellers, who embellished like fishermen, from kernels of truth, but few believers or psychologically-challenged projectors of hallucination, since neither were survival instincts that sat well in already emotional folk, so there was going to be a bit of a problem conjuring a dragon. Mh' rzcel could have made a potion that created visions, maybe even circulated in the air, although it would be a photonic flash in the brain rather than an actual chemical emanation, but it was deemed cheating, not *lahlic.* However, even a database can throw up the odd moment of inspiration, and Vygrail, who had carried on trawling through the list of the People of the Wolf while the others debated, suddenly came up with a name. 'Terry Rawlins!'

'Who's he?'

'He was with Gwener, in the Venus-parallel. He doesn't know it, of course. Anyway, here he's an ace tracker, of bats, conservationist, loves caves, so he'll be down in the leg somewhere. Point is, in Gwener-spacetime he saw real dragons, and, because of the way the multiverse lives in superposition, he has dreamed them, as vividly as if it was reality, because naturally, it was, it was tunnelling data. So he can be set to find us a dragon, and he will. Problem solved. Of course, since in his dream the dragon had a female's face and was queen of the world, you know whose head you'll have to chop off to save your people, so it'll be a challenge, alright. Still, if you can do that, you'll have indisputable *þegnlahriht.* Very fitting challenge. Symbolic, stuff of sagas for years to come. An excellent start.'

Vygrail might be pleased, Vi !sjn-ik was less so. Even in his wildest dreams Venus' face never appeared on anything he wanted to kill, only fuck. But he couldn't deny the iconography, which Mh' rzcel agreed was suitably Heraldic and would carry a Gist long after the Meat had been gnawed from the Bones. You probably couldn't ask for a better original myth on which to go forth into the story the future would write with you. It was already a Quest within a Quest, which always construed as fortuitous and meaningful, the compass that pointed the way to the destination.

The gauge was down. He could only pick it up or run away for eternity with his tail between his legs. Anyway, he'd given his oath to serve Her people. He was a Knight of the new *Nigredo.* He would wear Her Phoenix-colours until Her Dragon-Self burned them from him or he raised them as the Collar for his WolfPack, the tie to Terra that leashed their wildness in the wilderness.

Rowan was also in the wilderness, although his was more jungly and much more like WoodHame writ large, and it wasn't taming it nor his Consensus that was on his mind, but he shared the already-tamed desire to be validated by keeping faith with Venus' vision. Which in life would have surprised him, because he'd always thought of himself as the mentor in the relationship, but in HoloLife he knew his place. He'd hung around humans too long, got to think of himself as leader of his people, largely because of his instructional role for the Knights of the Augmentatio. It had been a Day-style hubris of which he would have been ashamed if that kind of self-indulgence was not counterproductive. It would also be hypocritical now, since, in this world he was the Voice of Authority.

Oh, the social model was still Wood, Consensus through mental sharing as ever, but it was agreed that of the few actual Woods on board, he was the most experienced and, since the Days liked to fixate on individuals, with their habitual cult of celebrity, he was the It-voice of the moment. He had to remember that fashions changed and that at any time he might have to give it up, but that would be fine too, since he'd have read the minds that chose and would understand their needs by then. At present he was just glad he had Cal with him. *Dear Cal! So loyal.* He was very glad to be forgiven for the deceit and infidelity he had slipped into by putting his mentorship before his love, but even more glad that Cal had chosen to be with him, though at the time of the *Judicium* he had believed that meant his own death, so that he could still tap the excellent common sense the man hid beneath the magpie surface chattering.

The people with them were, as in each ship, mostly Days, but these were the ones whose nature required them to be free but to be safe too, the ones who shared their distribution of the genepool more nearly with the Woods and bonobos than the rest of their own kin. They were not predators primarily, and would be happy to eat meneh and train trees to slowly grow habitations and to share everything in common, including access to their bodies. Only he and Cal were under any onus to restrain themselves sexually, but that was part of their fealty to one another, for everyone else liberation from the oppressions that had stifled all their creativities was the order of the Day.

There were many philosophers and cosmological physicists in this crowd, people whose journey would be spent in research without boundaries as they undertook the subjective experiment of living in the universe with wider horizons and new data. There were also many more artists than the Woods had ever produced, mostly from Days who had played as Termites, exercised their imaginations and could now make music and paintings and sculptures with broader brushstrokes than ever before. There were cutting-edge scientists from all disciplines, and many many IT specialists, especially games and web developers, despite the lack of historic Wood tradition in these fields. What there were few of were folk who tied things up in words, few journalists, lawyers, politicians or writers. The politics that was instantly apparent was that of freedom of speech and thought, so that individualism was definitely not subsumed into Consensus, although the democratic spirit remained alive as the individuals politely, if after suitably argumentative debate, would accept the majority verdict. As the debates were held within the metamindmeld of the Consensus format, with Rowan as Conduit, they were more informed with less posturing and no unnecessary verbiage and ultimately more fair than any system any of the Days had ever known.

What interested Rowan about the process was the shortcuts to decision humans were capable of taking. They could ingest the knowledge pertinent to the question, and, if they didn't have to fight through the tangled web of conscious words, their extremely sharp pattern-recognition enabled snappy reactions that would have enabled the Woods to have ruled the world if they could ever have emulated them. Such speed, such clever brains, built to satisfy primate curiosity with quick enough and good enough answers to allow them to go forward sharply. He had thought those Days he knew like Venus and Cal were exceptional, which in many ways was true, but now he noticed, perhaps for the first time, what the Archivist had also noted somewhat earlier, that all individuals were exceptional in their own way.

He had a diverse and talented people to steer across the galaxy but the direction was almost immaterial. They weren't on a quest for vengeance as predators, or for a planet to call home. Their thirst was for knowledge of the universe, so they would visit, not war upon nor colonize planets, and then move on, ronin-wanderers to the end. But they would want to report back their knowledge at some point, because they were flesh-lovers, and would want to return to the Nest, just like Mars, to give and receive before moving on again. It was a wanderlust he'd never felt before and yet it felt as natural as coming Hame, perhaps because, like snails, they were carrying Hame with them.

He began to get an inkling of what Venus had really been trying to save here. Oh, she wanted to give the planet a breather from the destructive power of massed Day predation, a thousand years of cessation of fossil-fuel use and resource-depletion, a thousand years for the planet to heat and change and stabilize again before any of the offenders could come back and take up where they left off: a thousand years of going forth to come back enlightened was her hope. She wanted the population reduced because it was already unsustainable in its present form, indeed, with its present habits it would be unsustainable on a planet of the same fecundity and geological wealth three times the size of Earth, but she didn't want to lose the species.

She did want the species to lose its innocence, its ostrich-like ability to ignore consequences, its arrogance as sole inhabitants of the universe, but not its *for want of a better word* 'soul'. Days were predatory yet not mere killers, curious yet capable of great and wanton ignorance, creative yet together stupid, fearful yet full of optimism. She didn't want them to stop telling stories either, just not to believe that everything they thought in their heads about themselves or the world or everything written down in black and white and not labelled fiction was truth. She wanted genuine thinking from a species she knew could do it, not just blind belief, but she hadn't eradicated those who believed, partly because that would have been conviction politics as bad as theirs and partly because the ability to create the imaginary world of the future requires a willing suspension of disbelief, for which at least the model of faith is required as a foil.

He knew this because she'd told him before she brought down the Tower. Not in words, not overtly, so the onlookers would not see, but she had held his hand to her holotemple one last time and said, 'You deserve the Coat Entire, but do not wear it until the time of the Foremost Knight of the Veriditas is also the time of the Days.'

He hadn't understood what she meant then, but he had obeyed her command not to view the upload until the time seemed right. He had been on the ship and reunited with Cal and voted the Voice of Authority by all the Day minds and engaged in the *Meditatio* prior to being Conduit, before becoming the Day-Song for the first time ever, when he had realized the time was now. He just hoped she had managed the rest of her vision as well as she had the escape of the ships.

Of all those shipboard, only Pereduri might have the answer to that, but search as she might on her vessel, Zelas could not find her friend nor Xl-arn'tz. This distressed her more than it should in the circumstances, since her beloved was here with her, having elected to go wherever she went and, being already dead, they could only continue their existence in holoform. But she had been cradled into that form through the sacrifice of Pereduri, whose body had been untouched in the IceBerga attack but whose mind had spiralled away for so long preserving the Ice and Ghost Queens that, despite Xl-arn'tz best efforts, he had lost all his companions. Since Venus had stipulated that no holoforms were to be allowed on Terra for at least one thousand years, Pereduri, and presumably Xl-arn'tz, must be on another ship. She had hoped their mingling in the *Coniugium* would have made them want to remain as aquanauts.

'Technically, we're all astronauts now.' Ranger pointed out, but it was hard to notice the stars from underwater. Perhaps, that was part of the challenge to the humans as well as the Hydraens aboard, to remember to look up and outward, not swim round one's tail forever. That kind of behaviour certainly hadn't favoured IceBerga survival, that was for sure.

Ranger was interfacing with the ship's mind, in a cavern that displayed a lot like the cabin of the Ghost-Hydraens' Cuttlefish-Knights. He was about the only one doing anything like work. Most people were playing, since most of the humans had never experienced water as anything other than recreational. Dakul and Flow were here, but since this was the first time they'd had compatible physiologies, they were still exploring the breadth of satisfaction their sexuality offered. They were the only beings that didn't look like any of the three types of Terran Hydraens. Humans, with their powerful imaginations, had surprised everyone by becoming this ship. For most of the game, the only Hydraens anyone could play were Whorlingas, since Venus didn't know about any others.

Apparently, being a Whorlinga was more popular with LandLubber Days than with the actual clan, whose depleted numbers had been vulnerable to extinction with one last shark attack. Here there were thousands of people looking like her. Even more interesting was the way the people who had survived the 'Rivers of Blood' episode, and been given the Coat Entire, had taken to the Ghosts and replicated here as them. So that, although few of that clan were left in the flesh on Terra, there were vast numbers here. Shockingly, there were also IceBergas too.

Ranger had tried to work it out, suggesting that there were plenty of people who retained the same tensions of being passive listeners just bursting to be predatory, and vice versa. 'You've been wild and free your entire life,' he'd said. 'Plenty of humans have spent their time in the frustration of listening to other people, in call centres for instance, or just sitting in front of a demanding computer screen. If you starved them too, they'd leap up and wreak havoc at some point, guaranteed. It would be carnage. I guess humans could have some sympathy with the IceBergas entrapment that you don't. And on the other hand (I should get used to saying fin or something), there's a long and honourable tradition, mostly Buddhist but also in individuals, of trying to tune in to the universe, so folk with those kind of aspirations are seeing this trip into the Void as their way of listening to the cosmos, as a means of seeking knowledge. What better way of doing that than in IceBerga form. They're the experts after all. And everyone wants to be farsighted enough to become a Tachyon-Siren in time. For which they'll need the guidance of both you Queens.'

'Am I Queen anymore? I don't see why I should be. So far my expertise has shown itself as bringing death to anyone who follows me. Wouldn't they all rather choose another?'

'Don't think it's shaping up like that, darling. They're all gameplayers who've just found themselves living inside the game, and when they get over the delight of being able to swim like fish, they're still going to be the really nerdy bunch that chose the most ancient traditions of the Quest to live by.'

'Does that mean they need a Queen? Because there's always been one, or one awaited in the future? Because even if that's so, there's no reason it should be me. There's Ouissocca, for one thing.'

'I've spoken to her and she's been out of the loop for so long, not to mention thawing out only to die and then to find she's not dead but in some LandLubber's version of an afterlife, that she's a) not really what you'd call a people-person and b) so shocked and humbled by what she now knows about the world, she's in no fit state to reign and she knows it. She doesn't want to return to Listening, although she's happy to teach others what she Heard and how to Listen and the Timbre of the Note, but she doesn't want to embody the Note. Mostly she feels too old. She'd have taken that role on, if required, for Terra, although she believes now that understanding Ice is no real substitute for understanding Land, especially Sunlit Land and its creatures, so she isn't sure her resonance would be rich enough in all of its Harmonics, but she is quite sure that on this young new world made of light itself, the Melody will be remade, the Orchestra will be different, and only someone young could hear the Note and Tune the world to it. She thinks that is you. And so do all the humans who followed you here.'

'They followed Me?'

'Sure, it was your story that got into the game, and it was your story that showed us the Ghosts and IceBergas at the end. Venus and Quogat and Peri were conduits to the Ydal, but it was you whose mind was shared with all us players. I recognized you the moment we met by the river. So did everyone else when they got the Full Blazon at the end. They might have wanted to live their avatars but they also sympathised with you and understood your aims and wanted to be in a world you could Fore-Sing for them. A world where cutting edge science meets ancient magics. Us nerdy types love new stuff to work on and dress up as Dungeon and Dragon-meisters to play.'

'How can humans do science here? There's hardly any land to beach on, and none to spare to build your labs.'

'I was chatting to a couple of lads who are on the other side of the world a little while ago and they're exceptionally excited by the potential for quantum processing in a world where, as a species, we can control water. They're already engaged in collecting the materials to reproduce the basics of the AI, so they can develop new programmes to extend its functions. And there's another team of, believe it or not, ex-marines, who have found eachother and are working on a way to use sonoluminescence to build habitats underwater and pipe air into them. So don't worry about the science buffs, they're going to work it out.'

'Well, what do they need me for, then?'

'They need you to do the Casting to determine where the ship should go. You need to Listen, find the Note, then find where it should Ring in the future. Then we'll set off in that direction. If it's far, you'll have to Cast for fish to get us there. Not food, obviously, but power sources, materials to scavenge, I dunno, depends where we're going.'

Zelas was silent. Listening. He was right. She could feel the anticipation in everyone's minds, even those who were playing, even those who were still confused, even those who were still fearful. And she had already felt the weight of them all looking to Her for guidance. Well, Tachyon-Sirens are born, and only hone or blunt their skills thereafter, and she and Ouissocca were all her people had. There were some *arpeggios* distilling out of the overall syncopation that might be developed into future-Sirens, but for now she was the only Tripodial of the Hydradesic. Anyone who had seen the future fixed in the current cannot duck their destiny. Plus, even without a true Cast, she could feel the pull on the line between her and the future. It was another Mind, a Siren Casting. Not Casting a lure on a tight line, but a net that trawled across vast acreages of spacetime looking for others of its kind. A transformed Planetary-style MetaMind, like and unlike Mars, and definitely not focused on something as individual and bounded as her. But she could feel that the crossing of their future paths would be between equals, that her ship would not be full of separated entities by then, that her people would transform, metamorphose, and become such a creature.

'Where's the nearest NetSpore communication conduit?' she asked abruptly.

Ranger snuffed into the AI and after a few minutes was able to tell her. 'Change course and head for it. I need to leave a message for Mars.'

'How do we do that?'

'I don't know. Get some of your people to work it out by the time we get there. I've got to make a proper Cast.'

'Yes, your Majesty!' he mocked, smiling with pleasure at the new decisiveness in her. 'Anything you want to tell me?'

'No. I determine the trajectory. I do not presume to know the events of the journey to the destination. That would be too much Queening. But I know the vague direction we're headed in, and I just want to be sure we meet an old friend when we get there. Mars ought to be told where to find his kin.'

She let Ranger think she meant Dakul. She knew she meant the other mind. The deepest and hollowest chord in the symphony of the world was ringing in her like a bell. Ouissocca, who was melded with her more nearly even than Ranger, despite and because of their history and regality, and who was ever a Listener on automatic, had heard through her. The chime resonated approval of her boldness and confidence in her monarchy. 'The Note was always made of

Light, not slow Sound, not fast Silence. I have Listened with my ears and I did not hear that Mind. You did. You are the rightful Queen and I offer you my fealty and all our hopes.'

No pressure, then! But Zelas was grateful for the endorsement and knew she would need the support of her erstwhile enemy, not to mention her ears for anything nearer than the distant future. It was also very very good to know that there was a future without death at the end of it, without her as the causal link between the two events, and with all of her people with her. It was astonishing how quickly the psychologically-induced somas around her could come to be taken as real. If they had wanted landfall on a new planet, the DNA of most of the crew would have decoded into original humans, but these people dreamed as mutations of transmutation. They were all Grail-Knights and she would offer them no less. But in the present, for the journey, there were forms to maintain.

'John, if I'm going to be Queen, we'll have to have a coronation. Not with a crown, of course. I've already got the dear mantis-shrimp, for one thing. One like I got as Ghost-Queen, but for all the clans, to unite and establish the Lore as our guidelines. It's got to be the best party anyone's ever seen.'

'Neat. I'll get the boys working on some fireworks. The guys exploring sonoluminescence have been playing with light and water and getting some pretty cool rainbow effects and bangs apparently.'

'Met any musicians yet? Cos some of the Whale-Knights can really blow. And I know some of the Octopus-Squires make sensational beats if you can find the right shells for them to drum on.'

'Well, this world isn't pliable, not to the imagination, the way the AI/Ydal suggested it might be. People here really want this to be real, so what we brought in our heads with us is all there is. At least until people start getting creative that way, if we do. Who knows. Point is the place is so new all the shells are occupied. Can't see any self-respecting conch wanting to volunteer to be drummed on by an overexcited octopus, can you?'

'Ah well, see what you can drum up. Ho ho.'

'I think Queens traditionally left the humour to their jesters. Perhaps it would be a wise act to follow, at least in public, dear heart.'

Somehow just being with him with something to do, even something as frivolous and important as the party, normalized the world for her. Normal must be even more important to establish for her people, for most of whom being aquatic was not normal. There was a lot to do and a lot to learn, but the future was bright and she could see it.

Pereduri, alone of all the translated on all the ships, could see too. Not the future, just the hopes and fears for it that all those who connected with their AI/Ydal on their separate ships could see. She hadn't had to die of the coma she'd gone into to ensure the continuance of the Ouissocca and Zelas, but she'd been troubled before that about sending the people away without any communication possible between eachother nor with Terra. Mother had not wanted to interfere with hominin evolution, whether culturally or physically, but her children already existed, Wood-Day hybrids and Dark-Day clones of Vi !sjn-ik, and she had cheated her way to success by using Wood technology to make the Ydal and cheated further by getting ideas from other universes through her. The Disappeared included all of the people her parallel selves had valued as contributors to their solutions, as well as a lot more, and they were onboard the ships, usually in the role of liason with the AI/Ydal initially, although whether they'd become leaders or mentors or pariahs was up to their handling of whatever situation they found themselves in. What Mother had not wanted for her final solution was the Ydal presence on Terra. She wanted the hominins to realize eachother's existence and cohabit peacefully, but she wanted them to do that for themselves, not because some superior intelligent machine made in her image told them to. So she had settled on dispersing the Ydal with the ships and in the Phoenix-alchemy. But Pereduri had lain in a coma, while her holoform graced the Tower and her siblings partitioned their MetaMind into an Ydal-supported visualisation for her and Ouissocca and Zelas, and she had seen the Exodus of the children. Oh, the ages of the people in the ships varied across the lifespans of the species translated, but in their new forms, their new societies, they were as children.

Heavens-to-Betsy, as Cal would say, there was even a Termite ship. I-*Mage* players whose desire for an ordered society was best described by the structure of the Termites, who were based on a real civilization in a fabricated parallel universe, and whose avatars were happily preset and whose aim was to find their way across the multiverse to join with those original Termites. When Mother had envisioned sending earthlings out into the galaxy to save them, to unleash them upon unsuspecting alien populations, to enable them to boldly go rather than stupidly die, she had not imagined how creative and diverse their choices for their holographic selves, societies and worlds would be.

It behoved the parent not to lose sight of the children, Pereduri had reasoned, and so she'd died and dispersed and become a hologram, because the Ydal-MetaMind partition had shown her how. So now, although she was here on this ship with Xl-arn'tz, one thousand light years from home, she was a part in the whole MetaMind, when her individual siblings engaged it, and a part in the whole AI/Ydal in each ship. It was only a question of ringfencing enough entangled photons to create a piece of mind that could upload the Cantor-dust of any glyph of any gist of any blazon of any coat, but the message could come in that way and Peri's mind, or that of the AI/Ydal contained sufficient processing power to decompress it. More to the point, she thought, was that she could reverse the process and send information back Home.

She missed home. Oh, not the look and feel and smell and sounds of Terra, the people she had come with were traditionalists in their own way, lovers of their planet who couldn't imagine living anywhere else, so they'd brought it in facsimile with them. But she hadn't brought her siblings and Mother was about to end her life in a blast that might even blow Peri's entangled mind apart. She wasn't leading the people with her, she was listening very intently to the World Service, so as not to miss the moment when all thereafter would be missing.

Xl-arn'tz kept coming in and out, checking on her, telling her things to whet her appetite for the now, about how things were going on board, how the people were settling without the kinds of technology that had powered their previous version of Terra, how they were suffering the remorse and regret of the dispossessed, how they wanted only to return home, how they were turning the ship straight around, even though they knew they couldn't locate Terra without it being a thousand years in the future at earliest from the point at which they left, but basically he was just worried about her. Perhaps about them all, wallowing in their nostalgia for a home that would not exist when they returned. They had no jump-power so it would take at least a thousand years at their current speed to get back, so they knew it was a long haul and they knew they couldn't wallow for the duration, and they knew they couldn't go home without changing themselves into worthy of the stewardship they would regain.

Xl-arn'tz had started off saying she was setting a bad example, but then, when she'd started reporting some of what she knew about the other ships and what was happening back home, and the people had been glad to hear it, he began to worry that her role was embedding as a living radio. 'Looking backward is not the way to order a society for the next thousand years or more.' He protested strongly, both in the Parliament of Equals and the Senate of Commons. Both civic authorities had been his idea, since the folk of this new world were in favour of democracy, rather than any form of enlightened dictatorship, and strongly against elevating individuals or even representative groupings to positions of power over the rest. They were interested in a brave new world, however much the landscape and buildings reflected the old one, but with the ability to share their minds had come new problems of decisiveness.

The Parliament, named after the talking shops of yore, was to be a monthly moment of Consensus to set the agenda for the forthcoming period, with the Senate, originally a grouping of elders, reviewing actions taken and reactions to them at the end of the month, also through total Consensus, to provide feedback and accountability. The people of New Terra, as they were already calling the sphere they had created as home, were split into two, randomly by the AI, and looped their minds into the Parliament or Senate as selected, rotating so that the system could not stalemate nor favour any aggregations of personalities or power bases as they might arise over time.

Pereduri had been the Conduit so far, but she was working with the people the AI/Ydal identified as best able to put aside their egos or those who had already experience of meditation to develop their talents for the role, specifically to avoid the human tendency to promote cults around celebrity that might ultimately lead to deification, which no one wanted, least of all Peri. Xl-arn'tz thought she was pushing her current acolytes rather harder than necessary, when, that is, she stirred herself to interact at all. Woods spent decades of their long lives becoming ready for Conduit, and the people here had no limit on their existences, so he found himself perturbed by her urgency, which he couldn't accept was justified by a fear of goddesshood. He suspected that she simply wanted to hand over the role and with it the only defined responsibility she had in this world. He knew she loved him, but her choice to be here was to be the link between the Diaspora and Home, and he began to feel insufficient to the task of engaging her other than as that connection.

She knew all this, of course, but he was right in that his anxiety and the needs of the people provided too little in the way of motivation for her. She was used to being able to think with her siblings as one mind, becoming a larger entity thereby, and all the shared thoughts of the little people, the individual mentalities that had barely risen above the concerns of the flesh and defaulted to thinking about food and shelter and sex when they should feel liberated by the end of these needs as holoforms, were not stimulating enough. She only felt like a true thinker when she was in the null-ego state as part of the distributed Ydal-Knight metamind. She couldn't see any point in surviving flesh if the aspiration to be bigger and better didn't survive with it.

'Well, we're here, and there must be a reason why we're on this ship rather than any of the others.' Xl-arn'tz pointed out.

'It's probably just because I want to go home as much as the rest of them.' she offered, finding the constraints of language tiring and uninteresting.

'I didn't. I wanted to explore. So why am I here? I mean, you're part-Ydal, you must know the way the *Judicium* went for everyone.'

'You are my Squire sworn. Even if you didn't love me, your *devoir* is to accompany the Knight who has accepted your fealty.'

'Does that mean you can shut me out?'

There was a note of hurt in his voice she hadn't expected. 'What's the matter?'

'Are you planning to leave us?'

'What? How? Stupid words! I don't know what you mean. Give me your ...'

'No!' He pulled his temple away from her hand and her probing mind could feel barriers erecting like walls tumbling backwards. 'I will have the Lapis on this. Word must be given. This is important.'

'Fine. Then tell me what you're talking about, so I can answer your stupid questions.'

'I can feel you waiting for Mother. I know you're only happy when you feel Knight-Mind. Even reporting on the other ships is like a hobby not a vocation. But we, us here and those in the other ships, are all we have now. Oh, at present, the Knights and Mother still exist and you can contact them, but they're in flesh and they'll die. Maybe not soon, but hundreds of years before you can get back. I'm worried that you think life will not be worth living for you when they're gone. Even if you're the only Knight left to represent what they stood for, what mind they were. I know you can choose to end your existence at any time. And you seem very keen to train up alternate Conduits. So I want to know what you're planning. Because something about leaving us is in your scent and I don't want you to go.'

'Oh, my poor dear. You think I would kill myself? No, never. It's not that. It's just ... well, I am waiting, for Mother's last trick, because if it works, with my mind entangled with the Knights', I may not be the person you know now. I may not even be a person at all.'

'You are leaving?'

'No. I'll always be here. But I've been distancing myself on a personal level, you were right about that. Partly out of taste, partly because it may be easier on all of us.'

'Us? You? Or me? Or the general population?'

'Oh, I want to have trained up some Conduits in time, but no. I thought this way would be easier on you and me. I thought if you got involved in the world, you wouldn't notice my moods as much. I guess I thought if we weren't as intimate *I'd* miss you less. But it didn't work, did it?'

'It's me you're missing? When I'm here?'

'I know. Bit like everyone else missing their past fleshy lives, I'm mourning my future lost hololife with you.'

'I hadn't realized. I thought it was the past. I thought we'd have time together.'

'Mother's dying. We've got till then. She's already lasted longer than anyone expected. It'll be anytime now.'

'Then let's make the most of the time we've got. No more pre-emptive mourning. Just be with me until you can't. Please.'

He was right, of course. The definition of being alive might no longer be the striving flesh is heir to, but the onus on living for the present, on being optimistic against future troubles, remained. Everyone else had got the idea, if only out of habit. She knew what she was facing and it wasn't living, even if it was life. But she did love Xl-arn'tz and he deserved to know what would happen to her, so he could prepare himself and, perhaps, be reassured that they would, in some way, always be together.

Maybe if you weren't born human, you could cope with all this, but Kean didn't feel he had it in him to accept Venus' final revelation as in any way comforting. Not that she was spending any of her last hours attempting to offer him any comfort. She might be in horrible amounts of pain and utterly exhausted, with constant nausea and intermittent vomiting, plus the beginnings of hair loss, but she was as busy as if her life depended on it.

Most of it was soothing the raised hackles of the intergalactic community who had been perturbed by the fall of the Tower. Just because the blip had lasted only for the seconds long enough for the ships to escape, and had been followed by the Ydal's looped holorecording of the place, did not mean the event had passed unnoticed. All the feedback loop did was allow time for the magnetic flux to dissipate so that the Cognimata could not learn anything from the ground to inform their understanding, and, of course, once the ships had left they'd jumped out of spacetime technically, with re-entry, outside anyone's field of monitoring reference, 1000 lightyears hence.

Of course, the Weapons had registered the magnetic bursts and demanded guidance, which was when they got the virus from the Ydal, via the complicit Archivist, and that, firstly, made them interpret the bursts as bearing the signature of Mars leaving the solar system and, secondly, made them allies. They behaved as programmed and vapourised the dead, but then they left their prescribed orbits in protection of Europa and in intimidation of Terra. Apparently, they dispersed to Lunar orbit, to an unknown black hole near the sun and to the heliopause Lagrange point, with lines of sight maintained between them by seeding the vacuum with transmitters and energy amplifiers.

The NetSpore queried the redeployment and got fudge back from the Archivist, but the Europans, once apprised of their lack of Cognimatan aide, demanded more robust assurances of safety. It was at this point that Venus tested the reverse-viral knowledge that the Ydal had been endowed with by the Weapons transfer. She blew one, just one, of the Weapons right out of the sky, and she did it from her moonbase, with an exceptionally-finely tuned laser blast.

And not one of the remaining smart munitions programmes retaliated.

That set the cat among the pigeons. Just when the solar system should have been settling down, with the population of Terra crippled technologically, Venus faced the community with a new threat. And, unless the Cognimata heard from the NetSpore and brought the Fleet through, there was no defence for anyone. So she had to convince the NetSpore that there was no danger, imminent or longer-term, from the remaining hominin races. She had, finally, to explain to it what her real plan was. She was concerned to reassure it about putting the power of the Ydal beyond the control of flesh, and to persuade it to oversee her demise by Riding both the facsimile and the real Venus. She'd managed it too, which made Kean even more uncomfortable, and, of course, she hadn't taken a moment to reassure him.

It was as if, now her health was terminal, even his professional skills were of no use to her, especially since, except perhaps for his pain medication, the Wood and Dark treatments for longevity extension were far more advanced than his own. Not that Venus was taking anything that really suppressed the pain, since morphine made her far too fuzzy-headed for her needs, but only humans had done research into radiation sickness, so, while, he was classified as the expert, Furze and Mh'aed were keeping her organs going by unknown means, and he could merely treat the symptoms. He had to concede his professional talents were not in the same league, since death was not his forte. So, since Venus seemed to want him around all the time, he had to conclude that she wanted him there for a different kind of comfort, but he was finding it particularly hard to give. His bedside manner was normally on automatic, but everything had changed recently, and nothing fell into the category of reflex anymore.

He couldn't look her in the eye since she'd been to see Dinah. His anger at her reflected his guilt over his wife, and perhaps vice versa. He was angry not least because he didn't think he should be the one feeling guilty. It should be Venus and Jake and Dinah herself, but in his heart he couldn't shake the incessant beat of shame. He watched Jake and Lily moving on into the regal status that designated them within the new world order as Voices for the human race in the multispecies Consensus. He watched Venus playing power politics even in her final hours. He couldn't accept that he should lose both

Dinah and Venus, even as he accepted that he'd never truly had either. But it was the loss of Venus that rankled most and whose loss would hurt intolerably. He'd talked to Furze and Mh'aed and they reckoned if she'd take treatment her life could be saved. Maybe the quality of it wouldn't be as she'd previously experienced, with her robust good health, but she'd be alive and he could look after her.

Of course, predictably, if he'd been thinking rationally, any attempt to stop one of her plans, even her final fatal one, *especially, given the implications for Terra,* ran headlong into her stubborn streak. He found himself pretty soon whining like the beggar he was.

'You've done enough. You've already saved the world. The danger is over. The NetSpore will be happy if you just destroy the Ydal and then it'll be galactic peace and you can live to see the people of the earth restore the planet.'

'You think that's what I want? To watch Terra lashed by global warming? To watch its people struggle with the exigencies of fleshly existence in an increasingly-hostile world?'

'Well, it won't be as bad as it would have been. We've got plenty of space now there's so few of us, so we won't be fighting for land and resources as the water rise and the deserts extend.'

'No, and we won't be carrying on regardless making it worse. No one's going to be rubbing their hands together in glee because the Arctic melts and they can get at the oil. That's all true. But why do you think I want to see it?'

'Because you've never been the suicidal type.'

'Did you think Dinah was?'

'No. But she was empathetic. Overwhelmed by what happened. Couldn't cope with watching so many people killing eachother.' He found it difficult to talk about her but the mantra he'd sold himself in his head as the only explanation came pat enough. It didn't impress Venus. She spat with disgust.

'So sensitive little Dinah can take her own life without your recriminations, except against me, but I can't?'

He'd never heard Venus be harsh about her friend, never heard her compare them as rivals for his approval. However, he'd been married long enough to a nuanced mind to recognize the hot water any answer would currently get him into.

'I didn't mean it that way.' was all he came up with. 'But you are ... stronger than her. Your attitude's are more ... rigorous. You don't shy away from the hard decisions.'

'Don't you think ending my life counts then?'

'Yes. Yes, of course. I just – why, for heaven's sake? I'm sure you can take the decision and see it through, that's what scares me. But I don't know why you need to. Why you can't just stay and enjoy the rest of your natural life, having warded off the end of everything?'

'This isn't about me. It's about you. You're the one not dealing with my death. Which, I might add, would already have happened if it wasn't for Furze and Mh'aed.'

'What does that mean? I should be able to save you? I should be your white knight on a charger? What about just being your lover? Isn't there any motivation for you to live that's to do with me?'

'Oh god, Kean. How many times do we have to do this? Of course, there's no future for us. Apart from the imminent death thing, and the fact that Dinah's marriage and death lie between us, you just don't seem to get it. You think you love me. You think you didn't really love Dinah. That's why all the guilt and anger. But the truth is you're a daft romantic who believes in soulmates. Me as yours, Jake as Dinah's. If you'd just been a bit more rational. If you'd just looked at the facts, instead of looking for a soulmate from a dream, but just looked for your own personal ideal woman, one who it suited you to be with, one with whom you were comfortable, with whom your relationship worked, you might have noticed you had all that in your wife. Oh, maybe in another universe there's a you and me, but in this one there was only you and Dinah. And you did love eachother, not madly, but well. We couldn't approach that kind of rapport, and since even passion itself wanes, especially when you're as ill as I'd be if I stayed alive for your pleasure, isn't it better I don't? You'll get over me. The question is really whether you'll get over Dinah? That'll be harder. She was the best of us. If you're honest, whatever other feelings you might harbour about me, you don't actually like me at all. So stop trying to cloud my mind with false hopes of love. I'm determined, but I'm only human, and just because you're only this world's shadow of a man another me loves well in another world doesn't mean I don't feel that seepage of attraction, you know that. But it wouldn't work at the best of times, and now is the worst. So please. If you love me a tenth as much as you think you do, just let me do this. After all, that way you really won't ever lose me.'

Perhaps he didn't love her as much as he protested, although he couldn't recognize that description of his feelings. Perhaps if he had, he'd have been able to put aside his (selfish?) need for her and just be at her side until the end. As things stood, he remained so angry with her, that he could no longer even manage civility, no longer even be sure his professional attitudes would see him through it.

Later, he would live to regret that the last thing he ever said to her was 'You are such a Bitch!' As an insult to the alpha-female of the entire Pack it lacked punch, especially to Venus with her soft spot for her dogs, not to mention the Dark influences, and she had merely laughed indulgently and patronizingly stroked his head, as if he was indeed a pup.

Much much later, when he and some of the others made their way back to Penzeen, he would see the laugh was on him, but, though he appreciated the irony, and sensed that Venus was enjoying it too, it never became funny.

So when she announced that she wanted to go home to die, he let her go without even saying goodbye.

Venus was relieved. Not because she wanted to leave on bad terms, but she'd take any terms other than constant harassment. Anyway, she'd had enough people to see her depart from WoodHame. There'd been the obligatory goodbye party, a ceremonial send-off full of Wood lights and colours, a raucous Dark Last Supper with *blodvin* and interesting potions that made the Wood glyph-dance into a bacchanalian religious experience, and a Day feast with *(gathered, so as not to offend Wood sensibilities)* floral decorations and massive fires and roasted game *(hunted in tandem by Dark teeth and Day flints, questing in friendly competition).* There was no hangover, courtesy of Mh'aed's brewing, and, after the festivities had drawn to a natural end as people fell asleep, everyone woke revived, even Venus, who had expected to pay for her excesses with increased nausea and pain, ready for the Last Rite. She felt vaguely uncomfortable about that, since it was an event instituted merely to honour her, but Lily had pointed out that symbols were important to all the peoples and that it would be an anniversary to unite them annually down the ages, so she'd been obliged to comply with a good grace. It wouldn't have mattered if she'd complied with a bad one, it was going to happen anyway.

They made a comfortable throne of moss on the cairn they built over the remains of the shattered pyramid-antenna. Representatives of every species lined up in a formal avenue in the Great Glade, except the Hydraens, who were too far away (and not LandLubbers) to attend, although, of course, they were sharing the moment through the Ydal's amplification of the Knights' telepathy. The Knights and Squires formed a semicircle around the throne and Furze and Mh'aed supported Venus as she walked up to it through the cheering people. She was the only one dressed. Everyone had taken their clothes off for the party but only she had been given a robe since. Jake and Lily held the long train of it, like bridesmaids, as they followed her procession. It was a beautiful garment for a shroud, she thought, although technically it was a coronation robe. It was made of a fine mesh of silk, so it clung fetchingly, but also fell like a curtain of water, making her walk flow rather more than fact and disease allowed. On it were feathers of every imaginable hue, iridescent fluttering accompanying her every step, and she was in the myth beyond the *Rubedo*, at the alchemical stage kept secret from all Day practitioners down the years, the stage that does not reflect chemistry but physics, the Lore of Light.

The robe flashed and distorted photons, cracking prisms into the eyes, and that was its Gist. The Coat Entire, the Full Blazon, was the Blaze of the Bright. The Lore was Light itself, established to reveal in simpler times the dependency of all Life on the Sun. Oh, the Dark instigators of the pseudo-religious iconography of alchemy had known about forms of life that did not require photosynthesis to be at the base of their ecological pyramid, but the lessons had been for hominins, who did. Lessons they encapsulated in the language of Lapis, the hierarchy of Heraldic, the art of Alchemy. Tears of pride were rolling down Mh'aed's face, as the mentor of the TransMutation. Venus would have felt rewarded for her years of study of the subject just by that rare, sweet smile, rarer than ever now since Bob's sad loss.

Furze, who had supervised the making of the Coat, was more inscrutable, but she too should have been proud of the effect she had achieved. The Coat of Many Colours was the *Prima Materia in Divisio* as she walked, light split prismatically, but when she sat on the throne, as the noontide sun hit its zenith, the albedo was pure white and the *Albedo* re-achieved, as in all cyclical traditions.

She sat and the remaining Terrans knelt or bowed their heads or genuflected or bared their jugulars or whatever their cultural mores suggested as appropriate obeisance. They accorded her her English due of a full three minutes of silence. Then, in the flurry of movement, as all rose, a few Woods brought round one of their flying boats and she was helped into it. She stood while it was readied around her, blew everyone a final kiss as it took off, waved as she rose into the canopy, and then she was alone.

The journey home was spectacular. She rode the jetstream in an enclosed bubble over the ocean, but the rest of the time she flew low enough to see the land, the empty land, the silent cities, the lonely fields, the deserted beaches, the peopleless earth. Animals and birds, beginning to realize they could come out in safety, were visible everywhere, although nature is harder to take when you've fucked with it and the sight of hungry dogs rampaging through city streets was depressing, with the rabbits in their local parks having a worse time than through myxomatosis. There were casualties of human intervention spread across the pastures, as cows bred to overproduce milk, bear udders stretched to hold 20 litres, rather than syphoned off regularly by their calves, died horribly painful deaths. Other farmed animals were starving where fenced in, but this would be the last generation to suffer such abuse, and the last to be born to feed the insatiable human race. The remaining people of the planet would turn away from farming and monocultures and return to hunting and gathering and meneh. It was small comfort to the suffering creatures, but they owed their artificial conceptions to the inhumanity of man and were mostly destined for slaughter anyway, but there was no more 'humane' humanity to deliver it, and naturally has always been a painful way to die.

Philosophical justifications were swept aside by her own human reactions when she flew over her native village. She'd seen millions die recently, including friends and family, but the quiet of the sleepy little village drove tears into her eyes. She landed the craft on the village green. The clock still ticking in the church tower and the twittering of starlings were the only things breaking the deathly silence. Every door was open - every door around the globe, since the call 'Home' had come embedded with some basics, like leave the doors open, let the caged animals out, put out all fires, switch off all appliances etc. It was very strange to walk down the street and be able to look right into folk's homes, and stranger to know they would mostly be dead wherever their homing instinct had taken them.

She passed the butcher's. He'd clearly got the message in full, as not only could she see his entire stock had gone from the front of the shop, but the open inner door to the freezer room showed a mass of gnawed bones on the floor and no rotting flesh on the hooks. At least the local dogs, cats, and, no doubt, foxes and rats, had got a head start before they had to depend on innate and unpractised hunting skills. *Much like most humans.* However, she made a stop in the village shop, which had never stocked anything anyone wanted to buy and was more a gossip-stop than store, and liberated a tinopener and all the cans of spam, ham, corned beef, cat and dogfood she could find. She carried them into the church, which would always be the coolest place, and laboriously sat and opened them all, placing their contents in all the saintly niches on chill marble tiles. Even as she left, she noticed a couple of cats slinking in.

But now it was time to go home. She wasn't looking forward to the empty house as much as she had been in absentia, and, of course, she was concerned to see if Morgan and Morgana were still around and well. She'd trained them to hunt for all their food, for this very moment, and they were used to her absences, so they were likely to be off on the moors on their own business, but she was rather hoping they'd come back in time for her to say goodbye.

She cut through the fields and came round the back of the old farmhouse into the orchard. The apple trees were heavy with fruit and the grass littered with their rotting siblings. The year had been a strange one for weather, unseasonal and more extreme, the harbinger of the future, but it was October now and for the first time nature seemed in sync with itself. Dawn was breaking and a chill condensation from the clear night had spread itself thickly over the paddock. Mist hung in a layer over the creek and curled in smoky tendrils up the treetrunks. The scent of decomposing leaves had begun to edge the soil with the acrid note of the coming winter. Heavy droplets of dew laced down reddening foliage onto her face and down her neck as she passed between the branches. Birds above began to mutter as they woke and the odd flighty woodpigeon crashed into the day with a startled clap of wings as they burst from their roosts.

Suddenly there was a howl from the open windows of the house that gave onto the rose garden adjacent to the orchard and the two dogs erupted into sight. There came a joyous five minutes of rolling over in a ball of fluff and flailing legs as they expressed their happiness at being reunited. Then Morgan rose and nudged Morgana and they led Venus back to her mother's erstwhile pristine sitting room. It was no longer an immaculate study in reproduction Georgian style. It was a kennel.

'You've got a pack!' Venus exclaimed in delight. It was clearly the poodles' pack, as all the other dogs were waiting for their signal before they leapt in delight and chorused their excitement at seeing a human. Venus managed to count twenty-two canines before the massed band vying for her attention pulled her into it.

Later, after they'd all calmed down and she'd remembered Cal's secret stash of dogfood in the larder and rewarded everyone's friendliness, she sat on the patio with a hand on each of her beloved poodles and explained the situation. She'd already told them what good dogs they were, but now she had to tell them she was going for ever. One of the things she had always done, easier in poodles and collies than many other dogs, was give them a vocabulary. So they recognized words and concepts broader than 'walk' and 'dinner'; they recognized 'dead'. *Mostly in the context of 'No! Don't eat dead things. Eat killed things.' Saves a lot of diarrhoea.* But they had sniffed her breath and recoiled, so she knew they already knew. Their heads went low, their ears flattened, their shoulders depressed when she told them, so she knew they knew that she knew now. When she got up, they stood, one on each side, nosing into her hands until she laid them on their shoulders and leaned on their support. Her tears fell then.

'You're the reason.' she spluttered. 'Not because the Woods told me so. You dogs. All you dogs. The one good thing humanity did was make friends with your wolf ancestors. The one thing that shows us we're in any way worthy to continue is your trust in us. Oh, we've abused plenty of you, I know. And you get eaten too. But basically, we showed we could be friends with one non-human species. And I thank you for that, because I thought about letting us all be exterminated, you know. It was a real temptation. It's a strong argument. The planet might well be better off without us. But the way we can love our dogs – well, it might be hope triumphing over experience, but that's all the future is to most of us. I am sorry to leave you. I am. But you're ready for it. You've got your pack. I feel better for that.'

They were through the rose-garden now and the rising sun had opened the year's last flowers with a heady scent of ancient summers. Morgan and Morgana were clearly in control of their fellows since not one had followed into their private moments.

Venus was going to walk through to the headland on which the lighthouse stood. She wanted her last view of the planet to be the wide open one of the sea and the horizon of light that joined land and ocean and all the peoples. But now the dogs were butting at her legs and trying to drive her back into the orchard. 'What's the matter?' she said, surprized at their insistent blocking of her path. Clearly they wanted to show her something, but she was rather hoping it wasn't the usual pride over a kill, another bloody corpse was not what she wanted in her final hours. Still, she had time and they had needs of her yet, so she allowed herself to be diverted.

They brought her to a twist of apple trees, in which a couple of unregulated saplings had grown up around the antique mother tree and woven a single thicket of branches. It was one of her favourite haunts as a child, not least because the oldest Wood she knew, Olive, had spent most of his hours wrapped around the trunk, communing with the trees too.

'Olive!'

Olive hadn't started out as short for a Wood, but the years and his habits had gnarled him like the trees he contorted his body around. All Woods make choices about which species they 'study', although their aim is not academic but is understanding, and Olive, despite the choice of his youth in the Mediterranean which had earned him his human name, had come to Cornwall and settled in the Penzeen orchard, because it had always been safe, given the local Dark early warning system, and because of the Penzeen women.

Locally, the Penzeen daughters had been looked on askance for generations by the villagers. Probably originally it was mere peasant jealousy of the people in the big house, but the whispers of witchcraft had been nearer true than false, as many a girlish diary locked in the attics alluded to the 'pictsies' seen and even danced with. One of the things that Venus had found out from Olive early on was that even her grandmother was not immune to his charms, although it is possible that her fanatical conversion to the Brethren dated from her shame at her enjoyment of his wandering hands.

Those hands had spent most of their time clinging to branches by the time Venus had become a nubile target for the isolated Wood and his mind had moved on from sexuality to fruition, from fingers touching to leaves waving, from leaping and dancing to rooting and branching, so their relationship had been much less dramatic, but nonetheless affectionate and intense. And, of course, he was still here. Here was Home, no matter all other Woods had felt called to Roraima, Olive was so bonded with his apple trees he was already there. Probably this was why he got on with humans, because he had remained apart and, as such, more individuated than normal. More apple than normal too, of course, which was also alienating in a whole other way, from all the hominin tribes, but, although his mind was almost slowed down to the working pace of sap, he was still crisp within his peel and he recognized that 'pip' Venus and opened wide arms and drew her up into his branches with a strength that creaked but was still vital.

She sat on his lap and he stroked her feathers and asked to know her. She shared her mind and then, like the child he made her feel, dozed in the warm sun while he processed the information. It must have been almost an hour later when she felt him stir at last. His spit touched her temple with a bony finger, although he could have shared through mere proximity as she had been altered by the virus to sense him, but he remained tactile in the old-fashioned way he knew best. 'I will Witness.' he told her.

And so began the last leg of her final journey. Supported on either side by dogs and followed by a walking tree, Venus walked to the edge of the cliffs and looked Beyond. The sun had risen to almost its full height and was hot and white in a cloudless pale blue sky. A half moon hung in the west, a pale imitation of the Life-Giver. The horizon was a line of grey between two blues that went on for ever. The granite cliffs shone black and roseate and the ocean kissed the shore eternally. It was her view, her Home, her planet, and she had to say goodbye and it was hard. She was glad that Olive was there to witness, because she almost faltered at the thought of leaving it, of leaving the dogs. She could almost run away with them and be hidden for the rest of her life, *if she didn't emanate another thought anyone could 'hear'*. But it was right to be sad to go, because it was for its beauty she had fought to this end. So she let the tears fall freely.

Her vision was blurred by the rain of salt but she kept looking and looking. Not for anything, just to see, just not to miss her last moments on her beloved world. A flicker of motion in the near-distance. And then it was more than a flicker. It was a boiling of the sea, surf upon the surface of the deep ocean, the unmistakable humped backs of whales and dolphins and porpoises, breaking into air, leaping and flashing, diving and displaying. The Hydraens could not attend from the southern hemisphere, but they had sent their sentient cousins-in-arms to Witness for them and for all mankind. Well, the sun-clock had ticked to the fateful hour of Noon, so she would not disappoint them.

She put her arms around her dogs and nuzzled a tearful farewell. She embraced Olive. She waved to the assembled, now-still, cetaceans. Then she put up the hood of her robe and raised her arms and the Coat flashed its finery for one last time and fuzzed over into the white shroud it was made to be, and she Called.

There was an answering flare from the moon, actually visible as the Ydal powered up all the nanobacteria and drained their energy, leaving no contamination upon or within the lunar body to speak to history of her existence thereon. There was an incandescent burst at the top of the atmosphere as the Weapons linked the solar system from sun to heliopause through the homecoming Lady and the *aurora orbis* scintillated from horizon to horizon, hemisphere to hemisphere. Then, as she looked upwards, a beam of light shot through, burning out her watching retinas, so that the moment of impact took place in inner darkness, before the world broke apart into Light.

Venus-Ygrail morphed, no longer humanoid, a rising of feathers, a ballooning of space, and the Phoenix rose. No one knows what the mythical bird looks like, so they had settled on a cloudiness of vaguely eagle-shaped beak and piercing eyes and world-spanning wings. They rose and rose until their shape was etched against every part of the sky viewed from the inhabited regions, the southern ocean and the Amazonian heights. They ingested the Weapons' input which was more than energy. It was a patterning at the cellular level, the pattern of the holoNetSpore on the Gwener-side of a quantum tunnel at the Lagrange extremity of the solar system and of the black hole radiation of the trapped NetSpore that was bound to Dawn in the Thursday-universe, all transmitted to them and to their Rider, the NetSpore Local Operative in the Venus-version. The subspace$_8$ traffic blew off anyone's scale.

Then, as the MetaMind of the Knights Augmentatio formed, taking the entranced Terran-hominins in Consensus into its broadening scope, they scrolled back through the figures of earth that the flight symbolized: Phoenix became archaeopteryx, became pterosaur, became dragon, became snake, became wurm, became amoebae, became plankton, became single-celled prokaryotes. Then the cloud of bright particles blew up into the stratosphere, swooped around the entire globe and fell like rain on land and sea, and each individual cell burrowed into whatever living thing was nearest, animal and plant alike, and the sigh of global knowledge went up from sea and hill as, voiced by the novel conjoined-hominin MetaIntelligence, seeded by three universes' worth of knowledge, birthed by the death of the Queens of the World, Terra Became.

New Terra Became too. Mediated by Pereduri in the Venus-role, reproducing the same imagery, taking the melded minds of her holopeople with her in her linkage through the MetaMind of the Knights and the Ydal. Oh, the power didn't fly from the old solar system via the Weapons and the lunar base, but, when your entire world consists of the projection from the surface of an Einstein-Bose condensate of entangled photons, you don't need much energy to rearrange its internal state. Matter requires much more power to change its nature, and Xl-arn'tz, watching the dispersion of his beloved, feeling her seed his little sphere of spacetime with old Terra's biodata and wondering if his head, however immaterial, would explode in attempting to co-contain all the knowledge the Planetary Intelligence was uploading through her, still found time to be truly amazed at the breadth of vision Venus had brought to her life's work. The computational genius might be originally Wooden, and only latterly, Day, from the Days in Fargo's employ that contributed the pieces of the puzzle that had been put together into the Ydal, but the political vision and determination and manipulation had been all Venus, or at least all Venus-Thursday-Gwener. So he wept for the sacrifice of the mother and the daughter, and he wept for himself and for all the people of the Terras, new and old, that had lost the personalities to gain the information.

But even as he did so, he could feel the change coming on. Individualism remained, as organs remain in the body, necessary specialisations of groups of cells, but egos rapidly receded. When you can sense inside the bounds of what you have previously called 'self' and find not voiceless organs but speaking creatures, a world of selfhood emerges, which has a quite different quality. Venus had cheated right at the end, it transpired, for she had broken her word to the Cognimata and the Net that had promised no Ydal leadership would remain on Terra. She had only broken the spirit of the oath, mind you. The letter was adhered to. The Ydal was cloned into the ships, but they were not on Terra and were so far away from the Legacy as to be no threat to Europa, but her explosion on Terra, into the particulate cells/spores, the mind-compression of holoNet Riderhood, given biological coats from the chemicals of Venus' flesh, was not technically the promised destruction. The earthlings had subsumed their egos into the HyperMetaMind resulting from the Knights leading the melded intelligences of all the hominins, but the status of Planetary Intelligence resulted only from those Riders feeding back information from the lowliest bacterium to the smartest cetacean into the single emergent consciousness. Pereduri had done a great thing for New Terra by joining them with this HyperMetaMind, not simply because the two could individuate and talk to one another, but because, unlike the only other example of such a creature they knew, Mars, Terra was still grounded in the material world of 3D flesh.

It had become apparent in a number of the ships that the worlds were populated by creatures of the transfigured consciousnesses' imaginations. This was a new normality that those living as their avatars were happy enough to explore, but here on New Terra, the folk wanted to see (the best of) what had previously existed in the old world. They found it disconcerting to realize that to see, say, a heron fly across a stream they all agreed was visible, the viewer had to want to see it, to imagine it, and that, unless it was a collective wish, only the individual mage need see it at all, at least without sharing it. Apparently people were readier to accept lack of detail in landscape and unmoving objects without question, without even the need to agree on the elements forming the background view, until they needed to fix a point, for instance for a meeting. Then, for some reason, consensus was still easier than Xl-arn'tz expected. They didn't seem to care if the valley they were in had more or less sloping sides as long as they all agreed it was a grassy valley, rather than a wooded one. For Xl-arn'tz, whose sense of smell would have told him which he was in without opening his eyes, this lack of interest denoted the fixation of Days on the action of 'looking', rather than the passivity of 'sight'. But they had begun to find it tedious to remember to 'look at' their dogs to know they accompanied them, because it took more concentration and visualisation than they were accustomed to give to viewing their world. Others worried they might forget what a particular creature looked like, the flash of a kingfisher might become just that, a blue-red streak, never resolvable into the arrow-shaped bird with its cheeky tipped beak and its piercing eye. It hadn't happened yet, of course, but time was never on the side of memory, and these folk so wanted to keep Earth's memory living.

But now, courtesy of dear Peri, kingfisher minds on old Terra swooped their flightpaths through Planetary Minds-eye and past actual ocular senses in the multispecies watching populations of the world feeding that Mind. So the New Terrans would neither be faced with forgetfulness nor with the need to concentrate the entire time, as they could holoform that kingfisher-mind here to have its own existence in New Terra. This was true TerraForming and they were excited by that almost as much as by the realization that they remained part of the old and its ongoing evolution. They could go forward into the future and stay part of their own history. 'Exciting times' was the general verdict.

Xl-arn'tz didn't disagree, he just had his own rituals to perform before he could get on with the life ahead without the personalized presence of Peri. Darks, modelling their behaviour on the pack, don't abandon their survival for long periods of mourning, but they grieve solidly for three days, first there is the deboning and consumption of the deceased in the Last Suppering ritual, followed by a vigil over the dead that requires fasting and howling, and later those who have taken the bones may ceremonially carve them into tools or instruments or bury them with flowers and seeds where no dog (or more likely Day) will ever dig them up. He could do none of this, except the vigil.

So he took the tunnels to Bite and sat down in the cave, beside the four Crystal Skulls, surrounded by fluorescing fungi dancing across the walls and ceiling in holopatterns that, without the geothermal power and wetware of Mind behind them had been meaningless but were now cosmic gistings, to Howl.

He was looking within, within himself, within his world, so he did not notice that in the great information overload of old Terra, he was not Howling alone.

Olive had watched the fireworks of the end of Venus and his rheumy ancient eyes had been unable to see the pips she'd scattered. He was still trying to unravel what she'd shared earlier about her intentions, although he'd gotten the fact that it was important and that he should Witness. To a Wood of his age, that role meant more than merely watch. It was part of Lore, as Days witness contracts of marriage and wills, Woods Witness death. Not by ensuring probity, not by looking on, but by mindmelding at the last breath to memorize in its entirety the mind that no more will be powered by flesh to consciousness. That mind is then entered, via the Crystal Skull, into the Wood collective mind, where it regains awareness briefly, then deselfs and its knowledge and memories flow into the ocean of the whole.

Olive was newly awoken from his own apple-laced stupor and could no more fail to do the full task on automatic than he could fail to breathe, even though Venus had specifically warned him of danger to himself and told him to stand well back. The timing was always difficult. People's last breaths could be slow and spaced and one always wanted to catch everything to the last brain-wave, but when Venus raised her arms and her eyes to the shooting star in the sky he extended his middle finger and held on for grim death.

Obviously, death itself did not arrive. He felt the powerful jolt of the energy beam, but then his mind floated up and outwards wearing the clothing of the Phoenix and he spread across the world and he felt time and evolution itself unravel within him and he exploded in the best pyrotechnics ever seen on earth and his ashes floated down around the globe and then he found himself lying prostrate on the cliff edge with Morgan and Morgana licking him back to wakefulness.

When he could make his brain believe it lived inside this cramped, gnarled old body again and had reminded it how to work enfeebled limbs, he sat up. The dogs were now sitting on their haunches, facing him, staring at him. To his surprize he knew two things instantly. One was that they had been leaning against him to support him when the lightning struck and the other was that they were all three transformed by the experience. It wasn't the normal protocol, since post-death consciousness through living in your carrier's head was strongly discouraged pre-absorption, but he had a strong sense that Venus was looking out of both of the dogs' eyes at him. He risked opening the package he was carrying to check.

It is a very strange sensation to find that another person is sharing your brain, using your eyes, and this was not the cellular-level-Riding Venus had intended, this was not a channel that flowed between the Ridden mind and the Rider Mind elsewhere, this was a selfed consciousness using Olive's body. She didn't take over, though. Perhaps through shock, but he noted her withdrawal from respect too. Perhaps because she didn't need him, as she squatted in two canine minds equally happily. It was as if she shut her eyes and went back to sleep, but he still experienced the endorphin cascade of her satisfaction with a job well done and its unexpected reward.

So he thought across to the dogs *(without having to touch them, without cross-species' translation problems),* and they went bounding off, returning, in less time than his body needed to recover, with the apple apiece he'd sent them to bring from his old nest. Then, because he knew that it was the last time he would see it, he swivelled around and looked at the place, sea and sky and land, Home. At length but before Venus had the chance to re-emerge and complicate matters further, he made his way out of the sunlight and into the tunnels that would take him to the Grail cavern underBite.

The dogs accompanied him all the way, which meant going the long way as, even with their enhanced minds, he couldn't see his way to encasing them in the turbochute foam. They knew the path of old, naturally, having been with Venus. He noticed that they mostly followed their noses as always, but when they all came to a junction at which canine noses and Olive's memory hesitated, suddenly both dogs strode forward together and he knew Venus had directed their steps.

Finally, they were in the Skull cathedral-cave. He walked round the walls, touching the hyphae into life, stroking the crystal domes of the Four, and then he leaned into the dogs and rubbed their heads. In his youth he would have enjoyed the newfound communication Venus had opened between all the species of the earth, would have delighted to know the minds of these dogs, now he was just grateful that they knew his better than any spit-carried message could have penetrated through hair. He had eaten one of the apples they had brought him on the journey. Now he picked the poison fungus, climbed into the Wood Skull-Tree, applied the gel-interface and inserted his cranium into the crystal cap and let Venus go. The walls went mad with the dataflow and he watched the pretty hallucinogenic dance of information as he munched alternately on the fungus and the apple, swallowing, as with the former, every last pip in the core.

Every now and again, as the lights ran down the walls and took his eyes with them, he saw the dogs, stationary, Witnessing for him. This was not the same kind of Witnessing he had done, he knew that, as did they, but then it was not the same kind of world, and when next he lived in it, it would be a very different experience, but he was looking forward and it was enough this lifetime's memories would go to be Absorbed. As the poison started to take hold, he felt his awareness slackening, the psychedelic effects increasing, but he was quite sure as he floated away into darkness that he heard the dogs announce *in English barks* his successful passage. 'Cycle Cycle'. And then came the Howling, such as would reach ships in the far heavens and comfort even the lost children.

It took them long to drag the carcass to the surface. It was night then, and Home was gone, though House remained. They pulled the body past the hopeful jaws of the pack with much warning growling and the odd managerial bite, that spoke of danger, although only the two leaders could conceive the idea of 'bad' food. Since they knew they could not eat Olive, not because he was not food, but because he was poison, they had no trouble with the instruction he'd given to bury him beneath the ancient apples in which he'd nested for so long.

They guarded the corpse and rested for the night, but at daybreak they rose again and dug and dug until they could roll him into a shallow grave. Then they kicked the dirt back over him, howled some more and laid down on it until hunger drew them to collect the pack and hunt.

Venus, watching from within, without any interference since this was between the dogs and Olive, was touched and impressed at their loyalty and determination. One day, when she and they had cohabited long enough for their minds to enmesh, hers growing more canine, theirs more human, she would be able to explain to them just what they'd done here today. If they lived long enough, they might even see the Olive-apple tree sprout and grow and develop in awareness. A completely new species: sentient apples. It made the canine-level of her mind want to giggle madly, and she had to control it as Morgan and Morgana were both quite cross, not to mention somewhat shocked, when their mouths barked simultaneously, seriously disturbing the hunt.

For now, well, for now, there was one. She had a Now. No responsibilites, no plans to make, no death to snuff out her awareness, just Being. Not, it appeared, MetaBeing, unless you count the Riders in the dogs' minds, which connected and might ultimately enlighten her with news from the rest of the world, but it would never be confined to the news of humanity again. No, she appeared just to be herself, sitting somewhere in the brains of two poodles, not fully separate but not integrated either. *Like a benign tumour without headaches. No, more like an idea that could be vividly dreamed, or a thought that could be dismissed, be tolerated, be explored, be dominant, or another personality as in MPD. Although even Ida Makepeace hadn't had her mind split between two bodies.*

Their bodies were certainly in better shape than hers had been recently. She thrilled to the muscles flexing as they ran, the current of air rippling sensitive whiskers and ruffling hair that gave dogs a sense of the liquid boundaries of their selves in motion, the unexpected excitement those currents brought into the nostrils, the distraction of distant rabbit, two-day-old fox, the young bitch in the pack coming into her first season *(Morgan and Morgana had quite different responses to that one)*, and yet the focus, the concentration that made her want to sneeze with the force building behind the desire for the chase, was all on one single scent: the blood oozing from the torn ear of the roe deer in the blackthorn thicket.

This was what all of life came down to. This was what she'd wanted humanity to find. This was why they had to embed Intelligence in the Flesh, the idea of the psyche in the material, because matter or energy, brain or holonet, it was all one. Forget the Grail, this was the Quest. Life. You could only count on one, but even if you got another, you'd better be prepared to Live it.

She could sense on the edge of her connectivity that most of the ships had taken the right attitude, and she knew that Terra itself was in a phase of accelerated evolution of its memepool, and possibly its genepool, if you included the hominin hybridizations possible.

Some of the ships, some of the Terrans would not survive, but the planet would and it would thrive. The NetSpore Local Operative had withdrawn its Riders of her and the Ydal just before they'd exploded, but it and the rest of the galaxy now had a new force to contend with. Not an aggressive one, she hoped, but with the strength of the predator as well as the thoughtfulness of the collective, and it was out there and it was unstoppable. The cosmic community would have to recognize Terra and its jumped-up hominins now. Even the Cognimata would have to accept that superior Mind could inhabit flesh.

But none of that had to matter to her anymore. Her posthumous life would have a different significance. Here. Now. The pack was closing on its prey, the siren-song of the quarry's scent had Called, the Cast had been played out and the Game won. She was the only Terran to have become an avatar of her own favourite Live creatures: the dogs' imaginary friend. Gave Life a whole new meaning. Come to that, in Morgana, it gave being a bitch whole new meaning.

The deer's death was meaningful too. It meant survival for the group, but this wasn't a mere linguistic Gist for Cycling. It wasn't even the shared Blazon of Mind as they ingested knowledge of deerhood, though now it was that too.

This was the Coat from which it all originated:

the Meat of Life.

She sank her teeth into it.

'I-MAGE!'.

ABOUT THE AUTHOR

ROWNEY MARSHAL EXISTS AS SCRIBE TO A BLACK KNIGHT WHO HAS TO RIDE OUT IN SANITY AND IN CORPOREALITY AND IN ARMOUR.

SCRIBES DON'T GET OUT MUCH, BUT THEY DO GET WITHIN, WITHOUT, WITHAL, ON QUESTS THAT TRANSCEND THOSE OF THE BLACK KNIGHT. HOWEVER, THE LATTER GETS TO BE GROUNDED BY FAMILY, FRIENDS AND DOGS, WHICH IS ITS' OWN REWARD.

BUT THAT'S ONLY IN THIS UNIVERSE, ELSEWHERE . . .

Heim Quantum Theory

Burkhard Heim was a real and extraordinary man. Disabled by an explosion in early life, he still went on to develop the theories fictionalised herein.

Heim theory remains relatively unexplored at time of writing but anyone interested in the overview of the application of his work can read:

Walter Dröscher and Jochem Häuser's paper 'Heim Quantum Theory for Space Propulsion Physics' at:
http://www.fileuniverse.com/spring/hqtforspacepropphysicsaip2005.pdf

If you're interested in the details behind this, try:
http://www.heim-theory.com/downloads/A_Abstract.pdf

or as published in the American Institute for Aeronautics and Astronautics journal 2002-4094
http://pdf.aiaa.org/preview/CDReadyMJPC2002_595/PV2002_4094.pdf